The Clowns Dance:

Love and Adventure in Ecuador

Lynden S. Williams

THE CLOWNS DANCE:
LOVE AND ADVENTURE IN ECUADOR

iUniverse books may be ordered through booksellers or by contacting:

iUniverse
1663 Liberty Drive
Bloomington, IN 47403
www.iuniverse.com
1-800-Authors (1-800-288-4677)

Because of the dynamic nature of the Internet, any web addresses or links contained in this book may have changed since publication and may no longer be valid. The views expressed in this work are solely those of the author and do not necessarily reflect the views of the publisher, and the publisher hereby disclaims any responsibility for them.

Any people depicted in stock imagery provided by Thinkstock are models, and such images are being used for illustrative purposes only. Certain stock imagery © Thinkstock.

ISBN: 978-1-4759-8959-5 (sc)
ISBN: 978-1-4759-8960-1 (e)

Library of Congress Control Number: 2013908164

Print information available on the last page.

iUniverse rev. date: 06/28/2017

During intermission, the bullfighters use their large red capes to direct the bull toward the clowns. Buffoons in baggy pants dance around the horns, and grab the bull by the tail. The crowd laughs, and the bullfighters smile down their noses like grammar teachers enduring the antics of children in the playground. But, the game is deadly serious. If a clown is gored or trampled, there will be a momentary hush while the man is carried out of the arena. Then, the serious business of bullfighting will continue.

EVERYTHING BACKWARDS: ECUADOR, MONDAY MORNING, AUGUST 3, 1957

"**B**oletos;" I squint and see the man tapping the visor of my baseball cap. The thought of slapping his hand away comes to mind; I hate being touched by a stranger, especially on the head. But, he didn't really touch my head—only the visor of my cap. There is a small piece of the dream left, and it fades with each conscious thought. I try to clear my thoughts.

The dream drifts back, slowly at first, and then it floods through my mind. All the circumstance and flavor surround and engulf, but there is no image. If I can just grab one small part, it will all come back. That conscious thought causes the dream to fade into the mist. I empty my mind and think of nothingness. A moment passes and then the dream takes control. I see my contorted face. That face fills me with disgust and shame. Why is your face twisted? You are left-handed, and your hair is parted on the wrong side. "You look stupid," I say to that face. Or was it the war? You have to find your radio, I tell myself; the Chinks will be coming up in force and will kill everyone in the platoon—it will be your fault. But I knew my radio had blown out of the bunker when the mortar round hit. There is nothing I can do; I have to save myself. Or was it the ranch in Texas? In those years prior to the Army, his family had never had enough money and he had never even dreamed of having any real money; but there he was living in a million dollar ranch in Texas. What great fortune had fallen to him when he married the daughter of a general. But the ranch isn't mine, and I know it will never be mine. Even his wife referred to it as 'my ranch.' Obviously it wasn't his ranch, but why couldn't it just be 'the ranch'? Why did it always have to be her ranch? In the stem of his brain there was a dog that always wanted to crawl out, growling and snapping at him. Some day he would have to fight that dog. Maybe he would jam his hand into the dog's mouth and grab his tongue and choke him to death. But maybe the dog would chew off his hand. Best to just push it back down in there.

The dream is gone, but I continue to think about my face. It never was a cute face GI, I tell myself. Girls that like cute guys pay little attention to it. So; we gave up on the cheerleaders a long time ago. Who cares about the cute cheerleaders and their cute preferences? We want girls that play football—not the cheerleaders! I become aware of talking to myself in my thoughts and the fact that I call myself 'we'. Stop saying 'we' GI, I tell myself, there's only one of us. And stop saying GI; you haven't been a GI for four years, and you weren't much of a GI then.

"*Boletos,*" the man says, and again he taps my cap. An oversized hairy belly is a few inches in front of me, displayed because the dirty shirt has the lower two buttons missing. I sit upright and think about punching him in the gut. The man seems to sense my thought and steps back. The big gut belies his stature. He is worn and gaunt; a front tooth is missing and the eyes are bloodshot and old. I am ashamed of having thought about punching him.

"*Boletos, boletos,*" the man says, as he turns and walks on down the aisle toward the back of the bus. He carries a leather bag full of coins in his right hand, which he shakes while requesting payment and the fingers of his other hand are filled with folded bills, with each finger holding a different denomination. Because both hands are occupied he cannot steady himself by holding the seats or rail mounted on the ceiling, so he sways back and forth down the aisle bumping his hips on the seats on each side, as the bus swerves to miss potholes in the road.

"He wants your ticket!" The female voice in English grabs my attention. "He wants your ticket," she repeats. She is in the aisle seat directly across from me. She is tall and strong looking, probably in her mid-twenties, about my age. Her sun-bleached hair hangs straight down, beatnik style, and her face is pleasant and calm. She's not wearing a bra, I tell myself. "Your ticket;" she motions toward my shirt pocket.

An Indian woman is sitting in the aisle seat in front of the American girl. The woman is asleep with a baby cradled in her arms. The child's head hangs over her arm so that the neck bends backward almost ninety degrees. Jeez! If your neck were twisted like that, your head would break off, I tell myself. The bus is crowded. All seats, except for the window seat beside me, are taken. A young Black man is standing in the aisle near the front, and several people are standing in the back. I am sprawled across two seats. They know you're a shit-head GI, I tell myself; they would rather stand than wake you. I sit up in the aisle seat.

Some of the passengers are Indians, dressed in homespun clothing, with ponchos or shawls, but most are Mestizos and Blacks. Some of the Mestizos are also dressed in wool clothing, suggesting that they, like the Indians, are coming from the cool highlands. The Blacks and most of the Mestizos wear factory-made T-shirts and cotton pants and dresses. The air is heavy with body odor. Indians and other Highland people occupy the rows immediately in front of me. They have the windows in their section of the bus closed, and many cover their mouths with their ponchos or shawls. Obviously, they think breathing the warm outside air, after the cool air in the highlands, will make them sick. I had become aware of the 'hot and cold airs' theory of sickness in Southern Mexico, and had recognized it again in Colombia. I theorized that the belief must have originated from Spain, since the Spanish culture is the only one the people of the various countries have in common. The body-odor comes with the territory GI, I tell myself; anyway, you don't smell so good yourself.

Fortunately, there are Blacks and others from the lowlands sitting in the front rows. They have their windows open, so some air does move through the bus. Blacks and Mestizos from the hot lowlands don't smell so bad; I figure they probably bathe more often than people who live in the cool highlands.

The front of the bus, including the top of the windshield and the dashboard, is elaborately decorated. Baby shoes hang from the mirror, along with a miniature hammock with the other end attached to the top of the passenger-side window. The hammock has the words *María me espera* (Mary waits for me) written on the side. The dashboard is covered with a dusty purple cloth. A plastic model of *Our Lady of Guadalupe* bobs up and down on a spring stand. Beside the plastic Virgin is a picture, also drawn on plastic, of *Mariana de Jesus*—the Saint breaking her chain bondage. I don't know what the chains are supposed to represent—perhaps sin, or escaping this world for heaven? Who knows? But, I saw it portrayed as a huge statue on a hill above the City of Quito, so it must be an important saint for Ecuador. On the inside of the passenger-side window is a picture of a nude woman with her large breasts thrust forward and her mouth open. There are a number of pin-ups, mostly showing breasts and panty-covered butts on the back of the driver's seat. Another bus celebrating womanhood, I tell myself; just like every other bus in Latin America.

The bus driver and his helper are both Mestizos. The driver turns every few minutes to say something to a young Mestizo girl who sits in the aisle seat in the front row. He is loud and laughing, and she doesn't respond. I can't make out the words, but I know they will be sexually suggestive and flirting. I try to guess his age, but he is in that age-less age—older than thirty and younger than fifty. He wears a greasy T-shirt, and a three-day old beard. How can they always have exactly three days of growth on their faces?

The destination is written at the top of the windshield. From inside the bus, the word appears right to left, in mirror image. *Esmeraldas:* We are heading for Esmeraldas, I tell myself. Going north on the coast road or west from Quito? The sun is getting high so it's not possible to determine the direction from shadows. From the window, I observe open savanna pasture and some African Palm groves, with tropical savanna vegetation farther from the road. We've passed Santo Domingo—headed west to the coast—it can't be far. I remember getting on the bus in the early morning darkness, after spending much of the night waiting beside the road outside Quito. I remember choosing the seat beside the sleeping American girl.

The ticket man shuffles toward the front of the bus. He stops just behind me, apparently hoping to avoid a confrontation. *"Boletos!"* he says.

"He wants your ticket," she repeats. She reaches over and takes the ticket from my shirt pocket and hands it to the man. He tears the coupon, and offers it to me. I don't bother to accept it. The man shrugs and gives the ticket to the woman, then shuttles his way to the front, stopping to pick up tickets from two other passengers.

"Better keep your ticket," she advises. "Sometimes, they pick up an inspector, and if you don't have your ticket, you have to pay again." My shoulders rise and fall, displaying the indifference I feel. "Well, it's no skin off my butt," she says.

I am looking directly at her eyes, and can't help glancing down, thinking about the skin on her butt. She seems to know what I'm thinking, and turns away. She is wearing a long full cotton skirt splashed with bright flowers, and has it tucked between her legs. Her arms are long and muscular, and bare from the shoulder. She is tall for a woman—probably about my height. Her skin is darkly tanned, and it contrasts sharply with her light brown hair and eyes, and that bit of pink-white skin I can see through the sleeve of her white blouse. She is casual and sexy, and has an air of self-confidence that radiates her personality into the space around her.

I puzzle to understand the source of the energy that surrounds her. Partly it's her physical strength, I tell myself; bet she's a really strong woman. Yeah, but there is something else—something even more striking about her. The expression on her face is the key. That tiny smile exudes self-confidence. The smile says, I enjoy life and have no hang-ups; and don't mess with me or I'll punch your lights out. Even these macho guys down here would be hesitant to screw around with her. She is mesmerizing. You should be trying to score with her, instead of trying to be the biggest shit-head in the country, I tell myself. To her I say, "Hey!"

"Hay is for horses," she says, not bothering to look in my direction.

"Hey, yeah; you took the words right out'o my mouth. Why am I trying to be such a jerk?"

"I give up," she says, turning toward me.

"Hey, I was just having this dream when that jerk came by and started poking me in the head." I am disappointed that I sound like a whining kid.

"Dreaming, huh?"

I want to keep her attention, but can't think of anything witty or stimulating. I continue with the dream. "I couldn't quite get it. It was as if… will, it was me, but everything upside down."

"So, you were standing on your head?"

"No, not like that, I mean…it was as if everything was opposite. See, I'm right handed, but in my dream I'm left handed."

"So, what are you doing in your dream, writing letters?" she says, sounding bored.

"Oh no, I'm just standing there. I don't know what I'm doing. It's sort of a recurring dream."

"So? If you're just standing there, what makes you think you look left handed?"

"Well, I mean…" I don't have an answer. "And, my hair is combed backwards. See, I comb my hair this way," taking off my cap and motioning from left to right, "but, in the dream it's combed backwards."

"For a fella' who wears a stupid baseball cap, you worry an awful lot about which way you might have combed your hair."

"So? Why is my cap stupid?"

"I don't see anyone else wearing one." She gestures at the other passengers.

"Hell, everyone in Texas wears a baseball cap. They have logos on um' that say things like, *Mack Truck*, or *Lone Star Beer*, or *What You See Is What You Get*. You know; something informative like that."

"Yeah; well, we're in Ecuador, not Texas. Someone should throw it out the window."

"Here take it." I hand my cap to her. "But, if you throw it out the window you'll make me cry, and then I'll go buy another one."

"They probably don't even sell them down here," she responds and hands the cap back.

"Sure they do. I bought this one in Quito. Some guy stole my other one. You know, it's a good thing I wasn't wearing that cap when he took it. He probably would have killed me for it. That's how valuable these caps are." She gives me an arched eyebrow look. "Really!" I say in a serious tone. "Someday everyone in the world will be wearing baseball caps!"

She rolls her head back, looks up and exhales, making the bullshit in the cloud above her quake like aspen leaves in a mountain breeze.

"Really; someday, the president of Mexico will step out on the balcony of the presidential palace on Independence Day, and say '*Viva Mexico*,' and he will be wearing a baseball cap." I give her my idiot look—wagging head cocked sideways, with tongue sticking out, and hands held up with palms forward.

She smiles at that, and I continue. "The girls on the volleyball team will all have baseball caps with their logo on the front, and holes in the back, so their pony tails will hang out. And, bank presidents will have baseball caps with spectacles mounted

6

in the bill, so they can count their money." Again, I do my idiot look. "And, the Chinese will make hundreds of millions of little-bitty baseball caps, and when their kids are born they will put them on their little bald heads." She giggles and shakes her head. "And, the old ladies down here will throw away all those little doilies they put on their heads when they go to church, and use baseball caps, with the bills turned backward, so they can cross themselves when they say their Hail Marys." I turn the bill of my cap around backwards, and demonstrate how they would cross themselves. "Hell, we should go to Texas and buy stock in all those baseball cap factories."

"We'd be rich in no time, huh?" She smiles and shakes her head up and down, as if to assure me that my silliness is not being taken seriously. "So you're going to Esmeraldas." She states, rather than asks.

"Yeah, I guess so." I respond.

"It means emeralds doesn't it? Did they find emeralds down there?" she asks.

"I don't know, but I doubt it. More likely, some dude said, 'Ya' know, this place wouldn't be so bad if the ground were covered with emeralds,' and they decided to name it that." She chuckles softly, and I continue, enjoying her attention. "You know, it's like every time you find a town named *Progreso* it's the most backward place in the country. And, never go to a place named *Esperanza*, cause' they only name a place *Hope* if there is absolutely no hope for it."

She nods agreement, smiling, and then turns forward and leans her head against the back of the seat. I try to think of something else to say to her, but my mind is a total blank. I think about the dream again. Look at you; you have your watch on the wrong wrist, and your face is screwed around backwards. I consider telling her more about the dream, but quickly reject that impulse. I check again to confirm that she is not wearing a bra. She has dozed off. Man, you just blew your last chance to meet a woman for the duration, I tell myself.

I think about the word *duration*. During World War II, soldiers were required to serve for the duration of the war. "I'm in for the duration," they would say; and, saying that would make each soldier aware of the fact that the enemy had to be defeated before he could go home. That gave a man an attitude about the war, and his part in it, that we didn't have. In Korea, you only had to serve a maximum of 18 months in the war zone, or less if you did time on the front line, and then you would be rotated back to the States. You never had the feeling that you had to finish the fight.

Nevertheless, we also used the word *duration* in Korea. Most guys learned it from the older soldiers who had fought in the Big War. For us it seemed to mean something else. Maybe it just meant 'a long time.' But, it also seemed to carry another connotation: It was like saying nothing will ever change, or you will never make it home, or you can't quit—something like that. I had heard Uncle Bob use that expression long before I was in the army.

Uncle Bob: Kentucky, autumn, 1952

After jump school at Fort Bragg, North Carolina, he received a thirty-day furlough and hitchhiked home to Mayfield Kentucky. On the way he stopped in eastern Kentucky to see his Uncle Bob. Bob had served with the Third Army in Europe during World War II. The Third Army, commanded by General George Patton, had engaged more enemy divisions and taken more enemy ground than any other Army in any of America's wars, as Uncle Bob had told him many times.

At Buzzard Hollow Road, he climbed down from the truck, and thanked the driver. He had spent the night riding through the hills of Virginia and Kentucky. The driver was a vet. "Hell man, I was just shoveling shit in Fort Huachuca, Arizona. That's the asshole of the fucken army," the driver said. "Wish I could do another hitch and see some combat in Korea."

No cars or trucks moved down the dirt road through Buzzard Hollow, so he walked. Dawn was difficult to notice through the dense valley fog. He remembered Dad saying Bob's house had burned and Bob had rebuilt on the same lot; he hadn't seen the new house—he hadn't seen Bob or his other uncles and aunts since his sophomore year in high school. His parents had continued to visit his Dad's brothers but he had always been too busy with football and dating to make the trip. Nevertheless, he was confident that he would recognize the lot, and thought he would be able to distinguish his uncle's house from most of the other houses along this road. His grandmother had always admonished her sons to stand above the 'trashy' people who have junk around their houses, and her sons' homes always appeared to be well-kept, with manicured lawns—at least, that was the way he remembered it.

He checked his watch: 7:20; he had been walking fast for an hour and a quarter—about five miles, he judged; should be close. Everything seemed much smaller than he remembered. The lake where he had fished with his grandfather was just a pond; the highwall of the abandoned strip mine, that seemed a mountain when he climbed it as a young boy, was no more than 25 feet high; the huge cornfields he hid in were just a few acres in size. He examined several houses along the road carefully; most seemed too junky and one was much too grand to be his uncle's home. In another fifteen minutes of fast walk he reached the curve in the road he remembered and saw his uncle's lot and house. The house was a double-wide manufactured house on a small but well-kept lot. There were rose bushes around the house and a small garden in back. He felt a bit disappointed to see how small and plain his uncle's home appeared to be, but the lawn and roses and absence of junk cars, told him it was the right house.

Bob hadn't recognized him at the door, but was happy to see the uniform. "Come on in!" Bob said. "You're who; Ray's boy? Son, that's the toughest outfit in the army." His Uncle had noticed the AA patch on his shoulder, which told him he was in the *All American* Eighty-Second Airborne Division.

Bob's wife Gloria rushed to greet him with a hug and kiss. "And your sister Barbara, how's she doing? How's her husband? He still got work? And, they tell me she's teaching school; well halleluiah, it's about time someone in this family got an education. And your mother; how's she doing? Still putting up with that no-good brother of Bob's? Well, I ain't seen your folks in a coon's age. What you doing in the Army son; last time I saw you ya' weren't no bigger than that," with a waist-high gesture with her hand, and giving him another hug and kiss.

Bob interrupted his wife: "Woman, will you give this boy a break; he just walked in the door and you're smothering him with all that kissen'. This boy didn't come all the way out here to hear your mushy talk. We're looking at a soldier here! Where's your car son? No car? You walked from the highway? Well hell, I woulda' picked'ya up. Woman why didn't you tell me this boy was walking from the highway; hell, I woulda' picked him up."

"How'ed I know he was coming?"

"Well come on over here and take the load off; tell me about the Army. Are they still as tough as they were back in the war? We were a tough bunch of sons'a bitches in those days son."

"Don't use that language in this house; I've told you that a hundred times," his wife said.

"Well hell, I don't figure it'll shock this soldier here; I reckon this boy has heard a few cuss words; if I ain't mistaken, that's about all they talk in the army. Ain't that so, son?"

Bob was more concerned with the uniform than kinship. He spread his old war maps out on the living room floor, and talked about battles in a grave, but proud, tone. Gloria interrupted a couple of times, telling Bob he needed to get some sleep; Bob worked the graveyard shift in a coal mine, she explained, and had just arrived home from work. "Let the boy relax and take a nap; he needs it after that walk. You can talk this afternoon."

"Go sleep yourself if you want to, woman." Bob said, and got back to his war stories.

Uncle Bob's stories triggered childhood memories. When Bob called his wife *woman*, Mom would glare at Dad, and fume like an overheated pressure cooker. Dad would try to correct his younger brother. "She has a name, Bob; treat her with a little respect!"

"What am I supposed to call her?" Bob would say. "She answers to *woman*, don't she?"

"Call her Gloria! That's her name!" Dad would say.

Mom didn't '*have much use*' for her brother-in-law. Once, through the back screen door, she had seen Bob and his wife rolling around on the floor. "He's going to hurt that girl!" Mom said to Dad, during the ride home from the family reunion.

"Nah," Dad chuckled, "they're just playing around."

"Well, what if he DOES hurt her; rolling around on the floor with her like an animal—and her pregnant?" Mom demanded, in a tone prepped for *I told you so*, if the predicted evil deed came to pass.

Dad had said nothing, of course. What could he say? Mom could absolve herself with that tone, and all future responsibility would rest squarely on Dad's shoulders. He had often wondered why Dad could not simply absolve himself first, and leave all the responsibility to Mom. Either Dad wasn't smart enough to pull it off, or the game just didn't work that way.

Gloria was only seventeen when she married Uncle Bob. Mom had been surprised when the tender girl married the ex-combat soldier just two months home from the war. But, he had not been surprised. Of course Gloria loved Bob. Any woman—other than Mom—would have loved Bob. He loved Bob. Bob was a hero.

Sunday family reunions at Grandma's house substituted for Sunday School and Church about every other weekend. After dinner, the adults would sit around Grandma's kitchen table talking, often with Bob telling war stories. Mom would shoo him and the other kids out of the kitchen because Bob would say bad words, and talk about killing people. He, and some of the other boys, would stand beside the door or outside the window and listen.

Sometimes, Grandma would become upset or sad. She didn't like hearing about her son killing Germans, and liked it even less when he talked about how he was almost killed himself. Grandma's mother had emigrated from Germany as a child, and had taught her children to speak German. Grandma had tried to teach her children German too, but being German was not popular in the late teens and twenties, and her sons had disregarded their German heritage.

"Those are my cousins you're talking about!" Grandma would say.

"To hell with the Germans;" Bob would respond, "I wouldn't give a nickel for a damn German."

Uncle Derek, another of his Dad's younger brothers, two years older than Bob, had been a soldier in the Pacific and had fought in the battle of Okinawa. But, Uncle Derek was not a hero. He didn't tell war stories. Bob did the talking: "Hell, if the Third Army had been in the Pacific, we would'a cleaned out them Japs in two months!"

"Them Japs shoot back Bob, and they weren't scared'a nothing!" Derek said, in a tone that seemed reverent.

"You think them Germans wasn't shooten' back at us?" Bob demanded. "Hell, we was fighting the toughest army in the worrrld!" He would drag that word out to indicate just how much of the world he was referring to.

"I just wanted to get home to my wife," Derek said. "It was her—praying for me back here—that got me home." No, Uncle Derek was not a hero.

"What was your hurry, Derek? Hell, them women over in France would kiss you all over." Bob's smile was audible through the wall, as was the shock on the women's faces. There wasn't time to consider what *kiss you all over* meant, as he scurried away from his listening post, and out of harm's way. Whatever it meant, Mom would careen through that door momentarily, like an overloaded pickup truck with a blow out, and God help any kid standing by the door.

Bob told about how, in a battle at such-and-such place, they had killed 10,000 Germans and taken fifteen prisoners. "When General Patton found out we took them prisoners he said, *you're taking too goddamn many prisoners*." Bob continued, "After that, the only time we took a prisoner was when we wanted to question him." He watched Bob's eyes shine with the thrill and glory of war, and enjoyed the elation of his Uncle's respect. Now, he was a soldier, and he was going to war. Maybe, he would be a hero like Uncle Bob.

He waited on the side of the dirt road for a ride. Hitchhiking in uniform was easy, especially in rural areas, assuming there was a vehicle moving down the road. Almost all drivers were men, and almost all men would pull over when a thumb attached to a uniform was presented. Rides down country roads would be mostly to the next farmhouse or crossroads, and the driver would apologize for the short ride as he stepped out of the vehicle. He felt respect, and sometimes envy, in their voices and eyes.

The morning fog began to dissipate. Suddenly, the wooded ridge to the west was visible. Within the dark green of the oaks and maples were patches of red and yellow, glowing brilliantly in the autumn sun. The grandeur and thrill of Uncle Bob's stories evaporated in the bright crisp air. A disquieting awareness of rebirth filled his consciousness. He was startled by his sudden metamorphosis. The second-string tight-end on the high school football team melted away in the sunlight. HE WAS A SOLDIER! Would he kill? Would he risk his life? When the door of the C47 opened the first time, he had shuddered in anticipation of commands that he knew would come: STAND UP! HOOK UP! STAND IN THE DOOR! Jumping became fun, but there would be other commands. Would he have courage? Would he be brave? He looked back down the dirt road: *Should have stopped to see Uncle Derek*, he told himself.

Then he knew the answer. There would be no question of courage or bravery. He would make no decisions. There would be commands, and he would obey. Perhaps he would shudder or cry or pray, but he would obey. He would stand up, hook up, and stand in the door. And, he would jump!

PATTERNS AND IMAGES IN THE DUST: ECUADOR, MONDAY AFTERNOON

The American girl across the aisle talks with someone in the window seat beside her. She reaches up to the rack above her seat, and fumbles to retrieve a small backpack. Through the sleeve of her blouse, I see the curve of her breast, and a hairy armpit. I repress an initial impulse of repugnance. It's okay GI; beatnik types don't shave their underarms, I tell myself.

"Señor, señor," she calls to the man standing beside the bus driver, *"el proximo calle nosotros salir el bus."* It's gringo Spanish and the man doesn't understand. He looks at her with a twisted, questioning face. I know exactly what she wants to say. She's getting off this bus, I tell myself; you have to get off too. I am anxious and disoriented. Do you have the time?

Who cares? There's no way I'm staying on this bus! I yell to the man in Spanish, *"She is getting off at the next highway."*

"A Atacames?" the man asks.

"You're going to Atacames?" I ask her.

"Yeah;" I nod affirmative to the man.

"You speak Spanish," she says.

"Some." My Spanish is very good, but I want to sound casual.

"How'd you learn Spanish?" she asks; her voice sounds friendly.

"I studied at Mexico City College, on the GI Bill." I want to correct myself immediately, but it's too late. Why did you say that? I ask myself. Why the hell did you lie to her? The words just came out, damn it; I didn't even think about it. Hell, I did study at Mexico City College! Lived in Tacubaya; took the Toluca bus to the College every morning from the Flower Market in the *glorieta*. I know that place like the back of my hand. Why do you think I'm lying? I ask myself.

I am confused, and talking to myself in my thoughts makes it worse. I know I have a puzzled look on my face. I had left the conversation hanging in the air. She is waiting for me to continue, but gives up, and turns to the person next to her.

Oh, shit! She has someone with her. Yeah, she said *nosotros*, I tell myself. The fellow rouses himself, yawning and complaining. Obviously, he is an American. He is taller than her and has his black hair is combed straight back, so it fluffs up and out on the top and sides, making his head appear very big. He wears Levis and a short-sleeved shirt. He's carrying too much weight; yeah, like most guys in civilian life, I tell myself. I think about him in boot camp: Sunny boy, you would put a smile on the Drill Instructor's face, just thinking about how long it would take to convert that two hundred and twenty pounds of flab, into one hundred and eighty pounds of muscle.

"Come on, Johnny!" she tells him. "This is our stop. Get with it, will you; and, don't forget anything."

"I have everything," her friend says, defensively.

I think about the two of them. They don't fit together. She's too tough, and he's too dainty. This stuff about opposites attracting is bullshit! They're together, but maybe not really together. She didn't look at you the way a girl does when she has a man with her, I tell myself. And, they don't talk to each other as if they were together—really together. And, even if they are, you sure as hell wouldn't need a crowbar to pry them apart!

The bus slows and pulls off the highway in front of a small *tienda*. The *tienda* is a combination store and restaurant, with a couple of tables out front. The layout is identical to *tiendas* located at virtually every crossroads in Latin America. There is a small Coca-Cola sign nailed to the outside wall near the door. That little splash of red, along with the tables, is the only indication that it is a commercial establishment. The Coca-Cola sign is also the only visual break in the dull brown color of the adobe walled and thatch-covered shelter. The dusty yard contains a single twig, about three feet high, bearing a couple of tiny branches with a few dusty leaves. There is a trickle of wetness, extending a foot or so away from the base of the would-be tree, which is more suggestive of dog urine than a deliberate attempt at irrigation.

The fellow stumbles off the bus, and walks over and sits at one of the tables in front of the *tienda*. The woman stands beside the bus, waiting for the man to open the bottom cargo door. The man removes a half-full duffel bag and places it on the ground in front of her. Forget it! I tell myself, that's as close as you'll get to a real woman for the duration. She is standing directly below me, and I can almost see down her blouse. I think about the curve of her breast.

She looks up and catches me looking. There is no way to pretend I'm not looking, so I look. She smiles and waves to me. I take my cap off and point to it, to remind her of my story. She mimics my idiot look in a less exaggerated form—tongue slightly out the corner of her mouth and head tilted, with hands moving back and forth, instead of wagging the head. I am thinking she looks cute.

No she doesn't, I correct myself. That girl isn't a cheerleader GI; she plays football! And, there is no way she is really with that guy! When she picks up the bag the front of her blouse falls down slightly. I remember the shape of the walnut topped Vienna white chocolate candies Mom used to make, especially the curve where the candies meet the cookie pan. Oh lord, were they good! I continue to watch her and wonder if she knows I caught a glimpse of her breasts. She looks up, smiles again and waves, and then carries the bag to the table where the fellow is busy drinking a beer.

To hell with it, I tell myself; we have things to do, and people to see, and miles to go before we sleep. Suddenly, I feel panic. What things to do? What people to see? Miles to where? I think about the dog in that hollow place in the back of my brain. She made the dog go away; when I looked at her breasts the dog went away.

You have to get off this bus, I tell myself. I find myself moving toward the front of the bus without realizing I have made the decision to get off. The bus is already rolling forward and the driver's helper is running along outside, about to jump aboard. "Hey!" I say. The driver pays no attention. "*Oye!*" That gets his attention. "*I'm getting off, too.*" I tell him, in Spanish. The bus slows.

The man climbing the ramp blocks my way. "*The ticket is for Esmeraldas,*" he says.

"I don't care what the ticket says," I say in English, and, "*Aquí*"; meaning, right here. The bus pulls off the highway again. I step down off the bus, and start back down the road toward the *tienda*. The woman and her friend have already crossed the highway and are walking down a dirt road. Apparently, they have not noticed me getting off the bus. She is walking ahead with the small backpack, and her friend goes along behind with the duffel bag.

Why would I want to go to Esmeraldas? I ask myself. It's the worse dump in the country. So, why were you going to Esmeraldas? The question is deeply troubling. I feel disoriented and alone. "What the hell are you doing?" I hear myself ask. Talking to myself aloud makes the confusion worse. I stumble on a rock, and almost fall down. There is a shrill whistle behind me. I turn back ready to confront the man jeering at me for stumbling. But, the man holds up a large brown bag and heaves it in my direction.

The bus starts rolling forward, and the man turns and runs for the bus door. These drivers always start moving before the driver's helper is on board, I tell myself. Who can be more macho? The man who jumps on and off the moving bus, or the driver putting him at risk? For some reason, the scene reminds me of the clowns in the bullring.

The bus churns up a cloud of dust pulling onto the road. When the dust clears, I see a shimmering image through the heat waves behind the bus. That bus had been my cocoon for a while, but now I watch it disappear. The loss gives me a feeling of apprehension of what may lie ahead, but at the same time there is a refreshing sense of renewal. I like not knowing what my next mode of transport will be.

I walk back and stand looking at the dust covered brown bag on the side of the road. You must be going crazy GI, I tell myself—walking away without your bag. The well-worn leather bag is only vaguely familiar. I pick the bag up, and turn back toward the *tienda*. It is almost mid-day and very hot. I take off my cap, and wipe the sweat from my forehead on the sleeve of my shirt. From thirty feet above, I observe myself walk to the table in front of the *tienda*, and drop the bag on top. Where the hell are you going? What are you doing? I ask the empty figure standing below.

"For the life of me, I can't remember this bag," I hear myself say aloud. But, I do remember it. A mestizo woman comes to the table and waits. "*Cerveza fría*," I say. I look toward the dirt road again, but the woman and her friend are already out of sight, around a bend. The *tienda* woman returns, and puts a bottle of *Bavaria* beer on the table. I turn the bottle up, and drink almost half without stopping.

"*Otra*," I say, and turn the bottle up again. She returns with the second beer as I take the last swallow from the first. I slam the empty bottle down on the table harder than I had meant to so it makes a loud noise; then I hear myself belch.

"*Que bruto!*" the woman says, softly.

16

That's a good description of you, I tell myself. Brutish! Why don't you stop trying to be the biggest shit-head in the country? *"Perdon, Señora,"* I say to her, and turn up the second bottle. The woman is obviously waiting to be paid. *"Cuanto?"* She just looks at me. *"The beers Señora, how much?"*

"Twenty. They are ten pesos each," she replies hesitantly.

"Ten pesos each?" I allow my irritation to show. That's about forty cents US, I tell myself. They charge that at a fine restaurant in Quito. A beer should be three or four peso in this dump.

"That's the way it is," she says. *"We are very isolated, and they charge for transportation."*

"Yeah, I'll bet!" I respond in English. "Well, I'm not going to sweat twenty pesos." I pull a wad of bills from my pocket. The wad of money is very fat, mostly fifty and one hundred peso notes, along with some US currency. No sweat, indeed! I am surprised by the amount of money in my pocket. The woman gawks at the wad of money. Hey stupid, I tell myself, don't show off your money. News of the rich gringo in the neighborhood will spread like word of a well-heeled ringer in a pool hall. I pull a twenty-peso note from the wad, drop it on the table, and put the rest away. I throw the bag over my left shoulder and with the beer in my right hand, turn back to cross the highway.

"Oye, la botella," she shouts.

"The bottle; I answer in English, "So how much do you want for the bottle?"

"Veinte pesos," she replies, as if she has understood my English perfectly.

"Twenty pesos; ten for the beer and twenty for the bottle, huh?" I say in English.

"Aquí estamos muy aislados," she whines.

"Yeah, I know. We are very isolated," I say to her, still speaking English. I take one more drink and drop the bottle to the ground. As I cross the highway I see the woman rush over to retrieve the bottle before all the beer runs out. Interesting how they can figure out what you're saying, even when they don't know a word of English, I tell myself.

Across the highway, I stop to examine a small sign at the dirt road, 'Atacames 7'. Seven kilometers to this place, I tell myself; isn't even worth a decent sign. Probably a fishing village or beach resort for the locals. I think about the woman at the *tienda* again, and turn for a look. She is putting the cap back on the partly-filled bottle. Still three pesos worth of beer left in the bottle GI, I tell myself. "God, I love these people!" I hear myself say aloud.

I can see about a half-mile to the curve in the road. The woman and her friend are not in sight. I have lost about fifteen minutes, so they can't be more than three quarters of a mile ahead—maybe less. I throw the bag over my back and slide my arms through the handles as if it were a backpack, and move forward at a quick trot. "Double time, HUAA," I call aloud to the invisible platoon of soldiers jogging along with me.

I feel good. We would jog three or four miles every morning before breakfast, just to start the day. In the field we would often walk fifteen miles or more, with full packs and weapons. My legs have never disappointed me. They have always done everything you've asked them to, I tell myself. I think about guys, some of them bigger and seemingly stronger, almost weeping from pain as they stumbled along, just trying to put one foot in front of the other. I love the sweat and the heat and the pain. Jogging four miles under a tropical sun: Like a bartender pouring himself a cold one at the end of the day!

It is hot—probably one hundred degrees—almost as hot as it can get in the high humidity of the hot wet tropics. The land on either side of the road is a grassy savanna with scattered palm and acacia trees. The small trees and bushes, growing along the road, are enough to choke off even the wisp of a breeze I felt out on the highway. Sweat runs down my face, and collects at the end of my nose, and the tip of the visor of my cap. Before the drops can fall, I blow them off with a quick puff at my nose, and they hit the ground a half step in front. I am in a rhythm; every fourth time my left foot hits the ground, I blow the sweat out in front.

Rounding the curve, I can see the girl and her friend about a half-mile ahead, about to round another bend. Moved faster than you thought, I tell myself. I stop to wait for them to get around the bend, and out of sight. A small tree nearby affords some shade. I walk over and think about dropping my bag, and then decide not to. "Screw it! It's the bipods!" I hear myself say aloud. I walk back and stand in the sun, enjoying the joke on myself. You're the biggest fuckup in This Man's Army, I tell myself.

As they round the bend I move out again at a quick walk. I don't want them to see me coming—don't want them to know how eager I am to catch up. Sweat collects on my nose and cap more slowly. Now I blow the sweat out in front every sixth time my left foot hits the ground. I see those dark splotches in the dust for half a second, before my left foot obliterates them. They make patterns and shapes—some with vivid detail.

There is a girl's face, with her hair blowing in the wind; the splatter of a clown's blood in the sand; a man with no head, suspended upside down; a peninsula appendage of a continent. There is a truck on its side in the muddy road, with soldiers scrambling away from the burning wreckage in all directions. I observe the scene from above, as if hovering in a helicopter, but I know one of the tiny specks is me, looking back over my shoulder at the burning truck. There is a girl, lying on her back; her legs are open, and she holds her arms up to me. Her eyes are half closed, and her lips parted slightly. As my left foot obliterates her image, I fall on her, and push my tongue deep into her warm mouth.

I think about the expression 'This Man's Army'. Sergeants and Officers used that expression when making the rules and regulations clear to the grunts. 'You fuck with This Man's Army and you'll be in a world'a shit!' 'Your soul may belong to God, but your ass belongs to This Man's Army!' they would say.

To me it had always been '<u>THIS</u> Man's Army', not 'This <u>MAN'S</u> Army'. It was not an army of men, but an army that belongs to THIS man; that is, to someone, somewhere else. The army didn't belong to the soldiers or officers and certainly not to me. Maybe, the army belonged to all the soldiers who have served in the past; or, maybe it belonged to God.

A MISFIT IN THIS MAN'S ARMY: FORT BRAGG, AUTUMN, 1952

The Korean War started when he was seventeen, just finishing High School. He talked to an army recruiter immediately and learned he could not join without his parent's permission until he was eighteen years old. He knew there was no way his parents would give permission.

He signed up on his eighteenth birthday, and volunteered for a combat unit. That disobedience was one of the few times he had acted against his parent's wishes. Korea was his war, and he didn't want to miss it. He reasoned they could have never understood his need to experience the war.

In the Eighty-Second Airborne, he was a misfit. He was from a good home and had done well in school. He loved to read and wanted to become a journalist. In school, he made good grades with little effort, and enjoyed learning. Most of the other guys in his outfit, and other hard-core combat units, were from poor families and many had not completed high school.

He had declined an opportunity for Officer Candidate School. That would have required an additional three-year hitch, and the war might have been over before he would finish officer training. Besides, there was a certain excitement in a hard life without decisions and choices. I made it today, he would tell himself, and whatever they throw at us, I will make it tomorrow. Before I fall down, the ground will be cluttered with guys like junk cars around the houses on Buzzard Hollow Road.

The first time he was assigned to CQ duty, he sat at the First Sergeant's desk for four hours during the night to respond to the phone and radio. He examined the list of names and codes under the glass cover of the Sergeant's desk. The men in the company were listed in alphabetical order by platoon, and each name was followed by two untitled codes: N or W, and a number. His own code was W 128.

Checking the guys in his platoon, he quickly discovered the meaning of N and W: Negro or White. Obviously, the First Sergeant, himself a Black man, needed to keep track of the race of his men. The army was integrated; there was no visible barrier between Blacks and Whites, but the barrier was there. The potential for race conflict was a clear and present danger to army morale.

Decoding the number was a bit tougher. Many of the numbers were in the high eighties or nineties, and almost all below 110. There were only four numbers above 125. One other guy in his platoon had a high number, Buck Sergeant Hart, a Black fellow in the first squad of his platoon. He thought about some of the guys who had numbers in the eighties, and then considered Sergeant Hart. Then, he knew what the numbers meant.

He made a mental note of the other two names with high numbers. He would try to get to know those guys. One was Patterson, in the second platoon, who later became his buddy—his best friend. He had not considered becoming friends with Sergeant Hart. Both the rank and skin color made that impossible. Nevertheless, he would always consider Hart to be an ally, and Sergeant Hart did turn out to be an ally.

He tried to make sense of the apparent insanity of the army way of doing things. Fall in! Fatigue uniforms and weapons! Restack weapons in armory, T-shirts and pistol belts with ponchos. Fatigue jackets and weapons, fall in on the double! Changes and conflicting orders came and went with little more moment than Amends and Hallelujahs at a tent revival. Prepare for the Inspecting General, polish your boots, footlockers must be in perfect order! Four hours later those boots were slogging through the mud. Hurry up and wait! No one seemed to be sure what the orders were. 'No one has the word,' soldiers would tell each other.

But, there was method in the madness. They were pushed forward and shoved back; insulted and then praised; abused and then rewarded. They were punch drunk—reacting to the lunacy without thinking. He was a participant, but also an observer. Most of the guys seemed to be unaware of the process at work. They simply reacted to the events that panicked and then soothed. They began to follow orders blindly—orders that made no sense, even to the officers and sergeants issuing them. That, of course, was the point of the apparent madness.

On those Sunday afternoons when the grunts were given free time, he would discuss the process with Patterson. They drank beer at the club, and considered the army way. Patterson had understood the process immediately, and even had a name for it: *Behavior modification training.* Much later he would hear the term *'brain washing'* meaning something the Chinese did to American prisoners of war. But, there was no doubt in his mind that the U.S. Army knew as much about brain washing as the Chinese.

Understanding the process at work, and recognize the symptoms among fellow soldiers, was comforting. But, he harbored a deep fear, never shared with his friend Patterson, that the behavior modification process was also affecting him.

He and Patterson worked out strategies to deal with the army. The first rule was stay in the biggest crowd. A sergeant could work one or two guys half to death. But, making a group of twenty or thirty soldiers work would require a whole covey of sergeants. "Don't let um' catch your eye or read your nametag, or you're dead meat," Pat would say. During Basic and Airborne training, Sergeants usually didn't know anyone's name, and would just say 'hey you', when catching a man's eye, or 'hey Jones', after reading the man's nametag on the front of his fatigue jacket. Casually looking away and covering one's nametag would prevent eye contact and name recognition.

Sergeants would come through the barracks after work and on Sundays, like barracuda through a school of fish, 'looking for volunteers'. A sergeant came into the mess hall on Sunday morning. "The WAC'S (Women's Army Corps) have a softball game in Fayetteville; anyone here know how to drive a truck?"

"Not on your fucken life, GI." Pat whispered, across the table. A soldier, smiling like a man with visions of breasts bouncing their way to first base stepped forward, and spent his Sunday scrubbing mud off trucks in the motor pool.

The second rule was to have fun. "Beat um' at their own game;" Pat would say, "fuck with their minds!" Whatever the situation, no matter how dismal, tiring, or purposeless, there would be something that could be made fun or funny. While marching, drag your right foot as if chained to the man behind. It's contagious; soon every man in the platoon, not being observed by the Sergeant, will join the chain gang. Loading up for a two-week field problem: "Come on Serge; give me a three-day pass—shit." The request is so bizarre the Sergeant can't even enjoy saying no. As a sergeant walks by, "Who's writing a letter to their congressman?" And, when questioned further by the anxious sergeant, "Hell, I don't know Serge; one of those fucken guys over there said something about it." Walk around with a clipboard looking at nametags, and scribble something on the pad. "Get my fucken name off that list!" a corporal said, knowing how terrible and irrevocable the consequences of having your name on a list can be—even a list drawn up by a grunt. Indeed, a grunt could walk around with a clipboard and pencil for days, avoiding all work, and few sergeants or officers would dare to ask what he was doing. Pick out something particularly stupid some sergeant or officer says, and repeat it endlessly: The Company's Commanding Officer (CO) ends his briefing for a field problem with the optimistic statement, 'There's no rain in sight!' At 3:30 the next morning the Company wakes to pounding rain, and twenty guys yell, as if rehearsed, '*NO RAIN IN SIGHT!*' The CO is tormented with his new nickname, yelled from a window or crowd of soldiers, for the remainder of his tenure as company commander. Indeed, the reason Captain 'No Rain In Sight' requested transfer may well have been because he couldn't live with his new name.

Inspecting officers could be intimidated. On the top shelf of the wall locker a soldier was allowed to have some personal item—usually a picture of a girlfriend or parents. Patterson recommended placing a book or two there, especially something heavy, like mathematics or philosophy. The inspecting officer's eyes would be drawn to those items, and everything else would be ignored. The notion that a soldier could read and think was sufficiently novel to intimidate, or positively influence, officers and some of the brighter sergeants. His choices were a dog-eared and underscored copy of <u>The Portable Nietzsche</u>, a book titled <u>The History of Mathematics</u>, and whatever paperback he happened to be reading at the time. The books worked like magic! Most inspecting officers would notice the books, and simply move on to the next man, as if he were contaminated with some lethal virus, or an Army Intelligence plant.

Once his Commanding Officer held a surprise inspection on Saturday afternoon with an apparent determination to confine anyone with a tiny flaw in their appearance or equipment to barracks for duty on Sunday. Reaching his bunk, the officer's eyes were drawn to the open locker and the books on the top shelf. The CO extracted the Nietzsche book and examined it carefully, as if he might have found a secret pocket filled with marijuana or pornographic pictures.

"You read this book, soldier?"

"Yes Sir."

His Commanding Officer replaced the book and moved on the next man, and he was among the few with Sunday off. Later, he was picked to carry the CO's radio on field problems.

He had been with the CO and the other officers while they discussed the case of Rand, a trooper in his squad. After following the CO around for a week with the radio, his presence was mostly ignored. That night there was no moonlight—a complete blackout—and the discussion of Private Rand took place as he, his CO, and the officers stood around a jeep. They spoke as if no enlisted man were listening.

Rand had been AWOL several times. He had been busted to buck private, then given hard labor, and finally sent to the stockade. One of the officers recommended dishonorable discharge; another suggested leaving him in the stockade with 'bad time,' since time spent in the stockade did not count toward a man's enlistment.

He responded to their discussion as if he were one of their colleagues: "Rand is just homesick and thinks he can get a medical discharge. Just go down there and tell him he has a choice of doing bad time in the stockade or coming back to the platoon. Hell, if you give him half-a-chance, he'll be the best soldier you have in this outfit."

There was total silence while the officers digested advice coming from an enlisted man. He waited for the reprimand, but his CO said nothing. The other officers, realizing the discussion had ended, drifted away. The CO finally turned to him. "Get some sleep soldier. I want you alert tomorrow."

"Yes Sir."

Rand was returned to the squad, and told his story. "The CO comes in to see me in the stockade and says: *Rand, there's two ways this can go down. You can do the rest of your three months here and come back to the Company, and when you fuckup, you come back here for another three months—all bad time—and we can keep doing that just as long as I'm breathing. The other way is you can come back to the Company now and shape up. It'll take you four months to get promoted from recruit to private; that's regulation. But, I'll give you the PFC stripe one month later. How about it?"*

"So shit man," Rand continued, "I figured I'd better get my ass in gear." Rand really did prove to be one of the best soldiers in the outfit. Indeed, he was the first White grunt in the squad to make corporal. Of course, making corporal wasn't a big deal, and lots of Black guys achieved that rank early. But, most White guys didn't figure on being in the Army long enough to make working for promotion worthwhile.

Rand was also the first trooper in his platoon to be killed in Korea. The truck hit a mine and rolled over. Everyone except Rand got out the back before the truck burned. The driver and a Lieutenant didn't make it out of the cab either. That nasty introduction to Korea came on their fifth day in the country. After that day, he would replay the scene countless times: He would observe from above, as if in a helicopter, watching the truck roll over and burst into flames. He would see himself and the other soldiers scramble away from the burning truck, and almost see Rand's hand grasp the tailgate. Maybe Rand's rebellion against the army had been a premonition. Maybe if he had kept his mouth shut on that moonless night when he stood by the jeep with the officers, Rand would have been in the stockade, rather than burned alive in that damned truck.

Many of the sergeants were Blacks, especially in combat units. His platoon Sergeant was typical—a tough Black man from Georgia. Sergeant Jordan was in his early 30's, and in his prime as a soldier. With only twelve years in, he was sure to make First Sergeant before completing his army career. Everyone said Sergeant Jordan had more combat medals than would fit on the front of his dress uniform. No one had ever seen a single one of them, but there was no reason to doubt the stories.

Jordan was self-secure. He was much respected by everyone in the unit, but he didn't seem to notice. He could dish out punishment with equanimity, and didn't need to get mad; indeed, it was rare for him to even raise his voice. Most of the troopers were in their late teens or early twenties. Sergeant Jordan usually referred to them as son or youngster.

Blacks made up only a small share of all non-Commissioned Officers during World War II, but they were far more likely to have stayed in the army. Black guys usually liked the army much more than most White guys. The reason was no mystery; the army treated them pretty square—almost as square as White guys. In the army a Black man could get a fair deal.

Most of the other noncoms were southerners—poor boys from Alabama, Mississippi, and Georgia. The army treated them square, too. The grunts called the career guys 'lifers'. They called themselves RA, a term derived from "Regular Army," the prefix attached to a volunteer's serial number. RA had come to mean a good soldier—a guy who fit the Army mold. If you said a guy was RA, it meant you could count on him to do his job; it probably also meant he was a lifer.

Black guys and the Good Old Boys from the South were RA. Seeing them work together seemed strange at first. He remembered the time Staff Sergeant Brooks, a White guy from Alabama, came in as replacement squad leader of the third squad. Brooks walked into the barracks, dropped his duffel bag in front of a bunk, and shook hands with Sergeant Jordan. "Now Sergeant, I ain't use ta'taken orders from you people," he said, with his Alabama accent and his Alabama smile on his face.

"Well, son," Jordan said calmly, "I gonna' give you five minutes ta'get use to it. An' if ya' ain't use to it by then, you'cn get yo' shit back up on yo' back, and get it the fuck out'ta my platoon."

"Hey, wait-a-minute, sergeant; I don't mean no disrespect. I know whose's in charge here, an' I do my job!"

"Then you and me gonna' get along just fine."

"Look sergeant, maybe I could buy you a beer at the NCO club tonight, and we can start all over again."

"We can start all over again right now, sergeant." The two men shook hands again.

"You can count on me sergeant."

"I intend to sergeant; this is the worst fucken shithole I ever seen an' I need all the help I can get." Jordan and Brooks got along fine after that—they were both RA.

I Don't Think It's My Bag: Road to Atacames, Monday Afternoon

As I round a bend I see the woman and her friend about fifty yards away. They are standing at a large red hand pump on a concrete slab, beside the road. She is pumping water, and her friend has his head under the spout. They have seen me, so I walk on up to the well.

"Who said you could take a break. We have four K to go," I say, trying to sound cheerful.

"Hey man, I'm carrying a heavy bag," he says. I lift the duffel bag, testing the weight, and let it drop. "So, you carry it, if you think it's so easy," her friend says.

"No thanks; looks like you need the exercise." Immediately, I regret my sarcasm. I learned a long time ago that when you say something like that to a guy, he will usually repay you one way or another. It's a stupid and nonproductive exercise, and sometimes it's dangerous.

"Get off him!" she says. But, she seems to be glad to see me. "So, you're going to Atacames, huh? Well, why not! We can use the company. Here, bend over and soak your head," she offers to work the pump. I slid my bag off and lean down to fill my cupped hands, and splash the water in my face. Then I fill my cap with water and pour it over my head.

"I'm Shirley; this is Johnny," she says brightly, and holds out her hand.

"Nice to meet you officially," I say, shaking her hand. Johnny has his hand out, but I am busy with Shirley.

"Maybe, he doesn't want to shake my hand," he says.

"Why not, Johnny?" turning to him, but he has pulled his hand back. "Whatever," I say, absent-mindedly.

"So?" she says.

"So...I thought I would just tag along with you to Atacames," I respond.

"Whatever," she replies, obviously mocking me. Seconds tick past and I am at a loss for words. "Want to introduce yourself?" She asks.

Somehow, I can't respond. I want to respond, but can't seem to say anything. Several long seconds pass. "Come on, Johnny. I'm sure Mr. Jerk can find his way to Atacames without our help." Her friend seems to enjoy this twist on the conversation. He picks up the duffel bag, and marches off behind her.

"Hey," I call after them, "I'm not trying to be a jerk; it's just that..."

"It's just that you can't help it, huh?" she says without stopping or looking back. I catch up with her in a few strides.

"No. It's just that... You know, I just don't know what to say."

"Who asked you to say anything?" We walk along in silence for a bit, and then she continues slowly, as if measuring the words carefully: "I just thought ...you might not mind ...introducing yourself."

"Well, no; I don't mind. I'm Ray."

"You just get out of the army?" her friend asks, looking at my boots.

"No."

"You weren't in the service?" she asks. I shake my head. "So what about Mexico City College and the GI Bill? How did you get the GI Bill, if you weren't in the service?"

"No, I didn't just get out. Yeah, I was a GI." I can't seem to make my brain work. There is another awkward silence.

"So, when were you in the army?" she asks.

"I was just thinking about it...just as I caught up with you guys. I was thinking about when I was in the army." I don't know what to say. The empty feeling reminds me of static lines trailing in the wind, behind the open door of a C47. All the troopers have jumped, and there is nothing left but an empty door and the cords that pulled the chutes open, flapping in the wind. If I could be alone I could think; but I don't want to leave her. What the hell is happening to you? I ask myself. A sudden wave of depression rolls over me, and I turn away from them.

"Oh, really; don't break my heart," Johnny says.

"Look," I say to her, "I'm just a little confused. I woke up on that damned bus and just didn't know where I was."

"How long have you been down here?" she asks.

"I don't know; about a month."

"And, before that?"

"I don't know. I've been kicking around Latin America for a couple of years."

"What do you mean you don't know? Don't you know where you were before Ecuador?"

"I said I was just kicking around. What the hell difference does it make?"

"To me, none; to you, I would hope it would make a difference."

"A couple of years, huh;" Johnny says, "so you're independently wealthy?"

"No."

"So, how can you afford to travel around here for two years?" she asks.

"I have a few bucks coming in, and I don't spend much. What the hell is this?"

"A few bucks coming in from where?" Johnny asks.

"That's none of your damned business; I didn't steal it!"

"No! I didn't think you would have stolen it. Guys who carry red passports are way too straight for that," he replies.

"Red passport; you think I'm a diplomat or something?"

"Yeah; or something;" he says, shaking his head. He picks up his duffel bag and marches on down the road, as if walking away from a drunken panhandler.

"So? What's his problem?" I ask. She shrugs, and seems as mystified as I am about Johnny's attitude. We pick up our bags and walk in silence for a bit.

Johnny has stopped and is waiting for us. He has his legs spread wide and his closed fists on his hips. He has the look of a Baptist preacher, about to spew fire and brimstone down on the backsliders. He needs to do something to restore his self-esteem, I tell myself. He won't need much of a victory; hell, let him have it.

"They must pay you pretty well for what you do!" he says.

I stop a couple of steps away. You feel better now Johnny boy, I am thinking; but he isn't finished.

"Saving the whole free world, huh? What is it, the DIA?"

The Defense Intelligence Agency accusation is as if he has slapped my face. I drop my bag, and close the distance between us. "Got to keep the military in power down here, right? Wouldn't want the commies to take over, would we," he says, as if shouting down to the sinners from the moral high ground.

"You're pushing your fucken luck!" I say, stepping toward him. He is three or four inches taller than me and probably outweighs me by forty or fifty pounds, but there is no question in my mind about the outcome of a fight between us. I let my right arm go limp and shake it from the shoulder. The maneuver is designed to disarm him and to prepare for my punch. I will jerk my fist toward his face, snapping my wrist, elbow, and shoulder locked at the exact moment of impact to maximize the thrust. The sound he will hear will be my yell, but he will probably think it is the sound of his jawbone being crushed. I will hit him hard enough to knock him down, and if he tries to get up I will hit him again. I want it over in a hurry.

He steps back and raises his arms with his hands open toward me. Apparently, there is no doubt in his mind about the outcome either. She grabs my arm, and jerks me back. "Cut it out, damn it!"

"So, why don't you show us your passport?" her friend asks.

She jerks my arm again, and I am surprised by her strength. "I've had about enough macho shit for one day," she says, giving me a hard stare. Then she turns to her friend, and gives him the same treatment. He hesitates, and then picks up his bag and walks on. I turn to pick up my bag, but she pulls my arm hard.

"Don't try to get physical with me jerk, or him either. I'm not afraid of you!" She is looking straight into my eyes, and squeezing my arm hard enough to actually hurt. Somehow the situation seems comical. I smile and try to shrug. She surprises me with a hard punch to my chest with her right fist. The punch doesn't really hurt, but it's a solid punch. I have raised my fists instinctively, in self-defense, but drop them quickly.

"Hey, you have quite a punch." I say.

"I told you, hay is for horses. My name isn't hay, and I don't take shit from you or anyone else."

"Okay. I can see that." I look down at her left hand on my right forearm, and she slowly releases her grip. I step back slightly and raise both hands, with my palms out toward her. "Okay, you're not going to get any shit from me," I say, surprised there is no tone of condescension in my voice.

We walk on. This is one hell of a woman! I tell myself. You have to like this woman, GI; hell, you have to love her! "You're one hell of a woman," I say.

She looks away from me. Hey man, don't piss her off, I tell myself. What could you do if she started hitting and kicking? Bet she could hurt you; couldn't hit her back; have to run. I imagine myself running full tilt, with her in hot pursuit. The thought makes me giggle. She can probably run fast. What if she catches you? What then? The scene is too much, and I burst out laughing. She walks slowly to the side of the road, and sits on grassy mound, fanning her face with her hand. I try to suppress my laughter, but a silly giggle continues for a couple of seconds. When I regain control, I walk over to her, again with both hands out and palms facing her—the universal expression of 'I give up.'

"You think it's funny," she says.

"No, I was just thinking, hey...no, wait a minute..." watch out for the 'hay' word, I tell myself, "I was just thinking that, ahh...I've never been beaten up by a woman and, ahh...there's always a first time for everything, and, ahh...better watch my step." My giggling starts again, but her look tells me she is not enjoying my joke. I control myself.

"So, what color is your passport?"

"I'm not with the DIA, damn it! I don't know where my passport is."

"Maybe it's in your bag."

"I don't know... Maybe... I don't think it's my bag." She gives me a raised eyebrows questioning look. That was a stupid thing to say, I tell myself. You know damned well it's your bag. What are you trying to hide? I drop the bag on a grassy area nearby, unzip the top and pull the bag open.

"Well, that's appropriate. Dirty underwear on top," she says.

I take out the underwear, and lay it on the grass. "It's not dirty, I just didn't fold it." I say.

Suddenly, I realize my passport isn't in the bag. "I don't carry my passport in my bag," I say, embarrassed. "I carry it here." I unbutton my shirt, and pull out the pouch attached to the chain that once carried my army dog tags. "I carry it here when I'm traveling, so it won't get stolen." I zip open the pouch, remove my passport, and hold it for a couple of seconds. I don't want to open the cover.

"Well, whada' ya' know; a passport." She says. We both look at the thick, worn, green-covered document in my hand. The passport is as familiar to me as my mother's face, and yet I am almost afraid of it. I offer it to her, but she doesn't accept. We stand looking at each other for a few more seconds saying nothing.

"You can look through my bag if you want. You're not going to find any DIA badges or guns in there." I say, still offering the passport.

She frowns, and brushes the air down with her hand, as if declining an offer to check my breath for the smell of onions. After a couple of seconds, she reaches over and takes the passport from my hand, and thumbs through the pages. There is an accordion foldout section that was added when all the original pages were filled with visa stamps. She shakes the passport and the accordion section drops, unfolding to the ground.

"Quite a traveler," she says. She picks up the foldout, and begins to read the country names on the visa stamps: Honduras, Nicaragua, Costa Rica, Nicaragua, British Honduras, Mexico, British Honduras." She stops reading, refolds the pages, and holds the passport out to me. "Well, shall we find out who you work for or, shall I just assume it's the DIA?"

"Go ahead, you're in charge." Again, we wait for a couple of seconds. I take the passport and open the cover page. The picture of my face seems to be contorted. On the line labeled occupation is the word 'student'. I hand the document to her.

"Raymond Lewis Richards, student; sounds like an aristocrat. Was your father's name Lewis?"

"No. His name is Raymond; Lewis is my mother's maiden name." I hear my voice shake, and feel ridiculous and ashamed. I want to brush off my silly behavior, but can't think of a reasonable explanation. "I'm sorry; I don't know what the hell was the matter with me. I just woke up on that damned bus and everything was so strange. I didn't know where I was." She waits for me to continue. "I've been traveling a lot and...; you know how sometimes, when you are traveling, you wake up and don't know where you are?"

"Yeah, I've had that feeling. But, I never forget which bag was mine, or where I'm going, or where my passport was, or who I work for!"

"I'm sorry, I didn't really forget. I was just confused for a minute." I turn away from her in embarrassment.

"Has this happened to you before?"

"No, no, never; give me a little break, okay?"

Her hand on my arm startles me. "Take it easy," she says. "You've had a hard knock; it's okay. Probably something happened back there and you're trying to repress it. It's going to be okay; just settle down."

"Thanks." I hear my voice crack, and hate the fact that I sound weak and helpless.

"Come on, we'll walk on and you can think. Just take it easy." I put my things back into my bag, and we walk on in silence for a bit. The past few minutes has been a shattering experience for me and I'm not sure what I should be doing or thinking.

"Atacames is a nice place; you'll like it." She says. "Why were you going to Esmeraldas?" I don't respond. "Why?"

"I don't know. I swear I can't remember getting on that damned bus." I have difficulty controlling my voice, and the embarrassment makes me wince.

"I have a friend in town—in Esmeraldas—she can help you. She has had medical training, and she's really smart."

"I don't want to talk to any of those damned people."

"What do you mean, those damned people? You don't know anything about her."

"I know all about those people."

"You know all about what people, psychologists?"

"Look, I just don't want some do-gooder working on my case. I just don't want to talk to her, okay?"

"Maybe you don't want to talk to me either," she says.

"Wait, I'm sorry I'm such a damned jerk. Sure I want to talk to you. Jeez, when you got off the bus back there I just couldn't stand... that's why I came after you." She waits for me to continue. "I don't mean I was after you. Hell, I'm not going to do anything to you—or to your friend either. I just want to tag along with you for a while, till I can..."

"Until you can get your head together?"

"Yeah, I can't believe I did that—that stupid memory thing. You're going to think I'm a damned psychopath."

"No I won't," she responds.

"And, I'm sorry for what I said to your friend. I'll tell him I'm sorry, okay?"

"You'll have your chance in a couple of minutes," nodding at Johnny, now only about fifty yards ahead of us.

We are walking faster than Johnny, and catch up with him after a few minutes. "Say, Johnny. I'm sorry for what I said back there." Johnny stops, and looks at us. "I'm not with the DIA; you can check my passport if you want to." I say, trying hard to be friendly. "Jeez, I don't know what came over me. That was really stupid."

"Yeah," he responds, "I'll bet."

We continued our trek along the dirt road. Soon we leave Johnny behind and are alone together again. "Why do they call soldiers GIs?" I know she is just trying to make conversation, but appreciate the chance to change the subject.

"They don't call all soldiers GI's; just American soldiers. It stands for Government Issue."

"Government Issue?"

"Yeah, all our equipment has GI stamped on it. You know, like a can opener: P38, one each, Government Issue, number 46739088776, for a lousy piece of metal, with a sharp edge for opening C rations, like this one: I have a P38 on the chain that holds my passport bag, and pull it out to show her.

"Just happened to have one with you, huh?"

"Yeah, you never know when you'll need to open a can of beans or a beer; nothing wrong with carrying a P38 is there?"

"Not a problem for me."

"Anyway, I guess during the War, Europeans noticed GI written on everything from underwear to tanks, and started calling Americans GI's. They were probably trying to insult us, but you can't insult Americans, you know. So, we start calling ourselves GI's."

"GI number 4739235673 for a can opener, huh?" She laughs.

"Yeah, the army is so stupid, they number everything, starting at fifty billion and counting backwards. They call the number of everything the nomenclature, and make the grunts memorize those numbers, when they have nothing more stupid to do. You know something? There probably isn't one man in the army who could define the word nomenclature." Joking breaks the tension, and I feel better.

After an hour or so, we reach a small cluster of huts, where the road turns right, and downhill toward the beach. Atacames is visible a couple of hundred yards away. The village is a row of houses facing the ocean. Most houses are thatched huts, but there are a few one or two-story concrete structures. The deep blue of the ocean contrasts with the blue-green water closer to shore and the foaming white surf.

"Looks like a fine place," I say.

A truck comes bouncing down the road behind us. The vehicle is a heavy-duty pickup truck, with a large homemade wooden structure on the back for passengers. The passenger compartment is very wide, so that it protrudes almost three feet wider than the cab on both sides—enough to knock a sidewalk pedestrian's head off, I'm thinking. It also has a tin roof to keep the rain off, but is open front and back and on the sides, so the air can blow through. Wood planks serve as benches that will seat five or six people each. The vehicle will probably carry thirty or forty people, including those standing in the back and crammed into the cab.

The truck and passenger compartment is painted in bright colors—red, blue, and yellow—and, it is covered with pictures and slogans. The inside windshield and windows are trimmed with cloth and lace. The Black Saint, Martin de Porres, is pictured with his broom on the passenger side door; below is a sign in Spanish proclaiming *'God is our guide'*. There is another sign on the front bumper: *'El Señor Chingón'*, which translates loosely as *'Mister Big Fucker'*.

The truck stops and Johnny jumps off his perch from the back of the tailgate. Johnny offers to pay the driver, but the driver waves him off; his ride for the last few hundred yards is free. I look at the sign on the front bumper and laugh.

"What's so funny?" she asks.

"You don't want to know."

"I know what it means!"

"No, I was just surprised at how blatant the guy is. Usually, it is something like: Here I come; lock up your wives and daughters," I say, still laughing.

"I don't see anything funny about that macho shit!" she says, and then continues, "Should have guessed the truck would be on time today; the one day we decide not to wait for the late truck, and it's on time."

"Want to ride the rest of the way to town?" I ask.

"We're staying down at Costa del Sol. It's only about a mile further down the beach; this trail is a short cut. They serve real cold beer—don't know how they do it. You can't even get a truck down there. Come on with us, if you want to. It's a quiet place; you'll like it."

The road we had been walking quickly becomes a two-lane path leading to a bridge over a small, but rapidly flowing stream. The bridge had been built to carry vehicles, but is now in disrepair. Most of the planks are missing, so we have to step over gaps, or walk along the beam supporting the planks. On the other side, we walk side-by-side along parallel paths that obviously originated as vehicle tracks. It appears that vehicles have not traveled this road for a long time. Shirley and I walk along side by side, with me trying to think of something witty to say, and not having much luck.

The road winds up hill through a pasture. From the top of the hill the beach and the community of Costa del Sol are visible. There is a series of small thatch-roofed houses located a hundred yards or so apart just above the beach for as far as one can see around the bay. About half way between the top of the beach and the water is a cluster of huts. These are also mostly small and have thatched roofs like the houses. However, the uniformity of arrangement and construction of these structures sets them apart from the homes of local people. The half-a-dozen small huts are arranged in a semicircle around one larger structure. All are constructed on poles so that they are five feet or so above the beach. The large central structure has an uncovered deck on the ocean side with several tables and chairs. Obviously, that is where the 'real cold beer' will be served.

We walk directly to the large structure, up the stairs, and out to the ocean side of the deck. The view is magnificent. The late afternoon sea breeze is strong. We are on the northern rim of a large bay. Atacames is out of sight, around the point to the northwest. There is another village across the bay to the southeast, perhaps fifteen or twenty miles away.

Evidence of human activity is rather sparse. An old fishing trawler lies on its side, some fifty feet from the water. A few children are at play in front of the houses further down the beach. Most of those houses have large canoes in front, with each resting on a log so it can be rolled toward the ocean when needed.

The water in the bay has several tones of blue and blue-green, depending upon depth and bottom cover. The bay appears to be somewhat protected but the surf is still strong. I hear the pounding waves, and feel the sea air, and almost expect to feel the spray from the surf. I think about the Pacific Ocean, and somehow I am reminded of my High School English teacher. She was eloquent and beautiful, and she was relentless. I always knew my work would never meet her standards.

I turn to look at Shirley. She smiles, and I realize I am smiling at her, too. The sea breeze evaporates the sweat quickly. The air feels cool and fresh. The wind blows her hair back, away from her face. She is beautiful, I am thinking. No, not really beautiful, but good looking and strong. I want to put my arms around her—to kiss her and tell her I love her. Your brain is playing tricks on you GI, I tell myself. You don't even know this girl. Don't be stupid.

"That's God's ocean," I tell her. Her smile broadens, and she nods agreement. I turn toward the bar in the back, and yell, *"Oye, dos cervezas."*

"She won't come out. You have to go rattle the cage," she says.

I go back and knock on the bar. There really is a cage on the other side of the bar, made of bamboo, like almost everything else. I walk around the bar and rattle the cage. A small oriental woman appears. *"Dos cervezas, Señora; bien frías, por favor."*

"You want two beer?" she asks, obviously speaking English, better than Spanish.

"Yeah, two beers, good'n cold—ice cold."

Returning, I find Shirley seated at one of the tables, overlooking the beach. I sit across from her, and continue to think about her. The woman brings two bottles of beer that are cold enough to frost the outside of the bottles immediately in the warm tropical air.

"A bottle of cold beer and thou beside me, singing in the wilderness."

"Omar Khayyam," she says.

"Why not;" I say to her, and to myself: Yes, Shirley is definitely our number one objective for the duration, GI. We will call it Operation Shirley Love!

"Can I rent a hut?" I ask the woman.

"Three dollar US," the woman replies.

"Three dollars a week?" Shirley questions. "We are only paying seventy pesos for the big hut."

"Okay, he pay seventy peso."

"That's too much," Shirley protests.

"It's okay; which one?" I ask the woman.

"That one," she points to a hut behind the main building, in serious disrepair.

"That hut is falling down;" Shirley says. "Give him this one," she points to a nearby hut.

"Not clean yet," the woman says.

"Well, hell," I say, "you clean it up, and I want a hammock on the porch."

"No hammock," the woman says.

"Look," I tell her slowly, "I'll pay three dollars. You *chogi* on over and clean it up, and put a hammock on the porch, okay?"

"I no Korea," she replies, obviously displeased.

"Sorry; *Nihongin desu.* I say.

"*Hai,*" she says.

"Sumimasin;" I say, nodding my head in a slight bow.

After a couple of seconds, she says: "I put hammock—you come after. You want shrimps? We have good shrimps. You want rice and shrimps?"

"Later." Shirley says, motioning the woman away. "We'll tell you, go on." After the woman leaves us, she asks, "Did you say something in Korean to her?"

"Yeah, but Japs don't like Koreans. She took offense at my assumption that she was Korean."

"You speak those languages?"

"Nah, just a few words; maybe ten words of slang in Korean, and three or four polite phrases in Japanese."

"You spent some time over there." Her statement does not call for a response, and anyway I don't care to respond.

Johnny comes up the stairs and drops his bag. "Hey, I almost fell in the creek back there, carrying this bag across that broken-down bridge—not that either of you would give a damn. Course, you might miss some of your stuff, Shirley."

I need to do something to atone for my sarcastic attitude, or have him hate me forever. And, I especially don't want anything to spoil the mood with Shirley. "Sorry about that Johnny; sit down and take the load off. Let me get you a beer." I give him a friendly pat on the back.

While getting the beer, I open my pouch and count my money. I have eighty dollars, and twenty-eight hundred pesos, plus what I have in my pocket. I have a Barkley's Bank account book, too. I open the small tablet and scan the last few pages. There are monthly entries of $215 and $150, and withdrawals of from one to several hundred dollars. Until the last page, the balance is increasing. Then the $150 deposits stop and the withdrawals increase. The last three withdrawals are for $200 each, drawn in Costa Rica, Colombia, and Quito, Ecuador. The current balance is over two thousand dollars. I remember each deposit and withdrawal. There is no mystery; I know I have had plenty of money for a long time, but somehow prefer not to think about why. Returning with three beers, I find Johnny friendlier.

He finished his beer first, and goes back to get a second. "Can I get you guys another?"

"No thanks, man. We're already working on our second one."

He returns and sits with us. He pours the beer down even faster than I do, and is quickly finished. He stands to leave us. "I'm going over to the hut. You kids take it easy here."

Johnny leaves, and we continue to sit and enjoy the wind and the view and, I think, enjoy each other too. We take turns using the outhouse. The structure has two doors side by side. I notice Shirley checking the male side before going in the other door. When my turn comes I understand why she checked the male compartment. A sheet of wallboard separates the sections, and someone has punched a hole through to the other side. There is evidence that the hole has been patched at least once, and reopened; now it is stuffed with toilet paper. Except for the whole in the wall, the outhouse is surprisingly clean and well kept. There is even a roll of toilet paper on a roller attached to the wall—probably the first I have seen in Latin America with the exception of private baths in hotels and upper class homes. Of course, the outhouse stinks to high heaven. I use the facility and return to the deck.

"This is a great place. How did you find it?" I ask.

"Yeah, I love it here. I discovered it last year."

"So, you were here last year."

"Yeah, I'm going to come down here and work every summer."

"What sort of work; DIA?" I snicker.

She slaps my arm casually. "Come on! I teach English at the school in Esmeraldas."

"You have a job teaching English here?"

"Nah, it's volunteer work," she says, "Esmeraldas is our Sister City—that is, it's San Jose's Sister City. I just help out teaching English, and they give me Spanish classes free. Actually, I think I learn more Spanish when I'm teaching English to the kids."

"Hey, that's neat. I never thought about that. It gives you some real good insight on the people, and you have something to do when you get bored."

"Yeah," she replies. "So, what do you do?"

"Oh hell, I'm just kicking around; trying to drink all the beer in the country."

"Yeah?" she says, obviously not buying my story.

"Well, you know. I'm trying to learn all I can about these countries, and the people. I'm going to write about it someday," I hear myself say.

"So," she says slowly, "you take notes on everything—keep a daily log on what you see?"

"Nah, I keep it all up here," I tap my head.

"You just remember everything."

"Yeah; I just want to experience all this, and write about it someday." She presses her lips together and nods her head up and down. "Look, that memory thing was completely crazy. I don't know what came over me."

"But, you don't want any help, huh?" she says, measuring the words. "You'll just tough it out, and everything will be fine."

I can't think of a response, and want to change the subject. "Are you guys the only customers here?"

"There are usually two or three families staying here on weekends, but that's about it; most of the time we are pretty much alone. Are you going to join us for dinner? The rice and shrimp is pretty good. She gets the shrimp fresh from the fishermen. They fish right out there," she points toward the sea.

"Sure!"

"Well, I'm going down to my hut, and clean up a bit," she says. "Why don't you get out of those high elevation clothes, and get with the tropics?"

She is right; I'm dressed for the cool highland climate, with boots, Levi's and a heavy long-sleeved blue work shirt. We walk down the steps, and part for our separate huts.

"I may take a nap," she yells back to me; "how about in an hour or so?"

"Fine, just throw a rock at my hut, when you are ready for dinner."

The hut has a porch with a hammock tied between the two corner posts, so that it blocks the top of the stairs. The hammock is made of hemp woven into a net that can be stretched out in width to a distance about equal to the length. It is the type of hammock people down here call *matrimonial*, because it is large enough to accommodate a married couple.

I step over the hammock and walk into the one-room hut. There is a single bed with an old mattress and worn-out springs. Neatly folded at the bottom of the bed are a sheet, a blanket, and a towel. One corner of the room is blocked off into a shower stall, with a plastic curtain at the opening. It is a closet-like space, with a pipe coming out of the back wall about chest high—an open pipe with no showerhead. A small mirror is propped on a shelf in the corner, also about chest high. The shower is a pleasant surprise. I had expected a tub of water with a dipper, at most.

I look at my face in the mirror. Three day's growth! Why do they always have three days of growth on their beards? I ask myself. People with a three-day beard should be taken out and shot!

I remove my boots and clothes, and taking soap and razor, step into the shower stall. After turning the valve, the pipe rattles and sputters for a few seconds and then spurts out cold water. I wet my face and turn the water off. Soap, cold water, and an awkward mirror are a formula for cutting myself, so I shave carefully. I open the valve again and wet myself from head to foot, dancing around in the cold water. I soap down from hair to toes, and then rinse quickly.

I put on a clean pair of drawers and T-shirt—both army issue. Jeez, you're probably the only maggot in the world still wearing GI underwear, I tell myself. I pull on a pair of Levi cutoffs, and go out on the porch to the hammock. Swinging in the hammock, the air feels cool and refreshing.

I think about the army. It wasn't all bad GI, I tell myself.

SOLDIER'S PLEASURES: KOREA, SPRING, 1953

It was a simple rule; the first guy on is the last guy off. He positioned himself to be close to the tailgate when the truck pulled in; he wanted to sit near the front of the truck. Some of the other troopers had the same idea, so there was always a bit of a scramble for the choice seats. That morning, he had managed to grab second place from the front of the truck, on the driver's side.

Immediately, he placed the bipods upright in front of him and braced the front edge of his helmet between the frame and sight piece. Within twenty seconds, and long before the last man had scrambled aboard, he was asleep. You could accomplish the same thing with an M1 rifle, by bracing your helmet between the sight and barrel, but you had to be careful. When the truck hits a bump your helmet could bounce off the sight and the barrel could poke you in the face or eye.

Ah, sleep! A soldier could fall asleep in a few seconds, and wake up one minute later having achieved a significant amount of refreshing sleep. A quick nap while on duty was referred to as ghosting, or cutting Zs. 'I'm gonna' cut ten Zs,' translates I'm going to sleep for one minute. 'I'm a ghost,' means kick me if the sergeant comes by, and a guy would flop in the bottom of a trench, asleep before his helmet hit the ground. Some guys could sleep while trudging down the road, with fifty pounds of gear on their backs. Indeed, the reason for sitting in the front of the truck was to continue sleeping while the guys closer to the tailgate were getting off the truck.

Sleeping was one of a soldier's greatest pleasures. Also, topping out the list of pleasures, were drinking and fucking. Of course, there was more talk about drinking than drinking, and fucking was almost all talk.

Laughing might also have been at the top of the list, if that were not so essential for survival. "They're going to tear down the old townhouse!" Sergeant Jordan roared. "BOOOO!" the platoon yelled back. "They're gonna' build a bar!" Jordon roared; and the platoon yelled back: "Yeahhh!" "Girls won't be allowed to wear miniskirts in the bar!" "BOOOO!" the platoon yelled back. "Just panties and bras!" "Yeahhh;" came the reply from 45 soldiers. "There'll be no fucking on the dancing floor!" Jordon roared. "BOOOO!" the troopers yelled back. "There'll be no dancing on the fucking floor!" "Yeahhh;" the men yelled. And, for a few minutes the men of weapons platoon forgot their pain and concerns as they struggled up Zebra Hill loaded with weapons and ammo under a hot sun, not knowing what the next day would bring.

Army talk might well have ranked among the top pleasures if it were not so pervasive and routine. Army lingo had been finely honed, by generations of soldiers, into an art form. He, and his buddy Patterson, had given considerable thought to Army lingo through the fog of half-dozen beers, and decided *Army* might be classed among tonal languages in South Asia. Inasmuch as the vocabulary is extremely limited, use of tones and gestures were essential for communication. They would keep notes, they told each other, for a definitive study of *Army* one day.

The terms shit and fuck, and derivatives of those terms, dominated the vocabulary. So dominant were those terms that without them communication would be choked down to a whisper. Shit could be used as a verb, noun, adjective, or adverb, or just be placed at the beginning and end of any sentence, to indicate the speaker has started or completed his thought. For example: 'Shit man, you don't know shit; that fucken shit is fucked up—shit'. The final term punctuates the sentence, and tells the listener to respond. He and Patterson decided that relatively few uses of that term in *Army* could be explained by diffusion from one's High School football coach.

Physical locations were mostly referred to as shitholes. All military bases were shitholes. Places where soldiers ate and drank were shitholes. Any commercial or public establishment, that would admit a soldier, was a shithole; places where soldiers were not allowed to go, were also shitholes. He and his buddy decided the number of shitholes known to a soldier, increased by a square of the number of months of service. One sure thing about shitholes: There would be many more of them at a greater range. The other certainty was, those nearby were invariably worse. Indeed, one could visit any barracks, mess hall, bivouac, bunker, or trench, at any time or season, during war or peace, and learn from the current occupant that he is in the worst fucken shithole he has ever seen.

Soldiers distinguish between fucken and fucking. Fucken is an adjective or adverb, modifying the previous or following word, as in: 'I'm gonna' fucken die if I don't get some fucken food in my fucken stomach—shit'. On the other hand, fucking was what most soldiers seemed convinced they would be doing right now, if they were not in this shithole.

Likewise, fuckoff is different from fuckup. Fucken off was normal behavior. Soldiers fucked off by definition when not on duty, and everyone not in the army was fucken off all the time. But, soldiers fucked off as much as they could while on duty. If soldiers didn't fuckoff on duty, there would have been no need for platoon sergeants.

By contrast fuckup—a verb or noun—is being caught fucken-off or the label for the soldier who was caught. Fucken-off was okay as long as you didn't get caught. For example, sleeping while on duty would just be fucken off, unless you fucked up and got caught, in which case, you were a fuckup. And, God help you if you were a fuckup. Even guys who were fucken off had no sympathy for fuckups.

He and Patterson had considered investigating *Black Army* as well. Of course, Blacks could speak standard *Army*, but they had developed a dialect of that language for use among themselves. For example, shit became shee'it, and fuck translated ma'fuck. He and his buddy had decided, the greater range of tones and body gestures in *Black Army* was explained by the fact that the vocabulary was even more limited than standard *Army*. Some Black guys seemed to be able to carry on whole conversations, with little more than shee'it and ma'fuck. Once he had stood with a group of Black guys and counted the number of times the term ma'fuck was used. "Three, four, five...six, seven, eight;" "Shee'it, this ma'fuck counten'; what the ma'fuck you counten' ma'fuck, shee'it?" "Nine, ten, eleven..."

Pat argued that study of *Black Army* was a waste of time because it would be impossible to document more than a few bits of the limited vocabulary, given that no system of writing that dialect had been, or ever would be, devised.

Trooper Garland planned his afterlife. When he gets out of the army, he will do nothing but sleep, drink, and fuck. Not necessarily, however, in the same order. By varying the order of these activities, he could retain the interest of his listeners for what would have otherwise been a repeat of the same story. Somehow, each variation was funny, and often a topic of conversation among the other guys.

"Shit man, I'm just gonna' fucken sleep—shit," someone said (which, as all soldiers would know, means just sleep—not fuck, sleep, and shit). The guys would consider the sleep-only option for a while, and then reject that in favor of sleeping, drinking, and fucking.

Often someone would try to elevate eating to the status of the other three pleasures. "Give me some fucken bacon and eggs man, and a big T-bone steak and fried shrimp, and a huge pile of fucken French fries—shit," someone would say. Much discussion would follow. Food was important, especially the kind of food you could get back in the world, and soldiers were always hungry.

But, Garland would argue resolutely against any adulteration of his three pleasures. "Ah shit man, you can fucken eat when you got nothing else to do. Sure you gotta' eat," he would respond, "but, you gotta' shit too, don't ya? So, whadaya' gonna' do, spend the rest of your life shit'en—shit." It was a tough call, but eating and all other pleasures, were usually rejected in favor of Garland's trinity.

Garland would allow only one modifying condition to his priorities for 'back in the world' life. During the Korean winter, soldiers were cold—cold all day and often cold all night. Thus, warmth would be elevated to the status of sleeping, fucking and drinking.

"My room will have a fucken fur floor," Garland would say, as we stood around shivering, "with fur on the walls and ceiling, and I'm gonna' have a TV set, with fucken fur all around the tube, and have big fucken fireplaces on all four walls, blazing all the time—shit. Man, I'm gonna' keep that place at 95 degrees, and just lay around naked, drinking and sleeping and fucking my women—shit."

"Four fireplaces?" someone questioned. "Shit man, you gonna' have to stoke those fires all the time, and every time you open the door to get wood, the fucken snow and shit will blow in—shit."

Garland would react angrily to attempted depreciation of his afterlife. "You don't know shit, man! I'm gonna' have electric fireplaces, and big fucken gas furnaces, and anyway I'll be down in Florida. There ain't no fucken snow down there—shit."

There are things all soldiers know and understand, but no civilian could ever conceive. Sleeping while off-loading from the truck is a prime example. That morning, sitting near the front of the truck, he had awakened several times, during the unloading process. He woke the first time when the tailgate crashed down, and Sergeant Jordan yelled. "Okay, move it! Move it! Let's go! Get off your ass Garland: Let go'a yo' pecker and pick up that rifle. Move it!"

He fell asleep for perhaps twenty seconds, and then checked the progress. There were still three or four guys between him and the tailgate. He slept for another ten seconds. He checked again. The fellow next to him still had not moved. Again he slept for five seconds. He checked again. There was no one between him and the tailgate, and the guy directly across from him had begun to lumber toward the back of the truck. Jordan was now yelling at him. "All right fuckup, let go'a yo' cock and get yo' ass outa' there."

There would not be time for even a two-second nap. He began the personal off-loading process. "Okay Serge, I'm coming; gotta' get all my shit." Slide your butt to the front edge of the bench, and check your equipment. "I have all this shit to drag off, Serge—shit." Slowly lift your butt off the bench, and take the first reluctant step toward the tailgate. Bump your helmet on one of the cross ties, that holds the canvas top of the truck. "Ah shit, Serge, I just fucken busted my head on this fucken thing; le'me go back with the truck Serge—shit."

"Move it! Move it!" Jordan never gave any indication he could even hear bitching by a trooper. "Get with it, maggot."

Two more hesitant steps toward the tailgate consume another two seconds. "Come on Serge, those fucken guys are still in there—shit." Consider that the two guys at the front of the truck are still sleeping. Determine to get the first seat next time. Jump off. "Shit Serge! I'm the only guy here who has to drag all this shit off, and you're always fucken yelling at me—shit." Serge doesn't hear. He's working on the last two men, still on the truck.

For the Platoon Leader, or anyone else observing the process, the off-loading would have seemed a model of army precision. Indeed, twenty men, along with about 1,000 pounds of equipment, were off-loaded in less than one minute! Who could possibly imagine that more than half those men had experienced significant peaceful sleep during that time, and some had slept three or four times?

MAGIC FILLED THE SPACE BETWEEN US: COSTA DEL SOL, MONDAY EVENING

Hey, Ray!" she yells from the bottom of my steps, "You having dinner with us?"

I sit up. "Yeah, I must have dozed off."

She is wearing shorts and a T-shirt; her hair is wet and hangs straight down. "Don't you have any sandals?" she asks. I shake my head. "There's a lot of broken glass on the beach; you can't go barefoot. I'll borrow a pair of Johnny's for you."

"No! I'm not going to use any of Johnny's stuff."

"Oh Lord! Okay, I'll get you my flip-flops." She turns back to her hut.

We meet on the path to the restaurant. "So, Mr. Macho can't stand to use something that has been touched by another man, huh? Well, you know, my stuff might be contaminated too."

"Yeah I know, but I need girl germs. My girl germ count is so low I've lost all my immunity."

"Funny, funny, funny," she says, but then smiles, and puts her arm around my waist, "come on, let's skip." And, we do—as if we were children, I am thinking. We scramble up the stairs to the deck, and take the same table overlooking the sea. The sun has just gone down, and the sky over the ocean is ablaze with color. The sea breeze is not as strong, but still lifts her hair from her back.

She is looking at the sunset, and I use the moment to examine her face carefully.

Her features are sharp, almost angular. She has high cheekbones, suggesting a bit of Indian blood. Her face does not have the soft look. She wears no makeup. There is nothing in her face suggesting submissiveness or tenderness—characteristics that I usually associate with feminine beauty.

She turns, and catches me staring. "Don't do that;" she says.

"Don't do what?"

"Don't look at me like that. It's as if you're thinking about trying to hit on me."

"Hit on you?"

"You know what I mean!"

"Hey kids!" Johnny calls from the beach, "I'm headed for Atacames to get something decent to eat. Want to come along?"

"Hey, thanks anyway," I yell to him, "I'm bushed. I think I'll just hang out here. You guys go on."

"Maybe, I'll stick around here with Ray," she says, to my immense relief, "we'll try to hold the fort down."

"Okay, Shirley baby; don't do anything I wouldn't do," he yells back as he walks on down the beach.

"So, what's the deal with Johnny?" I ask, trying to sound casual.

"What do you mean by that?"

"I don't know; he just doesn't seem to be your type."

"So, what's my type?" she asks, and stands. "Maybe, I should go with Johnny."

"Wait a minute!" I say, standing. "What the hell did I say? Okay, that's fine!" I put my hands out with palms forward. "I'm not trying to get between you two. It was just a simple question."

She sits down. I sit and try to keep my mouth shut.

"Anyway, Johnny and I are not involved that way. Look, Johnny is a good friend. I couldn't even be down here if he hadn't come with me. He pays half the rent, and he doesn't bug me. Besides, he keeps the macho boys away." I give her an inquisitive look. "I was down here last year alone. And, these local machos were hanging around here, day and night, like dogs after a bitch in heat. I couldn't stand it. With Johnny most of them think we're married and they don't come around. And, he spends a lot of time with his friends in Atacames, so I have plenty of time to myself."

"Well, I have no problem with it."

"You have no problem with WHAT?" she says in a sharp tone.

"No. I just mean it's great you have someone down here to look after you."

"I don't need anyone to look after me!"

"Well, I mean what you said—keep the macho boys away. Hell, Shirley! I'm not saying anything." I say, not wanting to dig my hole any deeper.

"You don't like Johnny, do you?" She throws the bait out.

"I like him fine. I just don't like him looking at me. It gives me the creeps."

"You're afraid you can't defend yourself?" she asks, in a mocking tone. "You look at me all the time! Guys are always doing that! And, touching—and their stupid suggestions—I get really sick of it! Has it ever occurred to you that a woman might not like that either?"

Her words are like ice water on a fire. I turn away to watch the sunset. "You're right, you know," I say. "I guess I just never thought about it like that."

Her hand on my arm startles me. "I really don't mind you looking," she says. "I didn't mean that for you. There's nothing wrong with a little bit of looking, and touching. But, please don't have problems with Johnny. Just live and let live, okay?"

I turn back toward her. "Sure! No problems at all."

The Japanese woman serves our rice and shrimp. "Do you have to wear that stupid cap while we eat?" Shirley asks. I hang the cap on a chair.

I have the feeling of absolute contentment. Everything seems to be perfect: the breeze, the sunset, the shrimp, the beer, and most of all, Shirley. The sunset is magnificent. The colors in the western sky are accented by occasional flashes of lightning from several thunderheads already building over the ocean. The sky is brilliant, with reds and purples in the west, and pinks streaked overhead and around toward the east. A kind of magic filled the space between us.

"You know, the artist would have been better advised to leave out those pink streaks across the sky; it would have been more realistic and believable without that."

"Yeah," she replies. "But, even without that, it would still be hard to believe."

"It's perfect," I tell her.

"Nothing is ever perfect, but this is real close."

At every opportunity, I look at her face. When she catches me looking I smile and say nothing, and she smiles back. I love her. I want to touch her face, and put my hand up tentatively. She turns away slightly, still smiling, and I drop my hand.

"I love you," I say suddenly, surprising myself.

"No you don't, but it's a nice thing to say." I put my hand behind her head, and try to pull her face to mine. She brushes my hand away gently.

Time to pull back and regroup, I tell myself. "I was in a place in British Honduras with a verandah overlooking the Caribbean," I tell her, needing to say something, "and we would watch the storms over the sea in the evening. We called it the light show."

"You know, it often storms over the ocean at night, but it rarely does during the day."

"Yeah, I noticed that too," I reply, "but, it storms a lot more along the Caribbean coast in Central America. They have big storms up there, even hurricanes. You know something I like about the tropics?" She nods her head up. "The sun comes up at the same time every day, and goes down at the same time. But, when the sun goes down it sure doesn't take long to get dark."

"Yeah, I've noticed that," she says.

"And, you know, the Ocean down here is cold. The Caribbean is warm, and that's a lot further from the equator than we are here."

"We are right on the equator here. Did you see the monument just outside Quito? They call it the Middle of the World Monument because it is exactly on the equator."

"Yeah; I wonder why the water is so cold."

"It's the same way in California," she says.

"I know, but that's not in the tropics. I didn't expect it to be cold down here on the equator." We continue to marvel at the wonders of this tropical land.

EXCEPTION TO THE RULE: COASTAL ECUADOR, SUMMER, 1957

The great ball of the earth turns toward the east, making a complete rotation once each day—actually it makes a complete rotation in 23 hours and 56 minutes; because the earth is also moving around the sun it takes another 4 minutes (on average) to bring the sun back to the same place in the sky. Thus, our 24-hour mean solar day includes one earth rotation and 1/365th of the revolution of the earth about the sun. The equator, an imaginary line circling the globe midway between the north and south poles, has the distinction of being the longest east-west line on earth. That line divides the earth into two geometrically equal parts, and thus defines the circumference of the sphere—about 25,000 miles; actually it is not a perfect sphere, but it's very close. All other east-west lines are shorter, diminishing to a point at the poles.

Because the earth makes a complete turn each day, the speed of rotation at the equator is a bit over one thousand miles per hour—25,000 miles in 24 hours. At the latitude of London, the east-west distance around the earth is only about 15,000 miles, or a bit more than half that of the equator. Thus, the speed of rotation there is only about 600 miles per hour. An east-west line four miles from the North Pole is only about twenty-five miles long. A point along that circle moves east only about one mile an hour as the earth rotates.

It is easier to appreciate the surface motions of the earth by considering a two dimensional analogy—the surface of a rotating merry-go-round. Obviously, the outer edge of the platform (the equator) moves faster than points located closer the center, and the center (the North & South Poles), is stationary.

We are not intuitively aware of our eastward movement by rotation. Rather, we observe this as an apparent movement of the sun, moon, and stars across the sky in the opposite direction. Nor are we intuitively aware of the fact that places north and south are moving eastward at a different speed. Nevertheless, the movement of the earth toward the east, and the differential speed of places located north and south are real and observable.

For example, a missile fired south toward the equator will follow a path over the earth that curves toward the west, as the surface moves more rapidly toward the east under it. This deflection, or Coriolis Effect, is not a minor detail. If the aim of missiles and other projectiles did not take into account the spinning of the earth, they would miss their targets, by a half-inch or so in the case of a rifle bullet over a distance of three hundred yards, by hundreds of feet in the case of long range artillery, or hundreds of miles in the case of an intercontinental missile.

The amount of deflection by Coriolis is dependent upon how far the earth turns while the object is in flight, which of course, is a function of the distance traversed by the moving object and inversely proportional to the speed. Things that move long distances very slowly with little friction, such as wind and ocean currents, are greatly deflected by Coriolis. Said another way, most of what we perceive as wind and ocean current is caused by the earth moving under the air or water, rather than the air or water moving over the earth.

The equator is also distinguished as the place where annual average solar energy is maximum, and seasonal variation is minimum. The sun rises at six in the morning and sets at six in the evening, every day of the year. This is because the sun illuminates one half of the earth at all times, and any circle that divides the earth into two equal parts (such as the equator) must be illuminated half the time every day of the year. The average angle of the noon sun, and thus the intensity of solar radiation, is greater at the equator than any other place on earth. And, the angle of the noon sun varies only 23.5 degrees from vertical from season to season, and is maximum—directly overhead—in late September and March.

Over land surfaces, the average equatorial temperature at sea level is about eighty degrees Fahrenheit every month, and almost every day, of the year. The temperature declines at night to the mid-sixties, as heat radiates away from the earth, and increases to the mid-nineties, during the day. Tropical oceans also have surface temperatures of about eighty degrees, but unlike air temperatures over the land, air over the water changes only little from day to night, as well as from month to month. The water temperature has almost no change from day to night or month to month. Much more solar energy is required to heat water because water is transparent so that solar energy is spread over a much larger volume, and because water has a very high 'specific heat'—a measure of the amount of heat required to raise the temperature of a given weight of a substance one degree—about five times that of most types of rock (by weight; obviously rock weighs more than water so by volume the amount of energy to heat water is only about double that of rock).

The huge volume of surface air that is heated by the tropical sun rises; the rising air produces low pressure and rainfall as the rising air cools below the dew point. When this air is aloft it is pushed north and south away from the equator. Because it has an eastward thrust of 1,000 mph, and because the earth is moving more slowly under it as it moves away from the equator, it becomes a tunnel of air moving east by the time it reaches about 30 degrees north or south. Being unable to break out of this tunnel and being joined continuously by more air from the tropics, it is pushed back to the surface of the earth. Thus, we have descending air, and thus high pressure, in latitudes of about 30 degrees north and south. These sub-tropical high-pressure areas are most intense in the eastern sides of oceans (off the west coasts of continents). Subsidence of air in eastern subtropical oceanic regions produces the world's great deserts on nearby sub-tropical west coasts, including the Sonoran-Mojave Desert of Northwest Mexico and Southwest USA, the Atacama in Northern Chile and Peru, the Great Sandy Desert of Australia, the Kalahari of Southwest Africa, and the western portion of the Sahara in North Africa.

Some of the air that subsides in the subtropics moves back toward the equator, in an attempt to fill the vacuum caused by thermal uplifts in the tropics. As air drifts slowly toward the equator the surface rotates eastward under it, producing a strong wind toward the west. Thus, tropical air crosses the surface mostly from east to west, becoming the great tropical easterly wind systems of the earth. Early sailors used the term Trade Winds, from the old English word 'trade' meaning trail or direction, because of the relative consistency of the direction of these winds. As these easterly winds cross the ocean, they bring moist air, and thus heavy rainfall, including giant tropical storms called hurricanes or typhoons, to the subtropical east coasts of Asia, Central America, and Australia. The Trade Winds drag tropical water westward across oceans, to bath tropical and sub-tropical east coasts with water at about 80 degrees.

One might expect surface water temperatures on the west sides of continents near the equator to be about 80 degrees as well. For the most part, they are; but there are exceptions. The most striking exception is found along the west coast of South America.

Some of the air that subsides in subtropical regions is pushed poleward across the surface of the earth, toward the Arctic in the Northern Hemisphere and the Antarctic in the Southern Hemisphere. As the air drifts poleward some of the eastward thrust of the air, caused by the more rapid spinning of the earth in the subtropics, is retained. That is, as the air moves away from the equator the earth rotates more slowly under it. Thus, the slow poleward drift of the air is soon converted to a rush of air from west to east creating a wind system we know as the Stormy Westerlies. The westerly winds drag ocean water along from west to east, creating an ocean current in higher latitudes we call the West Wind Drift.

Water moving across the North Atlantic is interrupted by Europe, and the current across the North Pacific plows into the North American Continent at about the States of Washington and Oregon. Thus cold water is pushed south along the west coast of California, as it is along the coasts of Portugal and Morocco. In the Southern Hemisphere, the west wind drift traverses the Atlantic Ocean and skirts mostly south of South Africa. That vast river of cold water continues across the Indian Ocean, mostly skirting south of Australia, and on across the South Pacific to become the strongest west wind drift on the planet. The southern cone of South America is the only land area that substantially interrupts the Southern Hemisphere West Wind Drift. That river of cold water plows into the west coast of South America and is forced up the west coast of that continent. The volume of water is so great that the flow continues all the way up the west coast of South America to the equator. Incredibly, Antarctic Penguins can sometimes be found in the Galapagos Islands located at the equator some 600 miles off the coast of Ecuador! Thus, the surface water temperature along the coast of Ecuador at Costa del Sol is a chilly sixty-five degrees, rather than eighty degrees.

A young woman sat looking out over the chilly water, and smiled at the man sitting beside her. Why did she tolerate this man? Why did she allow him to flirt with her? She had very little respect for men under the best of circumstances, and never tolerated flirting or touching. A man's advances would likely be met with a sharp punch to his chest. She had been warned several times that some man would knock her teeth out one day. But, no man had ever dared to challenge her, and she considered herself to be physically equal to any man.

But, she sat smiling at this man, knowing his thoughts and motives, and knowing she would normally have considered the situation to be loathsome. Why this exception to the rule? She had been moderately impressed with his Spanish proficiency, and had enjoyed his self-effacing wit. And, his amnesia problem conveyed victim status. Her prime role in life was to defend and care for life's victims. This one would be a simple case. She would sort out the problem quickly, and send him on his way mentally and emotionally recovered. If his case did prove difficult, she could always call on the expertise of her friend Norma.

But, there was something else that kept her sitting with this man. There was something that made his scheming and flirting fun. Suddenly, she knew the answer and her smile broadened.

"You think I'm beautiful, don't you," she said, confirming that conclusion for herself, and not expecting a reply. "Well, I'm not; you had better look again!"

"You look beautiful to me," he replied.

"Yeah, I know."

THERE IS A WAR GOING ON: COSTA DEL SOL, MONDAY EVENING

"**T**ell me about the army." I shrug my shoulders and say nothing. "You were in the service; in Korea; were you in the war?"

"Yeah, I guess so."

"You said you were a soldier; is that right?"

"Yeah, I was a GI. I'm not lying to you, damn it!" Then more softly, "I just don't know what to say."

"Did you go to Mexico City College?"

"Yes!" I say, hearing irritation in my voice, "Why are you interrogating me?"

"I'm not interrogating you," she replies, without changing her tone, "and you're scaring me, Ray. I don't think I like it."

"So what am I, some kind of freak? Look, I don't mind talking to that woman, but I really don't need any help from her. I'm okay now."

"Are you okay now?"

"Yes!" I say. "Why can't we just drop it?"

"I'm having a bit of a problem with your amnesia."

The word amnesia stuns me. "Amnesia? For Christ's sake, Shirley, I don't have amnesia." I want to walk away from her, but I can't. There is a long silence.

"I'm just wondering why at first you said it wasn't your bag, and then ten seconds later you said you didn't fold your underwear."

"What are you talking about?"

"Back on the road;" she says, not changing her tone, "you said you didn't think it was your bag, but then you said your underwear wasn't dirty; it just wasn't folded."

"What the hell is this, a Pinkerton investigation?" I hear my angry voice, but know I did say those things.

"Are you saying you don't remember that?"

"Okay, okay, okay! You've got me. So, what are you going to do now, call the FBI?" I stand, and turn to leave, unable to continue the cross-examination.

She stands and faces me, holding my arms. "It's okay, sit down. It'll be okay."

I sit. "I'm not lying to you." I hear my voice shake and hate it. The amnesia diagnosis makes me feel panic. I feel lost and dependent upon her. She's trying to help you, and you're a shit-head, I tell myself. "I'm sorry I'm such a jerk."

"It's okay, I'm not going to leave," she says. I know she can sense my anxiety, and fear of being alone.

"Hey," I say, and then put both hands up, palms forward after realizing I had said the *hay* word again. "Wait a minute, I was just thinking, if a guy were out on the plains

56

for years, or down in Amazonia, he might forget things. I mean, what difference would it make? He might just live from day to day and be happy."

"Don't try to rationalize it. You have a problem, and you have to deal with it. You don't have to get upset about it, but you have to deal with it, okay?" I remain silent. "Do you want me to be your friend?" she asks.

"Yes!"

"I'll be your friend, but only on the condition you start dealing with this problem in a serious way."

"What problem?"

"Don't tell me you can't remember that you can't remember!" she says sharply.

"Why can't you just leave it alone? I'm not lying to you."

"I believe you are telling me the truth, about not remembering things, and all. And, that means you have a problem—a very serious problem. I'm not going to stand by and pretend you're okay. If you want me to be your friend," she says, putting her hand on my cheek, "and, I will try to be your friend, but only if..."

"Only if you're in charge."

"Well, yes. I will be in charge of this problem you have. That is, I will be in charge of helping you get over it. And, you have to talk to Norma, okay?"

"Norma is the psychologist woman in town?"

"Don't call her psychologist woman; she's my friend."

"If I say okay, can we stop this for today? I'm really up to here with it." I brush the top of my head with my finger.

"Yeah, we can stop for now."

We sit silently for a few minutes. "So, you are going to give me therapy, huh?"

"That's right."

"Well, at least I have a pretty doctor to talk to." She gives me the eyebrows up, here we go again, look. "How about Norma, is she pretty too?"

"She's beautiful. But, don't think you're going to get away with any wise cracks with her. She will put you across her knee, and paddle your butt."

"Gee, I don't know, Shirley. If she's tougher than you, she should join the Russian Women's Hammer Thrower team, instead of talking with loony guys like me."

"So, you think I'm tough, huh?"

"Yeah, I think so. When you got pissed off at me, back on the road, I thought you were going to punch a hole in my chest."

"I didn't hurt your stupid chest. And anyway, I wasn't pissed off at you."

"No? Well, if you ever do feel that mood coming on, I hope you will let me know early on, so I can get some miles between us. Maybe, I'll put up a red flag over there, that says Shirley's Pissed Off, so all the folks along here can take cover." She puckers her lips and nods her head up and down. Actually, I think she enjoys my joke.

We continue to sit and talk, and look at the storms over the ocean for a while. I use the time to work on Operation Shirley Love. At this point I'm just sending out scouts to check the terrain and look for a weak flank or unguarded approach. Touch her hand or arm, put my arm around her waist, or both hands on her shoulders: Yes! Touch her face, kiss her, take a stroll down the beach: No! All in good time, my man, I tell myself, satisfied with the progress. I wonder if she knows there's a war going on. Hell yes, I answer myself. She wasn't born yesterday; she knows exactly what you are up to. Better throw her a curve ball, GI.

"Well, I've had a long day," she says, "and, I have to get up early tomorrow. Think I'll hit the sack."

We walk together to her hut. She thinks you're going to try for the kiss, I tell myself. Instead, I say, "It's been fun talking with you; I hope I see you again tomorrow."

"You'll see me—if you're here. I have to leave early in the morning, but I will be back in the afternoon. See you then." She goes into her hut, and I walk back to mine.

I decide to sleep in the hammock on the porch. I spread the blanket over the hemp fiber hammock. Facing away, I hold one side of the hammock high in my left hand, and the other low in my right hand, and then fall backward, and squirm around into the nest. I plan to dream about Shirley's breasts and the way her skirt curves out at the hips and behind. But that wasn't to be.

FIRE MISSION! KOREA, SUMMER, 1953

Fire Mission! He could not remember how many times he had said those words into his radio. Artillery shells whistled overhead and exploded on the hillside below with so thunderous a noise the ground under him seemed to shake. They're ours; no sweat man, he said to himself. He was crouched in the bottom of a deep trench, calling in artillery fire on the side of the hill below. Lieutenant Snider had his head over the top of the trench, with binoculars glued to his eyes.

He heard the single higher-pitched boom of a mortar round, much closer but to the right. That's not ours, he thought; and that thought was troubling. He wanted to believe the mortar round was ours, but he knew the mortars had been removed by the retreating platoon.

He didn't hear the round that hit a few feet in front of the trench. He was thinking about Donna. The smell of the explosion was thick. His head pounded, he saw blackness. His nose hurt. He heard his whimpering voice, "Oh no, God, oh no. God help me." He pushed himself up. His helmet had flipped forward, and smashed down on his nose. He pushed the helmet up, and felt warm blood run down his face. He tried to rub the blood out of his eyes, but his hands were covered with mud. The front of his fatigue jacket was covered with blood, and what appeared to be excrement. In complete panic, he felt his chest for a wound. As he moved his hand to his right side, there was a sharp pain.

Oh shit, you've been hit, he told himself. He opened his fatigue jacket and looked, but could not see the wound. He felt the back of his right side and cringed when his finger touched a small piece of shrapnel. You have to pull it out, he told himself. He did. The small metal sliver was razor sharp. He felt the wound again, and pulling his hand back saw his dark red blood. You have to bandage the wound. He took his field bandage from the pack on his pistol belt.

Then, he saw the Lieutenant hanging upside down, over the top of the trench.

There was no head, and one arm was also missing. Snider's dead, and you're alive, he told himself. He had respected Snider, but that wasn't Snider there now. It was just an empty sack.

He celebrated the fact that he was alive. "If you hadn't brought us out here, this wouldn't have happened, you goddamned shit-head!" He said aloud to the dead man. Then, he knew his face and fatigue jacket were covered with the Lieutenant's brains and blood.

"Ahh!" He heard his wail, as he rolled over against the wall of the trench, rubbing his chest against the dirt. Get it off me! His bandage had fallen into the mud. He thought about using the Lieutenant's bandage, but didn't want to touch the man with no head.

How long have you been here? They will be coming up. You have to call in fire, he told himself. Searching, he found his radio outside the bunker, smashed. The Lieutenant's radio had simply disappeared. "There is nothing I can do," he said aloud. We've stopped firing; they will be coming up. They're coming up now! They'll kill you. Run man, run, he told himself. He had crawled over the top of the trench, and was scrambling on all fours up the hill, before becoming aware of having made that decision. Get away! Be alive! He scrambled on, dropping to his belly with every distant explosion, to crawl to the nearest shell crater or low spot. Panic left no room for logic or reason. Run! Get away!

Reaching a deep hole he stopped, and tried to think. You don't know where you're going. You should have taken the commo trench up the hill. You could be running right into them. You have to think! But, he couldn't. Suddenly, he was completely disoriented. He was on the wrong side of the hill. No, the sun was on the wrong side. My God, the sun is setting. You've been here for hours. We'll pound the shit out of this hill tonight. Even if you survive the Chinks, you'll be blown away by our stuff. What can I do? What can I do? There was no room for logical thought in his panic.

His side began to hurt again. He wanted to feel the wound, but decided against that. Your hands are dirty; just make it worse, he told himself. You have to think clearly GI! You have to survive this fucken shit. Think man, think! But, he couldn't think. Suddenly, he realized he didn't have his carbine and pack. He could not remember if the rifle and pack had been in the bunker when he left. They probably blew out of the bunker with the radio, he told himself. The only weapon he had was his Kabar knife.

The knife is useless. If they catch you, you have to put your hands up. Let um' take you prisoner, man. Throw the fucken Kabar away.

Who says they would take me prisoner? Shit, they'd probably just kill me. He kept the knife and crawled up hill. You don't know where you're going man, think! I have to do something; he answered himself, and continued crawling. The sun set and daylight began to fade. Soon there were flares lighting the area for short periods. He would drop to his stomach and freeze in place. Occasionally a mortar round exploded, but always far from him. He expected heavy artillery to begin at any moment, but it didn't.

He couldn't crawl any further. Moving aggravated the pain in his back, and his nose hurt. Worst of all, his head pounded. Maybe, if I could sleep, he told himself, the pain would go away. He removed his poncho from the back of his pistol belt and wrapped it around himself. Fuck it, man; there's no place to run, and no place to hide. You might as well sleep here, and hope for tomorrow.

He slept for short periods, always waking with a start at the sound of a mortar round or the crackling sound and light of a flare. Sometimes he heard sounds that seemed to be nearby. The Chinks! He remembered the book *All Quiet on the Western Front*. Paul had been trapped between the lines, and an enemy soldier had stumbled into the bomb crater where he hid. Paul had stabbed the man, and had been forced to watch him die the next day, unable to leave the crater during daylight. Paul had decided to bandage the man's wounds, hoping that if the enemy captured him they would at least see he had tried to help the man.

What would he do if Joe Chink stumbled into his trench? He held his Kabar knife in his fist. He would kill the man. He would stab him many times to be sure he was dead. Then, he would crawl away and find another crater while it was still dark. The night stretched on through an eternity.

He woke and knew dawn was about to break. The pain in his back and his headache were worse, but he felt more confident. You have to find a good deep bunker that will take the pounding, and hope the Chinks don't find you. If they do, you're a prisoner. Don't die. You can do a year in a prison camp. Shit yes! Just live! Live and go home to Donna.

He formulated his plan. At dawn, he began to crawl up hill until he reached a lateral trench. There were bunkers at one hundred-yard intervals in major trenches, and he was confident the trench he was in was one of those. He moved down the trench on all fours, taking care not to show himself. As he crawled, his hunger and thirst became apparent, and then painful. His canteen was almost empty. He thought about saving the water, but then he pulled the canteen out and drank. He dropped the canteen, and thought about removing the canteen case from his pistol belt. "Fuck the goddamned army!" He said aloud. The canteen flopping back and forth had impeded his crawling. Then he decided against that, and put the empty canteen back into the case. Perhaps he would find water and need the canteen. He continued to crawl through the trench, with thirst and hunger gnawing at him. He regretted not searching for his pack, which had two cans of C-rations.

Think man, think! He knew he had moved at least two hundred yards down the trench, and there was no bunker. This must be one of the lower trenches. You have to move uphill, to the next trench; and you have to move right now! Soon the sun will rise and they will see you. He crawled out of the trench and began to move uphill. There has to be another trench, he thought, there has to be another trench! But, there was no trench. Tears came in his eyes. They're going to fucken kill me! Please God, help me.

Finally he did reach a trench and rolled in. A bunker was just twenty yards away. Oh shit, thank you God. He crawled to his safe haven. There was a poncho over the entry of the bunker. He pushed through into the dark space. He felt hidden and safe in the dark. The joy of salvation was as if a warm shower of water had poured over his body.

As the sun rose, a bit of light through the crack in the poncho-covered opening dimly lit the interior of the bunker. He began to scoot along the wall of the bunker, moving away from the door. He thought about finding food and water, and also about the artillery fire that would be coming in from our side. Suddenly, he recognized a dim outline of a man sitting against the back wall of the bunker. He moved back to the door and raised the poncho to get more light. He couldn't make out the figure sitting there, but knew the man was dead. He decided to wait for the sunlight.

He sat near the door of the bunker while the sun slowly illuminated the man some ten feet away. It was Doyle, a grunt in the second platoon. He had seen him many times but had not known him well. As the sun became brighter, he hung the poncho back over the entrance. Doyle is dead as shit, he told himself. Again, he felt the joy of being alive. His side began to hurt. He needed a bandage. He inched his way around the bunker to the dead man, and stopped beside him. He observed Doyle again. The dead man's eyes were wide open, and there was no sign of a wound.

"Hey Doyle," he said, in a voice he could not recognize. He reached over and pushed the front of Doyle's fatigue jacket, softly. He might as well have pushed on a sandbag. He pushed harder. Doyle's head flopped over, toward him, and remained in an awkward position. He pulled back. "Oh shit!" He sat, leaning away from the dead man, for a few seconds.

"Fucker's dead," he said aloud. Then, he knew no one was really there. He reached over and pulled out the dead man's field bandage. He opened the bandage and unbuttoned his fatigue jacket. "You're not needing this bandage man, and I'm fucken needing it."

He pulled the ties around his waist, and then pushed the bandage up to the wound he could not see. That produced a sharp spearing pain through his body. He gritted his teeth, and tied the ends together on his left side, as tight as he could stand. As he put his right arm down, the bandage slid down under the wound. He needed tape to hold the bandage in place, but didn't have any. "Fuck it," he said aloud.

His attention turned to his thirst and hunger. He unsnapped Doyle's canteen cover and removed the canteen. He drank, and drank again; the canteen was more than half full. He removed his empty canteen and replaced it with Doyle's. Maybe Doyle has food, he thought. The dead man had his pack on his back. He put his hand on Doyle's back and pushed him forward. Doyle was stiff. He pushed harder, and the dead man slumped forward. He sat for a minute, and then observed the pack on Doyle's back to be accessible. He reached over and opened the pack, and removed a rolled fatigue jacket. A cardboard box of C-rations was visible. He pulled the box out.

The package was almost complete: Two cans—one heavy and one light—plus a P38 can opener, a spoon, and a pack of Lucky Strike greens. Good old Lucky Strike greens, he told himself. They often received C-rations that were packed early in WWII, before Lucky Strike 'went to war' by changed their color from green to red, to save green dye for the Army. The old cigarettes were dry; sometimes guys would remove the cellophane from the packages and pack them in slices of apple to add humidity and improve the taste. But, it was no big deal.

He took the box and crawled back to the bunker entrance. He held up the poncho and read the label on the heavy can—tuna and noodles. He had never liked the tuna and noodle C-ration, but now he opened the can quickly and spooned the contents into his mouth as fast as he could. The taste was fine: "Like being alive!" he said aloud. The light can was fruit cocktail. He opened the can and drank the contents quickly.

He looked back at Doyle, wondering if he had anything else to eat. There was an M1 rifle against the wall to the left of Doyle. He retrieved the M1 and checked the chamber. Empty!

He looked around for ammo. There was a bandoleer on the ground, near the dead man; he retrieved it. It was a full bandoleer; he removed one clip from the bandoleer and loaded the M1. He was armed and safe.

I have an M1 and a full bandoleer; I can fight the whole fucken Chink Army. Again, the joy of salvation washed through his being. He lit a Lucky Strike and smoked.

"No GI; you can't fight the whole fucken Chink Army," he said aloud. He thought about leaving the M1; better to be a prisoner. But maybe I would be safer with the M1. Yeah, you can always throw the rifle away if you need to, he told himself. Just stay alive, GI. He kept the rifle.

He opened the poncho cover of the bunker again. It was full daylight. Why aren't we pounding the shit out of um, he asked himself? The routine of the stalemated war was to attack a hill with overwhelming force. Neither side had enough troops to man every hill against a determined attack. There were too many hills. So, the standard procedure was to retreat, and then counterattack with even greater force. Maybe that made sense to the negotiators at Panmunjom, but was hell for the soldier. Sometimes they would take casualties in retreat. And, there was hell to pay when they had to retake the hill. We always had lots of ammo on the hill. The rule was to fire everything, before retreating, or carry the excess out. In practice, the Chinks often captured lots of ammo. We carried 81-mm mortars, and they had 82's. They could fire our rounds, but we couldn't fire theirs. Not that we needed to; we had plenty. They didn't have plenty of ammo, but sometimes they would have lots of ammo available—our ammo—to fire at us, when we would counterattack. He had experienced that hell only vicariously from the stories told by other men, but now those stories made him shudder.

Why aren't we pounding hell out of this hill? Maybe, we gave up on this one. Oh shit, you're fucked, he told himself. But, there should be Chinks swarming all over this hill by now. What the hell is going on? Don't change the rules on me now.

He tried to think. If we're not coming back, you have to get out of here! And, you have to get out of here now! He picked up the M1. You have to get out of this shit, and get over to the other side. He pushed through the poncho cover, and into the daylight of the trench.

He stopped to assess his situation. No shelling. He had been on the northeast side of the hill, and had moved up hill during the night. You have to go uphill, and over the top, and then down southwest side. No time to lose. He left the trench, and ran in a crouched position toward the top of the hill.

He heard voices. Joe Chink! He fell to the ground and shuddered. The fucken Chinks, and you're walking straight into'um, he told himself. The voices came closer, and he realized, he was hearing GI's. Without raising his head, he began to yell at them. "Hey man, don't shoot! I'm in weapons platoon, Baker Company."

"Where are you;" came the call from above? "Stand up, so we can see you. Sling your rifle, and keep your hands up. Don't fuck with us man—we'll blow you away."

He knew he was in extreme danger. According to rumor, the Chinks would call out in English, maybe dressed in GI uniforms. No one was taking chances. He released the buckle on the sling and pulled the M1 over his shoulder. He put his hands up and slowly came to his knees.

"Don't shoot man, I have my hands up. Don't shoot." He got to his feet and walked slowly up the hill. They stared at him in astonishment. Some kept their rifles pointed at him. "Hey man, shit! I'm a fucken GI, put your rifle down—shit," he said. They continued to stare at him in disbelief.

"Where you coming from, man?" someone asked. He thought about the way he must look. His face and fatigue jacket covered with blood and brains. Blood had covered his right side, and had run down his leg.

"Helmsman, take this guy back to the Command Post," someone said. A young soldier stepped forward, and motioned for him to move up hill. As he walked up hill, he felt tears running down his face. He choked and stumbled. "What the fuck is the matter with you, man? Where the fuck have you been anyway?" the soldier asked him.

"Thought I was dead," he managed to choke out. "I thought you guys were the fucken Chinks."

"Ain't no fucken Chinks up here," the soldier said.

"Yesterday—two days ago," he couldn't remember whether one or two days had passed, "the fucken Chinks hit the hill," he said.

"The Chinks didn't hit the hill, man. Baker Company just bugged out. Shit, they just sent a patrol up, and half of Baker bugged out like a bunch of fucken old women."

"What the hell are you talking about? We were calling in fire on um'. They blew Lieutenant Snider away," he yelled at the man.

His reception at Charley Company Command Post was hostile. Where had he been? Why was he hiding? Lieutenant Snider dead; why hadn't he brought him in? Where is he? How do you know it was Doyle? Why didn't you bring in one of his tags? Where is the bunker? He was confused and disoriented. He could not locate the bunker where he found Doyle on the map. He was under suspicion of something, but didn't know what it was.

They think you're a coward, he told himself. Maybe you are a coward. You were running and hiding. His joy of survival quickly turned to shame and dread. A medic came into the bunker and examined his wound. "This man has to be sent down to MASH," the medic said.

"Fuck him!" The officer replied. "He has some explaining to do right here."

"Are you taking responsibility for this man Sir?" the medic asked the officer. He recognized the medic's ploy. If the officer accepted responsibility for a wounded man, his butt was on the line if the man died or had a serious problem. The medic couldn't tell the officer what to do, but he could put him on notice that he would be held responsible. There was stony silence for a minute, while the medic stood his ground.

"All right, get him the fuck out of here." The officer said, and to him, "We'll get to the bottom of this, you goddamn fuckup, and if you're lying, we'll stand you up in front of a firing squad."

He stumbled out of the bunker; his legs felt like numb posts. He was afraid he would faint. The ground seemed to move away from him, as he stumbled along. He felt many eyes looking at him, but couldn't see anyone.

"Don't sweat it, man!" The medic told him. "They're just trying to cover their own asses."

"What happened?" he asked.

"Ahh shit; it's the same shit," the medic said. "They got nothing on you. Don't tell um' anything—fuck the sons-a'-bitches. Tell um' you want a lawyer."

"Why do I need a lawyer," he asked, with complete puzzlement.

"Don't sweat it, man! Just don't tell um' anything." He decided the medic's advice was sound, and determined not to tell anyone anything.

They medevacked him by chopper to MASH 4. He had expected to be interrogated, but was treated with concern and kindness. The doctors and nurses didn't seem to know about the charges against him. At first, they were in a frenzy to find his chest wound, and not finding one, asked him how he got all the blood and tissue on his shirt. "Lieutenant Snider blew up in front of me," he explained limply.

They cleaned the wound on his side, and removed more shrapnel, and cleaned and bandaged the cut on his nose. Another doctor came in and shined a light in his eyes. A diagnosis of brain concussion was made, and he was evacuated to the hospital at Inchon.

He reached the hospital during the night. A nurse bathed him on a plastic-covered bed, and put a hospital gown on him. He was given a bed in a large ward. The nurse served him a hot meal, which he ate rapidly. Then, she cranked his bed down, and turned off his lamp.

When he opened his eyes Donna was there, hovering over him. She kissed him and barked orders to nurses and doctors. He was wheeled out, and placed in a private room. Several doctors came in to reexamine him. Donna seemed to be in charge. She would leave periodically to make a phone call, and then return to him. She examined and redid bandages. She yelled at and cursed doctors who were insufficiently attentive. She held his face in her hands, with tears in her eyes, and said, "You're my hero, baby.

I'm going to take care of you now. Sleep baby, let Mama take care of you." That was the first time she had referred to herself as Mama, and she was obviously playing Mama's role. He did sleep. He knew he was safe at last.

REMEMBERING TRIVIAL THINGS: Costa del Sol, Tuesday, August 4

I can sense that dawn is about to break. What a blessing to have a mental clock that almost always works. I have my clock set for a couple of minutes before daybreak now. It is one of many things I learned in the army that I will keep and treasure for the rest of my life.

There were forty-five enlisted men in the platoon but the latrine had only ten sinks and seven stools; some guys seemed to spend half their lives waiting in line to shit, shower, and shave. By waking up a couple of minutes before the CQ turned the lights on I was able to shave and not have to wait in line for a sink. Sergeant Hart and a few other guys would also wake up a minute or so early. We would finish our business in the latrine and then have time to make our bunks and take a five-minute nap before roll call. After the morning jog and exercise, all the men would shower, but most would face the task of making their bunks before breakfast. The early birds would be first in the chow line. After breakfast, we would have another nap, while the platoon finished breakfast.

I stay in the hammock and think about the dream. It wasn't a dream, I tell myself. The dream has drifted away. None of the images or places or names are there, but the feelings and surroundings are crystal clear. First there is the feeling of fear and hopelessness, and then relief the ordeal is over. I try to focus on when it was over and I am safe.

I watch Shirley emerge from her hut. She is wearing a full brown skirt and a white blouse, and her wet hair hangs straight down.

"Hey, Shirley!" I say, as she passed my hut.

"You're awake, huh?" She walks up the stairs to my hammock. "Well, get up ya' lazy bum! Come over and give me some company for breakfast."

"I'd love to. What does she serve?"

"I have coffee and hot *arepas*. I don't know what those things are made of, but they are good."

"They're just hominy cakes; I like um, too. Order me some ham and eggs to go with it. I'm going to take a quick shower," I say, walking into my hut.

"She won't have ham, but she can make fried eggs over rice," she yells back. "She usually has papaya too, or else a mango or orange juice."

"Sounds great, I'll be right there."

I shower quickly and put on my Levi cutoffs, a clean T-shirt, and Shirley's flip-flops. The woman is serving coffee when I reach the table facing the ocean. "You're all dressed up today." I say. "Going to a wedding or something?"

"I always dress this way for teaching. Have to get the eight o'clock out of Atacames, to make it on time. Want to come into town with me?"

"Nah, you go on. Think I'll check out these fishermen. Maybe I'll go fishing with them." The woman serves our breakfast. We both get a plate with a large slice of dark red papaya and hot *aprepas*. I also get my fried eggs, served over white rice. "Jeez, I had a really bad dream last night," I say.

"You see yourself backwards again?"

"Nah; well yeah, something like that. Actually, I don't know because I can't remember the dream. It was as if the bad guys were after me, and then I was saved, you know."

"Ray, I want to ask you something, and this is therapy, okay?"

"Go ahead."

"Sometimes you don't remember important things—like being in the army—and, then you do remember trivial things, like what GI means, and the can opener. It's like, when you said you didn't think it was your bag, and then you remembered you hadn't folded your underwear." I don't respond.

"There are other things;" she continues, "you remembered buying a new cap in Quito, and the verandah in British Honduras. You remembered you want to be a writer, and you were learning about these people down here. But, when I asked you about Mexico City College, you didn't even remember that at first."

"I've been thinking about that, too. You know, it's like I know everything, but when I try to think about it I can't. It's like, when you wake up and you know you were dreaming, but you can't remember what the dream was about. Do you know what I mean?"

"Sure, I know what you mean about dreams. I usually can't remember any of them."

"You know how, when you wake up, if you try to remember what you were dreaming about, you can't; it will go away. But, if you just clear your mind, sometimes the dream will come back."

"Yeah?" she questions.

"For me, it's as if my dreams and reality have switched or something, but they aren't dreams. It's actually when I'm just letting my mind wander—day dreaming. Do you know what I mean?"

"I don't know."

We finish our breakfast. "Well, I'm off to town. Probably see you in the afternoon. I usually take the three o'clock back out here, and get here about 4:30 or so if the truck is on time," she says, standing to leave. "You be careful out there, I feel responsible for you now that you are my patient."

"So, how does it feel to have a psychopath for a patient?"

"Well, if we didn't have psychopaths, we wouldn't need psychologists would we? So, how does it feel to have a quack for a doctor?"

"At least she's cute and sexy; you can't have everything, you know."

She taps his chest with her fist. "Don't get fresh with the doctor, fella'," she says. The chest punch is her signature, I tell myself; she's just dotting the *i* with that one.

I call after her, "Hey, Shirley! I wish I hadn't told you that stuff. That damned woman will probably have me committed to the loony bin."

She stops and walks back to me. "Do you trust me?"

"Sure."

"Then don't say stupid things, and don't call Norma that damned woman."

"Okay."

"Nothing I do, or Norma does, is going to cause you any problems. Do you believe that? Because, if you don't trust me, we might as well stop this right now."

"I trust you. And, maybe I'll try to trust this Norma, too." She turns and leaves for the second time. I watch her walk back to her hut. She is sexier in the skirt than shorts.

From the bottom of the stairs at her hut, she calls to Johnny, "You coming? We have to go if we are going to make the eight O'clock," and turned back up the trail, toward the crossroads. A couple of minutes later, Johnny comes down the stairs and hurries along after her.

The Oriental woman interrupts my thoughts, "Drink more coffee?"

"No, but I could use a lunch to take with me. Maybe I will go fishing with those men."

"I make rice and beans."

"And, water." I say.

"Water," she repeats. "You bring shrimps?"

"Yeah, maybe I'll bring some fish and shrimp, if we catch anything."

BE WARM AND LET THE PEOPLE LAUGH: COASTAL ECUADOR, SUMMER, 1957

The fishermen push their dugout canoes over log rollers toward the sea. The dugouts are over twenty feet long, and five feet wide at the center, and very heavy. The boats are fitted for lateen sails, but they would not be used on this trip. The wind would not be in their favor.

The fishermen wear shorts and, except for the two oldest, nothing else. The two older men also wear T-shirts. All are barefoot. They are called, and call themselves, *Negros*, Spanish for Blacks. The primary source of their genes was from slaves captured in West Africa, and transported to South America during the 17th Century. Many slaves had escaped from haciendas in the highlands and moved to this isolated coastal region. The men have very dark skin, and black kinky hair but, a West African in their midst would be almost as easily distinguished as an outsider as a European or an American

Indian. Mostly African in race, the people of Ecuador's north coast have sharp facial features, and abundant body hair, betraying their European admixture. They are mulattos—a racial blend of African and European, and some American Indian.

More fundamentally, in their thoughts and values, they are not Africans at all. They are Europeans. They speak a European language, as well as a dialect of that language that evolved over the two centuries of isolation on this South American coast. Their religion is European. Their cultural values are inherited from Europe—albeit a medieval, pre-industrial Europe. They know nothing of Africa. If there are residual cultural features traced to Africa, they are no more than subtle traits, awash in a sea of European culture.

Ranging in age from late teens to over sixty, they all have strong, sound bodies. An uninformed visitor, from a wealthy society, might assume these men carry genes that somehow preclude physical frailty and deterioration with age. Actually, there is a process of elimination at work in their community. Infant and child mortality is twenty to thirty percent. The weak do not survive childhood. Deaths due to accidents and disease are frequent. There is little that can be done to prevent such deaths and little interest in saving the life of a person who cannot contribute to the family and community. Only the survivor can be observed. Survivors are, by elimination, the strong and healthy. These Black people occupied the lowest rung in a society where the vast majority of the people have always lived in abject poverty. Over the past centuries, there had been almost no upward social mobility for anyone. Yet, they are no longer at the bottom of Ecuadorian society. Their social and economic position is distinctly superior to that of most Indians in the highlands.

For reasons of security, Spaniards and other slave owners in the Americas, purchased slaves according to tribal origin, always trying to avoid individuals that might share the culture and language of slaves purchased previously. With no common language or culture, slaves were forced to adopt the language and culture of their masters. The French in Haiti were the exception—bringing in slaves too fast to prevent cultural and linguistic connections. The result was probably inevitable; the slaves revolted and kicked the French out of Haiti.

In coastal Ecuador the Spanish language and culture gave Black people access to the limited educational opportunities that became available after 1930. Some of the men, and a few of the women, could read and write. The poor of Ecuador had little protection against abuse from the rich and powerful, but they had some rights, and these Black people knew how to use those rights. A man could talk to the Mayor or regional Prefect; he could report a crime to the priest, who might choose to punish the wrongdoer; with luck he could have an account of the offense printed in the newspaper, causing embarrassment for offenders. He had at least some recourse to law and justice. He was not completely helpless when his daughters were raped by wealthy persons or the police, or when his sons were forced to perform unpaid labor.

The contrast with Indians is stark. Lacking the European language, and knowledge of national culture, they were powerless. Their daughters could be raped; their sons could be pressed into forced labor. Their only recourse was revenge, and that would lead to certain death. The Indians had become closed in upon themselves, wishing most of all to be left alone. They did not understand the European culture, and could not compete with it. They wanted to avoid the European world, but of course, they could not avoid that world.

The contrast with the offspring of those West Africans who were fortunate enough to have escaped enslavement by Europeans, is equally stark. The Black people of South America, though poverty stricken and relatively powerless, nevertheless enjoyed a level of material well-being and freedom unknown among the common people of West Africa. Probably, no informed Black man in Ecuador would have willingly traded places with the average modern day West African. At the bottom of Ecuadorian society are the naked savages in the forest. They had no rights at all, and could be murdered almost indiscriminately. Yes, these Black men are certainly several rungs above the bottom of Ecuadorian society.

Six Black men pushed a canoe toward the sea, with three pushing on one side, and two on the other. The sixth man moved the log from the back of the canoe, to the front, to keep the boat moving. A young White man joined the weak side, and heaved along with them. The men did not acknowledge the White man. They knew he was not an Ecuadorian. No White Ecuadorian would have joined in their labor. They recognized this man as a foreigner—probably a *Norteamericano*. The only White men willing to join Blacks in physical labor were *Norteamericanos*—the strange, rich and powerful people, who did not understand cultural norms.

The power the *Norteamericanos* could command was legendary. If one of them were mistreated, even one with no money—and almost all were very rich—many policemen would investigate and punish any person thought to have committed the crime. These rich foreigners were not hated. The men often told each other, they should hate them, but the *Norteamericanos* were too naive to be hated. They walked through the villages, and mingled with local people unafraid—apparently secure in the knowledge that their government, or God, would protect them. They were wealthy, but somehow plain and accepting, as if they were equals, or ignorant of the vast gulf separating the upper-class from the poverty of the common people.

Although all Ecuadorians had been told the *Norteamericanos* were racist, they found little to suggest racial prejudice in these people. In Ecuador, as elsewhere in Latin America, segregation and discrimination are based mostly on social class, rather than skin color. Of course, most Blacks and Indians were poor, and most of the wealthy were White, or light-skinned Mestizos and Mulattos. But, that was explained by the absence of social mobility over the past five hundred years. The rich inherited their wealth, along with their light skin color, from Spaniards who had wealth to bequeath. Of course, most Blacks and Indians inherited the poverty, and dark skin color, of their slave and Indian ancestors. But, in those rare cases that Blacks or Indians achieved middle or upper class status—usually through marriage—the lucky individual would face no segregation and relatively little discrimination related to skin color.

For an Ecuadorian the thought of segregating, or discriminating against, a middle or upper class person simply because of the color of his skin is too aberrant to imagine. Thus, the Blacks of Ecuador had no measuring stick with which to judge the racism of the *Norteamericanos*. But the poor of Ecuador did have a measuring stick for judgment of discrimination based on social class. In Ecuador, and throughout Latin America, poverty marked a man as a member of a lower caste—a status his grandchildren would almost certainly inherit. If a man had the incredible luck to escape poverty, he would invent an aristocratic past for himself to avoid contaminating his children and grandchildren with poverty status. By contrast, the *Norteamericanos* came from a land where social mobility was commonplace. Being a 'self-made' man from a humble origin was a source of pride; even those who inherited wealth would often invent a history that traced their ancestors to log cabins and hard work. For the poor people of Ecuador, the absence of prejudice based on social class seemed to mean the *Norteamericanos* have no prejudice at all.

They called the *Norteamericanos* 'gringos'. That word, once intended as an insult, was adopted immediately by these strange foreigners who used the term to describe themselves. These people could not be insulted! Apparently, they could not conceive the notion that someone might think ill of them. Their superiority gave cause for resentment, and some local people would speak harshly against these *Norteamericanos*, who had so much money and power, and who pushed their religions and music and manufactured products, into the local culture. But how can you hate people who are friendly and laughing, who are generous, and will walk into a humble home and eat the food served to them? The people found it hard to hate these *gringos*.

Many of the young men liked their music, and enjoyed their friendship—so easy to acquire, and seemingly so pure and sincere. And, they liked sharing the fun and wealth the *gringos* could spread around. Many young women dreamed of the moment when they might be selected as a partner. If just for a day, then so be it. But, the chance to return to that other world of wealth and privilege was a reverie. Impossible? Of course! But, every girl had heard of someone who had accomplished that impossibility.

"How about me going out with you fellows? I'll help you fish." The men turned their heads away. Ignoring the White foreigners was usually the best policy.

The oldest man responded, *"We will be out all day. It is hard work, and dangerous."*

"No problem," he said. *"I was born here. Over there is my brother Juan, and there is my Uncle Jaime;"* motioning to the other boat.

The men laughed at his joke. Yes, he is a *Norteamericano*, they thought, only a *Norteamericano* would say such a thing. The older man shrugged, and it was settled. The young White man would join them.

The six Black men and the *gringo* pushed the boat into the surf and climbed aboard. One of the two older men was the captain. He sat at the stern and used his paddle as a rudder. The other men paddled furiously through the surf, which was unusually high given the early morning hour.

The captain shouted orders in the local dialect. The foreigner did not understand many of the words, but followed the lead of the man in front of him, paddling hard, pausing, and sometimes backstroking. Some of the breakers almost turned them sideways, and the sea poured into the boat. The surf was unusually strong, but the men were confident. The foreigner, but no one else, was surprised when they passed safely through the surf and into the bay.

They rendezvoused with the second fishing boat, and the men began to untangle a long wide net. *"Here is your brother Juan, and your uncle Jaime,"* the Captain said to the *gringo*, and pointed to two men in the other boat. All the men in the first boat laughed. The men in the second boat were not sure they understood the joke.

"Hello Tío Jaime. Hello Hermano Juan; how is Mamá?" The *gringo* yelled in Spanish to the men in the other boat. Now the men in the second boat knew the White man was a *Norteamericano*, making a joke.

"Mamá didn't tell me about any white babies. There must have been a gringo hanging around in the outhouse." One of them yelled back. The men in both boats laughed heartily. The joke would have been an insult to a White Ecuadorian, but this was a *gringo*. This White *gringo*, who probably had more wealth and power than most White Ecuadorians, was making jokes about kinship with Black men. They liked him.

The men in the two boats stretched the net out between them. Progress was slow. At noon the net was fully extended—about thirty yards. Finally, the men relaxed and allowed the boats to continue drifting north with the current.

The men ate their lunch, and laughed and talked. He ate his rice and beans, and drank his water. The men spoke their dialect. All of them could speak normal Spanish as well, but they preferred not to allow the *gringo* to understand.

He had time to think, and he did think about the Spanish dialect he could not understand. He could understand almost any Spanish, but not the dialect of Blacks along the west coast of northern South America. The rhythm and tone of that Spanish dialect was strikingly similar to the Black English he had heard in the army. Once, he had met an African from Sierra Leone who had spoken with an accent, which for him was similar to English-Creole speaking Blacks in British Honduras.

"How is it possible that your accent is similar to the people of British Honduras?" he had asked.

"It's not," the man had answered. "They speak very different."

Different for you, of course, but not for me. I hear the same tone, and the same rhythm. That was one of the mysteries he would understand and explain to the world one day.

The break was over, and they were back to work. The captain was at the rudder barking orders. The men paddled against the current now back down the coast. Their boat was further at sea, and the second boat, with the other end of the net, was skirting the coast. They paddled for an hour, making no apparent headway against the current. The young gringo was determined to do a fair share of the work, but his arms and back ached. He needed a short break every ten minutes or so. The other men continued to paddle, and seemed not to notice the slacking by the stranger.

The waves were high and the spray kept the men wet. Evaporative cooling from the wind chilled the skin, and the gringo, but no one else, shivered. He took a plastic garbage bag from his lunch bag and tore a hole in the bottom for his head and holes on each side for his arms, and pulled it over his head.

"Hey, gringo!" yelled the man behind him. *"You don't need to wear a dress here."* All the men laughed.

"I walk warm, and let the people laugh," he said, repeating an old Spanish proverb.

"You are right, gringo." The Captain said. *"Be warm, and let them laugh."*

It was a simple lesson that he had learned in Central America. To avoid wind chill, you must stay dry and avoid evaporative cooling. A plastic garbage bag would do that, and of course, he could afford plastic garbage bags.

The men paddled furiously for more than two hours, but there was no headway against the current. The restaurant deck at Costa del Sol was still a glimmering speck on the beach, a couple of miles or so south. The situation seemed hopeless. He stopped paddling and looked back at the captain.

"Take a break gringo, you are not accustomed to this," the captain said.

"We don't move south," he said.

"We are moving through the current. He goes north. He is filling our net. Soon, we will turn south—you will see."

After another hour of paddling, there was a call from the boat closer to shore. *"Okay boys, let's do it!"* The Captain shouted. The men redoubled their efforts—something he thought would have been impossible, given the effort already put forth. He worked hard too, not sure whether there had been an emergency on the other boat, or the call was part of the normal routine. And, then the boat did make headway to the south, or rather southeast, toward the shore. They were out of the current, and were swinging the net in a wide arc toward Costa del Sol.

The men in the second boat beached their craft, and began to pull the net from the shore. His boat continued at sea, paddling south and being dragged toward the coast by the men pulling the net. He forgot the ache in his arms and back, and worked along with the other men. As the boat was dragged into the surf, the men fought against the water with their paddles, trying to keep the boat perpendicular to the waves.

The captain yelled something to the men, and they threw the net over the side. The boat moved in toward the beach on the next wave, and the men jumped out to prevent the boat from being pulled back by the surf. Someone placed a log in front, and they rolled the boat up, away from the surf. After moving the boat about twenty yards the captain barked an order and all the men relaxed, and walked over to the net. He removed the plastic bag and joined them.

A large crowd of people had gathered to buy fish and shrimp. A young American woman was among them. The Captains of the two boats seemed to be in charge, but all the men were involved. The women buyers would yell to their kin, *"Cousin, sell to me!"* a woman would say, and one of the men would pick out some fish or shrimp for her. Most of the exchange was on a family basis. Some women paid nothing—wives and sisters of the fishermen, he thought. Other women paid a small sum of money—maybe cousins and aunts. Still other women haggled about price, and paid much more.

"Do you go with us tomorrow gringo?" the Captain asked, loud enough for all to hear. *"Or, have you become too tired?"*

"Tired?" he replied loudly in Spanish. *"Why should I be tired? And, where was the danger? We gringos send women and children out to do this kind of work. And, now you are charging these poor women for the fish you have taken with so little effort."*

The men smiled, and the women and children roared with laughter. *"Yes, listen to the gringo, you lazy robbers,"* one woman shouted.

The Captain had a small plastic bag he used to gather fish and shrimp for selected customers. *"Here, I will trade with you,"* he said to the Captain, exchanging his large garbage bag, for the Captain's small *one, "so that you would also walk with warmth."*

"Grácias, gringo; I will use it. If I am warm, why should it be important to me that the people laugh?" the Captain replied.

He picked up a large fish and nine large shrimp and put them into the bag. *"How much?"* he asked. The Capitan shrugged and turned away. He took the fish, and turned toward the restaurant. *"Thank you, Capitan,"* he yelled, *"and, thank you Brother Juan and Uncle Jaime. Tell Mamá I love her."*

The men laughed and hooted. *"I will speak with Mamá,"* one man yelled back. *"Who knows how many gringo brothers and sisters I may have."*

STOP TRYING TO CHARM ME: COSTA DEL SOL, TUESDAY AFTERNOON, AUGUST 4TH

Were they talking about me?" She asks.

"You? I wouldn't let them talk about you. Jeez, you must think I'm the biggest shithead in the world."

"But, they kept saying *gringa*, and they were looking at me."

"Sure they were looking at you. Who the hell wouldn't? But, they were saying *gringo*, not *gringa*; and, they were talking about me, not you."

She puts her arm around my waist. "Sorry. I know you well enough to know you wouldn't allow that. That was a really stupid thing to think."

"No sweat, love; I know where you're coming from. When I was first learning Spanish I often thought people were talking about me. Hell, it can drive you nuts—you become paranoid. They look at you because you are different, you know. Course, they look at you because..." I cock my head sideways and look her over. She smiles and gives me her fake signature punch.

"You always have so much fun with everyone. So, tell me what they were saying."

"Oh hell, this morning I told the captain of our boat that one of those Black dudes in the other boat was my brother—joking you know—and, this fellow says his mother must have had a *gringo* hanging around the outhouse, and he says, who knows how many *gringo* brothers I may have."

"You're crazy Ray," she laughs. "And, what did you say when the woman called them robbers?"

"Oh, the captain tried to talk me out of going with them this morning—said it would be hard work. So I told him hell man, I didn't see any hard work, and he shouldn't be charging so much for his fish."

"The fishermen didn't get mad at you for saying that?"

"Nah, everyone down here can take a joke."

We walk up the stairs to the restaurant. The Japanese woman is waiting. *"Si nos hace el favor, Señora"* I say, and then remembering she does not speak Spanish, I change to English, "If you will do us the favor, Señora, fix us three portions from this fish and two shrimp each, and the rest is for you."

"Thank you," she says with a slight bow, taking the bag and turning to leave.

"Doozo," I reply, and give her a deep bow. The woman turns back and stares at me. *"Ashita wa shitsurei shimashita."* I tell her, and repeat the deep bow. The woman bows and then turns and hurries away.

We sit at our favorite table. "So?" Shirley says, smiling: "tell me about that."

"That's three of my ten words in Japanese. I said, yesterday I did an impolite thing. She's just shocked to see some proper Japanese courtesy from a barbarian."

"They don't really bow to each other these days, do they?"

"You bet. Just exactly the way I did. And, they say '*sumimasen*', I'm so terribly sorry, and '*ohaiyo gozaimas*', gracious good morning, and '*shitsurei shimashita*', I did an impolite thing, heaven help us, and all this time, they are bowing. When I would run out of those words, I would just bow and say, 'kiss my ass', and bow again and say, 'go fuck yourself'. It seemed to work about the same way." She laughs. "You know," I continue, "they don't really expect foreigners to do polite things, because we are barbarians. So when you do, it's like heaping coals of fire on their heads. Sometimes, they turn around and run away from you." Shirley seems to enjoy my fun.

"I'm going to take a quick shower and put on dry clothes; I'll be right back. Here, you can hold on to my cap while I'm gone."

"I wouldn't touch that sweaty cap. Why don't you wear it in the shower? It could use a good rinse."

I shower quickly, and rinse the sweat out of my cap. When I return to the deck, I ask the woman to bring us a couple of beers, and sit with Shirley.

The woman brings two ice-cold beers and places them on the table with two glasses. She steps back with a nod bow of her head, and returns to the kitchen. Shirley seems to notice the special attention I get from the woman.

"You're so damned crazy, I love ya."

"Ya' do?" I ask.

"No! I don't mean like that."

"Well, it's a nice thing to say, anyway." I say, mocking her.

"You know what I meant. I just love the way you are always laughing and doing crazy things. It's as if you're on some kind of emotional high all the time."

"So, you don't love me?" She raises her eyebrows, looks up and exhales. "Do you kind of like me a little bit?" I ask.

"Stop it," she says, giving me a soft punch to the chest.

"Maybe, you don't hate me a whole lot."

"Stop trying to charm me," she whispers. "It won't work."

"It doesn't surprise me."

"What doesn't surprise you?"

"That you don't love me. Hell, I learned my lesson a long time ago. You can love them, but they never love you back. It's just like Peggy Rice."

"Peggy Rice? Who's that? And anyway, what does she have to do with anything?"

"I loved her, Shirley. I loved her for four years, and in the end she dumped me. Four years of my life blown away by her callous disregard for my feelings. She was an evil woman; she just used me and then pushed me aside—the way all women do after they get what they want from a man."

"Well, I'm sorry that happened to you." Shirley says with concern. "There are some people like that, but you can't let it bother you. You just have to pick yourself up and go on. And, it's not fair to say all women are like that."

"Ha! I bet all women are not like that."

She presses her lips together and frowns. "How long ago did this happen to you?"

I can't avoid a smile. "When I was twelve."

"Twelve! You were in love with a girl when you were twelve years old?"

"Well I was nine when I fell in love with her." I feel my smile broaden across my face.

"NINE? What the hell are you talking about?"

"It was in the fourth grade. She sat on the other side of the room; I was afraid to sit over there, so I sat on the other side and a couple of rows back so I could look at her. She looked so sweet and good—at least that's what I thought at the time. Ha! Sweet and good! Anyway, I knew we had to do something when we became girlfriend and boyfriend, but I didn't know what that would be. I knew it would be more than the kiss—like with Tom Sawyer and Becky Thatcher." She raises her eyebrows and presses her lips together, obviously getting ready to yell at me for saying something crude, so I quickly add: "And I knew for sure that it wouldn't have anything to do with pulling her panties down. I didn't even think about stuff like that in those days, Shirley."

She relaxes a bit: "So anyway, I finally decided it would be me looking at her breasts. You know, she would have to pull her blouse up and let me see her breasts."

"AT NINE YEARS OLD?" she demands.

"Well, how the hell could I have known? It's not like you could go to the library and look it up, you know. You couldn't ask a girl, could you? Or, ask an adult! If you asked a guy he probably wouldn't know either; or if he did know he would just start laughing at you like you were the biggest dumb shit in the world."

"Yeah, I can understand the problem," she says, smiling.

"So, anyway I knew she would be really embarrassed about letting me see her breasts, so I decided I wouldn't really look. You know, because I loved her so much, and I didn't want to hurt her."

"What a nice young man you are."

"Yeah, I am; but we never got around to that. Anyway, when I was twelve in Junior High School I had loved her for four years, and I decided I just had to talk to her."

"You hadn't even told her?"

"No! Jeez, how could I tell her something like that? She was one of the popular kids, and I was nobody. I had never even talked to her. But, I decided I had to talk to her because I couldn't stand it any longer." Shirley smiles; "I wasn't going to just blurt out that I loved her." She shakes her head. "I was going to say I liked our geometry teacher, because I knew she liked that teacher and I figured she would like me if I liked that teacher too." She nods agreement, still smiling. "So I walked up behind her in line at the cafeteria, and said, 'Hi, Peggy.' And, then she turned around and said, 'What?' with her face all screwed up like, who the hell are you? And, I didn't know what to say to her. You know, it would be stupid to say I liked that teacher or say hi Peggy again, and then I wouldn't know what to say after that anyway."

She has a big smile now, and is trying hard to hold back a giggle. I continue, "So I didn't say anything. And, she just looked at me, as if I were an idiot, and then finally, someone said 'Hey Peggy,' and she turned away to that person, cause he was one of the popular kids, ya' know, and she never looked back at me. She never even acknowledged the fact that I had said 'Hi Peggy' to her. So, that was the end of our love."

"So you were jilted by an evil woman, huh?"

"Yeah, I was. And, I walked right out of the school, right then, after I realized she would never love me. And, I went down to Thrifty's drug store, where we always went after school, and I had my twenty-six cents lunch money, so I bought twenty-six pieces of bubble gum, and I was going to kill myself, chewing up all that bubble gum."

The giggle she can no longer suppress spurts out and she covers her mouth with her hand.

"IT'S NOT FUNNY, SHIRLEY!" I say, trying to sound as serious as I can. She shakes her head. "But, anyway I couldn't get more than four pieces of that bubble gum in my mouth at once," she nods her head in agreement; "and it didn't seem like it was going to kill me," she shakes her head; "and anyway it seemed like a terrible waste of bubble gum." She nods her head in agreement again and chokes on her giggle.

"But, I can tell you I haven't forgotten. So, don't think you are going to run over me roughshod, and then laugh when you leave me crying in the rain. I know what it is to suffer at the hands of a hateful woman, and they don't fool me anymore."

She shakes her head and laughs quietly. "Ya' know something? You made a joke about this, but I think there really was a Peggy Rice," I nod. "And you really were in love with her, and you were hurt really bad when you realized it would never work out for you, huh?" I nod. "Even the stuff about the bubble gum; I think it really happened, huh?"

"Yeah, Shirley love, it really happened."

"I like you." She puts her hand on my face, and then rubs my cheek with her palm, "and, I would like you a lot more if you would shave once in a while. If I were to kiss you the road burn would be like falling off a motorcycle at sixty miles an hour."

"I'll go shave right now." I stand to leave.

"Not now! We're talking." She pulls me back to the chair. "Shave in the morning; and, do it every morning like a normal man. Didn't they teach you to shave every morning in the service?"

"Yeah, and that's probably why I don't like to do it. But I will if you want to kiss me."

"I don't want to kiss you!"

"You said you would kiss me if I shaved."

"No I didn't! I said IF I WERE to kiss you; that's a hypothetical statement—the subjunctive mood Raymond, in case you don't understand English. Just walk up to some guy on the street and tell him I want to kiss him, huh? You must think I'm the dizziest blond bimbo that ever came down the pike!"

"So you have never wanted to kiss a guy, huh?"

"Not bloody likely!"

"I'll bet you've wanted to kiss your dreamboat guy."

"I may have wanted to, but I certainly never told him that."

"Ah Ha! So, you want to but you don't want to admit it! I'll bet you're sitting there wanting to kiss me right now; and I don't even want to think about what else you might be wanting to do."

"LOOK BUSTER, IF I WANTED TO KISS YOU I WOULD DO IT!" Suddenly she stands and leans across the table and kisses me on the mouth. She sits back down. "I wouldn't just sit here wanting to do it. And, I can guarantee you I don't want to do anything else, so you can forget about that."

"Kiss me again."

"No."

"You did it too fast; I didn't even enjoy it."

"Life is tough Ray; get used to it."

"So, if you want to kiss me you just do it; what if I want to kiss you?"

"I didn't think you would mind."

"I don't. But, what about fair play; don't I get to do the same thing to you?"

"Okay, you're right; I shouldn't have done that. I'm sorry."

"Hey, being sorry doesn't change anything. How do I go about repairing the damage to my self-esteem? It's like I've been violated and can't do anything about it."

"Violated? Good Lord!"

"Well jeez, some woman just walks up to me on the street and gives me a big wet smacker, right on the mouth."

She chokes and laughs: "It wasn't wet!"

"Oh yeah, well what's this stuff drooling down my chin?"

She shakes her head and continues to laugh. "Nothing is drooling down your chin, you idiot!"

"Well, do I get to kiss you back or not?"

"Okay, okay, go ahead, before you decide to sue for psychological damages!"

I stand and bend over her. "Aren't you going to close your eyes? How about puckering up? I kissed you back, you know."

"Get on with it."

"Think I'll save my kiss for later."

"It's now or never, Ray."

I sit back down. "Huh uh; I get to collect when I want to. And I prefer later, when you've mellowed out on a few beers."

"I'm never going to mellow out, Ray!"

"You always mellow out after a couple of beers; showing some cleavage and stuff."

"Cleavage? I don't have any cleavage!"

"And you wiggle your butt around, and accidently brush up against me."

"Raymond! I have never done anything like that in my whole life! And if you don't stop saying things like that I'm going to walk away from here right now!"

"Hey, I'm just bullshitting; I know you wouldn't do that—unfortunately." I go back to the cage to order more beer. When I return to the table she has a serious look and changes the subject.

"Tell me about when you were in the service."

"Jeez," I say, turning away.

"Were you in the service?"

"Yeah, I guess so."

"This is therapy Ray; you have to tell me about it."

I sit back and try to think, and then just let my mind go blank for a few seconds. "Second squad," I hear myself say. We are quiet for a few seconds.

The Clowns Dance:

"Second squad?"

"Yeah, second squad, weapons platoon, Baker Company, fucken Eighty-Second Airborne."

"Before you said you were in the army," she says.

"The fucken Eighty-Second is the army."

"Why do they call it airborne? Did you fly around in airplanes?"

I choke back a laugh. "Not long, love."

"So, why do they call it airborne?"

"Didn't you ever read a book about the war, or see a movie?" I ask in disbelief.

"No, I hate that stuff."

"Well, let me tell you some of the facts of life; there's two kinds of things that fall out of the sky, and only one of um' is bird shit."

She thinks for a few seconds. "You were a paratrooper? You jumped out of airplanes?"

"Yeah, we jumped out of perfectly good airplanes."

"That explains a lot about you, Ray. Did they shoot at you while you were floating down?"

"Only in the movies," I laugh.

"Looks like you would be a perfect target, floating around up there."

"In combat, you try not to jump in their laps, and anyway you come in low. You're only up for half a minute; so, if they aren't right there waiting for you, they aren't likely to get a shot. Anyway, I never made a combat jump."

"How many times did you jump out of airplanes?"

"Twelve."

"Did your parachute always work?" I hear myself sigh. "That was a really stupid thing to ask, wasn't it? The fall would kill you if your parachute didn't work, huh?"

"Nah, the fall wouldn't kill you, even if your parachute didn't work."

"Sure it would."

"Nah, it wouldn't even hurt you." I tell her, enjoying my joke. She shakes her head in disbelief. "Of course, that sudden stop when you hit the ground—that would kill the shit out of you." Shirley glares at me. "Little airborne joke." I say.

"It wasn't funny Ray," but she has to giggle. "You're interrupting the therapy, Ray."

I start singing an Airborne song to the tune of Glory, Glory, Halleluiah: "There was blood upon the risers, there were brains upon the chute, his intestines were a dangling from his paratrooper suit.."

"Will you shut up; I don't want to think about your intestines dangling around."

Johnny is below on the beach. "What's up kids?"

"Come on up and have dinner with us, Johnny," I yell back, hoping he will decline.

"I was thinking about walking up to Atacames, and get something decent to eat," he replies.

"Come on up, Johnny," Shirley yells to him, "Ray was out fishing today, and brought back a beautiful fish, and some big shrimp. Come on up and join us." To me she says: "We'll continue the therapy later, and be nice to Johnny. And, by the way, you were right about not having amnesia. You're just blocking some things out."

"Is that what Doctor Norma told you?"

"Yes! That's what DOCTOR NORMA told me!"

Johnny comes up and sits at our table. "I've never had a decent meal here yet, and frankly, I have some real serious doubts. Maybe I'll just have a beer with you kids, and head on up to Atacames."

I go back to the cage and get a beer for him. "You actually went fishing with those guys?" Johnny asks. "I'm surprised you made it back. Hell, half of um' don't even know how to swim."

"You're right, some of them don't," I respond, wanting to make conversation. "You know, once I was down in Central America taking a dory—you know, a dugout—across the bay, and the boatman didn't even have a paddle in the boat. So, I said, don't you have a paddle? And, he said, hell man, I don't need a paddle, I have an outboard motor." We laugh.

"And, these fellows would probably say, hell, I don't need to know how to swim, I have a boat," Shirley adds. We all laugh.

"God, I love these people." I say.

"You really do love them, don't you," she says, putting her hand on my cheek.

I turn and look into her eyes. "I surely do, Shirley love, I surely do." Her smile is mischievous, as if she and I have something secret between us. What would that be? Probably, that she knows you should be locked away in the loony bin, I tell myself.

The woman serves our meal. Each plate had a large fish fillet and two shrimp, with rice and fried banana. She gives each of us a cloth napkin and a full set of silverware.

"Jeez," Johnny says, "I've never seen anything like this in Costa."

The fish and everything else is very well prepared. "Jeez," Johnny says, as if to himself, "this is the best fish I've had in Ecuador." And, then to us, "How did you guys manage this?"

"Ray managed it;" Shirley says, "he charmed that Japanese woman."

"Charmed that woman?" Johnny replies. "It would take one hell of a snake charmer to charm her."

"He charmed her." Shirley says, smiling at me.

"Well," Johnny says, "you've made a believer out of me."

We finish our meal, order more beer. We take turns using the outhouse, and watch the flashes of lighting over the ocean. Shirley and I mostly look at each other.

Johnny breaks the silence. "Seems that woman is not the only one being charmed."

"What are you talking about?" she asks.

What am I talking about?" Johnny repeats. "Well, I'm talking about you sweetheart—my very own, never-give-a-fucking-inch, Shirley. And, I am suggesting maybe you are being charmed by this gentleman, sitting here between us."

"So? Since when did you take charge of my life? And, what makes you think I can't take care of myself?"

"I just feel responsible for you," he says, "and, frankly I don't like what I'm seeing."

"WHAT ARE YOU SEEING?" she asks, angrily. "Who told you to take responsibility for me?"

"Okay!" Johnny replies, "and, don't start hitting me. It makes a bruise you know, and I don't like it." Johnny gets up. "I hope you are coming back to the hut with me tonight, Shirley."

Shirley is up and in his face immediately. "Okay, okay, okay!" Johnny says, "I'm not telling you what to do." He puts his hands out, palms forward, and brushes the air down, to indicate he is finished. He turns and walks away.

"I can't believe it!" she huffs, after Johnny leaves.

I know she's embarrassed. "Sit down, love. Don't sweat it. It's no big deal." But, she doesn't sit. There is an awkward silence.

"I'm going back to my hut. It's been a long day for both of us. I'll see you in the morning." She turns to leave.

"Shirley, don't be upset about him; there's no problem."

"I'm not upset! I have to teach tomorrow, and I need to get a good night's sleep. I'll see you in the morning," she says, and walks away immediately.

I go to my hut and get into the hammock. I consider Johnny's "never give-a-fucking-inch" description of Shirley. Maybe you're making some backhanded progress on Operation Shirley Love, I tell myself. For some reason, I am reminded of the time I slugged it out with the whole fucken Army—standing toe to toe, no quarter asked and none given—and came away a winner.

THE BIPODS: KOREA, SPRING, 1953

Weapons platoon had three 81 mm mortars, each with a forty-four pound set of bipods. Each mortar also had a twenty-one pound tube, and a two-piece base plate, each weighing a bit over twenty pounds, so four men were needed to carry all the parts of one mortar.

The bipods were the worst. First, there was the additional weight, and second, they were terribly awkward. The only thing you could do was put them across your shoulders and put your arms over the top. The bipods, along with the weight of the pack, one or two canteens of water, an M1 rifle or carbine, and full ammo ration, was painful. In theory, the gunner carried his bipods, but in practice Sergeant Jordan often assigned the job to the fuckups, as punishment.

Richards and his buddy Patterson had been in the medic's hooch drinking grape juice laced with medical grain alcohol—a concoction known to the GI's as Purple Jesus. They called it Purple Jesus because it was purple, and after the first swig, most guys would say *Jesus!*

"Thought I'd catch you here, fuckup," Jordan said to him, and to Patterson and the medics, "You youngsters better get some sleep; we pullen' out in the mo'nen," and motioned for him to get a move on. He knew Jordan wouldn't report the other guys; why should he? They weren't the Serge's problem. He was Jordan's problem, and he knew he'd be loading up the bipods in the morning.

Sergeant Jordan wasn't vindictive. Anything you could get away with was fine with him, including things that could send you to the stockade. But, he had a "sense'a duty," as he called it: "You youngsters gonna' be back out on the block (meaning civilian life) one'a these days, and I gonna' still be right here. This my job; you fuckup, I gonna' land on ya."

"Hey Serge, can I carry the bipods?" Everyone in the platoon turned to look at the idiot that had volunteered for the bipods.

It was 3:30 AM, and the platoon was standing at ease after roll call, mostly bitching about everything. It had rained all night and the day was sure to be hot and steamy.

There would be a bumpy thirty-mile ride in a duce-an'a-half truck, and a seven-mile hike to the top of Zebra Hill, where they would replace Charley Company.

"You got um, fuckup." Jordan said.

Had um' anyway Serge, he told himself; just didn't want to give you the satisfaction. He hoisted the bipods over his shoulders.

"Ain't leaven' yet, son," Jordan said.

"That's okay Serge; I just want to start getting used to it."

The trek up the hill was tough that morning. Footing was poor, and boots were almost pulled off feet by the suction, trudging through the mud. Jordan called short breaks every thirty minutes or so, but PFC Richards had not taken a break, or even taken the bipods off his shoulders.

"Take a break, son," Jordan said. "You gonna' need yo' energy, them Chinks come whooping up Zebra."

"It's okay Serge; I just want to be ready to move out."

Jordan was suspicious. "What you up to, fuckup?"

"Nothing Serge, shit, I just want to do my duty," he smiled, and several troopers nearby, laughed. There wasn't a moron in This Man's Army who would have taken that seriously, and Jordan was no moron.

"I don't know what you try'en to pull fuckup, but if you try it, I gonna' break yo' fucken back," Jordan said.

Two weeks later at 3:30 AM the platoon was again in formation, at ease, and bitching as usual. They would repeat the ride and climb to Zebra Hill to replace Charley Company. "Hey Serge, can I carry the bipods today?" he heard himself say, in a cheerful voice. The whole platoon fell silent.

"You got them bipods for the duration!" Jordan yelled, "an' I don't ever want'a hear no more'a yo' shit! You got that, fuckup?"

He shouldered the bipods with a giant smile. The trek up the hill that morning had been hell. He walked in the rain, and stood alone with the bipods on his shoulders, when the platoon took breaks. There was little moral support from the guys. Jordan was pissed off—or as close to pissed off as Jordan ever got—and no one wanted to cross him.

During the week on the hill, several troopers had asked him if he was going to volunteer for the bipods again on the next trip up Zebra. He had not responded. He didn't know if he would be able to muster the strength to volunteer again. The first trek up Zebra with the bipods had left his shoulders sore and blistered, and the second time they were bloody. He had plastered bandages over his shoulders for the second trip, but it hadn't helped much. Very likely it wouldn't matter, since Jordan would probably assign him the bipods regardless. So, the word had spread through the Platoon. 'He's gonna' do it again!' 'Nah, he won't do it.'

It was 3:30 AM two weeks later, but this time the platoon was not bitching. They were listening and watching. "Hey Serge, can I take the bipods today?" His voice had sounded almost matter of fact and he regretted the lack of levity. Jordan turned toward him, obviously pissed off. He took the bipods from the gunner and hoisted them to his shoulders. They can kill you GI, he told himself, but they can't eat ya'.

At that moment, a miracle happened. Miller, a guy from his squad, spoke up: "Hey Serge, can I carry bipods too?"

"Miller," Jordan yelled, "you goddamn fuckup, I gonna' break yo' back!"

"I just want to carry the bipods, Serge." Miller said, with a broad smile.

Jordan turned to Corporal Rodgers in the First Squad, "Give this fuckup your bipods," he commanded. Rodgers did as told, and Miller hoisted them onto his shoulders, smiling.

Then the second miracle happened. "Hey Serge, can I carry bipods too?" It was Rosenski, the smallest guys in the platoon.

Jordan responded in a tone of a hangman, with more volunteers for the noose than rope to hang them with. "Well, I'll be damned if this ain't the most fucked up shit I ever seen!" He turned to Jackson, in the Third Squad. "Give this maggot your bipods!"

It was at that moment that the true goodness of the Lord blessed all the fuckups and maggots that ever served in This Man's Army. Jackson, a Black guy, responded to Jordan: "He ain't get'en my bipods."

Jordan walked back and faced Jackson: "Don't fuck with me corporal!" The Sergeant spit the words in his face.

"I ain't given him my bipods, Serge; he fuck um' up."

"How he gonna' fuck up yo' bipods, boy?" Jordan asked, now deadly serious. Jordan usually only used the term boy when he was talking to a Black guy, and there was a feeling, he really would break his back.

"They fuckups Serge. They gonna' fuck um' up, shee'it!"

The Sergeant stood for a moment contemplating the big smile Jackson couldn't hide and the giggling that spread through the platoon, and then walked away. Jackson shouldered his bipods, and laughed quietly.

There was a great deal of tension in the platoon. Everyone knew the rules. There are two kinds of army funny: There is White guy funny and Black guy funny, and the two don't mix. The bipods thing was clearly a case of White guy funny. Would Jackson cross over? That was rarely done, and Jackson was no fuckup. He had made corporal in record time, and would almost certainly make the army a career.

The Squad Leader for the fourth squad, a Black Sergeant, kicked Jackson in the butt. "Get the fucken bipods off your shoulder," the Sergeant snarled at him.

"Don't be kicken me, Serge," Jackson said, but he lowered the bipods to the ground and stopped laughing. Blacks and Whites had learned to live together, but they usually kept the rules strict and correct. Whites could laugh at Black army funny, and likewise, Blacks could laugh at White army funny. But, actually taking part in the fun just wasn't done.

But, rules are made to be broken. On the first break Jackson remained standing with the bipods on his shoulders, along with himself and Miller. He and Miller stopped laughing, and tried to take the situation seriously, knowing Jackson had his neck sticking way out with the other Black guys. The Fourth Squad Sergeant was still upset with Jackson; he walked out and yelled: "Yo' fucken up Jackson; get yo' ass back here."

But Jackson's pride was still smarting from the kick in the butt: "Who you think you talking to Serge? You get them fucken strips off your sleeve an' we see who's kicken' who in the ass." Suddenly, it was no longer funny. Jackson was not just insubordinate; he had issued a challenge that neither man could back away from.

"Don't fuck with me Jackson!" The Sergeant strutted out to meet the challenge. But, Sergeant Jordan had heard the exchange and intervened.

"Hold on there Sergeant; I'm still in charge here." Jordan walked out and stood between the two men. "What's this insubordination going on here Jackson?"

"I ain't taken this shit from Sergeant Watson, Sergeant; ain't nobody kicken' me in the ass." Jackson said.

"I'll decide who's taking shit from who around here, Corporal Jackson! You think I need help run'en this platoon?"

"No, Sergeant."

"Then you just back off here son and let me run my platoon." Jordan motioned for Jackson to back up and then turned to Sergeant Watson. "So what's this about kicken' corporal Jackson in the ass?"

"I didn't kick him; I just pushed him with my foot."

Sergeant Jordan leaned forward toward Watson: "What you mean puten' yo' foot on my corporal, sergeant?"

"Jackson's out'a line Sergeant, an' I'm set'en him straight."

"How's he out'a line sergeant?" Jordan demanded.

"He's carrying them fucken bipods around with that bunch a' fuckoffs."

"If Jackson wants to carry them bipods around—LIKE A FOOL—then that's his problem;" Jordan turned to Jackson, "and maybe it's gonna' get to be my problem;" he turned back to Sergeant Watson, "but I don't see how that gets to be none of yo' problem. You think I need help run'en this platoon sergeant?"

"No sergeant."

"I guess if there is any ass kicken' in this platoon, I the man gonna' be doing it. You understand me sergeant?"

"Yes sergeant."

"If you don't like work'en for me, I find someplace else for you to go."

"I like working for you, sergeant."

Jordan turned to Jackson: "That goes for you too corporal. If you don't like your job as gunner I can take care of that problem for you."

"I like my job sergeant." Jackson responded.

"Well, I can tell you right now, ain't no NCO's in my platoon taking no strips off their sleeve and doing no fisticuffs, and I ain't putten' up with no insubordination in my platoon. Now, you got any problem with that?"

"No sergeant, I ain't got no problem with it."

"Well, I don't want to hear no more'a this shit. If I hear any more'a this we ain't gonna' be talking about no sergeant and no corporal; we gonna' be talking about a corporal an' a PFC; now, either you men got a problem with that?"

Both men shook their heads and turned away. Sergeant Watson joined his squad and Jackson joined up with the bipods fuckups. The platoon leader, who had been observing from a distance, finally felt it safe to step in and take charge. "Sounds like insubordination from Corporal Jackson, Sergeant; looks to me like a little company punishment is in order here."

"I took care of it, Sir." Jordan said.

"We're in a war zone Sergeant; we can't put up with an insubordinate corporal."

"I ain't finished with him yet Sir;" Jordan responded, "an' if there's anything left'a him when I get through, I' turn him over to you."

"Well, good work Sergeant." The lieutenant turned and yelled to the platoon: "Off and on! Let's get to work! There's a war going on here, in case you men haven't noticed." The lieutenant pranced off as if he had taken care of the problem. We all knew he wasn't about to get involved between two Black guys in the mood for a fight.

Jordan had defused potentially serious situation, as he had so many times in the past. The outcome of a fight between the Sergeant Watson and Corporal Jackson would have been uncertain. Jackson was probably the better man, other things being equal, but the sergeant had maturity and an immense pride at stake. If he could not best Jackson, his career as leader of the fourth squad would be over. He would have been fighting for his life, and you just don't want to fight a man who's fighting for his life. On the other side, Jackson's pride would require him to make a serious stand—which would bring us back to the sergeant fighting for his life. Absent Jordan's intervention, there was just no way around a very serious problem. The threat of being demoted provided the excuse to back away that both men badly needed. There would still be a bit of tension between the two men over the next week, but being in different squads they could mostly avoid each other. Later, Jordan will get the two men together at the NCO club for a beer and a hand-shake, and the hatchet would be buried.

Jackson was in good spirits again. The other two bipods fuckups provided the approval he needed: "Good show, Corporal." "Don't take no shit from Watson, man. You let that son-of-a-bitch know the score, man." "Way to go, Corporal; Watson's got no right to be kicking nobody; Way to go, man."

The three fuckups continued to walk around during breaks with the bipods on their shoulders. On the second break he and Miller could hold in their mirth no longer, and Jackson was having a hard time remaining serious. By the third break, Jackson was a co-conspirator. The three of them walked around in a small circle laughing. At times, they laughed so hard they could hardly remain standing. They stumbled to the center of the circle, and leaned together for support while they giggled and laughed. The platoon looked on, and gave moral support. Even the Black guys enjoyed the scene.

Only Rosenski dared to join them during breaks—having earned that right with his request for the bipods at roll call. "Come on, Jackson; let me carry your bipods," he would say.

"Shee'it," Jackson would respond, and the platoon would howl.

Jordan and the other NCO's sit stone silent. Everyone knew the fuckup grunts had won a major psychological victory and there was nothing the forces of order could do about it. The only man in the platoon who didn't know what was happening was the platoon leader. The Lieutenant told Jordan, "I think it's commendable of the men to take on the extra burden." Sergeant Jordan grunted and turned away. Taking orders from morons was not novel for Jordan, but having his authority undermined by fuckups, certainly was.

When Bravo Company arrived on Zebra Hill Jordan kept his platoon in ranks, and called them to *Attention*. "Rogers, where yo' bipods?" He yelled to the gunner of the first squad.

"Miller's got um', Sergeant."

"You don't like yo' job as gunner corporal?" Rodgers nodded yes. "Well, you get them fucken bipods, an' I don't ever wanta' see you without em' again." Rogers retrieved his bipods from Miller. "That goes for you too Myers," Jordan yelled to the gunner of the second squad, and Myers retrieved his bipods from Richards. "I won't have a man with me 'can't do his job; you don't need two stripes on yo' sleeve to shovel shit Corporal Myers; you don't like yo' job I find something else for you to do."

"I like my job Sergeant." Myers responded.

Jordan walked back to the third squad and faced Jackson: "And I don't want a' see no gunner carrying his bipods around LIKE A FOOL when we on break; if you like worken' so much I find some more work for you to do. You understand me Corporal Jackson?"

"Yes Sergeant!"

"And I ain't putten' up with no insubordination in my platoon: You understand me corporal?"

"Yes Sergeant."

"WHAT YOU MEAN YES SERGEANT?" Jordan yelled.

"I mean I understand you Sergeant."

The sergeant turned slightly toward Sergeant Watson in the fourth squad; "Ain't no man putting his foot on one'a my soldiers: I the man do' the ass kicking around here! You don't know what ass kicking is till you get me started. Now, any man 'don't understand that, he just' step up here right now!"

Jordan stood and waited as if Sergeant Watson might consider challenging him; then he walked back to the second squad and stood in front of Richards for a full minute before yelling: "CLEAR THAT WEAPON SOLDIER!" Richards snapped his M1 up, opened the breach and extracted the round from the chamber and the clip, and then returned to the position of attention. "PRESENT ARMS SOLDIER!" Jordan yelled. Richards snapped his M1 up, opened the breach with his left thumb, quickly glanced down at the empty breach and snapped back to an erect position.

The Sergeant thrust his right hand out to grab the weapon and just as quickly Richards dropped his hands to his side allowing the weapon to fall into the Sergeant's hand. The Sergeant slammed his left palm into the butt of the rifle spinning it around and inspected the breach and barrel: "THIS WEAPON IS FILTHY!" He yelled in the soldier's face. "LOOKS LIKE YOU BEEN DRAGGEN' IT AROUND IN SOME GODDAMN RICE PADDY!"

"Yes Sergeant!" The soldier yelled back.

"WHAT YOU MEAN YES SERGEANT? YOU SHIT IN YOUR WEAPON AND ALL YOU GOT TO SAY FOR YO'SELF IS YES SERGEANT?" Jordan yelled even louder.

"No excuse Sergeant!"

"Night guard duty till further notice; outer perimeter wire!"

"Yes Sergeant!" He yelled back.

"And, you can report to me when you get off guard duty; you like worken' so much we see how you like shoveling shit all day!"

"Yes Sergeant!"

"WHAT' YOU MEAN YES SERGEANT?"

"I mean we are going to see how I like shoveling shit all day Sergeant," Richards responded smiling.

The mummer of chuckling swept through the platoon, and the Sergeant yelled at the closest man: "YOU AT ATTENTION SOLDIER," to stifle the laughing.

He turned back to Richards: "There's just one thing I don't understand Richards."

"What's that, Sergeant?"

"I don't understand why the biggest fucken fuckup in This Man's Army 'got to be in my platoon."

"Just luck Sergeant." He said. Jordan put his fists on his hips and leaned toward him. "I mean bad luck, Sergeant; bad luck for you, but good luck for me—for having the honor to serve in such a fine platoon." The mummer of snicker rolled through the platoon again, and this time even Jordan was forced to chuckle.

"At ease men," Jordan said, and then to Richards: "Well I'll say this for ya' son; you sure as hell are entertainin 'un."

The snickering turned to giggling and then laughter. Rosenski called to Jackson: "Come on Jackson, let me carry your bipods."

"Shee'it," Jackson replied, and the platoon hooted and howled. Even Jordan and some of the other sergeants laughed. The disorder was such that Jordan walked away without dismissing the platoon.

Miller and Rosenski walked over to him, and they shook hands. "You did it man!" Miller said.

"No, we did it! You and me, and Rosenski, and Jackson." The three of them walked over to Jackson. "Can you feel the glory man?" He asked.

"I don't see no fucken glory; shee'it!" Jackson replied.

"You ain't looking right, Jackson." Miller said.

"I feel the glory!" Rosenski said.

"Well," Jackson said, smiling, "we did some shit."

"We did some shit all right!" He responded: "We did it for the whole platoon; no, we did it for the whole fucken army. When the history of This Man's Army is written, it's gonna be in two parts—Part One will be titled *Before the Bipods*, and Part Two will be *After the Bipods*."

Jackson chuckled. "shee'it, man; I gotta clean my bipods," He said, turning to walk away.

"We won't forget you, man." He called after Jackson.

"Shee'it."

Jordan lost that round and the grunts won. From that day forward, in Jordan's weapons platoon the gunner would carry his bipods—no exceptions! The bipods would no longer be used to punish the fuckups. The battle had been waged on behalf of all the soldiers who had ever carried a rifle, or sword, or spear, and the grunts had won. He was proud to have served his fellow grunts in so grand a manner.

YOU WANT TO KNOW WHERE I'M FROM? Costa del Sol, Wednesday, Aug. 5

I wait for the first hint of daybreak. The moon had set earlier, but starlight is sufficient to make out the outline of the central hut and deck. Dawn is only minutes away and I can hear the woman moving around in her kitchen. After washing my face and urinating, I go over and order coffee. About twenty minutes later, Shirley walks down the steps of her hut. She is freshly showered and dressed as on the previous day. She stops in front of my hut.

"Up here, Shirley!" I call to her.

"You're up early today," as she sits down; "are you going fishing again?"

"Yeah, I thought I would. Do you teach every day?"

"I usually teach Tuesday through Friday, but this Friday is a holiday, so I will have a four day weekend coming up."

"Really; why don't we go someplace together—maybe visit the village across the bay?"

"Sure, we can go Friday," she responds.

"More like Saturday or Sunday. Those men will probably be using their boats for fishing on Friday."

We finish our breakfast, and she stands to leave. "Ray," she says hesitantly, "I need to borrow your passport."

"Borrow my passport?"

"Yes!" she says, and repeats, "Borrow your passport."

"Why the hell do you want to borrow my passport?"

"Norma wants to see it; she wants to check on some things."

"Check on what things? Look Shirley, I don't want that woman prying into my life."

"So, what are you—some kind of criminal?"

"That's not the point. I just don't want her calling my family and scaring the shit out of them."

"She wouldn't do that. She isn't going to call your family or anyone else you know. No one will ever know she did anything. And, even if you WERE a criminal, she wouldn't do anything about it." I don't respond to her. "Why can't you just trust me on this?" I don't respond. "Then, you come into town with me, and talk to her."

"No!" I reply flatly.

"You promised you would."

"Not today! I'm going fishing."

"Then give me your passport," she says.

I leave the table and walk down the stairs and over to my hut. She is waiting for me on the path; I hand her the passport as I walk by and continue down the beach.

"Don't worry about it; I'm not stupid! I'm not going to let anything happen," she yells to me, but I have decided to ignore her.

The fishermen move the boat down to the water. I have my lunch wrapped in a plastic garbage bag, which I drop into the boat, and help with the work. It is a repeat performance of the previous day, but much easier. The surf is calm, and we negotiate it easily. We laugh and joke during lunch, with most of the men speaking normal Spanish now, so I can join their conversation.

I marvel at the simple elegance in the style of these men. No one has asked me where I am from, or why I am here. They have not asked why I want to fish with them, or even asked my name. They don't need to know my name since I can be identified as "gringo." By contrast, I do need some names. The captain can be "*Capitan;*" but I cannot simply call everyone else "*Ecuatoriano*" or "*señor.*"

Nevertheless, I don't ask them personal questions. These men do not talk of their wives and children, or of their hopes and dreams, which I assume they must have. They mind their own business, and expect everyone else to do the same. I love these people, I tell myself.

There is less wind when we turn into the current, and we don't have to work so hard. I am thankful for that, because my arms are sore from yesterday. I don't even need my plastic garbage bag. The captain does put his on, but I figure that is to prove he isn't concerned about people laughing at him.

The captain had told me the catch would be good today. The moon is getting better for fishing, he told me, and would be good for the next couple of days. Apparently, fishing is thought to be better around full moon. I asked whether fishing would also be good during the new moon, and was told that it will be. Just why the moon affects fishing is a mystery for me, but I don't discount the theory. After all, the moon does affect the tides and tides might somehow change the current or something else.

After we beach our boat and return to the net, I find the captain is correct about the catch. We have more fish and shrimp than yesterday. The women purchasers also seemed to have anticipated the larger catch, since there are more of them.

*"**I** would like to visit the village across the bay there,"* I tell the captain, motioning to the southwest, *"maybe on Saturday; can you help me find someone with a boat I can rent?"*

"Maybe your Uncle Jaime can," he says, turning to one of the men from the other boat. *"I present Felipe, your uncle,"* the Captain says. I shake hands with Felipe.

"So, it's Tío Felipe, rather than Tío Jaime," I say, smiling at the man.

"I can be Jaime or Felipe, as you wish," the man says.

"I was hoping to get a boat over to the village on Saturday—with the gringa, and maybe another gringo—just to look around for the day. Do you have a boat?"

"Yes, but I have promised to spend the day with my family."

"Well, bring them along. We can have a picnic together," I tell him. *"I will buy the food and beer, and soft drinks for the children, and I expect you to charge me for your boat."*

"It would be very kind of you to provide the food. I have many children, so I cannot charge you for the boat."

"Shall we say Saturday at eight?" I ask.

"Well, yes; that would be fine," he responds.

"Good, and where shall I meet you?"

"I live down there," Felipe points south. *"You will see my boat near the water on Saturday morning. It would be better to leave at seven o'clock; the wind will be in our favor."*

"Then, it is settled," I say, shaking his hand, *"Saturday at seven o'clock."*

I pick out two large fish, and about a dozen shrimp. I hold the bag up for the captain to see. The captain gives a side wave of his hand. *"Gracias,"* I say, *"until tomorrow Captain. Tomorrow, Tío Felipe and Hermano Juan,"* they all laugh and wave to me, *"and, don't cheat these poor women,"* I say, turning to leave, *"t*hey have to feed their children with this miserable fish you lazy men drag in here."*

The crowd of women and children roar with laughter. *"Yes, you thieves, listen to the gringo,"* they yell.

Shirley is not there to meet me and I wonder why. I walk up the beach to the restaurant and give the fish to the woman. She offers to pay, but I decline with a deep bow, and several of my polite words in Japanese. She has rented two more huts and has a large crowd to cook for; I'm glad I brought extra fish and shrimp for her. I notice she has blocked off our favorite table for us, by putting the chairs on top of the table.

Johnny is sitting in the hammock on their porch reading a book. I go over to check on Shirley. "Say Johnny," I say from the bottom of the stairs, "where's Shirley?"

"She hasn't made it back yet. The damned three o'clock probably broke down again." Johnny looks at the sun low in the sky. "It's going to be dark in a couple of hours. Maybe I should walk over to the road and meet her."

"Read your book Johnny; I'll meet her."

"Okay," Johnny says, reluctantly.

I walk the half-mile to the Atacames road at a fast pace. Checking at one of the huts, I learn the truck has not passed. Not wanting to wait, and not being sure the truck would be coming, I decide to walk on toward the Esmeraldas road. I consider jogging, but decide against that because I don't want to look silly to Shirley if I meet the truck coming the other way.

About a mile into the walk the truck comes bouncing down the road toward me. I flag the truck down, and after checking to make sure she is there, climb aboard. The truck is crowded with people, and all the bench seats are filled. I stand at the back holding onto the tailgate. She joins me.

"What are you doing here?"

"Just taking a walk." I say.

"You were worried about me, huh?" I shrug. She smiles, shaking her head slowly. She has the expression of a woman accepting her child's gift from the grammar school art class.

"I just couldn't wait to see you, love."

"We like to flirt with each other, don't we?" she says, moving close. The truck hits a bump and her breast touches my arm. I react with a snap of tension, and then quickly relax, but she has noticed. She moves closer so her breast touches my arm again. I have never liked the word 'flirt', but I do like the feel of her breast touching my arm. I don't respond to her question, but think about how she says things, and follows with a request for agreement.

"It's fun, huh?" I nod. "Would it take all the fun away for you, if I told you you're never going to hit that homerun?" she asks.

"Would it take all the fun away for you, if I told you I'm really a queer, and don't like girls?"

"Ha!" She laughs loudly, and moves away slightly. "You can fool all the people some of the time, and some of the people all the time, but honey, you could never fool me on that one. If there is one thing about you I would bet my last dollar on, that's it!"

We get off the truck, pay the driver, and take the trail toward Costa. After crossing the old bridge, we walk down the old road side by side—each walking in one of the parallel paths originally made by vehicle traffic sometime in the past.

"How was fishing?"

"Great! Hey, I lined up a trip for us, to the village across the bay—I forget the name of the place. The man I called my *Tío* Jaime is going to take us. His name is really Felipe. He is going to take his wife and kids along too."

"Great," she responds with enthusiasm, "on Saturday then." She starts laughing again. "I was just thinking about you telling me maybe you didn't like girls," she says. And, then more serious, "You know something—something I really like about you? You really do like girls. And, you like me, don't ya?"

"Hell, Shirley. I love you."

"Nah; but, you really do like me. I can tell. It's not just your hormones humming. You like being around me, and talking and flirting and... don't ya?" "Ahuuuuu!" She yells, jumping away and pointing toward the ground. I catch the movement of something through the grass and step back to have a look.

"Don't do that Ray; get over here!"

"I just want to check him out, love."

"If you pick up that snake, I swear to God you'll be walking back to Costa by yourself!"

"I just want to look at his eyes."

"LOOK AT HIS EYES? Oh lord, that's it!" She turns and starts down the path, and yells back, "I won't put up with insanity, Raymond."

I see the snake and approach cautiously. It remains motionless until I am quite close and then quickly coils. It is more than four feet long and can get its head about a foot off the ground. The round pupils of the eyes are easy to see. It is almost certainly non-poisonous, but it's putting up a good bluff. It hisses and strikes toward me. "Go on; beat it!" I say to the snake. "I'm not going to kill you." I take a step back, and the snake darts through the grass in the opposite direction. "I may be a shit-head," I tell the snake, "but I'm not that big of a shit-head."

Shirley is fifty yards or so down the path, and walking fast. I jog to catch up with her but she continues walking ahead without looking back, "You better not have that snake, Raymond!"

Just for the hell of it, reach down and nip her butt with my fingers. "Ahuuuu!" she screams, turning toward me and grabbing my hands. Her fright becomes a nervous giggle. "You idiot; you almost made me pee on myself! I have to hold your hands just to make sure you won't pick up a deadly snake."

"So, you're afraid of snakes."

"No! Well, yes, of course; everyone's afraid of the snakes down here. They're deadly! You're the only one who isn't afraid of them, and that's because you're whacko."

"Why did you think I would pick it up?"

"I know you're crazy; you jumped out of airplanes, and I saw you out in the ocean on that little boat when the waves were ten feet high. The next thing you will probably do is pick up a deadly snake."

"I wasn't going to pick it up."

"Why couldn't you just leave it alone? And anyway, what conceivable purpose could be served by looking at a snake's eyes?" She drops my hands, turns away and yells to the sky: "DEAR LORD HAVE MERCY!"

I find her comments humorous and have to chuckle. She turns and gives me her hard stare. "In Texas, all the poisonous snakes are pit vipers;" I say, and then add, "except for that little coral snake."

She folds her arms and cocks her head up so she looks at me through squinted eyes, as if trying hard to be patient. "This is going to have something to do with looking at a snake's eyes."

"Well yeah; pit vipers have slit pupils, like a cat. That one had round pupils. So, it probably wasn't poisonous."

"This is not Texas! How many times do I have to tell you we are in Ecuador! This is a tropical rainforest on the equator! How do you know the vipers down here don't have round pupils? Maybe they are mound vipers instead of pit vipers! Did you ever think of that?"

"Doesn't look much like a rainforest; a savanna maybe, before they made it into a pasture."

"It's the equatorial tropics, and it's full of deadly snakes! Don't split hairs!"

"So you figure they are mound vipers down here, with round pupils, huh? Well, it makes sense; slits in the pits and round on the mound." I say, laughing.

I get the raised eyebrows and stare again, but then she also breaks into a chuckle. "That was real cute; okay? I love your humor, and I admit that was a stupid thing to say. But, even if your theory were true, why would you have to RISK YOUR LIFE trying to find out if it's poisonous? Why couldn't you JUST WALK AWAY from it?"

"You mean just turn and walk away? Without even checking on whether or not it's poisonous?"

"YES!"

"Well jeez, I've never thought about it like that. But, yeah it makes sense. You know, if you just walk away you would never know if it was poisonous, but I guess it wouldn't matter because it probably wouldn't bite you."

"Is it hard for you to understand that, Raymond?" she asks, as if the thought is painful for her.

"No; I can see you're right on that. Of course, the snake would never know whether I'm poisonous either, but that wouldn't matter because if I walk away I probably wouldn't bite him." She presses her lips together and nodding her head as if to summon patients. "It's a win-win situation for everybody! I win, the snake wins, you win because you don't have to see me stagger around and foam at the mouth, and drag my lifeless body back to Costa. I swear Shirley, your suggestion is simply brilliant!"

"I can guarantee you that your lifeless body will rot exactly where it falls!" Her scowl slowly changes to a smile. "A very smart woman once told me, you never try to make sense with them. Anyway, in your mind you were probably trying to save me from the snake. First you come out here to save me from the bad guys and then you save me from the snake."

"I should get a reward for that."

"Yes you should!"

She steps forward and holds my face in her hands. I put my hands around her waist and kiss her; she kisses back. "That's the kiss you owed me." I say.

"No, that one was mutual."

I pull her to me and kiss her again. I rub my hand down the front of her blouse, keeping my palm flat. I can feel her nipple on the palm of my hand.

She pushes me away. "Just because I'm kissing you doesn't mean you can feel me up."

"I wasn't feeling . . . and anyway not there."

"I KNOW what you were feeling!"

"I was just touching. There's a big difference between feeling and touching."

"Is that so?"

"Yes! And anyway it wasn't up"

She gives me a puzzled look; then, as if the light just came on, her look turns to something between shock and disgust. She exhales loudly and puts her hands on her hips: "You try that and see what happens!"

"I wouldn't dream of it, love. And anyway, I don't see why you make a big deal just because I touched your breast."

"I didn't make a big deal;" she responds, and then continues: "there isn't enough there to make a big deal about."

We continue down the path; soon she is in a good mood again. She tells me this is the fourth snake she has seen on this path, and she suspects a lot more than four snakes have seen her. "The snakes down here are really bad, aren't they?" she says.

She doesn't expect an answer to her question. Again I wonder why she ends her statements with a question she doesn't want answered? She's lecturing to her students, I tell myself. "You teach high school in the States, right? What subject?" I ask her.

"Guess."

"Math and science?" She smiles and shakes her head. "English; physical education?"

"Not phys'Ed. You were right the second time; English. But, I do coach the girls' volleyball team, on my own time."

"I wasn't far off, was I? Do you teach creative writing?"

"Nah, I wish I could. We have an old fart who has taught that course for a hundred years, and he won't give it up. He's about as creative as brain cancer. I've been waiting for him to trip and fall down the stairs—may have to help him along one of these days."

"Bet you would be good in creative writing. You know something? I was always in love with my High School English teacher."

"Were ya? Did you leave her little notes and put flowers on her desk?"

"Hell no; she would have stuffed them down my throat!" I say. "Do the guys leave you notes and flowers?"

"No! Well, actually I have received a couple of anonymous love notes, in addition to the usual sex stuff. But, they better not let me find out who they are."

"Because, you would stuff it down their throats, right?"

"You bet!"

When we reach Costa del Sol we head toward our respective huts, and I call to her: "I brought some good fish for the woman, and she is going to fix it for our dinner. Ask Johnny to join us."

In my hut, I strip and rinse quickly, and then soap down and rinse again. Then, I decide to shave and soap my face. I hear her in my room. "Ray? What's keeping you?"

"I'm shaving, so you will kiss me." I am surprised by a hard slap on my bare butt.

110

She has reached through the curtain to slap me, and then jumped back. I put my head through the curtain.

"I've always wanted to slap a guy on his wet butt." She laughs. "But, don't pay me back, okay?" she adds, with both hands up.

"Hey, what is this? You can hit, but I can't hit back? Is this girl's rules?"

"No! And, don't pretend that hurt, or care if I see your butt."

"It hurt like hell; and my mother told me not to let strange women see my butt. Throw me my towel," I say, not wanting to walk into the room nude. She hands the towel through the curtain. I towel off, and walk out of the shower stall holding the towel over myself.

"My, my, such modesty," she says, and walks out to the porch and sits on the steps, looking the other way.

"There is nothing uglier than a naked White man, Shirley."

"Oh yeah; so, what are you, the expert on naked White men?"

"I've seen hundreds of um, and if I ever see another one I'm going to throw up." She laughs.

I put on a pair of drawers, clean Levi cutoffs. She walks in the room and puts her hands on my chest. "Naked white men don't look so bad to me." She rubs my chest and then bends to kiss my nipples. "Look your little nipples even get hard."

"Can I do that to you?"

She hesitates and then looks back at the door, as if to see if someone may be watching. "If you want to." She says.

I put my hands under her blouse and feel, and then lift the blouse and kiss each nipple. "They're wonderful."

"They're tiny." She says, "I don't know why you even want to do it."

"They aren't tiny; they are small, but they have the perfect shape."

She pushes my hands away. "That's enough; you're going to get me going."

"I want you going."

"I don't want me going." She sits on the bed and crosses her legs. "So, what do you do; just go around and find the girl that was the ugliest one in the class and put the make on her? What's your success rate, 95 percent?" she asks.

"Were you the ugliest girl in the class?"

"YES! And don't tell me you don't know that!"

"Well, maybe the ugliest girl and the ugliest guy should get together." I say.

"You're not ugly! You're beautiful, for crying out loud!"

"Beautiful? Talk about not seeing straight; jeez Shirley, you need help."

"You're handsome and strong, and self-confident—that's what I meant—the way a man is supposed to be."

"So, you're handsome, strong, and self-confident."

"Girls aren't supposed to be like that! They are supposed to be petite and pretty, and have big boobs, and be submissive."

"Submissive? Where the hell have you been? When is the last time you've seen a woman with a nickle's worth of brains that was submissive?"

"They are supposed to act that way, Ray."

"Well, the acting stops at the bedroom door."

"There isn't going to be a bedroom door! Raymond, that thing is sticking up in your pants! I'm getting out of here before you start trying to pull my panties down." She gets up and walks toward the door.

"Shirley, if your panties come down it will because you pulled them down—not me! I'm not a rapist!"

She walks back to me; "I know that Ray. Do you think I would be hanging around you if I thought you would try to do something to me? Ray, I'm sorry I said that. I'm sorry I slapped you on the butt, and I'm sorry I did that to your chest; and I'm sorry I let you do that to me. It doesn't mean anything; I'm just being really stupid."

"Why are you sorry? Anyway it was nothing. That is, what you did to me was nothing; what I did to you was really something. I know it doesn't mean anything, and I am the one that is being stupid."

"I don't want to hurt you Ray."

"You are not hurting me, damn it."

"I'm leading you on; making you think you are going to get something from me, and you aren't. I'm just having fun with you, and it isn't right."

"I'm having fun with you too; why the hell are you sorry about this? If you are going to stop talking to me I'm getting the hell out of here."

"I'm not going to stop talking to you."

"So what are you going to stop doing?"

"I'm going to stop leading you on, Ray! You want to have sex with me and you aren't going to do it. I'm just going to stop leading you on with this."

"Half the people in this world want to have sex with you Shirley."

"Half of the people in the world; what are you talking about?"

"All the men in the world want to have sex with you, and probably some of the women—how does that make me any different?"

"Raymond?"

"Look Shirley, if you aren't going to let me kiss you I'm leaving this place. You are the only reason I got off that bus and you know it. If you don't want me here I'm leaving."

"I do want you here Ray—and you can kiss me!" I grab her shoulders, pull her to me and kiss her. She has a shocked look. I kiss her again and she still has that look—so I kiss her again. "Ray?"

"You said I could kiss you."

"Not ten times!"

"Why not ten times?" I kiss her again. "Oh Ray, what have I done to you?"

"Nothing—nothing that I didn't want you to do."

"I'm causing this Ray; I'm just having fun with you and it's not fair."

"You are causing what? You are not in charge of me Shirley! You are in charge of your panties; not me. You don't control what I think or how I feel, and you are not responsible for me. I'm responsible for me. Will you get that through your thick head! You are always saying I have a thick head; well what about you? I fell in love with you the first day we met, and you wouldn't let me kiss you or even touch you. So stop thinking that you control me or thinking you are responsible for me!"

"That thing in your pants went down, didn't it?"

"Well, what the hell do you think? After you give me this shit."

"Ray, that's the first time in my life—in my adult life—that someone has just told me I am completely wrong and shut me up. Actually, it's the second time. Norma told me I was wrong and shut me up; of course, she did it in a nice way. But I thought about it and knew she was right, and so I had to change the way I was thinking. You are right too Ray, so I have to stop thinking that I'm responsible for you."

"Thank you Shirley. I'm sorry I was not nice about the way I told you that."

"You don't need to be sorry." She turns and walks back to the door.

"Hey Shirley, wait; I'm going with you." I put on a tee-shirt. "Hey, I'm running out of clean underwear."

"Well, I'm glad to hear you recognize that as a problem," She says, tuning back, "That Japanese woman will do your laundry. She will probably fold it for you too," Shirley responds. "Knowing you she will probably give you a discount. By the way, here's your passport." She hands me the document as I come out on the porch. I go back in and put the passport away. We walk down the stairs and across the path to the restaurant.

"So, did she get my rap sheet? Is the FBI coming in to pick me up?" Shirley turns away from me, and doesn't respond. "So, what did you find out about me?"

"Norma isn't going to tell me anything, unless I need to know it. She's professional; and anyway, I don't give a damn about your past life."

The twenty yards up the beach to the restaurant is sufficient to change the mood. She puts her arm around my waist and pulls and laughs, and dances around me. By the time we scramble up the stairs, I have forgotten my anger about the passport ordeal and our argument.

"Isn't Johnny going to join us?"

"No. He's going to Atacames. Anyway, I wanted to talk to you. You know, therapy."

"Oh shit, do we have to do it now"? I ask.

"Yes! But, I don't want you to get upset, okay?" I don't respond and she is quiet for a few seconds. "You're married, aren't you?"

"So, Norma figures I'm married, and warns you to stay away from me. Is that it?"

"She didn't have to tell me you were married. It's obvious from your passport." She waits for a response, and then says: "Well?"

"I was married, but she left me. We aren't together anymore."

"She left you?"

"Hell, I don't know. Maybe I left her. What difference does it make? Anyway, we aren't together anymore."

"Her name is Donna."

"Yeah, how did you know?"

"It's written in the front of your stupid passport! Come on!" We are quiet for a few seconds. "Tell me about her." I don't respond. "Look, it doesn't bother me. I was married once too, and it didn't work out. That really doesn't matter to me, except I think it may be important for you."

I really don't want to deal with the question and look away from her. "This is therapy, Ray. You promised you would do this. Norma said you have to deal with your past. We have to find what is bothering you. Maybe it has something to do with Donna, or maybe it's the damned war. We have to start somewhere."

The woman served our dinner. The food and table are even more impressive than the previous day, and we eat quietly, enjoying the meal and the view of the sea. Two other families join us on the deck for dinner. The woman brings out a record player and plays scratchy 78 rpm records with Colombian *sausa* music.

I think about Donna and my dream: "I had a dream about Donna. Maybe it wasn't a dream; it really happened and I was just thinking about it."

"Was it a bad dream?"

"Yeah, it was. But, the bad part didn't have anything to do with Donna. In fact, Donna saved me. They were going to kill me and Donna came and saved me. She was acting like Mama—kissing me and taking care of me. That's when I finally felt safe."

"Like your mother?"

"No, Mama is her mother—Donna's mother. It's just that, it was the first time she acted like her mother. It wasn't until then that I realized she was like her mother."

"So, you liked what she did?"

"Oh, sure; they were going to kill me, and she saved me."

"Who was going to kill you?"

"I don't know...the army. Hell, I don't know." I tell her.

"You mean the enemy—the Koreans—they were going to kill you?"

"No, it was the fucken army. I don't know... It's this terrible dream I have sometimes." A few seconds pass and I realize, what I have said makes no sense at all—even to me.

"Where were you?" she asks. The question puzzled me. "In your dream, where were you?"

"I don't know," I respond.

"What kind of place was it?"

"It was like in a prison. They were going to execute me."

"Have you been in prison?"

"No! Jeez, I'm not a criminal. I've never done anything to anyone. Will you stop it? I don't want to talk about this."

"You have to talk about it. Where were you in the dream? Were you in prison?"

"No, it was a hospital."

"They were going to execute you in a hospital?" She questions.

"I know that doesn't make sense," I say.

"You said it really happened."

"Yeah, it really happened, and I was just remembering how it was. But, now I can't remember anything. I swear, that's a total blank," I say, and feel myself shudder.

"Tell me about Mama."

I am relieved at the change in subject, and suddenly my mind flows freely. "Mama is like...She has a lot of power, and controls everything, and she will do anything for Donna. You wouldn't believe that woman—she is wild; she is always yelling, and waving her arms in the air. At first, it was like a mad house. I couldn't hear myself think," I laugh. "You wouldn't believe Mama. The first time I met her, she runs into the room and grabs me around the waist, with her big boobs pressed into my chest. And, she starts yelling about how I was so pretty, and she starts kissing me—right on the mouth—right there in front of Donna and her husband. And, she says to Donna, 'go get yourself another one, I'm keeping this one for me.' I mean you can't believe this woman."

"Sounds like a neat lady," Shirley says. "I think I would like her."

"Yeah, you have to like her. Hell, you have no choice. She runs everything and everyone. Her husband—Donna's Dad—is a general, and since Mama runs him, she runs the army too." Shirley is silent, and I continue. "They have this big ranch down in Texas, and Mama's out yelling at the Mexicans—the workers, you know—and, then she runs back in the house, and is yelling about this or that. The only way you can get away from her is to go into the bathroom, and lock the door, and even then she will probably come and bang on the door. You know something; I don't think we ever got through dinner together without Donna or her mother yelling or crying about something." We both laugh.

"How did you meet Donna?"

"It was in the hospital at Inchon. She was with the Red Cross."

"Pretty nurse taking care of the wounded soldier; how romantic!"

"Nah, I wasn't wounded. I just cut my leg with a machete clearing brush on Zebra. That's a hill we were holding. It wasn't really bad, but I had hit the bone," I turn my chair so she can see the scar on my leg just below the knee, "and, the army has this rule, if you hit the bone, you have to stay in the hospital for three days. Anyway, she wasn't a nurse. She was a volunteer nurse's aide, but it was pretty romantic." "Tell me about it," she says. She had leaned forward with her elbows on the table and her hands cupped under her chin. "I want to know about the pretty nurse and the soldier, and don't leave out any juicy details."

"You don't want to hear about my love life."

"I want to hear about it. Maybe, if it's romantic enough, I'll get interested," she says, "and, this isn't therapy any more, okay?"

"Well, she just sort of picked me out for a lot of special attention," I explain.

"Love at first sight, huh? Tell me about her, what does she look like?"

"Well, she looks a lot like Mama, black hair and big dark eyes, and olive skin." I look at Shirley, making the mental comparison. "She's kind of short, and soft... Not so strong... She's not plump, but..."

"Kind of round," Shirley fills in for me.

"Yeah," I agree.

"With big boobs and a nice soft round butt."

"Yeah, like that," I respond.

"Let me see if I get the picture, you're lying there in a hospital gown, and she rubbing your tummy, huh?"

I laugh. "She would change my bandage, and it would just about blow my mind. Jeez, I'd been up at the front forever, ya' know, and to have a girl touch you—man I was dying."

"Was it a private room?" She arches her eyebrows.

"Nah, at first I was in the ward, but she had me changed to a room with one other guy. But, they had a curtain she could pull around my bed while she worked on my leg."

"Keep going; sounds like we're getting to the good part."

"No, that was it," I say.

"You didn't make love with her?"

"No! Jeez, Shirley! I just knew her two days there, and anyway she was not about to...we just kissed. But, I was really blown away by her."

"You told her you loved her, huh?"

"Yeah, I did."

"You do that a lot," she says with a 'just as I thought' nod.

"I guess I like girls," I say, sheepishly.

"I can tell. Look, it's okay to tell a girl you love her, as long as you're not just trying to hit on her," and then adds, "and, you don't say you can't remember saying that the next day." I don't respond to that. "So, then you went back to the Zebra hill, huh?"

"Yeah, she called me though, the next week when we were back in reserve at bivouac. It was really strange, they called me into the First Sergeant's hooch and let me use the phone, and he was pissed as hell. I found out later, she had her Mama pull some strings. Anyway, she said I should ask for a three-day pass, to visit some guy in the hospital I had never heard of. I told her there was no way they would give me a pass. She said I should make the request up the chain of command—you have the right to do that, you know. If your platoon leader turns you down, you can ask to speak to the company commander, and they have to let you do that. If the CO says no, you can ask to see the battalion commander. But, they get really pissed off, and they never override the local commander. So I said, jeez, this is not the Red Cross, it's the fucken army. But, she said, do it, trust me, and gives me the details on this guy who was supposed to be a close friend, who was paralyzed from the waist down. So, I did. When I made the request to the Lieutenant he said, *go to hell*! So, I said, 'permission to speak with the Captain, Sir'. The Lieutenant was so pissed he could hardly breathe." I stop to laugh, remembering the scene.

"So, he marched me down to the Old Man's hooch, and goes in to talk to him first, and then calls me in. So, I make this ridiculous request for a three-day pass. And, the Captain said permission denied. So, I said, request permission to speak to the Colonel, Sir. Well, they both just about pissed on themselves. And, the Captain said, and I continue in an authoritarian voice: 'Lieutenant, take this gentleman down to headquarters to see the Colonel, and then bring him back to me. I have something I want to tell him when he gets back.' So, we go to see the Colonel, and I'm thinking, oh shit, I've had it, you know. And then, the most amazing thing happened."

"The Colonel approved the leave," she fills in.

"Yeah, he said, real serious like, 'Soldier, I want you back here when Baker Company relieves Charley on Zebra.' That was four days! And, he told me to report to his tent in thirty minutes for a jeep, leaving for Inchon. Lieutenant Snider was so pissed he almost died, but I didn't give a damn. I would have given anything for four days in Inchon with ..."

"With Donna," Shirley fills in. I nod. "So, then what happened?"

"Well, hell, I went to Inchon and met Donna, and we spent the whole four days together."

"Tell me about it." She says, obviously enjoying my discomfort.

"I'm not telling you anything. It's none of your business."

"Well, that's your loss honey," she says, with a sly grin. "It's just not juicy enough to make me interested." We are silent for a few seconds, and then laugh together. "So, why did you leave her?"

"Maybe she left me. No, maybe I did leave her. I was having this problem. Maybe, she was just fed up with me."

"You mean your memory problem?"

"Memory problem?" I ask.

"Your memory problem; stop telling me you can't remember that you can't remember!"

"No, I didn't have that problem, and I'm getting over that now. I remember everything—Donna, and everything."

"So, you don't have a problem anymore, huh? And, you don't need any of my therapy, or any help from Norma, huh?"

"Yeah;" I respond. "Okay, I had a problem, but I'm okay now." She turns away and is silent for several seconds.

"You want to know where I'm from?" Her question is posed in an off-hand manner.

"Yeah, where are you from?"

"You want to know why I come down here?" she continues. I nod. "Why haven't you asked?" I can't think of anything to say. She waits a few seconds, and continues. "You didn't ask me if I'm married or if I have any kids."

"Well, yeah; I want to know."

"Do you want to know if I have a boyfriend? You even told me you were in love with me, but you didn't want to know anything about me, and you still don't want to know, do you?"

I am stunned. It seems strange that I had not wondered about where she came from, or about her life, before I met her.

She continues. "I'm not a psychologist, but frankly, I've never heard of amnesia so selective for the things you really don't want to deal with." I remain silent. "Look, I'm not stupid, okay? Either you have a very serious problem, or you're one of the best bullshit'ers I've ever come across, and I can tell you I've met a bunch of um'."

"I know there was something wrong with me." I hear my voice shake. "But, I'm not trying to pull anything on you."

She waits a bit and then asks. "Where do you get your money? The money you use to travel around here?"

"I have a few bucks," I say.

"How much?" she asks.

"I have a couple of hundred bucks and some pesos, too. Why?"

"So, what do you do when the money runs out?"

"Why are you asking me this?" I am apprehensive.

"According to your passport you haven't been to the States for almost two years. Did you start off with a couple of thousand bucks and work it down to a couple of hundred? Then, why aren't you headed back home now? What happens when you have no money left? That just doesn't make sense. Someone must be sending you money," she says.

I have a hard time focusing on the question, and am suspicious about her motive. "You've given this a bit of thought, Shirley. How did you manage to ferret all this out?"

"I didn't ferret it out. Norma did, but that's not the point. The point is it doesn't make sense."

"Maybe, I'm with the DIA."

"If you are with the DIA, you can go straight to hell." She says, rising to leave.

"Look, you know that isn't true."

She remains standing. "If you are not going to deal with this in a serious way, then I don't want to be your friend. And, I really resent the implication."

"What implication?"

"That I'm trying to get your stupid money!" She says sharply.

"I didn't say that."

"It's written all over your face, Ray." She remains standing and waits: "Well, are you going to tell me where you get your money or not?"

"I get a check from the VA every month."

"Who's the VA?"

"The fucken Veterans Administration."

"They're still sending you money for college?"

I don't respond. She sits, and we are silent for a minute, watching the storms over the ocean. The magic comes back, and seems to be a more special magic.

"**W**hy do you call me love?" she asks.

"Because it fits you; it fits..." I continue in a lower voice, "It fits the way I feel about you."

She smiles and gives a soft punch in the chest—more like a little push with her fist. That's her super fake signature punch, I tell myself. "Do you mind me calling you that?"

"No, I like it." The surf is very quiet, and the last of the sea breeze keeps the deck fresh. It seems almost incredible that there are people in the States who live their entire lives without experiencing the beauty and pleasure of a tropical sea breeze. I tell her that, and she agrees.

"We like each other, don't we," she says smiling.

"Hell, Shirley. I love you."

"No you don't," she responds. "You are like a kid who is scared in the dark and trying to hold on to someone," she says.

"That's the damned psychologist woman talking." I say.

"Stop saying that! She's not some psychologist woman. Her name is Norma! And, YES! If you want to know, Norma did tell me that."

We are quiet for a minute. "Can we stop poking at each other?" I ask.

"Yeah, maybe we poke at each other because we are so much alike."

"Alike? Hell, you don't look like a shit-head to me."

"You don't look like a shit-head to me either, Ray."

We sit talking and drinking beer, occasionally taking a trip to the outhouse. "Let's go for a swim," I suggest.

"I don't think so. I'm not going to take any clothes off while you have that look in your eye."

"What's the matter, love? Afraid you won't be able to defend yourself?" I ask, rubbing an old wound.

"Ha! That'll be the day when some man rapes me."

"Maybe we could just take a walk down the beach," I suggest.

"Okay." We walk slowly along the beach through the surf, arm in arm, and sit on the sand, watching the surf for a while. She sits leaning against me, and I kiss her cheek and ear.

"I think I'm drunk," she says.

"Good," I say, and continue caressing her cheek.

"That doesn't mean you will hit the homerun, you know."

"I know." I pull her head around to me, and kiss her. We fall over into the sand, and continue kissing, and I put my hand under her blouse.

After a few minutes, she pushes me away and sits up. "We had better go back," she says.

"What's the hurry?"

"I'm teaching tomorrow. I don't think the kids would enjoy seeing me in this condition," she says. We walk back, arm in arm. "You're trying to charm me."

"I'm trying, but not making any progress."

"I'm not so easy to charm, honey. I know what men are and, they don't put anything over on me."

That irritates me. "So, what am I trying to put over on you?"

"I didn't mean that for you. I'm talking about men creatures in general," she says, with a slur in her voice that suggests she really is a bit drunk. I leave her at the bottom of the stairs of her hut with a good night kiss.

I decide to sleep in the hammock again. I want to think about something pleasant and consider Shirley's breasts. But, I think about Donna, not Shirley. The memories flood back and I recreate the scenes in my mind.

GET THE HELL OUT OF MY HOSPITAL: KOREA, SPRING, 1953

At MASH 4 he was examined, and referred to the hospital in Inchon. He had cut his leg with a machete while clearing brush. The blade had hit the top of his boot and he had noticed the cut in his shin only when his boot had filled with blood. The medic sent him to MASH 4, and from there he was taken by truck to the hospital at Inchon for a three-day stay. The wound was not serious, but the blade had touched the bone and army regulations required a three-day hospital stay, to prevent infection.

At the Inchon Hospital, he was given a shower and a gown to wear. He was placed in a ward with some twenty other men, with wounds of all kinds—almost all far more serious than his. An orderly cranked the back of his bed up so he could sit upright, and placed a table in front that he could use to write a letter, or have dinner.

He watched the girl moving from bed to bed toward him. She was pretty, and sex blossomed from her face and body. "I'm the angel of mercy," she would say, passing out candy to the guys. Those who were conscious enough to appreciate her presence mostly stared dumbfounded as if she were an apparition. At the bed next to his, he read her nametag. "Hello, I'm the angel of mercy," she said, offering him a candy.

"Hi Donna, I've missed you. Why haven't you written?" he replied in a cheerful voice.

"Do I know you?"

"Sure Donna!" He spoke softly, trying to keep the fellows on either side from hearing. "I was on the football team when you were a cheerleader. We went to the drive-in, remember?"

"I was never a cheerleader, and I sure didn't go to a drive-in with you. You read my name tag." She said, putting her hand over the tag.

"Gee, you look just like her."

"And, her name just happens to be Donna too, right?"

"Yeah, really; but she never wrote to me. I guess that's all over now," he smiled broadly. She smiled back at him. "Ah, yai yai," he said, as if in pain, "be careful."

"What?"

"When you smile it hurts my leg."

"What are you talking about?"

"Really, it gives me goose bumps all over, and then the bandage starts hurting my leg."

"Boy, I've heard a lot of stories, but you are really full of it." She replied, still smiling, and turned away.

"Hey wait," he said. She walked back to his bed.

"Will you come back?"

"Tomorrow."

"Ah gee, can't you come back later today?"

"I have work to do honey. There are a lot of guys here who need help—a lot more than you do."

He was thrilled that she had called him honey. "I just thought you could help me write a letter to my mother." He was trying hard to think of something to say, and wishing he had come up with something better.

"I don't see anything wrong with your hand."

"No, I just don't know what to say to her, and I thought you could kind of help me put my feelings into words." He knew she wasn't buying his story.

"There are a lot of wounded guys here, and part of my job is to change their dressings and empty their bedpans, so maybe you better write your own letter."

"You know, my bandage needs to be changed too. It's too tight, that's why it hurts," he responded, trying to be serious this time.

"I'll look into it." She said, walking back to check the clipboard at the foot of his bed, and then continued her 'angel of mercy walk' down the row of beds.

He watched her as she moved away, captivated by the curve below her waist, and the bottom of her white dress brushing the backs of her knees. The guy in the bed next to him growled, "Stop trying to fucken take over the Angel of Mercy, man. She belongs to everybody—shit."

"Hey man, I really thought I knew her."

"Shit! If bullshit had wings, you could fucken fly out'a this fucken place—shit."

That afternoon she did come back. "Well, let's see about your bandage." She removed his tray, pulled the sheet down, and began removing the bandage on his leg. "You're Airborne, huh?" He nodded. "My Papa says anyone who would jump out of a perfectly good airplane is as dumb as a rock." She said, without looking up at him.

The guy in the bed next to him laughed. "Yeah, fucken dumb as rocks!"

"Well, yeah." He responded to her. "Your Papa got that right."

"So, what's your excuse?"

"Well, I'm really a reporter with the New York Times—doing undercover work."

"And, your assignment is to find out if they really are as dumb as rocks," she said, continuing her work.

"Nah, we already knew that. There is a rumor, the fucken Eighty-Second—aha, excuse me, I didn't mean to say that," he stuttered. "I mean the Eighty-Second Airborne may be paying the Chinks off to leave their positions alone. Paying them off with ammo, you know, so they can hit the Jarheads over on another hill," he explained, with a broad smile.

The guy next to him spoke up again. "Yeah, that's right. The fucken soldiers ain't doing shit, and we gotta' fight the whole fucken Chink Army." Obviously, the guy was a marine.

"Hey man," he said to the marine, "watch your language."

"Don't worry about it," she said. "I hear that word a couple of thousand times a day. The New York Times, huh? I don't see anything wrong with this dressing."

"Is there any infection? It feels kind of funny."

"Nope, looks clean as a whistle."

"How did you know I was Airborne?" he asked her, in a low tone.

"I checked on ya," she whispered. "PFC, Weapons platoon, Baker Company, white and a test score of 128."

"You got me."

"I'm not sure I want you."

"Give it a chance," he said, touching her arm.

She looked down at his hand on her arm. "You aren't... supposed... to touch... the nurse," allowing her voice to rise slightly with each phrase.

He removed his hand. "Sorry, I just want to talk to you," he whispered, "and, I can't because all these fuc.... all these marines around here hate soldiers. Can we go outside, and have a smoke or something?"

"I don't smoke."

"Hell, I don't care, anything!" He said, almost in desperation.

"I'll see if I can get you transferred," she whispered. She finished redoing his bandage, replaced his tray and left.

At 9:30 PM, a few minutes after lights out, two orderlies pushed a wheel chair down the aisle, checking names on the clipboards at the foot of beds.

"Richards? You're being moved; don't put any weight on the leg." The two men helped him into the wheelchair and pushed him down the aisle and out of the ward. He was placed in a small room with two beds, each with a curtain that could be pulled around for privacy. The orderlies pulled the curtain around his bed and helped him in, again admonishing him not to put any weight on the leg. They pulled the curtain back and left him.

His heart pounded. The anticipation of her entering the room was almost overwhelming. The man in the other bed breathed heavily, groaning and occasionally crying out weakly. He decided the other man was dying, and hoped that would not happen while she was there with him. The vision of her face, the curve behind, and the bottom of her skirt flowing across the back of her knees, filled his fantasies. He was desperately in love with her. He lay awake for several hours, and then drifted into a fitful sleep.

He felt spasms of pleasure, and woke realizing his hand was on his penis. He turned on the lamp near his bed and pulled the sheet down. His gown was wet, and he felt wetness on his stomach.

The thought of her seeing that filled him with disgust. He went into the small bathroom. He took the gown off and turned on the shower very slightly. Cold water dribbled out. He rinsed himself carefully, trying to avoid getting water on the bandage. He toweled off and wrapped the towel around his waist, and walked out of the room and down the hallway to a nurse station. A large Black woman was asleep at the desk.

"Hey," he said. She looked up at him. "I got my gown dirty; it fell in the toilet. I need a clean one."

"They will get you one in the morning," the woman said, sleepily.

"I need one right now. I'm cold."

"What are you doing walking around. You are supposed to be confined to bed. You are in room nineteen, aren't you?"

"I don't know what the number is, damn it! But, if you don't get me a clean gown, you are going to hear about it tomorrow."

She gave him a gown and offered to help him back to his room. "No! I can make it okay by myself." And, then thinking about what this one might say to Donna, he added, "Look I'm sorry I was impolite. I'm not trying to give you a hard time, okay? And, I really appreciate your help."

He returned to his room. What to do with the dirty gown? He put it by the dying man's bed.

Donna arrived with a doctor at six AM. The doctor was busy with the other man and Donna came to him. "How are you feeling this morning?" she said, business-like, putting her hand on his forehead.

"Fine," he said sheepishly.

"Let's check that infection." She pulled his sheet down and removed his bandage.

The doctor came over and examined the wound briefly, and picked up the clipboard from the back of his bed. "I don't see a problem here," he growled.

"I would just like to keep him here for observation—if you don't mind," she responded to the doctor, in a soft voice.

The doctor looked at him with a mixture of boredom and disgust. "I take my work seriously girl," the doctor told her. She said nothing, but continued looking at the doctor. He checked something on the clipboard, and walked out. She pulled the curtain around his bed, and sat next to him.

"I was thinking about you all night," he said.

"I was thinking about you, too."

"Jeez, I hope I didn't get you in trouble."

"Nah, it's no problem," she said smiling.

"How did you do it?"

"I have connections."

"So, why are you doing this for me?"

"I think I like you," she responded. He put his hand behind her head and pulled her to him. They kissed passionately. "I think I like you, but I'm not sure." She said.

He pulled her to him, and they kissed again. "When will you be sure?"

"I'm checking on you honey, and if you have any skeletons or pregnant girls in Kentucky, you might as well spill it out right now."

"How can you do that?" he asked.

"I'm doing it! I know all about men. My Mama told me everything, and I've been watching Papa for a long time. I know everything." He pulled her face to him and they kissed again.

"God, it feels good to kiss you. I love it."

"Me too," she replied. She stood and opened the curtain around his bed. "Gotta go now, honey."

"When will you be back?" he asked in desperation.

"I'll come back to check on your infection this afternoon."

That afternoon she pulled the curtain around his bed, even though the man in the other bed could not have heard and seen anything. She removed his sheet and began to undo his bandage. He took every opportunity to pull her face to him and kiss. "It looks Okay," she said, redoing the bandage.

"God," he said, "I can't stand it." She left his leg and sat on the bed facing him. He pulled her down to him and they kissed again. He moved his hands over her body, but each time he was close to something interesting, she gently pulled his hand away. After a while she pushed herself away from him, and went back to the leg bandage.

"I love you, Donna." She looked at him and said nothing. "Can you come back this evening?" She said nothing. "Look Donna, I'm not going to try to... Jeez, I'm so lonely I'm dying, and I love you."

"I'm going to the PX later, can I bring you something?"

His heart jumped, and he was sure she could hear it beat. "Yeah, anything; a couple of beers would be great."

"I don't know if I can get beer in here. Anything else?"

"Anything Donna, anything; just come back."

Shortly after 9:30 when the lights were turned out, she came in the room and closed the door. She pulled the curtain around his bed and turned on the small reading lamp. From a paper sack she extracted three bottles of coke and two paper cups, and from her purse, a half-pint of rum.

"How about a rum and coke?" They sipped the drinks and kissed. He was surprised she was as passionate with her kisses as he was, and allowed him a greater range of touching—but only through her clothes.

When the rum was finished, they sat side-by-side leaning against the cranked up back of the bed. They talked—mostly she talked and he listened. She talked about Mama, her mother, and Papa who was a general in the army. She was a volunteer nurse's aide, and had come to Korea to please her father, who had always wanted a boy who could be a soldier. They had a ranch in Texas. She asked questions. "What's your father's occupation?

"He is a welder; works at a machine shop in a mine."

"How many brothers and sisters?"

"One; an older sister."

"Did she go to college?"

"Yes, she teaches science in High School."

"What is your religion?"

"None."

Oops, wrong answer. "You are not a Catholic?" she asked. "That's bad."

"It is?"

"Yes!" She said, as if surprised he didn't grasp the problem immediately. "Maybe you could become a Catholic."

"Yeah, maybe;" He would have agreed to become a communist, if she had requested, but he didn't understand what becoming a Catholic had to do with petting, and drinking rum and coke.

She checked her watch and said, "Gee, I have to go. I have bed check in twenty minutes." She quickly put the bottles and cups in the paper bag, withdrew the curtain from around his bed, kissed him again, and rushed out.

She was with the doctor at six AM the next morning. Again, the doctor attended to the other man and she attended him. The doctor came to his bed. "I've already checked him," she said, and held the clipboard out, indicating the doctor should check a particular box.

The doctor glared at both of them, and checked the box. "He has a three day stay. Tomorrow is the last day, and I want him the hell out of here," the doctor said, and left the room.

She stayed with him for a half-hour. "Got to do my angel of mercy rounds, honey; see you later." She stopped briefly again in the morning, and stopped twice in the afternoon, leaving at six PM. "I'll see ya' after lights out."

In the evening there was no rum and coke, less talk, and more passion. She kept her buttons buttoned, and didn't let his hands under her dress, but everything else was fair. She reached down and touched him through his gown. He moaned. She moved her hand up under his gown. He moaned louder. "Am I hurting you?" she whispered.

"No, no, no, no!"

"Do you want me to do this?"

"Yes, yes, yes, yes."

A bit later he lay exhausted and gasping. He looked up at her. Her eyes were dull, with eyelids half closed, and she breathed heavily. He rolled toward her and pressed his face against her, trying to pull up her dress. She pushed him away slowly. "I can't stand it," he said.

"I can't stand it either," she said in a raspy voice. She turned and left him.

It was six AM and the doctor was working on the other man. She began to remove his bandage. "You're going back today, ya' know."

"Yeah, I know. I'll never see you again Donna."

"Maybe you will; I'll call ya."

"Call me? I can't get to a phone up there."

"Trust me."

The doctor walked over and looked at the wound. "Okay soldier, get out of here!"

Donna frowned at the doctor. "There's nothing wrong with you," the doctor yelled at him. "Get the hell out of my hospital!"

"Okay, where's my uniform?"

"I don't know where it is! Just get out the hell of my hospital!" The doctor replied, with a wave of his hand, and to Donna, "I take my work seriously girl, so don't ever do anything like this again!" The doctor left them.

"Jeez," he said. "I hope I didn't get you into trouble."

"Don't worry about it honey, I can handle him. I can handle you too, and don't you forget it!"

"I just want to see you again."

"Ray, there are whore houses up there. I don't want you going to those places."

"I won't go there."

"I swear Ray, if you do I will know about it, and I will never speak to you again."

"I won't, Donna!"

"Okay, I'll call you. And, there's something else I want to tell you. I think I'm in love with you."

GO WITH GOD: COSTA DEL SOL, THURSDAY, AUGUST 6

My thoughts and dreams during the night flood back. I recreate each scene in my mind. I know daybreak is more than a few minutes away, but decide to get up. I can hear the woman moving around in her kitchen, so I go over and order coffee.

I sit at the table, facing the ocean on the deck of the restaurant and sip coffee. Have I lost Donna's love? That had not been in my thoughts during the night, and I didn't want to cloud those memories. I force myself back to thoughts of the first days with Donna, and our marriage in Japan. Thoughts of those last days on Zebra try to crowd in, but I push them back, and concentrate on Donna. How could I have let her love go?

Shirley comes down the stairs of her hut, and notices me on the deck. She joins me. "What's the matter?" she asks, with her hand on the back of my head. I am embarrassed she has noticed my melancholy state.

"It's nothing, love. It was my dream last night. Maybe it wasn't a dream. I was just lying there thinking about Donna. How I met her at the hospital, and the time we spent together, and about how sad it was, when I went back to the front." Shirley sits beside me and remains silent. "I was an innocent babe in those days, Shirley. That was before I became a shit-head. It seems like a million years ago."

"You're not a shit-head," she says, softly. I don't respond, and she continues: "Do you still love her?"

"Yeah, I guess I will always love her. But, it isn't going to do me any good, is it?"

"I don't know."

We have our coffee and breakfast saying little. "Are you going fishing again today?" she asks. I nod. "Are we still going to the village on Saturday?" I nod. "If I am late tonight, are you going to come out, and save me from the bad guys?" she asks, smiling at me.

"Bet on it, love."

The day on the boat is a repeat of the previous two days, but now I know what to expect. When the time comes for the final pull against the current, I am ready and feel I am doing a full share of the work. I still have some soreness in my arms and back, probably because the rowing uses muscles I usually don't exercise much. But, I am as strong as they are. If I had to I could make my living fishing with these guys for the rest of my life. That thought makes me feel good. But, that it also tells me I have relatively little more to learn from them.

Shirley is waiting with the other women and children on the beach. I confirm the Saturday boat ride to the village with Felipe again, and take two large fish and some shrimp.

"Okay Captain," I say in Spanish, *"I will not fish with you again. May you go with God."*

"May you also go with God, my friend." The Captain responds, holding up his garbage bag to show he doesn't care if the people laugh.

"May all of you go with God," I say to them.

"Vaya usted con Dios tambien, gringo," they answer.

"Good-bye brother Juan. Take care of Mamá."

"My brother, it will be as if she is resting in the arms of Jesus," the man responds.

"Saturday, Tío Felipe;" I say.

"Saturday, amigo;" Felipe answers.

"How was your day?" Shirley asks, as we walk back toward the restaurant arm in arm.

"Great, but it was kind of sad to tell them I wouldn't be fishing with them anymore," I respond.

"You told them *'vaya con dios'*, didn't you? And, they all said that to you, too. It's really touching, the way you just mix in with them like that. You really love them, and they love you, don't they?" I don't respond. "And, you told your brother Juan to take care of Mamá. What did he say? It wasn't a joke, was it?"

"He said it will be as if she is resting in the arms of Jesus. And, no—he didn't say it as a joke."

"That almost makes me cry. You could go with them tomorrow, or next week," she says.

"Nah, I've already done this fishing thing. I know the routine. I have some other things I want to do and see here on the coast," I tell her, as we walk up the stairs and sit at the table.

"Like?"

"Like visit San Lorenzo up the coast, and maybe Tumaco across on the Colombia side, or take the old train from San Lorenzo to Ibarra. And, I want to go back down to the *Oriente* again—the Amazon side—and take one of those boats down the Napo River."

"How long will it take you to do all of that?"

"Oh, the San Lorenzo-Ibarra thing could be done in three or four days. It would probably take a week to do the Napo River," I respond, and add, "I wish you would go with me."

"Sounds like great adventures. But, I kind of promised Norma I would teach for three more weeks."

"Can't you get out of teaching?"

"Yeah, I could, but I'm not sure I should."

I give the woman the fish and shrimp, and return to the table with two beers. I finish mine quickly. "I'm going to take a quick shower."

"Better lock the door. Someone may come in there and slap you on the butt."

"You are welcome in my hut any time, and for any reason, love," I yell back to her.

Our dinner is again spectacular. The woman serves a bottle of wine, and gives us real wineglasses. Shirley is amazed and delighted. "Where did she get the wine?"

"I asked her to get wine for us a couple of days ago. I told her we wanted Chilean wine, and this is the best of the best: *Casillero del Diablo—the* Devil's Locker—by Concha y Toro!"

"Why do they call it that?"

"I haven't the foggiest notion, but it sure sounds exotic, doesn't it?" Shirley is enjoying the wine and not being sure the woman has another bottle I switch to beer and leave the wine for her.

"Flirt, flirt, flirt;" She says, giggling.

"Don't say that! Jesus Shirley, you make it sound like we're teenagers."

"Well, we are acting like teenagers. Why shouldn't I say it?"

I want to change the subject. "Do you like being a woman?"

"Yeah; don't you like being a man?"

"Sure. But I wouldn't want to be a woman—have some son-of-a-bitch pawing at me all the time."

She laughs as if that is the funniest thing she has ever heard. "Is that what they do? Paw at you?" She uses her hand to paw at my arm. "Mua, mua, mua;" She says.

"I don't mean like that."

"No; you mean they grope you, and try to feel you up; that's what you mean, huh? Is that what you are thinking about doing to me?"

"I'm trying not to act that way." I respond.

"Oh, thank you so much for trying not to do that; otherwise I would have to put up with you groping me and feeling me up all the time." Again she laughs.

"I have the feeling you wouldn't put up with that."

"NO SHIT! ...I'm sorry to say a bad word, but it will be a cold day in hell when some man just walks up and starts feeling me up!" She laughs again: "I'm so glad you told me how you feel about that. And, I was just thinking about pawing you; imagine that! I was going to run my fingers through your hair and..." she uses both hands to run her fingers through my hair; "and feel all your muscles.." she feels my arms and chest; "and pull up your T-shirt and feel your little nipples.." she does that too; "and maybe even feel your private parts. But now I know how disgusting that would be for you, so I won't do it."

"That wouldn't be disgusting."

"Oh, I see; so being a man and having some woman paw at you wouldn't be so bad, huh?"

"Nah; and anyway that wouldn't be pawing."

"Sweetheart, has it ever occurred to you that if you were a woman and loved a guy you might enjoy having him touch you and love you?"

"Frankly, no; that has not occurred to me."

"How does it feel to walk around with your brains hanging out all the time, so everyone knows what you're thinking?" she asks.

"I know as much about what you're thinking as you know about what I'm thinking."

"HA!" she says, "That's a laugh! I could be planning to murder you and you wouldn't have the slightest idea."

"Murder me, huh? Better watch your step, girl. Airborne soldiers are the meanest sons-o'-bitches that ever walked—slit your throat in a second, and never look back."

"Mean? You're not mean! Do you think I would be hanging around with you if you were mean? Oh, I know you were going to hit Johnny back there on the road that first day, but you were glad I stopped you, weren't you? And, you tried to make it up to him later, huh?"

She feels my arm and runs her fingers through my hair again, smiling broadly. "You know," she says, "that's something I've never understood about men. You know what would have happened if you had hit him, don't you?" I don't respond. "You know, don't you?" I nod yes. "Well, go on and say it!"

"You would never have spoken to me again."

"That's right! And, that's the only reason you got off that bus in the first place, isn't it? And, you would have had to just turn around and walk back down that road and get back on a bus and go away...FOREVER, wouldn't you? So why would you do that? It's not because you're mean, and it's not because your stupid, is it? So what is it? It's the same reason you would go to the war, isn't it?"

"You wouldn't understand."

"TRY ME!"

"It's honor, Shirley."

"Hitting someone is honor? Even if it means someone you like is never going to speak to you again in your whole life?"

"I guess I figured that if I had to I could get along without you speaking to me; but, I couldn't get along without me speaking to me."

"So you wouldn't be able to speak to yourself if you didn't hit him? That is the most STUPID thing I have ever heard in my entire life!"

"I told ya' you wouldn't understand."

After a few seconds she continues: "Well, at least it is an explanation. I always thought it was just instinct, left over from the caveman days."

"**D**o you have bad dreams about the army—about the war?"

"Sometimes; is this therapy?" She nods. "Yeah, and when I have those dreams, it's almost like a big dog comes out of a hollow place in the back of my head—down in the bottom of my brain, and then I have to fight it."

"A dog?"

"Yeah," I respond. "I thought about that damned dog the other day on the bus when I woke up. That's why I was so confused."

"Did the dog go away?"

"Yeah, well, you made it go away."

"How did I do that?"

"It was your breast, love," I laugh. "When I saw your breast, I couldn't think of anything else but that."

"You didn't see my breast."

"When you reached up to get your bag, I could see through the sleeve of your shirt."

"Jeez, Ray. That's really pathetic. That's like peeking at me."

"I couldn't help seeing you; you were right there." She presses her lips together and nods her head up and down. "Hey, I was just putting you on about the dog thing. Jeez, you're going to think I'm a psychopath."

"No I won't. I think I understand what you are saying." We watch the sun setting over the ocean. "How old were you when you joined the army?"

"Eighteen; on my eighteenth birthday in 1951."

"Why did you join on your birthday?"

"That was the first day I could join without my parent's permission. My Mom and Dad were mad as hell, but they couldn't do anything about it."

"1951? The war was already going on, wasn't it? Why did you join?"

"I guess it was because of my Uncle. He was a soldier in Europe, and he was always my greatest hero. I guess I wanted to be like Uncle Bob."

"The Korean War has been over for a long time, and it still bothers you?"

"Yeah; more than ever."

"Really; can't you just forget about the war—put it out of your mind?"

"At first I did forget. But, later it got harder and harder to forget. It just started coming back."

"Is your Uncle Bob still your hero?"

"No, not any more."

"Tell me how Donna saved your life."

I don't want to think about that. "I can't remember."

"You said you were in a prison or hospital or something and Donna came in with her Mama and saved you."

"No, Mama didn't come in. Mama was in Texas. But, she pulled the strings for Donna. Donna was talking like Mama—she even referred to herself as Mama. She hovered over me and said, 'don't worry baby, Mama's going to take care of you,' just like Mama would have."

"You were in the hospital? You were wounded?" I nod. "It's that scar on your back isn't it?" I nod. "What else did she say?"

"She said the officer who accused me would be crucified; Mama probably did have him crucified."

"What did the officer accuse you of?"

"I don't know, probably cowardice, of running and hiding—trying to save my ass."

"Did they arrest you?"

"No, they gave me a medal."

"Seriously, what did they do to you?"

"Seriously; they gave me a medal! I'm a fucken hero! Didn't you know?" Immediately I regret my mocking tone. "I'm sorry, love. None of this has anything to do with you."

"A hero huh?"

I am disgusted with myself for having spilled out the hero stuff. "Just forget about it. That has nothing to do with...I'm sorry I said that, okay? Just forget it." She isn't forgetting. "Oh shit," I say. "This is just some of my GI shit. Will you just forget it?"

"No, I won't. Tell me about the medal," she says softly.

"Damn it, Shirley! Will you just get off it?"

"No, this is therapy. Tell me about the medal."

"I didn't get a medal, okay!"

"Tell me about the medal."

"Oh shit, Shirley! I don't remember anything about that." I hold her hands and speak to her very seriously. "Please, love; don't do this now."

She is quiet for a minute. "You had to fight in the war, didn't ya?"

"I didn't do shit in the war."

"It's something about the war, isn't it?"

"What Shirley, what; will you get off my fucken case?"

"It's about the war, isn't it?"

"Jesus, Shirley!" I get up and turn to leave.

She holds my arm. "Call me love." She says with a smile, pulling me back to the seat.

"Oh shit, Shirley—love, please don't do this to me now."

"Okay, not now." We sit quietly for a few minutes. She has the sly smile again, as if we share some secret.

"You're off my case, huh?"

"Yeah; no more therapy."

I put my hand on her cheek. "I really like you like this."

"I like you like this too," she replies. "Sometimes, we can be really nice to each other, can't we?" Her statement doesn't seem to need a reply. I brush her cheek with my hand and look at her, enjoying the mischievous smile. "We really care for each other, don't we?" Again, no reply seemed to be called for. "Let's go for a swim."

We walk down the stairs and down the beach. I put my arm around her waist and hold her close, and she doesn't seem to mind. We walk along the shore, about a few hundred yards down the beach away from the huts. The almost full moon is exceptionally bright, reflecting off the sea and sand. She stops and looks back at the huts. Apparently, judging them to be far enough away, she kicks off her sandals, pulls her blouse over her head, and unzips her shorts. Her shorts drop and her panties come off; she is completely nude in the moonlight. She turns and runs into the surf. I remove my clothes quickly, and join her.

We play in the surf, first struggling to get into deeper water, and then allow ourselves to be carried back toward the beach, tumbling in the waves. At the first opportunity, I put my arms around her. She averts my kiss. I slide my hands down her back.

"Don't get personal with me. And, you might as well disarm that thing; you aren't going to use it on me."

"Shirley, that's totally involuntary. I can't control that—ask any doctor."

"Involuntary, huh? Well, rubbing it against me is not involuntary."

"It is, love. It's instinct; just like little babies start sucking when they're first born."

"Instinct; poking that thing against me is instinct?" she asks in a disgusted voice, pushing herself away. "You're so full of...; how can you say things like that with a straight face?"

"Well hell, it's true."

"Let's get dressed; I'm cold." She wades out of the surf, and then turns back. "Don't just stand there; come on."

"I'll be out in a minute."

"Embarrassed huh? Well, you should be!"

"I'm just cooling off a bit," I say.

By the time I reach her she already has her panties and shorts on, and is pulling her blouse over her head; she is shivering. "Get dressed Ray, I'm cold. Let's get out of the wind." I pull my boxer drawers on and pick up my Levi cut-offs. She amuses herself with the strings hanging from the top sides of my drawers. "What are the strings for?" she asks, taking them in her hands and laughing.

"I don't know, they come that way."

"You just sort of rope it in here when it gets out of control? Here let me tie a bow for ya," she is busy tying a bow in the side of my shorts, and having a good laugh.

"I guess if your waist is smaller, you just use these strings to make um' fit," I say, embarrassed.

"So, why not just buy underpants that fit you in the first place?"

"It's kind of a one size fits all thing in the army," I respond, now pulling on my Levis.

"You are still wearing army underpants?"

"Well, yeah. I buy shorts and T-shirts at the PX. Hell, they're cheap, and I got used to wearing GI stuff."

"They still let you buy stuff from the PX?"

"Yeah, I have a ..." I had almost said disability. "I guess I'll always be hung-up on my GI shit." I respond, wishing I hadn't.

She seemed to pick up my sour tone. "Here, kiss me baby!" She puts her hands around my waist.

I resist the irresistible. "You're playing with me, Shirley."

"Sure, I'm playing with you! What the hell do you think you're doing with me?" she asks, pushing me away. "What gives you the right to play with me, and think I can't play with you back?" She turns away, and starts up the beach.

"Okay, you have a point," I say, walking after her. She continues walking up the beach. "Hey, I didn't mean it like that. Wait a minute, will you?"

We walk, mostly in silence, back to her hut and go inside. It is similar to mine, but larger, with a small room on the right side. She goes into the small room.

"This is my room. No one is allowed in here but me." I stand at the door. "You're in the other hut—and don't think about coming into my room."

Her tone irritates me. "So, what do you think I am; some kind of rapist?"

"No, I didn't mean that; I'm sorry I said that."

"Can I have that kiss now?"

"No!"

"Am I ever going to get to first base with you?"

She sits on her bed and looks up at me. "We've already been on first base. First base is when we treat each other in a civil manner," and adds, "at least some of the time. Second base is when we actually enjoy doing that—so I'd say we've been on second base, too. Third base is when you can touch a person or maybe even kiss without the other person getting mad, so maybe we've almost been on third base. What you really want to know is, are you going to hit a homerun. The answer is no! Get out!" She gets up and pushes the door closed.

"Hey," I say, from the other side of the door, "can I see you tomorrow, maybe on third base?"

"You'll see me tomorrow," she says, and then opens the door slightly. "Ray, if I ask you to kiss me, are you going to refuse, and make some stupid comment?"

"No, love; that ploy didn't work very well."

"Well, come back here and kiss me then." I do. "You know, for someone who can't remember where he's going, and can't even remember he can't remember, you're not so bad. Go to bed. I'll see you in the morning."

I turn back to the porch, down the steps and go to my hut. I lie in my hammock and clear my mind and thoughts of the army and Donna flood in.

NOW THERE ARE THREE OF US: KOREA, SPRING, 1953

He knew that somehow Donna really could manage the impossible phone call. After a week on Zebra, he arrived back at the bivouac on Monday evening, and spent the evening drinking beer with his buddy Patterson.

On Tuesday morning someone yelled through the door of his hooch, "Richards, report to the First Sergeant on the double." The First Sergeant motioned for him to answer the radio-phone.

He listened to her instructions and was flabbergasted when the plan succeeded. He had just enough time to grab a pair of clean fatigues and underwear, and give Patterson the thumbs up sign, before the Colonel's jeep left for Inchon.

"Go get it man," Patterson had said. "And, bring me back a sticky finger."

Donna was waiting at the depot. He rushed to her. "God, I love you Donna," he said. They went to a hotel she had arranged, and directly to the room. When the door closed, they began to caress and pull at each other's clothes. After, they lay together exhausted.

"I gotta tell you something honey," she said.

"What?"

"You want to know how I know how to do this?"

"No," he said. "You don't have to tell me."

"You are my first lover. I'm not saying I was a virgin, but you are my first real lover."

"Okay."

"No," she said, "I want you to know you are my first real lover."

"Okay, I believe you."

"Mama told me you wouldn't believe me. She said, when you get your man, he will want to know how you knew about it before. She said men always want their girl to know everything, but don't want them to have learned it from someone else."

"I really don't need to know about your past life, Donna."

"Yes you do! I want you to know how I know about all of this sex stuff."

"Okay," he responded, puzzled.

"My Mama told me everything. She said the only thing dirty about sex, is when you don't love the guy you are doing it with."

"Your Mother told you that?"

"She told me everything, and told me how to do it. She said, when you find the man you want, ya' have to tell him how you knew, because he would think you learned it with some other guy."

"I don't think that."

"Good. You are my first real lover, and I'm going to keep you." That gave him pause. "Don't you love me honey?"

"Yeah, I do."

"Then, we will get married and have babies, okay?"

"Jesus!"

"Not right away; after the war is over. Then, we well get married, okay?"

"Jesus!"

"You do love me, don't ya?" she questioned.

"Sure, I love you."

"And, you want to stay with me, don't ya? Spend your life with me?"

"Sure I do."

"I will always love you, and I will give you everything and take care of you," she promised. "Honey," she said, as they lay facing each other, "I want to share something with you."

"Yeah, what is it?"

"Me; I want to share myself with you, and I want you to share yourself with me, okay?"

"Sure," he said.

"Are you sure?"

"Yeah, I'm sure."

"Then, we are together forever," she said, holding him tight. "We will be married and have babies, and we will always be together even when we are old and stupid."

It was mysterious and magical. He had never known so much pleasure. During the first day with her, he had experienced more sexual passion than in his previous twenty years of life, by a factor of hundreds. Indeed, the totality of his previous sex life had been confined to fumbling with buttons and zippers in the front seat of his car at the drive-in, and four trips to the whorehouse in Korea. He had found encounters with whores to be very unsatisfactory and even shameful. On his last visit he had been unable to get an erection. He had paid the woman and decided he would never return.

With Donna, sex had been totally different. The following three days were long, and filled with passion and excitement. They were together almost continuously. The seemingly impossible expectations he had fantasized were exceeded beyond his imagination. Her body was becoming as familiar to him as his own, yet the excitement did not diminish—it grew. There seemed to be no limit to his desire for her. A force, stronger than chains or walls, bound him to her, and he wondered how that had happened.

On Sunday afternoon, she walked with him to the depot. "Don't you dare go to one of those whorehouses. Those women make sex cheap and dirty, and they have terrible diseases."

"I told you, I never go to those places." Her look said she didn't believe him. "Look Donna, I did go before, but I didn't like it, and I decided not to go back—and that was long before I met you."

"Okay," she said. "What you did before doesn't count; but from now on, I'm the only one."

"Sure."

"You guys go back to Zebra on Sunday?"

"Yeah."

"And, then back at the bivouac the following Monday?" I nod. "I'm gonna' see ya' on Saturday, at the NCO Club guest housing, at Eighty-Second Division Headquarters."

"Donna, I can't get into the NCO Club."

"Trust me, honey."

During the ride back to the front, he felt as he had leaving Uncle Bob's house. Suddenly his life had changed. He would never be the same person again. He thought about his new life. She was lovely and beautiful, more desirable than he had ever dreamed. She was more important than the army, and his dreams of journalism and fame. She was more important than his life.

Reaching the bivouac area, he was already lonely and sad, and could think of nothing but her. He wanted to avoid anyone he knew, and wasted time on a few beers at the club hooch, till lights out. Then, he went to his hooch. He didn't want to talk to anyone. He especially didn't want to talk to Patterson. He had shared his previous experiences in the hospital with Patterson, including her masturbating him. They had discussed the impossible dream of requesting his three-day leave, up the chain of command. Patterson had said, "Do it man! What do you have to lose? Shit, I'd go AWOL for a chance at some real pussy."

When his leave came through he had taken the time to find his buddy, to let him know the plan had worked. Patterson had been almost as happy for him, as he had been for himself. He knew Patterson would be dying to hear all the details, and he knew he wouldn't and couldn't discuss Donna—even with his best buddy Patterson.

It was a strange feeling. Having a buddy was very special. Someone who did not understand the army might have had the incorrect impression that the buddy relationship was sexual. Perhaps only soldiers could experience and understand the buddy relationship. During the past year, Patterson had become his best friend. They shared everything, and hid nothing. They had considered the possibility that one might be called upon to risk his life for the other, and they were fully prepared to do that. He knew everything about Patterson's life and dreams, and Pat knew all about his. He had believed he would always be closer to Pat than any other person on earth. He could not think of a future life that did not include his buddy.

Suddenly, that was changed. What he had with Donna he could not share—even with Patterson. He didn't even want to talk and joke with Pat about girls. His mind was filled with Donna, and anything else would take away time and space he needed to think about her.

On Zebra, Patterson found him. "Hey Rich, how was it? Did you get in her pants?" his buddy asked. He brushed the question off with a grunt. "Come on man, give me the low down—shit."

"I don't want to talk about it, Pat."

"What's the matter, Rich? She give you a bunch of shit?"

"Nah, it was great, we spent four days together."

"No shit? Four fucken days! Man, I'd trade my ass for four days fucking a real chick."

"Look Pat, this is serious, okay?" he responded, hoping to end the conversation.

"Hey man, pussy is pussy. Put a sack over their head and they all look alike. Hey man, what gives?"

"I told you Pat, I don't want to talk about it. And, I don't want to talk about women, okay?"

"You don't want to talk about fucking? Hell Rich, you're fucken sick. You better go see the medic and take some pills."

"Look man, I love her. I'm going to marry her."

"You're going to FUCKEN-A WHAT? You couldn't have knocked her up that fast, and she sure as hell didn't get knocked up, giving you that hand job." Four days previous, he would have found nothing offensive, or even different, in Patterson's language and attitude. Now he was disgusted. He stretched his arms with palms out, and fanned the air, as if to say I'm fed up with you, and walked away.

He tried to avoid everyone, and be alone as much as possible. He didn't want anything to interfere with his daydreams and fantasies of Donna. The guys in his squad picked up those feelings, and they soon left him to himself.

Sergeant Jordan was concerned. "What's yo' problem, youngster?" Jordan asked him privately.

"Nothing, Serge."

"I don't want you going off the deep end on me, son. I don't plan to lose no more troopers in this shithole; you hear me?"

"I hear you, Serge. Nothing's wrong."

"Want to tell me what happened at Inchon over the weekend?" The sergeant waited for an answer and then continued, yelling in his face: "I don't want no suicide in my platoon, boy! I'll pull yo' fucken weapon! I'll have yo' ass digging latrines for the rest a' yo' fucken life. You hear me, boy? I'll break yo' fucken back!"

He was startled that his behavior had provoked the suicide-watch treatment, and the word boy, coming from Jordan, told him nothing less than a real explanation would satisfy the sergeant. "Hey Serge, really, there's nothing wrong. Look Serge, I have a girlfriend, okay? A real girlfriend; she's a white... she's an American," he explained, knowing that falling in love with a local whore was automatic grounds for a suicide watch, "and, I just don't want these fucken guys talking about her. I just want to think about her, instead of this shit. I've never been happier in my life."

"Don't fuck up, son!"

"I won't fuck up, Serge."

"You fuck up, I gonna' land on you so fucken hard, you wish you never heard a' no girlfriend!"

The second evening, Patterson found him on guard at the outer perimeter. "Halt; password!" He said, releasing the safety on his M1.

"It's me, man, shit."

"Come on in, Pat."

Patterson moved through the trench crouching to keep his head down. "Hey Rich, second platoon got beer rations." He put six half-quart cans of beer and a pack of cigarettes on the sandbags above the trench.

"You did all right, man." He took two cigarettes out of the pack and squatted in the trench to light them. The sand bags were a foot above their heads, but scuttlebutt had it that the Chinese could detect a glowing cigarette two or three feet below their line of vision, so guys always squatted at the bottom of the trench to take a drag. It was a silly idea; if the Americans didn't have that kind of technology, the possibility that the Chinks had it was ridiculous; but no one wanted to take chances.

"Yeah; I grabbed four like always, and got Johnson to take his two and sell um' to me. He's a Mormon, you know. I'm gonna' pay him ten cents a can on payday; I get his cigs too, for five cents a pack."

"Good thinking, Pat. I'll split the cost with you on payday."

"That's okay, man; don't worry about it."

"Hey man, we split it—right down the middle—just like always!"

"Look Rich, I don't MIND doing a favor for my buddy; okay? I'm not like some guys."

"I'm getting fucken sick and tired of your bleeding heart sacrificing, Pat. We split it or you can fucken drink your own beer."

"Okay; we'll split it." Patterson used his beer-can opener to pop two holes in the top of two cans, while his buddy ducked down to take a drag on his cigarette. "My bleeding heart sacrificing, huh; for twenty-five fucken cents, huh?"

"It's the principle of the fucken thing, Pat!"

"Hey man, I'm sorry about what I said about your girl—shit."

"It's okay Pat, don't worry about it."

"Well shit, Rich! We've been buddies since we got into this shithole, and then she comes along and steals you away in four fucken days—shit."

"Come on man, it's different; she's a girl. It has nothing to do with the fucken army."

"Are you sure you want to jump into this shit, Man? Hell, you just met her. Shit, she could be..." his voice trailed off. "I'm just thinking about you, Rich. I don't want you to get fucked up."

"Yeah, I know."

"Someday I'm going to fall in love with a girl," Patterson said, looking away through the wire. "I think about it all the time."

"It's better than anything you've ever thought about Pat; it's a thousand times better."

"Are you sure you know what you're doing, man? That girl has her fucken hooks in you, and you don't even know it."

"I know it, Pat! I want her hooks in me! I know what I'm doing, and I'm doing what I want to do—what I want more than anything I've ever wanted!"

"Yeah? So you're hooked! And, instead of a buddy I got a fucken guy who is fucken hooked on a girl. Maybe I'll just drink my own beer next time."

"Hey man, thanks for the beer. We get our ration tomorrow, and I'll share with you—just like always."

"So, we can still be buddies, huh?"

"Sure, just like before."

"No! Not like before; now there are three of us in this fucken shithole."

THE SNAKE DOCTOR CURED HER: COSTA DEL SOL, FRIDAY, AUGUST 7

Moonlight flickers on waves and illuminates the white sand. The moon is low in the west, over the ocean, and I know dawn is about to break. Thoughts of Donna are fresh in my mind, and I try to continue thinking about her. Have I lost her love? The question frightens me. I swing my legs out of the hammock and go down the steps and around the side of the hut to urinate and observe the eastern sky. There is no hint of daylight, but it can be only minutes away. Shirley won't teach today, and will sleep late. I decide to walk down the beach. When I reach the water the first light appears in the east. The tide is low, and I walk along the mud flats digging silver dollar clams with my toes. There is a strong land breeze, but the ocean is very calm, with small waves just lapping along the shoreline. Several hundred yards down the beach, I meet Felipe and five other men carrying their nets and gear; they will fish again today. We talk briefly, and confirm the trip to the village on Saturday. I continue down the beach for a while, mostly thinking about the good times in the army and with Donna, and repressing thoughts about the bad times.

I return up the beach to Costa del Sol. From the deck, I watch the men launch their boats, and then order breakfast. At about eight o'clock Shirley joins me and I am happy to see her smiling face. I have more coffee while she has breakfast. We talk and joke. Everything seems to be perfect.

About nine-thirty or so Johnny emerges from their hut, and comes over to the deck. He calls from below, "I'm going down to Atacames to get something decent to eat. Want to come along?"

"Sure!" She responds. Before I can object, she pulls me to my feet.

Johnny walks on along the beach and we follow. She wants to play. We follow the surf out as the water recedes, and run back as the next wave comes in. We skip along holding hands, and generally act like children. Johnny turns occasionally to jeer.

"Oh, aren't you cute? You two make me sick. Why don't you go back to the hut and play with each other?"

I don't care what Johnny says, and she doesn't seem to either. We begin to chase each other, splashing in the surf and rolling in the sand.

"Stop it!" She pushes me away. "We're having fun, and you take advantage of it."

"I didn't mean to do that," I say, unable to hide my smile. "I just had my hand there, and when I pulled it up, it went up there."

"So, you thought you would feel around a little, huh?"

"Well, yeah, as long as I was there." I close my eyes and wait for the signature punch. It's worse when you know it's coming. Bang! "Okay, love. We're even."

"Play fair, damn you!"

"I'll play fair."

I am easy to catch and tackle, and even easier to hold down, if she wants to force a kiss on my lips. She sits on top of me holding my arms down: "I could rape you until you beg for mercy." She says, with a big smile.

"Don't show me any mercy Love, I don't deserve it."

She slides down from my waist to kiss my mouth, and then jumps back and off me. "Well, you sure took that threat seriously," pointing to the rise in my shorts.

"Come on Shirley; I can't control that."

"That wouldn't happen if you weren't thinking about having sex with me!"

"Shirley love, that would happen if I were thinking about taking you to Sunday school."

"I don't believe you!" A minute later she says "Can you run when that thing is sticking up like that?" I shrug. She grabs my cap and runs down the beach. When I catch up with her she dances around Johnny, holding him between us. "Keep him away from me, Johnny." She says. "He's trying to molest me."

"Oh sure;" Johnny says. "I can see how hard you are trying to get away from him." He walks along with his arms folded, trying hard to ignore us.

"I'm not molesting her, Johnny. I'm just trying to get my cap back. She's had her eye on that cap from the beginning; next she'll be after my OD tee-shirts."

"Well, I was going to give it back to you before, but now I won't!" She says, and puts the cap on. "And don't try to grab it off my head!"

"I have a lot of friends in Atacames." Johnny says. "And, if you two are going to act like teenagers I'm not sitting at the same table with you."

I am behind her and she tries to crawl away. Through the bottom of her shorts I catch a glimpse of the curve of her butt and her pink panties. The view is only a couple of inches away, and I can't resist closing the distance.

"Stop it!"

"Okay. I'm sorry, okay?"

"And anyway, that was really gross, Raymond."

"It's not gross."

"Kissing my butt is not gross? Then, what is gross?"

"I wasn't kissing your butt."

"Well, what do you call that?" She asks.

"I was trying to kiss your pussy, if you want me to spell it out!"

She turns back to me; "Well, you can't do that; and you certainly can't do it from the back side."

"Can I do it from the front side?"

"NO!"

"It seems less certain that I can't do it from the front side."

"You CERTAINLY can't do it from either side!"

We continue the game, and are hot and sweaty when we reach Atacames. We sit at a beachfront table. The place is just a bamboo shack with a table and stools on the sand under a thatch awning. I ask the woman what she has for lunch. She has fish, shrimp, and beef.

"Better ask her how much is it," Johnny says. "They charge you double if you don't check the price first."

"She won't raise the price. Anyway, it's on me." I say.

"Well, I'll have the fish, if it's fresh."

"Well, of course it's fresh Johnny, there's the ocean right there." I say.

"I'll have the fish then."

"Me too." Shirley adds.

I ask the woman if she has good fresh fish. She assures me she does. I ask her to serve us three fish fillets—no bones, skin, or heads, and cooked to perfection—and I tell her I want to leave an extra tip. The woman smiles, and says, *"Sí señor, por supuesto."* She returns immediately, with three very cold bottles of beer.

"What the hell did you say?" Johnny asks. "I didn't understand a single word."

"Just ordered our fish."

"You really do speak Spanish!" Shirley says.

"Yeah, some;" I say, trying to sound modest.

"You learned all that in Mexico City College? How long were you there?" She asks.

"Mexico City College?" I hear myself ask.

"Are you going to start that again? Look! You said you studied at Mexico City College." She says. "Come on!"

"Yeah, I did. I just haven't thought about it for a long time. I just came down here bumming around, and stopped thinking about all that stuff."

"How can you just stop thinking about things?"

"I just didn't want to think about it."

"So, what difference does it make where he learned it?" Johnny says, as if taking my side. "He speaks this lingo like a native. Why don't you get off his case about this fucking Mexico City College?"

"This is none of your business, Johnny!" She says, and turns to me again. "So? I'm still waiting to find out how long you were in Mexico City College!"

I let my mind clear and listen to myself speak. "I went down there two years ago, when I left Donna. I was there for a year and a half. Then, last January I decided to do some research in British Honduras. I was supposed to be doing research on bush medicine used by the Black Caribs and Maya people. They even kept sending my GI

Bill check for a while." I laugh, and continue, "But, hell. I never sent any paperwork back to my Prof in Mexico, so they finally cut me off. I was just having a good old time, with those Carib and Maya guys, fishing and hunting, and running around in the bush looking for old Maya ruins. Then, I came on down here."

"So, you left Donna."

"Yeah; well, actually I didn't just leave her. I wanted her to go with me, but she wouldn't go. For the first couple of months I called her every week, and asked her to join me. But, she wouldn't, and wanted me to come home. And, I wouldn't. And, then... Well, I just stopped calling her."

"How can you just stop calling your wife?" I shrug. "You mean she doesn't even know whether you are alive or dead!"

"I just stopped thinking about it. Anyway, she knows. Mama always knows everything. A couple of months ago in Bogota the US Embassy had the police pick me up. I had to sign a statement that I was traveling around of my own free will. I know that was Mama's work."

"How can you just stop thinking about things!" She states, rather than asks, and exhales loudly. After a minute she says, "Studying bush medicine, huh? You mean like witch doctors and herbs?"

"Well, yeah. I thought it was a lot of hocus-pocus when this anthropology professor told me about it. But, you know, some of that stuff works. There was a little girl in a Maya Village down there that was bitten by a really bad snake. It got her on the toe. Can you believe it? People would have a little girl running around barefoot in a village surrounded by rainforest? Anyway, this was a bad snake. Even an adult would be in a coma in minutes, and this was just a little girl."

"And, the witch doctors cured her?" She asks.

"They call them snake doctors, or bush doctors. I don't think you would call anyone a witch down there. They are all very religious, and really superstitious about witches. But, yeah, the snake doctor cured her."

"How did she do it?" She asks.

"It was a he. I told you it wasn't a witch." I say, smiling. I get the wrinkled brow look, and lean away from the table to avoid the signature punch. "No. I'm joking. Anyway, I don't know how he did it. He wouldn't let me watch. There was a lot of prayer and magic, but he had some herbs and stuff, too. All I know is the girl was running around in the village a couple of weeks later."

"I guess you kids want to be alone." Johnny says. "Excuse me." Apparently he feels excluded in the conversation.

"Just try to be a little bit civil, will you Johnny?" She tells him. I am beyond concern about Johnny, and enjoy watching her command every situation. I am glad he is with her; there is no competition.

"This is the best fish I've had in Atacames." Johnny says, obviously wondering how that had been possible.

She pulls the visor of my cap down so she has to cock her face up to look at me. Her sly smile excites me. We have three beers each, and are laughing and joking. I pay the bill. Johnny excuses himself, and walks on into the village. Shirley and I hang around the beach area, having a couple of beers and watching the kids play in the waves.

Later, we watch the gigantic orange disk sink into the Pacific Ocean. The full moon rises in the east a bit later. We head back to Costa del Sol, walking arm in arm and she continues asking me questions. "So, you traveled around in Colombia too?"

"Yeah, I spent most of my time in the Llanos; that's a savanna region east of the Andes. I was on a cattle ranch down there and rode horseback all over. It was great." We talk about my adventures in Colombia, and about my plan to go down the Napo River to Coca.

"Coca?"

"Yeah; that's a town down on the east side of the Andes, the furthest one out in the bush—sort of Ecuador's port on the Amazon—that is, on the Napo which is a tributary of the Amazon. Actually, the town is named *Orellana*, or something like that, but everyone calls it Coca. Anyway, there was nothing moving on the river, because there had been a huge storm in the mountains. But, I'm going back down there one of these days. That's going to be one hell of a ride, down the Napo River to Coca. Someday, I'm going to just stay on the river and go all the way to the Atlantic."

I put my arm around her shoulder and hold her close as we walk along the beach. She puts her arm around my waist and holds me close too. My brain is racing, but I am determined to be cautious. I decide to risk trying for a kiss. She kisses back, and stands close so I can feel her breasts pressing against me.

She pushes my arms away and steps back. She pulls her T-shirt over her head and drops it on the sand, and then unbuttons her shorts and lets them drop. After a few seconds she pulls her panties down and kicks them off. The light of the moon is very bright but her face is shadowed and I cannot see her expression. I decide my best strategy is to do nothing. It isn't necessarily a homerun; she had stripped before for a swim and all I got was, '*don't get personal with me*'.

"Ray?"

"What?" I remove my T-shirt and shorts, and go to her. Her kiss tells me it is a homerun. We stand together for a minute, and then fall into the sand.

She runs into the surf and I follow. The water is chilly and we quickly came back for our clothes, shivering.

"Don't start acting as if you own me; as if you can have me anytime you want, okay? Because, you can't!"

"What are you talking about?" I ask.

"Look. We've had some fun together, okay? But, that doesn't mean you own me."

"I'm not trying to own you. I just want to love you."

"Well, you can't!" she says, and turns away down the beach.

"I've never met anyone like you. What the hell is this?"

She stops, and turns to me. "I'm not your girl!"

"I want you."

"You can want all you want, but I'm not your girl!" She turns and continues to walk down the beach.

I catch up with her and pull her around to me. "I just don't understand you. Why are you doing this?"

"It's very simple, Raymond; I don't want to be your girl; okay."

"Was it that bad?"

"I didn't say it was bad; for me it was the best ever...I don't want to talk about this Ray!"

We walk to her hut: "Maybe we should just call it a night," she says.

"No! I want to talk to you," I insist. "Come up to the deck and sit with me for a while, jeez."

We sit at the table, me drinking a beer, and her just watching the moonlight flicker on the top of the surf. "You said you liked it; you said it was the best. You know what that means," I say.

"Yes! It means you're an expert at sex!"

Her reply makes me mad. I grab her shoulders and shake her. "That's not fair, Shirley; tell the truth." Immediately I regret having grabbed and shook her; I wait for her harsh reaction, but it doesn't happen. Apparently she recognizes that what she said was a silly lie.

"It means we clicked," she corrects herself.

"Yes, WE; both of us!"

"You don't know how much we clicked."

"I know! It was the same thing for me!"

"You have no idea," she says, and it's true, I have no idea of what she is talking about.

"Okay, so I have no idea. Then tell me about it."

"I have a guy, Ray."

I deflate, as if having taken a hard punch in the stomach. "You are in love with him?"

"I have a guy," she repeats.

"Do you want to tell me about it?"

"He's good to me. I live with him on weekends in Frisco. I guess I would move in with him—marry him you know—if I had a job up there."

"Do you love him?"

"He's good to me. He has two boys. His wife died when the oldest was just twelve years old. She was my friend. He just couldn't deal with it, and somehow I fell in there. And, I love his boys. He has always been so good to me, and he loves me, and wants me to marry him."

"Are you going to marry him?" I ask.

"It's so good being with him, and the boys. I wish I had a job up there. I just can't leave my job, without having something else, ya' know? He gives me a lot of space, like letting me come down here, ya' know. But, I have to have my own income."

"I asked you if you loved him," I insist.

"Love doesn't have to be like that."

"Like what?"

"Like what you are thinking—that big emotional thing," she says. I am mystified. How could love not be a big emotional thing?

She continues, "Martha—that was his wife—she always told me about how she would take the boys to Little League practice on Saturdays. Well, when she died, I thought about those boys without their mother, and I just couldn't stand it. I called him, and told him I wanted to take the boys to practice, and he said fine. He said she— Martha, ya' know—always made them pancakes for breakfast on Saturday morning. So, I went over and made pancakes for them, and took them to practice."

"And, then one thing led to another," I fill in.

"Yeah, it did. He was terrified being alone, and the boys were really too much for him. She—Martha, ya' know—had always taken care of all that stuff. It was a new life for me. Do you know what I mean? Taking care of those two boys, and they love me so much, and need me. Do you know what I mean? I wasn't trying to take their mother's place or anything like that. I just wanted to be sure they had someone close by to take care of them, if they had any problems. Do you understand what I mean?"

"You aren't sleeping with the boys, Shirley." Immediately, I recognize my words as hateful, and regret them, but the words have already been spoken. She stands and turns away, with her arm over her face, as if I have slapped her. "Hey, I didn't mean it that way."

"I know exactly what you meant!" Her voice sounds is if she is choking back tears.

I stand, and put my arms around her. "Please, love. Don't take it that way."

"I just wonder how you can stand to be around a whore like me." She tries to pull away from me.

I can't let her leave me this way, so lock my arms around her, forcing her to stay. "I didn't mean that. Please, don't take it that way."

"You make me feel cheap. You insulted me, damn you! And, you meant to do it. You don't have the right!"

I hold her, and won't let her go. "Yes, I did. I did it on purpose; it was my damned jealously. But, I didn't mean what you said. Really, I didn't. I'm sorry I said that. You have to forgive me. Really; I couldn't stand it if you didn't forgive me."

"No!" She struggles to get away from me, and I have to let her go. I want to cry for being a stupid shit-head. I expect her to leave immediately, but she doesn't. She continues to stand, facing away.

"You just have to know, I didn't mean to say that. You have to forgive me."

After a long minute, she says, "Okay."

I put my arms around her again. "And, you have to forget I said that."

"How can I?"

"You just have to. Otherwise, you will always think I was thinking about you that way, and I wasn't."

"Okay." She turns around to face me, and rubs her eyes with the back of her hand. "We can't even get through one day together, without poking at each other, can we?"

"I guess not." I reply.

I walk her back to her hut, and stand at the bottom of the steps, while she walks up to the porch. "Shirley, I'm never going to think about what I said."

"Okay," she replies.

"You say that too."

"I'm not ever going to think about what you said, and I know you don't think that way about me."

"I really admire you for taking those boys to Little League. And, if you have a man who loves you, and treats you good, then you are lucky. That's a hell of a lot more than anyone could ever say about me." I turn and walk toward my hut.

"Are we still going to the village tomorrow?" She calls after me.

"I hope so." I say, looking back at her.

"I'll see you in the morning." She says.

I return to my hut and crawl into the hammock and watch the moonlight dance on the waves.

No One Blamed Her: San Jose, California, Spring, 1950

From the upstairs bedroom window the sixteen year-old girl watched her father's car turn from the street into the driveway. She examined the woman who stepped out of the car. She had never seen this woman before, but she knew it was her aunt—her father's sister. The aunt's visit had produced much argument between her parents.

"Margaret is a woman of the world," her mother had said; "I don't want her around my daughter." The girl had listened silently to her parents argue about the 'woman of the world' and she was filled with interest. She wanted very much to talk with this 'woman of the world'. In the end her father prevailed and Aunt Margaret was allowed to come for the visit.

The girl was tall and thin. Her features were angular and masculine. She was not a pretty girl, and she would do nothing to enhance her looks. She refused to wear make-up, or have her hair permed. She preferred to wear jeans. Her breasts were small, and she didn't need to use a bra. Instead, she would wear a T-shirt under her blouse, making the small mounds almost disappear. Her mother worried endlessly about her, and talked to her often about trying to be more feminine. The girl refused.

She had not told her mother that she had been molested on a school bus, three years before. She had been the last child in the bus, and the driver pulled the vehicle onto a side road. The man forced her to touch his erect penis; he squeezed her tiny breasts, and forced his finger inside her. Her screaming caused the man to stop. The man dropped her many blocks from her house, and she was late getting home. Her mother was angry with her for missing her bus and being late. But, she said nothing.

During the three following years, she developed a deep hatred of men, and decided she would never allow another man to touch her. She avoided the caresses from her father she enjoyed so much before. In her fantasies, she thought of punishing men, and especially the bus driver. One day she would kill him. She has told no one about being molested. But now, perhaps she would tell this woman of the world.

On the second day of her visit, Aunt Margaret borrowed the family car for a drive into San Francisco. She needed to sign divorce papers at a lawyer's office. The girl wanted to go. Her mother said no. "Please, Mom."

"Let her go with me, Helen. I'll take good care of her." Mother agreed reluctantly.

A few blocks down the street, Aunt Margaret tried to make conversation. "Do you have a boyfriend?"

"No, I hate boys."

"Well honey; there's no future in that," her aunt chuckled. "Don't worry, you'll get over it."

"No I won't! I will always hate them!"

"Really; how about the real cute ones? Don't you like them a little bit?"

"No, I hate all of them."

"Are you trying to tell me something, child?"

"A man made me touch his thing. He squeezed my chest and put his finger in me." The woman pulled the car over to the side of the road and stopped.

"When did this happen?"

"Three years ago."

"Did your mother go to the police?"

"I didn't tell her."

"You didn't tell your mother?" The girl shook her head. "Your father; your teachers?" The girl shook her head. "I am the first person you have told?"

"Yes."

Her aunt sat for a moment, dazed. "Oh, my poor child." The woman said, and put her arm around the girl's shoulder. "I'm so sorry, I'm so sorry."

That was not the reaction the girl had expected. The pain and humiliation had been inside her so long, she could no longer cry about it. And, why was Aunt Margaret sorry? The man was responsible, not Aunt Meg.

"We have to take care of this right now," her aunt said.

"What do you mean?"

"We have to tell your mother, and go to the police."

"No!"

"We have to. We have to do that for you. And, we have to do that for all the other children out there. Don't you realize this man has hurt you terribly?"

"Yes, and I'm going to kill him someday."

"Child, that man has to be put away. He may be hurting other children. Don't you know you have to do this for yourself, and for all the other children?" The woman turned the car around and headed back home.

"But, your divorce papers?"

"My divorce papers can wait. This cannot wait. Not one more day, and not one more minute."

The girl's mother became hysterical. She called her husband at the office. The father came home. The girl watched her father sit and weep quietly. She didn't hate all men; she didn't hate her father. She went to her father, and put her arms around him. "I'm sorry, Dad."

Her father hugged her. "You don't need to be sorry baby, you didn't do anything wrong. It was me; I should have protected you better. I'm so sorry I let that happen to you, baby. I hope you will forgive me for being a bad father."

"But, it wasn't your fault, Dad. You have never been a bad father." The girl was astonished by the reaction of her parents and her aunt. They didn't blame her. They didn't think she was dirty. They didn't look at her with disgust. They didn't blame her; they blamed themselves. *She felt sorry for them.*

Aunt Margaret called the police. The father and his sister would go to the police station to fill out the papers. Mother would stay with the girl. Later the girl would have to tell her story to a policewoman and identify the man. There might be a trial, and the girl would have to repeat the story on the witness stand. Facing the man might be a traumatic experience for her. Would she be able to cope?

There was no problem at all, the girl said. The terrible burden had already been lifted from her mind. She would not have to kill the man. She would help to save other children. There was no problem at all.

The girl and her aunt were inseparable. She insisted Aunt Margaret's bed be moved into her room. They talked into the night, and spent much of the day together. The woman seemed to know everything about life, and the girl wanted to learn.

Aunt Margaret had been in Paris when the German occupation began. She and her lover had escaped to Lisbon and taken a ship to Brazil. They had grand adventures, and loved each other so much. The woman related hours of their adventures in Brazil, and told how they had loved and laughed and had fun together. She left him when he wanted to marry and settle down. She wanted to continue living her life of adventure. She lived with other men, and had been married twice.

When Aunt Margaret's week visit ended, the girl couldn't be separated. She would go with Aunt Margaret to San Francisco. "No!" Mother said. Aunt Margaret's visit had to be extended. The woman really had no place to go, and a time to rest and share with the girl, was a welcome pleasure. The girl listened and learned.

YOU WANT US TO PRETEND: COSTA DEL SOL, SATURDAY, AUGUST 8

What is it?" There is just a hint of daylight when I knock on the window of her room from the porch.

"I thought you might want to have some breakfast before we go." I tell her.

"Just a minute." She comes out to the porch wearing shorts and a short-sleeved top, made of a silky material. "That's moonlight; the sun hasn't even come up yet," she says.

"I know, but it will come up in a few minutes, and we are supposed to meet Felipe at seven." I put my arms around her. "And, I love your outfit. I can see and feel right through it."

"It isn't an outfit. What you're feeling is my PJ's, not me. And, you can't see through them. And, don't kiss me; I need to brush my teeth."

"Okay, love. I'll wait for you on the deck."

"I'll be right there."

I go to the restaurant to confirm our early breakfast, and picnic food and drinks. The woman serves us breakfast, and brings out our picnic order. There is a large icebox with beer and soft drinks, and a huge basket of food. I had not thought about how we would carry everything down the beach, but the woman had. She has three boys coming to help. The boys arrive, and I send them ahead with the icebox and food. We walk along the beach near the surf, arm in arm. I feel closeness not there before.

She tells me more about her man. She likes him just the way he is. He gives her a lot of space. If she marries him, she is afraid he will change. She isn't sure she can get a job in San Francisco, and there is no way she will become dependent upon someone else's income. I listen, and I'm super careful with my comments.

Felipe wasn't kidding about having lots of kids. There are eight. The boys are in short pants, and the girls in dresses. No one in the family has shoes. They range from about six to the oldest boy, about seventeen. I recognize the boy as one of the fishermen in the second boat. Felipe's wife is a short round woman, with a permanent smile. The oldest girl is Margarita, perhaps fourteen or fifteen, and she's bursting out of her dress. She latches onto Shirley, immediately.

Shirley is delighted with the family and the boat, and the attention from Margarita. She will practice her Spanish with the girl, she says. They sit together in the front of the boat. I sit at the back with Felipe at the rudder. The oldest boy handles the sail.

We sail out on the land breeze, far past the village on the other side, and then come about, and tack back toward the village. I watch Shirley and Margarita. They sit close with their arms around each other and talk. The girl feels Shirley's hair and touches her nose. I wonder what they were saying to each other. I talk with Felipe, and think about the beauty and simplicity of life on this tropical coast.

At the village, we decide to split up—they to visit family, and we to explore the village. Margarita insists on accompanying us; *Mamá* says no. *"Let her go with us,"* I tell *Mamá*. *"She can show us around."* I really want to be alone with Shirley, but I know she is enjoying Margarita, and I want to please her.

Shirley and Margarita walk together arm in arm, and I tag along. The girl wants me to tell or ask Shirley this or that. I translate as little as possible, knowing Shirley is enjoying practicing her Spanish. Anyway, many of the questions are quite frank and embarrassing for me to repeat: Is Shirley married to me? Will she marry me? Do I give her money? Why doesn't she have children? Would she like to have a maid? I skip around the questions, and let language confusion fill in gaps.

We meet the family at the dock at mid-day. Both the wind and current are in our favor now. We stop at a shallow spot at the head of a small bay and fish for a while. They use hand-lines with old sparkplugs for weights. Felipe and his older sons catch a fish almost every time they drop the line into the water. They are perch-like fish, eight to ten inches long. Felipe says they are 'good eating'. Shirley and I try our luck, but without much success. The fishhooks are rusty and not very sharp. It takes a perfect jerk when you feel the nibble. We jerk a fraction of a second late, or jerk too hard.

Soon they have more fish than we can eat. Felipe explains he will pack the extra fish in the icebox after we finish the drinks. We sail to an isolated spit of sand and palm trees, and beach the boat. We have our picnic. The boys build a fire and roast fish to go with our sandwiches and drinks. There is no way to get Shirley away from Margarita, and I content myself by just watching them. Felipe and I drink beer and talk. The kids swim and play on the beach. Felipe walks away with *Mamá,* down the beach, and I sit alone watching the kids and watching Shirley.

On the ride back, Shirley remains at the front of the boat with Margarita, and I sit back with Felipe. She continues to talk with the girl, but she looks at me. She looks very deliberately, with no indication that she acknowledges me looking back. I feel something different in her eyes, and that feeling makes me want her very much. There seems to be a new magic between us. We beach the boat and roll it over the log away from the surf. Shirley tells the family the day was wonderful. Felipe will have his kids return the icebox. Margarita tries to hold on to Shirley and cries when we leave.

"You let me spend the day with Margarita, didn't ya?" I don't respond—not wanting to risk saying something that might make the magic go away. "It was wonderful, being with those people. It was something I never thought I would experience. You love all these people, don't ya?"

"Yeah."

"It's so wonderful. I've been down here, but I have missed so much. Do you know what I mean?"

"I don't know."

"No, I mean you really get into these people. I've never done that. Do you know what I mean?" I don't answer.

She stops and looks up and down the beach. There is no one in sight. The sun has set, and twilight is fading fast.

"Ray, I want to make love with you."

This new magic is real. It is late when we walk back to the huts. She talks, and I say as little as possible, not wanting to repeat any of my past mistakes. The Japanese woman has turned out the lights on the deck. I walk her to my hut.

"I have to go back to my place," she says.

"Stay here with me."

"Johnny will be coming home, and I don't want him to see us here."

"Just stay until he comes. Please."

"Okay honey, I'll stay for a while. Get in there, and I'll snuggle up with you." I get into the hammock and squirm around to straighten myself, and then hold my arms out to her. She rolls into the hammock and into my arms. I wrap my arms and legs around her and hold her. She closes her eyes, and I kiss and lick her eyes and nose, her cheeks and mouth.

"I've figured you out," she says.

"Oh, yeah? Well, I've known me for twenty-four years and I haven't figured me out yet. So, lay it on me love, I can take it."

"You want to play the 'let's pretend' game." I don't understand her. "You want us to pretend we are in love, don't you?"

"I'm not lying to you."

"I know you're not lying. You're just pretending, and you don't know you're pretending."

"How do you know that?"

"Ray," she frees her arms and takes my face in her hands, to force my complete attention. "How many times have you told me you love me?"

"Maybe, three or four times, and, I really do."

"Three or four times? You've told me that ten times at least."

"Not ten times." I say.

"At least eight times, maybe more. You told me that before we knew anything about each other. There's no way you could fall in love with me so quick. Talk about love at first sight!"

"You shouldn't make fun of me for saying that."

"I'm not making fun of you. I'm just explaining to you why you're doing it."

"I do it because I love you."

She pushes my face up a few inches away from hers. "You want me to pretend I love you too, don't you?"

"I want you to love me."

"No you don't! You want us to play a game—to pretend we love each other. That's what you want!"

I turn away from her and lie back on the hammock. She squirms around in the hammock until we are lying on our sides facing each other, with our foreheads touching.

"Look, it's not a bad thing to pretend. It's fun. Sometimes I like to pretend, too. Maybe, I would like to pretend I love you too, okay?" I remain silent. "Wouldn't it be great for us to be in love—completely in love with each other—for a while?"

"It would be great if you loved me for ten seconds."

"Well, that's what I mean. We could have a lot of fun together, and no one would get hurt."

"I wasn't planning to hurt you. But, of course, you're hurting the hell out of me all the time."

"No I'm not. I just haven't been playing the game with you. Maybe I will play."

Suddenly, I'm very interested. "Really; are you are going to pretend you love me?"

"Maybe."

"Really; and, can we be together? All the time together and I can have you?"

"Maybe."

The thought makes me dizzy. "Yes, love! Please, yes!"

"But, there are conditions. Both of us have to admit, from the beginning, we are just pretending."

"And, what if I'm not just pretending?"

"THEN YOU WILL JUST HAVE TO FACE THE TRUTH AND ADMIT IT!" She continues, "And, we both have to agree that when it's over we're not going to make some big thing out of it. You aren't going to send me flowers on my birthday." She changed her tone to express disgust and boredom, "And, you're not going to call me six months from now—none of that bull."

"How do we know when it's over?"

"It's over when you want it to be over—or when I leave you, honey. And, it's definitely over in three weeks, because I'm going home. That's it; fin! Kaput! I'm gone; you're out of my life! Don't stand in my road honey, or I'll run you down! Get the picture?"

"Jesus!" I am shocked at her frankness, but more than ready to accept her proposal. "Tell me you love me." I say.

"Wait a minute. There's another condition. We can't cut Johnny out."

"What do you mean?"

"Look, he's away most of the time doing his thing. I just mean we have to include him when he is around."

"INCLUDE HIM IN WHAT?" I ask, in shock.

"Oh, come on! You have a filthy mind, Ray!" She turns away and exhales loudly. Then she continues: "Just have lunch with him sometimes, or invite him for a beer or something."

"Well, I have no problem drinking a beer with Johnny once in a while."

"And, there's another condition."

"Another one; Jeez Shirley, how many conditions are there?"

"Just one more; we are going to work on your problem."

"What problem?"

"Don't do that again! Don't tell me you can't remember that you can't remember. I'm not going to put up with this denial. We are going to work on your problem. Do you understand me?"

"Hey love, we'll work on my problem."

"Your memory problem, remember? We are going to continue the therapy, and you will have to talk to Norma."

"Okay".

"And from now on, when we do therapy you have to take it seriously, and tell me the truth, okay? And, I mean the whole truth. And, if you don't make progress, I'm going to leave you; cause, I'm not going to be in love with a psychopath, okay?"

"After you fall in love with me, are you going to keep hitting me in the chest, and having conditions on everything?"

"No, honey;" she cups my face in her hands, "I'm going to just love you and hold you and kiss you." She gives me a special kiss as a demonstration. "But, you have to play the whole game, with all the conditions."

"Let's play."

We lie together quietly for a long time, and I wonder what's going to happen.

"**R**ay, I love you."

"Really?"

"Yes honey, I do. I just want to be with you, and close to you, all the time."

"Really? Really?"

"Yes, my love. I want to be your girl. And, I want you to be my guy."

I kiss her, and she kisses me back. "I can't believe it. We are really in love, and I can have you."

"Yes, but Johnny's going to be coming back soon. We can wait until later."

Johnny is later than usual. We sleep for a while. It must be well after midnight when I hear Johnny stumble past, obviously drunk. Immediately, Johnny is back down the steps of his hut, seemingly recovered from his drunken stupor. He runs to my hut.

"Ray, wake up! Shirley's gone!" He yells.

"Shirley's right here."

"Oh, that's fine." He says, turning back to his hut and then adds loudly, "I wasn't spying on her, Ray; I always check on her when I get home. I just want to be sure she's okay."

"I know, Johnny. Thanks." For the first time I really appreciate him.

"Thanks for that," she whispers.

"For what, love?"

"For what you said to Johnny."

I feel so much contentment, and try to breathe in all the pleasure I can.

Her smiling face is a few inches away. I caress her face with my right hand, and she does the same to me with her left—our other arms being wrapped around each other. "I love you," she says. "How many times have I said that now?"

"Two."

"Gee, I have a long way to go to catch up, don't I?"

"I have plenty of time. Did I snore?"

"No. You make some noises, but it doesn't bother me. Did you dream?"

"Yeah, I always dream."

"What did you dream about, honey?"

"I had visions of sugar plums, dancing in my head."

"Seriously," she says.

"I was dreaming about the army again, but it wasn't bad. I can't remember now, but it was a pleasant dream."

"So, the army wasn't all bad, huh?"

"No. Nothing is ever all bad, and nothing is ever perfect. Isn't that right, Shirley?"

I try to kiss her, but she turned away. "If you are going to kiss me, I'll have to go brush my teeth."

"Is that a hint about my bad breath?" I ask.

"No. I don't care about yours; I just worry about mine. Anyway, if I were concerned about that, I wouldn't hint—I'd just tell you. It would be okay to just say that, wouldn't it? We aren't just dating. We are in love, so we can just say things like that to each other, huh?"

"Sure." I respond.

"And, you have to tell me if something bothers you, okay. You know. Like bad breath, or my clothes or something. Otherwise, I would always have to be worrying about that."

I want to tease her. "Perhaps, I could just say, please consider some oral hygiene before French kissing." She giggles. "Or, perhaps you could show a bit more cleavage in front, dear."

"Cleavage"; she laughs, "I don't have any cleavage. I'm surprised you even noticed I had anything there."

"It's not size, love; it's form."

"Is that right?"

"Yeah, and this is the sexiest part here—right along the bottom. Once, I saw a girl with her tee shirt cut off and no bra, and when she moved you could see this bottom part. That was one of the sexiest things I ever saw."

"Really? I always thought men wanted to look at the top part—the cleavage."

"No, no, no. The bottom part is a million times more sexy."

"I'll file that away under useful information," she says.

"And, the sexiest part of all is right here—just above the top of your leg."

"You are really into the bottom edge of curves, aren't you?"

"I guess so."

"Johnny says we act like children. We really aren't very adult, are we?" She says.

"Who said we were adults?"

"We're not teenagers, but we sure do act that way, don't we?"

We untangle ourselves, roll out of the hammock. The shower is cold, "Kind of takes the shine off, doesn't it honey?" She asks.

"Yeah, sure does." We wet ourselves and stand away from the cold water. I lather soap in my hands and cover her body. For the first time I can really see and touch her body. "Go ahead and rinse."

"No, let me do you first. If I rinse, I'll be too cold to enjoy doing you." She goes through the same ritual. We rinse and shiver, dry and dress.

We have our breakfast mostly in silence. Just looking at her seems to be enough. Words are not needed, and I feel, would be in the way. We touch and smile at each other.

"Why don't we see some of the country together?"

"Sure! What about Johnny?"

"We'll invite him along. What's the possibility of you getting some time off your teaching job for the next three weeks?"

"I really hate to quit completely. Maybe, I could just cut back some. I could ask for Fridays off, and we would have four days each week."

"How about Tuesdays and Friday off? We would need at least five days to get down to the Amazon side and back."

"I'll check with Norma."

"So, the psychologist woman is your boss, huh?"

"Don't say psychologist woman! But, yeah, she's the principle of the school."

"I have an idea. Let's go into town and take the boat to San Lorenzo. We can check that place out, and if you could get Tuesday off, we would have time to take the train on to Ibarra. We can catch a bus back here on Tuesday afternoon."

"I don't know. I would have to tell Norma I would not be in on Tuesday, and I don't think we should just pull out on Johnny. We haven't even told him we are in love yet."

"Well, let's tell him. And, invite him to go with us; and you can call your boss and tell her you will be late."

Johnny finally appears on the porch of his hut, and comes over for breakfast. "Well, thanks a lot for telling me you wouldn't be home last night, Shirley." He says.

"I'm sorry. We really meant to tell you when you got back, but we were asleep."

"So? What am I supposed to think when I get here and you're gone?" He asks.

"We said we're sorry Johnny," she repeats. He glares at me.

"Hey," I say. "Actually, I was awake when you came by last night—she was sleeping. But, I didn't think to tell you she was with me. That was my fault. I'm sorry about that."

"Johnny," Shirley says. "We're ... Ray and I are in love."

"Oh shit!" He responds. "You promised you wouldn't do that." I haven't the slightest inclination to intervene, and remain silent.

"It's not a forever love, Johnny," she says. "We just want to be in love for a while—maybe for three weeks. And, then we will go on home—you and me—and that's it. You can understand that, can't you Johnny?" She reaches across the table and holds Johnny's face close to hers.

"I can understand it, but you're playing with fire here. You don't know who..." He glares at me again.

"Don't worry about Ray," she says. She gets up and walks around behind my chair. She puts her arms around me. "He's my baby." She says, caressing my chest and putting her face next to mine.

"Oh Christ, you're sick! You should see yourself!" Johnny says, with disgust.

"There's nothing sick about it. We're just in love."

"I can't believe I'm talking to my Shirley, my very own Shirley. What the hell is this guy doing to you?"

"He loves me."

"Oh wow!" He says, and then with resignation. "Well, I guess you want me out of here, huh?"

"No, we don't. We want you to stay. We just want you to know we're together. That doesn't bother you, does it?"

"Why should it bother me, baby? It's no skin off my ass. If you want me to scram out of here, I'll go. But, I feel kind of responsible for you, and I don't like it, okay?"

"We don't want you to scram. We want you to stay. Then you and I will go home, just as we planned."

"So what am I supposed to do? Sit around and watch you two play house together?" He gets up to leave.

"Wait a minute," she tells him. "Have your breakfast. Then, maybe we can all take a little trip."

He sits down. "Where?"

"We want to go to San Lorenzo—up the coast. It's supposed to be a neat town. Then, maybe we will take the train to Ibarra, and come back here by bus on Tuesday afternoon."

"You are supposed to teach on Tuesday." He says.

"Yeah, but I'm going to ask Norma to give me Tuesdays off—and Fridays, too."

Johnny begins his breakfast and is quiet for a minute. We wait. "I don't want to go to this San Lorenzo place. And, I especially don't want to go and watch you two play house together."

"It's okay if you don't want to go," she replies.

"I'll go if you want me to," he says quickly. "Look, I worry about you. What do I do if you don't come back?"

"Don't come back?"

"Yeah; how could I ever find you in there? This guy knows this country like the back of his hand."

"Jeez, Johnny, he's not kidnapping me."

"How do you know? For that matter, how does he know? Hell, he doesn't even know where he's going himself, half the time." Johnny replies, as if I am not there.

"You know I can take care of myself. What is this?"

"No, Shirley; I know you used to be able to take care of yourself. Now, I'm not so sure."

"Is this going to be okay for you?" She asks Johnny.

"Oh shit! Who cares about me? I'm just the idiot standing around watching you two slobber on each other."

She licks my ear and cheek. "Yummy, yummy," she says to Johnny.

"And, I can tell you," Johnny continues. "It's really sickening."

We return to our respective huts to pack for the trip. I dig out my small pack and throw in a couple pairs of underwear and socks, and an extra shirt, along with my toilet kit, map, and guidebook on South America. I change from my beach outfit to Levis and tennis shoes, and put my passport and money in the tobacco pouch. I am changed and packed in perhaps ten minutes, but Shirley is already waiting at the bottom of my stairs. She wears her long skirt and blouse, and has her small backpack.

"Did you remember your passport?" I ask her.

"Yeah; but why? We aren't leaving the country." We are already walking fast down the path.

"The law requires us to have the passport and visa with us at all times. I had my butt locked up in jail in Colombia for not having my passport with me."

"Really; what happened?" She asks.

I tell her the story as we walk down the path to the road. "I was in a village in the llanos—that's a savanna region east of the Andes. I got a room at a dumpy hotel, but didn't have my passport; I had left it in Bogota. So, I guess the hotel owner called the police, and a couple of guys in dirty tee-shirts with guns under their belts picked me up. They figure I'm with that bunch of missionaries down there, and they have no regard at all for missionaries. So anyway, they take me to their jail. Hell, it was a bamboo cage with a muddy floor—I couldn't even sit down. And, they tell me they are going to keep me locked up until Monday morning, when they can get a radio message to Bogota and check on my visa—no phones down there, ya' know. Fortunately, I was the only person locked up in there, but it was Friday night, so I figured they would be throwing the drunks and lunatics in there with me soon."

"So anyway, these two guys are sitting under a shed beside the cage playing cards, and by that time, it is about ten or eleven o'clock at night. And I said, hey man, can I buy you fellows a beer? And, this dude says, sure! You know, that's a funny thing; they didn't take my money. In fact, they didn't do anything illegal. So, I give him enough money to buy a whole case of beer, and he trots off and comes back with twelve of those big bottles of beer they have down there. I wanted to keep um' happy, and get em' to know I wasn't a damned missionary, ya' know."

"So, these fellows are sitting there drinking my beer, and giving me one too, ya' know. Well, it must have been about one or two in the morning when this jeep pulls up, and a Colombian Army Officer gets out. He has a clean uniform, and I know he is *gente decente*—decent folk you know, educated and middle-class. And, I know this is my chance, so I call this officer over. I said, hey man, I shouldn't be locked up in this fucken place. Well, actually, I didn't say that. I said, pardon me officer, I'm an American citizen and I have a passport and a valid visa, and just didn't have it with me. And, I told him I was a combat vet in Korea, ya' know, and he was impressed with that."

"So, he tells those guys they should let me out, but they said, hell no, he is *indocumentado* and he stays here till Monday morning. Actually, they are just going by the law, ya' know. I was wrong and they were right, and they were just doing their job. Anyway, this officer finally gets tired of asking them, and he orders them to let me out. They are really pissed off, but he out-ranks them, so they let me out. And, the officer told me I could stay in the hotel that night, but had to spend the Saturday and Sunday with him, until he could check my visa on Monday morning."

"So, what are we doing tomorrow? Well, guess what! He had a military exercise out there, and a company of soldiers were going to parachute in. And, I said, hell man,

I was with the fucken Eighty-Second, let me jump with your troopers. And, he said, sure, why not? Well, here I am in jail one minute and the next minute I'm going to make a jump with the Colombian Army! Hell, it can't get any better than this, I'm thinking. And, then it did!"

"Well, you know, there was a lot of wind on Saturday, and they had to cancel the jump and the whole exercise. So, this guy and the other officers wanted to go out to a hacienda, about thirty miles out from the Andes, so he could get TV reception, and watch a soccer game between Colombia and Argentina. And, of course, I went out there with them. And, I didn't care much for the soccer, so they gave me a huge horse and a *llanero* kid—a cowboy ya' know—and we rode all over the savanna. It was fantastic! I have never been on a horse that was so strong, and just wanted to run. We crossed creeks so deep the horses almost had to swim, and over hills and ya' know there are no fences for a hundred miles, and oh shit, it was wonderful."

"And, when we got back they had a big barbecue going. They had killed a beef and strung the meat on poles like a tee-pee with a big fire under it, and we just stood around with knives and carved off big pieces and ate it. And, they had these llanero fellows playing their harps and singing, and everyone was drinking beer and happy as hell. I couldn't believe it. It was one of the best things of my life, and all because they threw me into that pig-pen jail." She seems to like my story.

We are lucky at the crossroads. A pickup truck is headed into town and gives us a lift. We stand in the back of the truck and enjoy the wind. The truck drops us at the Plaza and we immediately take a bus to the dock. The boat is still there. I knew it was scheduled to leave 12:30 but counted on it being late. We get tickets and learn we will be delayed until two PM—another hour. We go to a nearby *tienda* and have a bowl of soup and a beer.

"Why don't you like the missionaries?" I give her a puzzled look. "You said, you didn't want them to think you were a missionary."

"I said they don't like the missionaries. Hell, I have no problem with um'. I just didn't want to get my butt in a sling by them thinking I was a missionary."

"So, why don't they like the missionaries?"

"Well, all these people are Catholics and the missionaries are *Evangélicos*, ya' know.

These Protestant preachers from the States are screwing all over the local culture, because they have a lot of money and they can provide services the local church can't."

"That's terrible. I don't blame them for not liking the missionaries."

"I don't blame them either. Hell, it's none of my business."

"What do you mean, 'none of your business'? You tell me the missionaries are down here trying to destroy the local culture, and you have no opinion on that?"

"Hey, we're just observers down here. Anyway, it all comes in one big package. You are just looking at the ribbons and wrapping paper on the box. It's never that way; there's always two sides to every story. For example, one reason the local people don't like the missionaries is because they are trying to save the wild Indians. The government and the farmers want those wild Indians dead and gone."

"What do you mean, save the Indians?"

"Well, they have medical clinics and give the Indians vaccinations, and give them antibiotics when they have infections. And, they make a big stink when the army or local farmers kill the Indians. My anthropology Prof in Mexico said all the wild Indians would die of disease or gunshot if it wasn't for the missionaries."

"Then, the missionaries are not bad! They're saving the Indians!" She exclaims.

"I didn't say they were bad. Anyway, good and bad depends on what side of the fence you're on. And, me? I'm not on either side of the fence. This is not my country."

"HOW CAN YOU SAY THAT?"

"Hey, we're just observers down here. They don't come up to the States and tell us how to think." Her look tells me I had better explain myself. "There are only a few thousand wild Indians out there in the Llanos, and only a couple hundred thousand in the whole Amazon basin. What right do they have to keep millions of people from going down there and farming that land?"

"The Indians were there first!" She exclaims.

"The Indians down there probably took the land from other Indians a few years ago, who took it from other Indians before that. So, how is this any different?"

"I CAN'T BELIEVE YOU!" Her eyes are wide and her head thrown back.

"So, what do you want me to do? Go out there and shoot wild Indians, or shoot farmers?"

"I don't want you to shoot anyone! I just want you to care about them!" she says.

"Okay, love. I'll care. We'll care together, okay? We can care about the wild Indians today, and then tomorrow we will care about the farmers. No, we should care about the farmers for a whole week, since there are a hell of a lot more of them to care about."

She stands and exhales my ideas right through the thatch ceiling and tile roof of the *tienda*. She walks outside and stands at the door with her arms crossed, and glares at me as if looking at a worm.

I go to the counter to pay the bill, continuing to drink my beer. *"How much for the soup?"* The man behind the counter shrugs. I figure the soup would be about ten pesos, but I drop a twenty-peso note on the counter. He opens a drawer below the counter and rakes the twenty peso note in. The drawer is filled with coins and paper money scattered about, without order, in piles and wads. *"And the two beers?"*

He shrugs again, and says: *"She is mad at you,"* shaking his head up and down, as if to confirm his statement. I nod, and think about asking him if he understands English. But, of course, he wouldn't need to understand English to know she is mad. *"Don't pay any attention to them,"* the man continues. *"They will make you crazy."*

I drop another twenty on the counter, knowing the beer is probably only four pesos each. Again, he opens the drawer and rakes the bill in. *"And, this if for the advice."* I tell him, dropping another ten-peso note.

The man rakes the ten pesos into the drawer too, and opens a bottle of beer for himself. *"Can you imagine?"* The man says. *"One so rich he sells beer, but so poor he cannot drink it himself?"* A woman yells from the other room—probably their living quarters: Why is he standing around drinking beer in the middle of the day; doesn't he have anything better to do?

"And, if this gentleman is the best client we have had in a week?" He yells back to the unseen woman. *"And, if he has paid twenty pesos for soup, and ten pesos for each beer, including this one? Shall, I tell him to keep his money and go away?"* I hear the woman

exhale loudly, obviously ending their conversation. The man shrugs. We tap our bottles together, and drink to each other.

"The human condition does not vary greatly, from one side of the earth to the other." I say.

"Not even this much," he responds, holding his thumb and index finger a quarter inch apart.

I meet Shirley outside, and we walk back to the dock. She keeps her arms crossed and her forehead wrinkled, and glares at me. It's like being a worm under that myopic vision of a robin standing above with his head cocked sideways. Twenty seconds of the stare exhausts me.

"I'm sorry, Shirley. Let's not talk about this. There's nothing we can do about it anyway."

"Okay, OBSERVER!" She says the word as she might have said rapist or plunderer to a criminal whose conviction was set aside because of a technicality. Rather than dig my hole deeper, I shut up.

We are back at the boat in plenty of time. The boat leaves at 2:45. The craft is an old sailboat with an inboard motor for use in the channel, and when there is no wind. Making the few miles up the coast will take almost four hours. The boat is crowded. Almost all the people are Black, speaking their Spanish dialect, and making jokes about the gringos on board.

There is a group of girls from the San Lorenzo school, all wearing their uniforms, returning home after a field trip to the big city of Esmeraldas. Like kids everywhere, they may be shy alone, but are super confidant in their group. They crowd around us as the main attraction.

Shirley is delighted. I let her practice her Spanish, and translate as little as possible. The girls are mostly interested in Shirley. They feel her hair and touch her skin, screaming and laughing to each other. I tell the girls we are movie stars, and we plan to make a movie about their school, and they will play the lead roles. They know I'm not telling the truth, but enjoy the fun.

Shirley is still not quite over my observer status. "If you tell them we are missionaries," she whispers, "you are going to regret it."

"I won't. I was just joking with them."

One of the girls asks Shirley if her nipples are also white. *"Cochina,"* the teacher yells at the girl, and swats her on the butt.

"Why did she hit her?" Shirley asks me.

I have to laugh. "That girl asked you if your nipples were white."

"Well, that's no reason to call her a pig and hit her."

I leave her to the girls. The teacher comes over to me. Who are we really; she wants to know. Obviously, very few gringos travel these waters. I tell her we are learning about the country, and want to see their town and take the train to Ibarra. What can we do for her school, she wants to know. She needs books, maps and paper—indeed, she needs desks and chalkboards and chalk. There is nothing we can do, I tell her.

Shirley calls the girl that had her butt slapped and pulls the front of her blouse down so she can see the nipples. "They are brown; like us!" the girl informs her friends. Several other girls rush over for a look, but Shirley has had it with that sort of examination, and pushes them away. Apparently, the price of seeing Shirley's nipples is a swat on the butt.

I think about the teacher's request and my observer status. *"Wait a minute; maybe you should speak to my woman here,"* I tell her.

I invite the woman over to where Shirley is sitting with the girls. "This is Ines; she is the teacher for this group of kids. She needs teaching materials for her school. Maybe you can help." Indeed, Shirley can help. From the conversation, part of which I translate, Shirley seems prepared to adopt the whole school. She tells the teacher of the Sister City relationship with Esmeraldas, and her connection with Norma at the High School. Can the Sister City arrangement be extended to San Lorenzo? Shirley is sure that can be arranged.

I have lost her attention for the boat ride, but I enjoy seeing her so happy, and hope she will get over being mad at me. Besides, remembering her time with Margarita, I figure it's an investment that will pay off big time later.

In San Lorenzo, we are forced to visit the school, and then, to my dismay, Shirley agrees to have dinner with the teacher in her home. I protest that we have to find a hotel, but the teacher will send someone to take care of that for us.

The dinner is rice and beans with "hen". Apparently, the woman thinks the older the hen the better, and has really put herself out for us. The bird must have been laying eggs when the Spaniards defeated Atahualpa; the meat is black and so tough you need excellent teeth and jaw muscles to gnaw off a sliver. Shirley gives up on the hen after the first try, but that doesn't dampen her enthusiasm. She will arrange the Sister City connection with San Lorenzo, and come down next year to work with the school, she tells Ines.

Between translations my eyelids flutter and I drift off. My head falls forward and then jerks up with a start. There is a huge grandfather clock against the wall that ticks off the seconds. I seem to do at least one head jerk every five to ten ticks. If I ever get Shirley back, I may be too old and worn-out to have sex with her. Time drags into an eternity! Finally, I pull Shirley aside.

"I wanted you to be with me!"

"I am with you."

"First you get mad at me, and then you spend the whole afternoon with this woman, and now you are going to stay all night!"

"We are going to the hotel after dinner, and we will be together in bed. Isn't that what you want?"

"I want you to be with me all the time, Shirley!"

Apparently, what I said is significant. She holds my face in her hands and looks into my eyes as if peering down a well for some hidden object at the bottom. "What do you see in there; my brains?"

"I like what I see in there," She says.

"Well, can we go?"

"Indulge me for a couple of hours; I'll make it up to you." She says. "Tomorrow, I will be with you all day. And, I won't get mad at you, even if you say stupid things."

'A couple of hours' is starting to sound like a real long time, but I muster all my strength and determine to survive the ordeal. We are finally able to leave the woman at 9:30. I regret introducing Shirley to the teacher, but am glad to see her so excited and happy. She has broken through another layer of isolation, to a new and more desperate level of need. She will bring the gospel, according to John Dewey, to this outpost of humanity.

At last, we reach the hotel arranged for us. The hotel is an old wooden structure, with cracks in the walls of our room. Shirley insists on turning off the lights. People will be peeking through the cracks, she says. The hotel has two common toilet stalls side by side and a single shower. There are cracks in the walls between the toilets and shower stall. Shirley has me stand outside while she uses the toilet to be sure no man goes into the other stall. In our room, we undress in the dark and get into bed. Shirley is ecstatic. She smothers me with kisses, and tells me she loves me.

Later at night, she lies asleep with her head on my chest. I think about the boat ride with Felipe and his family that led to the 'I want to make love with you' beginning of our new relationship. Shirley wants and needs to be with common people, especially people to whom she can be of service. She wants to help, to be of use—to be used—by real people who need her help. The more desperate the need, the more she wants to fill it. I have provided her with an opportunity to serve people who are several tiers below the level of poverty and isolation she has been able to contact previously. She loves me for it.

I think about those traits she demonstrates so clearly. You don't have that, I tell myself. I have always been content to observe. It has not occurred to me that I could make some kind of difference in the lives of the people I meet. Shirley does have that. She wants to make a difference. Of course, it won't work. The gap is too great. Just as there is White guy funny and Black guy funny in the army, there is rich guy stuff and poor guy stuff down here and the two won't mix. But, obviously success is not the point. Shirley finds pleasure in trying to help—wanting to help. I begin to think about her in a different way, and that makes me love her more.

PROMOTION TO CORPORAL: Korea, June, 1953

On Monday morning Baker Company was relieved on Zebra, and by late afternoon he was in his hooch in bivouac. Someone yelled through the door of the tent: "Richards, report to Lieutenant Snider, on the double." He rolled out of his bunk and hurried to the Lieutenant's hooch.

"PFC Richards, reporting as ordered!" He said, in a very loud voice. He saluted and stood at attention.

"At ease, Richards. From now on you're carrying my radio. You're assigned to Sergeant Fellows, in Headquarters Platoon, here in bivouac. You familiarize yourself with that fucken radio. I'm coming over there to check on you, and you better not be fucken off. You hear me, Richards?"

"Yes Sir."

"You pick out two of the best radios he has over there, and bring them back here to my hooch. You got that? I don't care if you have to steal um'. I want the best radios he has. This fucken shit isn't worth shit!" The Lieutenant said, and kicked the radio beside his desk. "You got that, soldier?"

"Yes Sir."

"And, I want four new batteries."

"Yes Sir."

"From now on I'm going to carry the extra radio, and a spare battery. You're carrying a spare battery too—YOU CAN GET SOME OF THAT GODDAMNED SHIT OUT OF YOUR PACK, AND PUT THAT SPARE BATTERY IN THERE. Are you following me, soldier?"

"Yes Sir."

"You're moving in with Corporal White. Get your shit over to his hooch tonight."

"Sir, excuse me. I would rather stay with the guys in my hooch."

Snider stood, "Soldier, do I look like someone who gives a fucken shit about what you want?"

"No, Sir."

"Then, you get your fucken shit over to Corporal White's hooch tonight. Now, did I make myself perfectly clear on that, soldier?"

"Yes Sir."

The Lieutenant sat, "And, I don't want you drinking with that son-of-a-bitch. If I catch you drinking whisky, or anything else, on the hill or in his hooch, you'll be in a world of shit. You got that?"

"Yes Sir."

The Lieutenant hesitated a moment, and then continued red-faced… "I'm putting you in for Corporal. You get those fucken stripes on your sleeve by roll call tomorrow; you hear me?"

"Yes Sir."

"The papers will come in later. You are not getting paid for Corporal this month. That doesn't start till all the paper work is completed. But, you get those stripes on now! You got that?"

"Yes Sir."

"And, no one needs to know the paperwork hasn't come through. Especially, Corporal White doesn't need to know. And, don't be fucken around with the grunts. You're an NCO, and fraternizing with grunts is off limits. Are you getting this?"

"Yes Sir."

The lieutenant was silent for a full minute, and then continued in a low voice: "From now on, while we are here in biv, you get Saturday and Sunday off. You will go to the NCO Club at Division, and stay in the NCO guest quarters."

His mouth dropped open in amazement, and then a broad smile began to spread over his face. She did it! She walked down the hallway, with her starched white dress brushing the backs of her knees, and raised the phone to her pretty face, and said gentle and innocent words. And, then an invisible hand reached out, and down the throat of the United States Army, all the way down to the lower intestine of that beast, to find the Eighty-Second Airborne Division. And, there in the muck of Zebra bivouac, located Second Lieutenant Snider, and jerked on his chain.

The Lieutenant stood, hardly able to contain his fury at the smiling soldier standing in front of him. "And, you don't go anyplace other than the NCO Club and the Guest Quarters. You are there to see your sister! And, you don't see anyone else but your sister! And, you don't go anyplace else! Do you hear me?"

"Yes Sir."

"If I catch you even thinking about fucken off, you're going to wish you had drowned in the biggest shithole rice paddy in this fucken country." The lieutenant sat. "That's all Richards, and I want to see those stripes on your sleeve at roll call."

"Yes Sir." He saluted, turned sharply, and left. Once outside the Lieutenant's hooch he broke into laughter, and a spasm of choking. He went to his hooch and packed his gear quickly.

"How do you rate promotion to corporal?" Corporal White asked.

"I don't know, Corporal. Maybe Snider just wants to see another stripe on his radioman."

"Yeah; well, fuck that son-of-a-bitch. Here, you want a drink?" The corporal offered him a half-full pint of whisky.

"No thanks, Corporal. The fucken Lieutenant says he is going to be checking to make sure I don't drink with you here in the hooch, or in the field."

"Yeah; well, fuck that son-of-a-bitch. And, don't call me corporal. You're gonna' be a fucken corporal tomorrow."

"Okay, White. Say White, you have any extra corporal stripes?"

"Yeah, I got a whole fucken foot locker full of um'."

"Can you let me have a couple of them? The fucken Lieutenant wants me to have them on tomorrow morning."

"Ah shit! Why not? Take everything; I don't give a shit." White kicks at his footlocker. "It took me five years to make corporal the first time; and it takes me about two months to get busted back to corporal every time I make buck sergeant. Shit man, corporal is the best rank in the fucken army. Nobody gives you any shit, and you can get into the NCO Club. Fuck all of 'um!"

He had known men like Corporal White, but rarely had an opportunity to share a personal conversation. Corporal White was typical of lifers—as career enlisted men were called—who were short on both intelligence and ambition, and long on Army regulations and whiskey. The Corporal was absolutely correct with superior NCO's and officers. He was a good soldier, and was prepared to walk into hell if commanded—indeed, he had done so on several occasions; he was RA. But, the Corporal's real attitude toward the army, and almost everything else, was best expressed with the phrase used to punctuate many of his statements: "Fuck all of um'."

He had wondered how inclusive 'all of um' really was. Clearly, everyone in the army and government was included, as were all the enemies and allies of the United States. Careful attention to the Corporal's use of 'fuck all of um' statements revealed that representatives of all public and private organizations were also included, as was anyone with a title in front of their name, all owners and workers in industry and business, all persons who earned their living providing services of any sort, and even most members of the Corporal's own family. He was able to identify only two exceptions, to the 'fuck all of um' rule—the Corporal's mother and himself. He had been blessed with that status, he reasoned, because a hooch-mate was as close as Corporal White ever came to forming a buddy relationship.

He remembered an occasion that typified Corporal White's attitude toward life. While in temporary bivouac, the men paired off and pitched their tents. He was paired with Corporal White. From his pack he extracted his shelter half and rope, along with a three-piece tent pole and five pegs. That's half a tent—standard issue. With the same components from Corporal White's pack, they could make a tent.

But, of course, Corporal White didn't have a shelter half in his pack, or a pole and pegs, either. Corporal White had other things to carry around with him: two onions, a bottle of Louisiana Hot Sauce, three cans of beans & franks, and two bottles of whisky. White scrounged around and somehow came up with an extra poncho and some commo' wire. The wire was used for secure telephone communications to outposts, and could be found abandoned just about everywhere. However, the poncho had to be stolen from somewhere or someone. He used the poncho along with the shelter half to jerry-rig a lean-to. It started to rain, so the Corporal immediately quit working on the lean-to, and crawled under and into his sleeping bag.

The lean-to was so poorly built, the bottom half quickly collapsed, and the bottom of the Corporal's sleeping bag was in the rain. The Corporal simply placed his helmet over his feet at the bottom of the bag, and left them in the rain. Disgusted with the Corporal's shoddy construction of the lean-to, he gathered more commo' wire and busied himself trying to stabilize it.

"What the fuck you' doing out there in the rain, Richards?" White asked.

"Shit man, there's a storm coming and this fucken thing is going to fall down in the middle of the night," he responded.

"Leave it alone—shit! The Corporal yelled to him. "The goddamn thing is gonna' be hell to tear down as it is!"

The corporal's logic was so apt he stopped his work and laughed himself to sleep in the storm. So, here I am, a Corporal, he thought. The best rank in the fucken army; fuck all of 'um!

POSADA SAN MARCOS: COASTAL ECUADOR, MONDAY, AUGUST 10

We are out of the hotel before sunrise. She wanted to dress early, so no one would peek at her through the cracks in the walls. I stand in front of the shower and toilet while she uses them. I had never considered how difficult it was for women to travel in outback places. I know men all over Latin America will peek at women at every opportunity, but didn't realize what a terrible burden that would be for the woman.

We have breakfast, and are at the train station at 7:30. The train leaves late, as we expected. The train is crowded, and we sit together on a short wooden bench with another man. Shirley takes the window seat, and I'm in the middle, so she won't have to worry about the other man touching her, she tells me.

"You think this guy would touch you, with me sitting right here?"

"They do it real subtle. They just let their leg or arm rub against you, and when you move they crowd over and do it again. You know exactly what they are thinking, and it's really uncomfortable." Again, I think about the burden of being a woman in Latin America.

Another bench faces us, with so little space between we have difficulty avoiding the knees of persons on the other side. The toilet is a wooden seat with a hole open to the railroad ties below. I tell her about the toilet, and she wants to see it for herself. Returning, she informs me she has just peed on half of Ecuador.

Most of the people on the train are traveling short distances, to villages along the way, so the train begins to empty. Soon, we have our bench and the one facing us, to ourselves. She moves to the other side and sits facing me, "So I can look at you," she says. We look out the window and at each other. I detect yet another look in her face.

Her face is more expressive than any person I have ever known. She is able to communicate without speaking. I consider her repertoire. First, there is the slight smile, calm face—her normal—which suggests happiness and self-confidence. Second, is her arched eyebrow look, that might say, I'm on to you, but I'm still enjoying your story, or if the mouth turns down slightly, I'm on to you and you better be out of town by sundown. Third is the, 'we have a secret' look, eyebrows down with mischievous grin, which she flashes at me occasionally. I think the secret we share now is sex. Fourth—the one I enjoy at the moment—is also eyebrows down and a broader smile. It says I love you. She punctuates that look by curling her lips into a tiny kiss to me. And, of course, there is the hard look that does not acknowledge a response. When I saw that look the first time, on Felipe's boat, it said I want you. It is a determined and certain look. I find it exciting, but I wonder if she would have that same look if she were holding a shotgun and about to blow my brains out.

We have a quick lunch and soft drink at Ibarra. She wants to look around, but I am in a hurry to get her to the *Posada San Marcos* in the highlands. We go to the telephone office, and Shirley makes her call to Norma about not teaching on Tuesday and Friday. Then, we take a bus headed south, into the mountains.

"What kind of place is it?" She asks.

"It's just another place, love—no big deal. I just want to check it out again. I'll explain it to you when we get there." In fact, Posada San Marcos is one of my favorite places in Ecuador, and I want her to experience the place as I had—just walking in from the road wanting a place to sleep for the night.

The bus stops in Otavalo, and we get off and have a coke. "This is a great town." She says, noticing the Indian flavor.

"Yeah, it is. We'll come back here, but we have to go on to the *Posada*."

The bus stops at the road leading to the *Posada*, and we get off. We walk down the cobblestone road past pastures and groves of eucalyptus trees. Across the fence are cows, sheep, donkeys, and a couple of horses. The *Posada* is about a half-kilometer down the cobblestone road. As we approach, we can see the high adobe wall that encloses the compound. The huge wooden doors are open, and it frames a picture of colonial Spanish America.

"It's beautiful!" she exclaims.

Just outside the wall Otavalo Indian women have sweaters and ponchos spread out on the grass for sale. The grounds inside the adobe wall are filled with trees and flowers, with cobblestone paths and arched passageways. From the entry of the main building, Andean music drifts past us. Flutes and drums, whistles and soft voices, perfume the air.

"Oh!" She says, as if losing her breath. "Oh, it's so beautiful."

That had been my feeling, when I happened by a month earlier, and I enjoy her reaction. We walk through the entry way and into the interior patio. An Indian band is positioned on the covered porch that faces the open patio. The cobblestone patio has several tables, some with people eating and drinking. Shirley walks into the patio to an empty table, and turns to me beaming her I love you look.

"I'm going to get us a room. Order for us; I'll be right back."

We listen to the music and eat fried pork, with cassava and plantain. Shirley is thrilled. She has never seen anyplace so beautiful. I have tricked her into thinking the place would be another dump. The room must cost a fortune. The music is haunting and exotic. She cannot tolerate so much pleasure and happiness. Have I ever experienced so much happiness?

Yes, I have tricked her into thinking the place would be another dump, because

I want her to feel the way I did when I first came here. No, the room doesn't cost a fortune; the tourists haven't found this place yet. Yes, the music is haunting and exotic, and I also love it more than I can stand.

"Let's look at the gardens." We walk around the grounds, hearing the music and feeling the serenity of the place. We go into the tiny chapel and examine the rustic beauty. We examine the field of produce and flowers behind the main structure. We go back to the entry garden and walk through all the arched passageways. We examine the cacti growing on top of the old adobe walls that surround the compound. We go out the gate, and buy a sweater from the Otavalo Indian women, and then look back through at the picture the gate frames.

After sunset we return to the patio and listen to the music and talk. We are in bed by 8:30. We have a real bed, and a shower with warm water. The air is cool. We snuggle together under two blankets. Andean music drifts through the window and the magic of the *Posada* surrounds us. Our night together is wonderful.

LEARNING ABOUT MEN CREATURES: SAN JOSE, CALIFORNIA, SUMMER, 1950

Aunt Margaret's stay with the family was extended for a week. Mother continued to be apprehensive about her daughter spending so much time with the 'woman of the world'. But, she could see her daughter's transformation and wanted that to continue. Her daughter was less withdrawn, and more open to her and her father. For the first time in several years, the young girl seemed to be happy. She was smiling again.

At the end of the second week, Aunt Margaret's stay had to be extended again. Two months later, when school started in September, Aunt Margaret finally said good-bye. Over the two and one-half months, the girl and her Aunt spent hundreds of hours together. They talked. Mostly they talked about men creatures. Aunt Margaret didn't hate men.

"But, you are divorcing your husband."

"Yes, because I couldn't control him. But, I'm going to find another one."

"Why do you want one of them?"

"I'm going to get old, honey. This is my last chance to find a man I can live with, and grow old with. There are some good men out there. They can give you a lot of pleasure, and they can help you. It's really tough to be on your own. There are a lot of freaks that will take advantage of you. But, if you have a good man, he will protect you, and he can make a lot more money than you can."

"How do you know if he's a good one?"

"Well, who the hell am I to tell you, honey? I just made a bad mistake—I've made a lot of mistakes. But, the truth is, all my men have been good ones. If you follow the rules, you're pretty safe."

"What are the rules?"

"Well, men are kind of dumb—I don't mean stupid. Sometimes, they're real smart—you know, maybe a lot smarter than you about most stuff. But, they are really dumb in the important things. You can usually tell what they're thinking. And, that's the first rule: If you don't know what he's thinking, stay away from him. That's usually the kind that turns out to be a real bastard, and he can hurt you really bad."

"What will he be thinking?"

"Well, when you first meet a man, he will just be thinking about getting your panties down."

"That makes me sick! That's why I hate them."

"Whoa, honey. There is nothing wrong with them thinking that. You are the one that gets to decide whether your panties come down or not. And, they can't help thinking about it. The point is, it's easy to read their minds. So, you know what they are thinking, and they don't know you know. See? That's your advantage. They don't know what you are thinking, but you know what they are thinking—right from the get-go."

"How can you stand them?"

"I'm not going to tell you they are easy to put up with, but it's not all bad. And, there are a lot of things about them that can be good. I mean real good!"

"What? What is good about them?"

"I'm not going to tell you about sex, because you had a terrible thing happen to you, and it's going to be a long time before you can think about that."

"Is that the only thing that's good about them?"

"No, there is a lot of sharing and fun. It's really great to share yourself with someone, and have that person share himself with you. Love can be really fulfilling. And, they are lots of fun; it's so easy to trick them, because they are dumb, you know. So, you can pull all kinds of stuff on them that would never work with your girlfriend."

"Like what? Give me an example!"

"Like, one time while I was with my first lover, down in Brazil, I just said, I'm leaving you, and started walking out the door. You should have seen him. He was on his knees begging me to stay, and I said, hell honey, I'm just going down to the market to get a bottle of wine, and started laughing. It was so funny." They laughed. "Sometimes you just say, you don't love me anymore, and it breaks his little heart. It's so funny. One time—with my last husband, you know—I was talking to my mom on the phone, and when I hung up I said, Dad lost his job, so he and mom are moving in with us. His mouth just fell open. He was in a state of shock for a couple of minutes, and then I just started laughing."

"Do they try to trick you back?"

"Yeah, but he always has this big stupid grin on his face, so you know right away. But, you play along with it, because otherwise he wouldn't think it's fair when you do it to him. Yeah, I can tell you that I am going out and find myself another man to live with—a good one. To have someone who really wants you, and needs you, is really important. I can tell you."

"How can you be sure he will be a good one?"

"There is no sure sign, but I can tell you some of the things to watch out for. And the main thing is that he wants to be close to you. And, he wants that even more than he wants to get your panties down."

You Never Understand Anything: Ecuador, Tuesday August 11

"**W**here are you going?" She is on her side facing me, with her arm over my chest. I had tried to move her arm carefully, to avoid waking her.

"To the bathroom." I answer.

"No!" She holds me with her arm, and throws her leg over me.

"I have to go to the bathroom, love."

"No! You're going to run away from me."

"Run away from you? What the hell are you talking about?"

"I'm not letting you go!" She says, holding me tight.

"Shirley? I just want to use the bathroom." I hear her choking; she seems to be crying. "Jeez, Shirley; I'm not going anywhere. I just want to use the bathroom." Then, I realize she isn't crying—she's laughing. "Damn it, Shirley!" I push her away and go into the bathroom.

She laughs and calls to me through the door, "Please don't run away from me. Can I come in and hold your hand?"

I don't think she is funny, and tell her. "I jerked on your chain a little bit, didn't I?" She says, continuing to enjoy her joke.

"I really don't see why you think that's funny, Shirley. I wouldn't do that to you."

"Oh no? You do your deadpan idiot stuff all the time."

"You knew I was joking about that stuff."

"That's because I'm not dumb enough to be fooled by it. But, it's so easy to trick you." She is still having a big laugh.

"Don't joke about that." She gives me an inquisitive look. "Don't joke about us being in love. You can joke about anything else, but not about us caring about each other, or about Donna."

"Donna?" She becomes serious. "I wouldn't joke about... Any more that you would..." She gives me the long exhale treatment. "Talk about me thinking you are the biggest shit-head in the world. What must you think of me?"

"I know you wouldn't joke about Donna. It's just that—well, damn it Shirley, you shouldn't joke about us loving each other."

"I didn't joke about us loving each other. And, I don't want you to do that either. I just didn't want you to run away from me. That's fair." She starts giggling again, "It's so easy to trick you, and you take it so seriously. One of these days, I'm really going to jerk on your chain."

Would she really do that to you, GI, I ask myself? Hell yes! She has motive and opportunity. What's she going to pull? I try to put myself on alert, but it's no good. It's like trying to be prepared to step on a snake in the bush. You can't even enjoy the walk, and the snake is going to startle you anyway. You know that snake is out there man, and you know it's going to startle you eventually. But, there isn't a damned thing in the world you can do about it, I tell myself. You might just as well stomp on through the bush, and enjoy yourself.

When I wake Shirley is looking at me; she doesn't have her usual morning smile. "What's the matter, love?"

She waits for a bit and then responds, "We are really something together." I nod. "Why is it so much for us?"

"It's because we love each other."

"You're trying to make me..." she pauses, as if to think of a word, "want you."

"I want you to want me."

"Stop trying to do that!"

"Don't you like it?"

"I love it!" She exhales the words, and changes her expression to the—I'm either

200

going to rape you, or blow your brains out—determined look. I am not sure what she is trying to tell me.

"We have been together for a whole day." She says. "Together continuously since Sunday night, that's thirty-six hours. We haven't even talked to another human being."

"You are making up for spending all that time with Ines on Sunday, huh?"

"How can we stand it?"

"Don't you like it?"

"Yes! But, how can we keep doing it?"

"Keep doing what?"

"Being together all the time! If we keep this up, one morning we will wake up and won't be able to stand to look at each other anymore."

"No we won't." I don't enjoy her discussion, and cover her mouth with mine. We make love.

"I want to talk to you."

"Not therapy now!" I respond. "We can do that later. We will be lucky to make it in time for the last truck to Atacames."

"This is for me; and, we have to do it now. I want to ask you some things, okay? Will you be serious about this?" I nod. "You want to be with me, don't you?"

"Sure."

"You want that even more than you want to make love with me, don't you?"

"Jeez, Shirley; without that, there wouldn't be anything. Are you going to stop making love with me?"

"No! I know we couldn't be close without making love. But, we could make love without being close to each other all the time."

"Why would we do that?"

"Lots of men do that! They just want to make love with their wives, and then go out with their friends. They don't want to spend their time with her. Maybe they would rather just go to a whore house, and not have to bother with being around a woman all the time."

"Well, I wouldn't want to just have sex with you."

"Why not; that's what makes you feel good! Why wouldn't you want to just have sex with me and then go out and have fun with your friends?"

"You are my friend. And anyway, if you didn't enjoy it, I don't think I would either." I tell her. She holds my face in her hands and looks at me intently. Once again, I have said something significant.

"So, you want me to stop hanging around you all the time?"

"NO!" She responds emphatically. "You never understand anything!"

The bus is roaring up and down mountain roads, and she is sitting at the window seat beside me. "I have to tell you something," she says. "Look honey, Norma and I had already decided that I would be in charge of your day to day therapy, and I would report to her. That was before we fell in love. But, I didn't fall in love with you because of that. And, I was going to make you promise to do the therapy, and see Norma, even if we hadn't fallen in love, okay?"

"Sure."

"Anyway, I'm in charge of the day to day business. Like, I'm on the front lines you know, and Norma is the general back at headquarters, running everything. I explain it to you as if it were military, so you will understand it."

"I understand it."

"Well, anyway when the time comes, she's the surgeon. You'll have to go in to see her."

"Surgeon; what the hell is she going to do? Give me a lobotomy?"

"It's just a figure of speech. You know what I mean. You just have to talk with her. But, that's not going to be easy. She told me it would be hard for you to come in to see her, and even harder to sit down and deal with it. And, she said it would be a waste of time, unless you were completely prepared to deal with it. That's my job. To be sure you are prepared to deal with it." She lets that sink in. "There is something else; I have to tell her we are together now. It won't be easy to tell her that, but I have to."

"Why? I don't see why that should concern her."

"Look honey, we have to tell the truth, and tell the whole truth. Otherwise, it's just a waste of time. Anyway, when I tell her we are together, she may take me off your... she may think that would disqualify me doing therapy with you."

"Well, you can tell her I don't want anyone else on my case. And, don't think I'm going to talk to anyone else about this stuff."

"You promised to talk to Norma."

"Okay, with Norma. But, not with anyone else but you and Norma! And, I still don't see why our personal thing is related to this therapy stuff."

"I told you honey, you have to tell the truth; otherwise we are just wasting our time on this. Besides, Norma is my friend. I always tell her everything, and she gives me advice." She continues, "I think I already know what her advice is going to be, and I don't think I will take it." I know what Norma's advice will be, and I hope she won't take it. "Johnny will be worried sick." She says.

We are lucky with the buses. We reach the Esmeraldas crossroads by eleven AM and get an Esmeraldas bus less than an hour later. With luck we can make the Atacames crossroads before the last truck. We sit close and talk and nap, and talk again. "We haven't done therapy for two days." she says.

"You're giving me a break, huh?"

"No. We just haven't had any good opportunities. You can't do it on a bus or train because—you just can't do it."

When we reach the Atacames crossroads, the five PM truck had already passed. A light rain begins, and it looks like there will be more coming. I take two trash bags out of my pack and cut head and arm holes. We put them over our heads and walk in the rain. I am worried. The sun is setting and daylight will be gone soon. The moon will not rise till nine PM or so, and the clouds will even block the starlight. I don't mind stumbling along a road in the dark, but am not sure how she will react.

We are lucky again. Just three kilometers into the walk, a pickup comes by and carries us to the Costa trail. We are in Costa by 7:30 PM.

Johnny is waiting and worried. "Don't put me through this again, Shirley. I can't take it." He says.

"Put you through what, baby? We didn't put you through anything."

"Oh shit! I was about to head into town and call the FBI. They probably have his prints on file in every office in the country. Course, it would take the CIA to track you down in there."

"We're just a little late, Johnny. What is this about the FBI? You would think I'd been kidnapped or something."

"Yeah; or something!" He storms away to his hut.

We go to my hut—our hut now. "What do you say, love; hmmock or bed?" I ask her.

"Honey, I love the hammock, I really do. But, my arms go to sleep when you are lying on them. Maybe we could sleep in the bed tonight. Will that be okay for you?"

"Shirley love, that will be perfect."

She insists on taking a quick shower alone and comes out wearing her pajamas.

"What the hell is this?" I ask.

"I thought you said you liked my PJ's. You can see and feel right through them, remember?"

"I can see and feel better if you don't wear anything."

"You can't touch me tonight." She says.

"Can't touch you; why not?"

"That's none of your business!"

"How about tomorrow morning?"

"No!"

"Oh; you're menstruating."

"Why do you have to say it?" she huffs.

"I know about that; it's no big secret, you know. Anyway, it means you're not pregnant."

"I know how to take care of myself! And, that's none of your business either." She rolls over on her side, facing away from me.

"And, anyway why do you have to wear the top? That has nothing to do with it." She pulls the top off and throws it in the corner. I snuggle up against her, so I can feel her butt against my thighs.

"I'm warning you, Ray!"

"Can't I even be close to you?"

"Yes. But, if you try to touch me, you're going to be sorry."

THESE WOMEN WILL DRIVE YOU CRAZY: Korea, Summer, 1953

Life became a repeating, three-part drama. First, there was a week on Zebra Hill. He would follow Lieutenant Snider, in a crouched jog, down a 'commo' trench—a lateral trench connecting the Main Line of Resistance to an outpost. In the outpost he would sit at the bottom of a trench or in a bunker, repeating commands from the Lieutenant into his radio, and try to snatch a moment to think about Donna. Second, was the five days of doldrums in bivouac, pretending to work in the radio shack, and drinking beer with Patterson at night. Third, the Friday evening rides to the Division Headquarters, and Donna.

She would meet him in the lobby of the NCO Guest House with a key. Often, he would hardly speak to her as they hurried to the room. She seemed to feel the same way, and words were not needed. Later they talked. That is, mostly she talked and he listened and petted her face and body.

Good-byes became tearful events on Sunday evening. She was concerned about the increased level of fighting at the front. The war had intensified, ironically because the peace talks had begun to make progress. Indeed, two hills in his sector had been hit—taken by the Chinks and retaken by the army—with a huge number of casualties. The MASH units, supporting two other Battalions, had been pressed into service to support MASH4, and the hospital at Inchon was flooded with wounded and dying men.

Donna wanted him transferred out of the Eighty-Second. He refused, and refused to discuss the issue. "I was in the fucken Eighty-Second when you met me, and I'm staying in the fucken Eighty-Second. Don't sweat it babe, I just have five months to go. I've made it this far, and I'm going to make it all the way. And, don't try to work it without telling me. Nobody but nobody is transferred out of the Eighty-Second, without him requesting it, and even then they wouldn't let um' out. So, if anything happens, I'll know you did it."

He worried about his motives. He needed support, and sought that during a beer drinking session with his friend.

"I'm not doing it because her father is a general." He told his buddy.

"I know that, man. But, why shouldn't you take advantage of your good fortune?" Pat responded. "Maybe her father will get you a job at Division. You could get out of this shithole, and spend all your time with her."

"I'm not trying to get out of it, Pat!"

"I know you're not trying to get out of it. But, why should you be stupid? There's nothing wrong with taking advantage of an opportunity that falls right in your lap."

"I'm not trying to take advantage of it! I just want to see her, and the only way I can do that is to be an NCO." His friend was silent. "Well shit, Pat, you act like I'm just using her to get a soft job, and get out of this fucken shithole. Next you're going to say I want to marry her for her money—shit!"

"Hey man, it's not me that's saying that; it's you. You've got a fucken hang-up GI. You better get over it. This gal's had connections and money all her life. If you can't deal with it you better forget her and go down to the whorehouse with the rest of us."

The war continued to intensify. There were peace talks and lots of sparing on the ground, to gain some unknown advantage. On Wednesday one week in bivouac, he was called to the First Sergeant's desk to answer a telephone. He stood in front of the First Sergeant and spoke nervously.

"I had to call you honey," Donna said softly. "I'm pregnant." He couldn't respond. "Is someone there?"

"Yes."

"Okay, I'll do the talking. Honey, we have to get married right away. Do you want to marry me?"

"Yes."

"We are going to get you a two week furlough to Japan. My parents will be there. We will be married in Japan. Is that all right?"

"Yes."

"I don't know how long it will take. Papa is in Washington, and can't get away now. Mama's coming over to Japan next week, and I'm going to meet her there, so I won't see you next week."

"Okay," he replied.

"As soon as Papa can get away, we will arrange your furlough, Okay?"

"Yes."

"I'm sorry honey. I swear I was using the diaphragm just like they told me. But, it didn't work."

"That's Okay."

"I wanted us to have a couple of years together before we had kids, honey."

"So you could decide if I'm the right guy?" He responded. The First Sergeant raised his eyebrows, and began to tap the desk with his fingers.

"No, I know you're the right guy. I just wanted us to have some more time. I love you."

"Me too," he said, and hung up the phone. He left the First Sergeant's tent in a haze, unable to think. He wanted to share this revelation with Patterson, but didn't. Everything was happening too fast.

Two days later, he was called to the First Sergeant's tent again, for another phone call. The First Sergeant was obviously pissed off.

"Hello," he said.

"Honey, I'm not pregnant. My period came this morning. I had to call you," she said. "Are you alone?"

"No."

"Then, I will talk. Honey, you don't have to marry me. I'm not pregnant."

"I want to."

"It's as if I'm forcing you. I don't want it like that."

"No. It isn't that way. Do you want to?"

"Yes, but I want you to be sure about it."

"I'm sure."

"You think about it for one day, and I will call you back."

"I don't think they will allow that."

"They will allow it. You have to think about it for one day. I will still love you if you say no."

"I won't say no."

"Bye honey, I love you."

"Me too," he said, and hung up the phone.

The First Sergeant stood up. "You think I'm running some kind'a Girl Scout club here Richards?"

"No, First Sergeant."

"Then, get your fucken ass out of my office!"

He dreaded the call the next day. The First Sergeant stood in front of him and glared, as she spoke to him on the phone.

"Did you think about it?"

"YES SIR!" He responded sharply, in the First Sergeant's face.

"Do you still want to do it?"

"YES SIR!" He shouted again.

"Jeez! You're yelling 'yes sir' at me. Are they watching you?"

"YES SIR!" He shouted into the First Sergeant's face, looking him directly in the eyes.

"Right there in front of you?" She asked, incredulously.

"**Yes Sir**!" He shouted, even louder.

"Okay, I'll do the talking. Are you absolutely sure? I will still love you, even if you don't want to do it now."

"**Yes Sir**!" He shouted.

"We have to postpone for a while. Papa is still in Washington and can't get away for at least three weeks. Mama's still coming over to Japan next week, and I will meet her there. We will arrange your furlough. I will call you from Japan, to let you know the dates."

"**No Sir**!" He shouted.

"Okay, I won't call. When your furlough comes through, you will know it's on, okay?"

"**Yes Sir**!" He shouted, in the First Sergeant's face.

"I'm sorry if my calls have caused you problems there."

"Yes Sir," he said more softly.

"I love you."

"Yes Sir," he said, this time in a low tone, and hung up the phone.

"Richards, I don't want to hear any more'a yo' shit!"

"Yes Sir."

"What do you mean Sir; I'm no fucken officer."

"I'm sorry sergeant, I was talking to a general, and I got confused."

A month later he visited the First Sergeant again, this time to pick up furlough papers. He was to represent the common soldier at a meeting of high-ranking officers and VIPs in Japan. The First Sergeant was beyond anger and had resigned himself to a grudging admiration of the power this young trooper was able to command.

Donna met him at the gate in the airport in Tachikawa, Japan. They went directly to a hotel she had arranged. The next day, they took a taxi to Camp Drake, the US Army base just outside Tokyo. "I told them you were arriving today," she explained. He wondered how she could explain her absence for the past 18 hours. The taxi took them to a large house in the General Officer's section of the base. They walked into a lavish home.

"This is Mama." Donna said. The woman was short with olive skin and large black eyes. She rushed to him, throwing her arms around his waist, and pressing her very large breasts into his lower chest.

"Oh Sweets, he is so beautiful!" Mama said, to everyone but him, and kissed him on the mouth. Mama pulled his cap from his head and felt his flattop haircut. Her voice was loud and filled with laughter and her dark eyes darted between him and her daughter. "He's so pretty," the woman continued, and moved around behind him with her hands around his waist, her breasts now pressed against his back. "I'm keeping this one for me. You go get another one." Mama spoke to Donna as if he were a new toy.

Donna came over and pulled him away from her mother. "This one is for me, Mama." She turned to her father. "This is Papa."

The middle-aged man gave the impression of enormous dignity and self-assurance. He wore dress army uniform, with two stars on his lapel. He stood very straight, making him appear taller than his six-foot stature. He retained most of what must have been a very athletic body in youth. His face was as if made of leather and his blue eyes were bright and alert. He would have conveyed the bearing of a man in total control, were it not for the obvious fact that in this household, he was not in control. Mama was in charge, and maybe even Donna was in charge. But, there was no contest, and Papa was not threatened.

"How do you do, Sir," he said stiffly, shaking the general's hand.

The general shook his hand, spilling some of the drink he held in his left hand. "No one calls me sir around here, son. Can I fix you a drink?"

"Yes sir."

"What will you have; a martini?"

"A beer would be fine, Sir."

"Mama, we have any beer around here?" And, without waiting for an answer, "Here son, let me fix you a real dry martini."

"Thank you, Sir."

"Stop being so military; this is Papa." Donna crowded between the bar and her father. She kissed her father's face several times. "And, I love him so much." The man seemed not to notice her attention, but concentrated on fixing the drink. "And, I especially love him for what he did for us." Donna continued kissing his lips and cheek.

Mama crowded in behind the bar with the two of them, apparently unable to miss out on the kissing and hugging. He was flabbergasted. They all talked at the same time. Whether or not someone was listening did not seem to be a major concern. They touched and caressed, kissed and shouted. Mama, someone would say, and the woman would run—not walk, Run—to attend to this or that. Mostly, she attended to Papa and Donna. Apparently, they were in almost continual need of being combed, brushed, led about the room, and pampered.

The General told him stories about the Big War, and he tried to listen. He looked over at Donna and her mother, who sat on the couch with their arms around each other whispering and laughing. "These women will drive you crazy, son. Don't pay any attention to them." The general said. "Hell, who knows what they talk about? Ready for another drink, son?"

"No Sir. I'll just work on this one." The drink was almost straight gin and he already felt dizzy.

Donna and her mother surrounded him, and talked about him to each other, as if he were unable to hear them. They touched and petted him, laughed and squealed. He tried to listen to the general, who apparently took no notice of the women. This place is an insane asylum; he thought, and began to laugh. The general gave him a twisted look, as if he were laughing at what the general had said.

"Excuse me, Sir," he said quickly, and by way of explanation, "They are poking me in the ribs."

"Yeah? Well, don't pay any attention to them."

"Yes Sir."

Papa certainly heeded his own advice. Indeed, Papa seemed to be oblivious to their talk and pampering. The fact that the martinis had him several sheets to the wind probably helped, but something else was clearly at work. During one incredible ten minutes, as he rambled out a war story, Mama decided he was too hot, and removed his coat, and then decided he should have the coat on during dinner, and replaced it. She combed his hair to cover a bald spot, and brushed cigarette ashes off his pants. During the same period, Donna sat in Papa's lap, and while kissing his cheek, ran her fingers through his hair, which Mama promptly re-combed to cover the bald spot. Incredibly, Papa seemed to notice none of this, and continued his story without missing a beat.

After dinner, and more drinks, Mama announced bedtime. He and Donna were assigned separate bedrooms. A few minutes after the door to Mama's bedroom door closed, Donna came to him. They lay together whispering.

"How do you like Mama?"

"Jesus!"

"She's kind of loud and pushy, but you will get used to her."

"Did she really tell you all about sex?"

"She told me everything."

"Everything?"

"Yes, everything!"

"Jesus!"

"Well, why would she want me to be stupid?"

"No, she's right. There is no reason to keep it a secret."

"No, of course not! And, stop saying Jesus all the time. You make it sound like we're crazy."

'Jesus!' He said, under his breath.

The wedding was a formal military affair. He wore a tailored uniform complete with spit-polished boots and a blue silk scarf at the top of his shirt. Many high-ranking officers were there, all of whom seemed to know and love Donna.

The commanding general of the Eighty-Second Airborne attended, and offered—more like ordered—him to take a job at division headquarters as a personal aid. He refused the offer, and stated flatly that he would prefer to remain in his unit for the duration of his stay in Korea. Donna was furious, and Mama brought to tears by her daughter's concerns. But, his division commander and Papa had been as proud of their soldier as they would have been of a new hunting dog, bringing back its first bird.

They spent their honeymoon riding trains around Japan, staying in Japanese-style hotels, eating sushi, and mostly loving each other. The furlough over, she flew back to Korea with him in a military plane. They parted, hoping to meet at the NCO guest quarters in two weeks, this time as husband and wife rather than masquerading as siblings.

SOMETIMES THE BAD GUYS SHOOT BACK: COSTA DEL SOL, WED., AUGUST 12

I watch the daylight slowly reveal her face. She is on her side facing me. She has her normal calm look, but slightly more relaxed. Her breathing makes a low hum. I examined her face carefully. I have looked at her so much during the past days, but I have never really seen her face. I just read the expressions she passes me. Now, I can look at her in a different way.

Shirley is not a pretty woman, I tell myself. No, her face is way too strong to be pretty. There's definitely a little bit of Indian blood, or maybe oriental, just enough to raise her cheekbones, and push her mouth out slightly. Her beauty is in her strength and self-confidence. Yes, and that she is so comfortable with herself. She thinks of herself as a beautiful woman. I smile, and as if moving my facial muscles is sufficient to wake her, she opens her eyes. The slight relaxation in her face disappears, and her expression changes to normal-calm and then to the 'we share a secret' look. Her face dissolves into that expression.

"How long have you been looking at me?"

"A few minutes—since daylight. I woke up at dawn, but I couldn't see your face until a couple of minutes ago."

"It's not a pretty face is it?"

"It is a very beautiful face." I put my hand on her cheek.

"You think so, huh?

"Yeah; you think so, too!"

"I do, huh? Well, as long as you think so, that's the main thing."

She wants to shower alone, and I know I had better not suggest otherwise. We have our breakfast on the deck and leave for town. From the truck stop in Esmeraldas I walk her to the school.

"Want to come in and have a look around?"

"No thanks, love. I wouldn't care for brain surgery today." She gives me a tiny signature punch.

"What are you going to do today?"

"Maybe try to get a boat up the river. They cut bamboo up there somewhere; I've seen them load it on ships in the harbor. I'm going to try to be back here to pick you up at three. We can eat here in town, and then get the five o'clock truck. But, don't wait for me. If I'm not here at three, you just go on back to Costa, and I will catch up with you there."

"Okay honey. Don't kiss me. I don't want the kids to see that."

At the dock, I locate a boat going up river. There is a lot of traffic on the river—more than the road. Mostly there are small dugouts, with fishermen or people coming and going to the market in town. Some dugouts are very large—thirty or more feet long and six feet wide and have outboard motors. Smaller dugouts are paddled or poled along the river. There are also flat pontoon boats used mostly to move hardwoods down from the forest—tropical hardwoods being too dense to float. And, there are small tugboats pulling or pushing barges used to bring bamboo down to the harbor.

I climb aboard one of the tugboats, and talk with the pilot, gathering all the information I can about bamboo. Obviously, bamboo is a major resource for the region, and is used throughout Ecuador, and exported to Peru. I am told that export of bamboo was the major reason for building the port facility, which preceded the road from the highlands by many years. I learned that production had been greatly stepped up over the past decade, especially for export production to Peru. No one seems to know what the Peruvians do with so much bamboo, and I decide I will go down there and find out some day.

I stand on the bow of the boat, and watch the shoreline. There are houses built at water's edge, mostly on bamboo stilts. The shoreline is a mess—saved from environmental disaster, I reason, by the relatively sparse population in the region. That will change with the current average of six or seven kids per family. Given the fact that ten to twenty percent of the kids die before reaching age one, family size will probably grow as health care improves. At that rate of growth it wouldn't take long to fill all of South America.

I examine all aspects of cutting and transporting bamboo, and try to gain some perspective on the number of people employed in the industry. I make notes on some of the details in my Guidebook to South America, and figure I will remember the other important facts.

I take a boat back down stream at one PM, so I can meet Shirley at three. I meet her coming out the door with a crowd of children.

"Don't kiss or hold hands," she says, "or, these kids will have a field day with it." We walk to the main street, and catch a bus to the beach.

"There is a good restaurant out here. It's called Casa Garibaldi." I tell her.

"Yeah, Johnny has recommended it to me."

I laugh. "I'm not surprised Johnny sniffed that out, after seeing the guy that owns the place." I put my hands up, before she can snap at me. "But, that doesn't bother me, cause I'm pretty sure I can defend myself, and he serves real good food." She gives me the arched eyebrow look.

The owner immediately guesses Shirley's name, and promises a very special dinner for 'any friends of Johnny's.' Dinner is very special. We order chateaubriand-for-two and a fine Chilean wine. The owner serves us personally, cutting the meat at our table, and expertly serving potato and vegetable, with two large spoons held in his right hand. He assigns a second waiter to be handy, just in case we need a wineglass refilled, and comes back to check on us occasionally.

Two glasses of wine in the afternoon makes Shirley giddy, and she displays another of her looks. She has a bubbly giggling smile that caused her to put her hand over her mouth, after saying something silly. For the first time I notice that she can be cute, as well as beautiful. We stay longer than we had intended, and take a cab back to the truck stop, thinking the cab could catch up with the truck, or even drive us all the way to the Costa trail, if necessary. Actually, the truck is still there—leaving late as usual.

The truck ride, and walk back to Costa, is sufficient to sober Shirley up, but she remains happy and bubbly. We get off the truck at the trail-head to Costa del Sol, cross the bridge and walk along the trail. I'm telling her about an adventure in Colombia, and for some stupid reason say: "... I just got fucken used to it." She is looking the other way and misunderstands.

"What did you say?" She says sharply. She stops and gives me the wrinkled brow look.

"You've heard me say that word before Shirley, Jeez."

"You better not say that word to mean what we do!"

"I didn't mean that. I was just talking about ... hell, give me a break, Shirley; I've never called it that. I never had any reason to call it anything, but if I did I would say make love to you."

She turns and huffs out a loud exhale. "Okay Shirley, this time I'm completely innocent. You are getting mad at me for no reason at all."

"You don't do it TO me. No one does anything TO me. We do it together. You make love WITH me, Ray."

"Well, that's what I meant. Don't be so touchy about one little word."

We walk in silence for a hundred yards or so, and then she seems to be happy again. She says she wants to invite Johnny to join us for a beer on the deck, and tell him we have met his friend.

At Costa, I wait on the deck. They emerge from the hut a few minutes later, he reluctantly, and her pushing him along. We sit at our normal table, overlooking the sea. "So, you met Roberto," he says to me, and adds, "the owner of Casa Garibaldi."

"Yeah, he really gave us first class treatment. He said any friend of Johnny's deserves the best."

"Roberto has a lot of talent," Johnny says. "You will find him down in the market every morning, buying fresh meat and produce personally. And, he oversees all the cooking."

"That was our number one meal in Ecuador, Johnny." I say, hoping to be a bit friendlier with him. We have a beer together, and soon Shirley is giddy again. She tells jokes, and laughs at ours, spewing beer on the table in a spasm of laughter.

"Well kids, I'm off to Atacames. And, I'll bet you two don't want to join me."

"Thanks Johnny." Shirley says.

"Thanks for what?"

"Thanks for joining us for a beer. Thanks for having friends that serve us good food. Thanks for worrying about me. Thanks for understanding."

"I understand, Shirley baby. Just be careful." He replies, and leaves.

We walk down the beach to an isolate place and I start to strip for a swim. The moon is not up, but starlight sparkles on the surf. "Wait," she says. "It's going to be too cold after we get wet." We sit on the sand berm overlooking the surf. I don't know what she has in mind, but know for sure that it isn't sex.

"Let's do therapy."

"Oh shit."

She ignores that. "You remember that dream you told me about when we first met—about seeing yourself backwards and all?" I nod. "Tell me about it again."

"Well, it's just the way I said. I always see myself—my face, you know—and everything is backwards."

"How long have you been having that dream?"

"Jeez, I don't know; for a long time. That was one of the reasons Donna got fed up with me."

"Did Donna understand the dream?"

"Yeah, I think she did. Well, actually, I never told her about the dream. But, she sort of knew."

"How did she know if you didn't tell her?"

"I don't know." I say.

"She loved you, didn't she?" I nod. "If she knew, why didn't she try to help you get over it."

"She did. I guess I was just a shit-head. Maybe, she was more concerned about Mama and the General."

"Do you know what the dream means?"

"No." I reply. "Do you know?"

"No, but Norma does. She knows why the dog bothers you, too."

"How the hell could she know anything about that?"

"She knows about it because I told her! Look, she's the general. She's running the show. And, I'm just the soldier on the front lines just like in your fucking Eighty-Second army." I burst out laughing. "That's what you call it," she says, defensively.

"Yeah, I know. But, it sounds funny to hear you say it. Did Norma tell you to use this army metaphor thing?"

"Yeah; she said it would help you to understand what we are doing." I give her a skeptical look. "Look, she's not stupid."

"No, but, she thinks I am."

"No! She hasn't even met you."

"Hey, love; if you are going to be a grunt soldier in a shooting war, you have to plan on taking some incoming."

"What's incoming?"

"Well, hell; the bad guys shoot back sometimes, ya' know."

"Yeah," she says, and is pensive for a moment. "Norma told me you would shoot back sometimes. She said I should remind you that I'm just following orders, and maybe you won't shoot at me so much."

"She said that, huh?" I am beginning to gain some respect for this Norma character.

"She's really smart, honey."

"Yeah; she's already playing with my brain, and I haven't even met her."

"She already knew almost everything you've told me. I don't mean the details. She just knew how you were going to feel about everything, and how you would feel about telling me."

"Shirley love, I don't mind you telling her that stuff. I just can't believe she could know why it happens."

"She knows, honey. She knew right away. She wasn't even surprised."

"Jesus!"

She is quiet for a whole minute, and I wait for the next shoe to fall. "You get disability money from the army, don't you?" I don't respond. "That's the money you get every month, isn't it? That's why you can run around down here for years, isn't it?"

"Yeah."

"Norma says you would be better off if you didn't get that money. Then, you would have to stay home and work, wouldn't you? You're supposed to be taking medication and counseling, aren't you?"

"Yeah."

"Norma says depression is very dangerous." She looks up at me. "She says, someday that dog will come out and you won't be able to get it back in there."

"I'm not going to hurt anyone."

"You might hurt yourself. Norma says you might hurt someone else who happens to be around you—not because you would want to, but just because they happen to be there. She says, you're already hurting all the people who love you, and someday you may hurt them a lot more." She continues more softly. "You don't want to do that, do you?"

"No."

We sit quietly for a long time, "There's one more thing I have to tell you. This isn't therapy anymore, okay?" She continues, "Norma says, being in love with the person you are giving therapy to, is a conflict of interests. She says I should either give up one, or the other."

"What are you going to do?" I hold my breath.

"I told her, I would have to give up both or keep doing both. I couldn't stay with you without the therapy, and I couldn't be around you doing therapy without loving you." I remain silent. "She said I'm making a big mistake. She said, it is common to become emotionally attached to people you are trying to help. And, that the emotion of therapy would cause people to become physically attracted to each other. She said, the first rule for a professional is to avoid a physical or emotional attraction to your patient, at all costs."

She stops for a few seconds, and then, "She said, what I feel for you is caused by your dependency on me—by me wanting to help you. I don't think that's true Ray, do you?"

"Yeah, love. I think it's probably true."

"She said, your love for me is also because of your feeling of dependency, and fear of being alone. Do you think that's true too?"

"No."

This Norma character intrigues me. "Does Norma know you tell me all this stuff? I mean, telling me about your personal conversations with her?"

"At first, I didn't know how much of this I should tell you, so I asked her what I should say, when you asked me about it." She is quiet for a few seconds, and then turns to face me. "She said, when you deal with people, you have to have a very simple rule about what to tell them, and what not to tell them. It has to be a rule you can be sure you will never forget, and it will work regardless of the circumstances. Otherwise, you will make mistakes, or forget what you said last time. You know what the rule is?"

"No, what?"

Again, she is quiet, as if trying to control her emotions, "She said...you tell the truth. She said it works the same with all other relationships, too."

She uses the back of her hand to wipe tears from her eyes. "Jeez, Ray; she says things that are so simple, but so eloquent and wise. I told you she was my friend, but that's not true. With friends, you try to help each other. But, I could never do anything to help her. She doesn't ever need any help. It's more like she's my mother or something. Sometimes, she doesn't like what I do, and she tells me. She gives me advice, but if I don't take her advice, she doesn't hold that against me, and never mentions it again. She wants to help me, but she never wants anything in return. Have you ever known anyone like that, Ray?"

"I guess not. Is she married?"

"No."

"Maybe she's a lesbian."

"NO! I told you, she doesn't want anything! Sometimes, I really hate the way your mind works. Anyway, that's how I knew I could tell her about your problem. I knew I could tell her everything, and you would never have to worry about any problems from that." After a few minutes she says, "You're going to trust her too, aren't ya?"

"Yeah, I guess so."

"Let's do our swim," she says.

Later we lie on our sides in the bed facing each other. There is no light and I cannot see her eyes, but I know she is looking at me too. My love for her is boundless. I am even beginning to like her therapy sessions, but I do that for her, and for her love. I don't really care about my problem; maybe I don't have a problem anymore.

You have less than two weeks left with her GI, I tell myself, and then she will be gone forever. That makes me shudder. "What's the matter?" She says softly.

"Nothing, love; I was just thinking...it's nothing, love."

"Really, tell me."

"It's nothing, love; really."

AUNT MEG TELLS IT LIKE IT IS: SAN JOSE, CALIFORNIA, SUMMER, 1950

The girl and her aunt lie in their beds and talk. She is no longer shocked by her Aunt's talk about men. She wants to learn more.

"Tell me about how you can read his mind."

"They have a huge fragile ego, and they are sentimental and emotional so they get embarrassed, and have their feelings hurt easily. And, their emotions show, plain as day, on their faces. They blush and pout and brood and whimper and laugh and growl and giggle and snarl, and it all shows, plain as day, right on their faces," her aunt stops and laughs, "they really aren't smart at all, and it's easy to control them."

"You tell him, you won't let him get your panties down, unless he does what you say?"

"No, honey, that never works. You always have to make them think you like sex as much as they do. You have to make them think they are doing you a favor. See; they only enjoy it, if they think you are too. You give them all the sex they can stand—more than they can stand—that way they won't be looking around for some other girl all the time. And, that's another one of the things you have to watch out for. If he isn't sentimental and emotional, and if he can enjoy having sex with a girl that doesn't want it, he's no good."

"So, how can you control him?"

"First, you always make them think they are in control. Yes, dear; whatever you say, dear; please tell me what I should do about this or that, dear. And, you try not to nag and bitch at them, cause that doesn't work either. You just make sure he knows what you want on the important things, and if he doesn't do it, you just act like you are really hurt, and sit down and start crying. That kills um'." She laughs again. "And, that's another thing to watch out for. If it doesn't kill him, when you act hurt and cry, you better get away from him."

"Gosh Meg, it sounds as if you are just manipulating him."

"Well, you are; and, that's fair. They are a lot stronger than you, so you have to use the tools God gave you," the woman points to her head. "There is nothing worse than a weak man, or a stupid woman, and you never forget who's stronger, and who's smarter. The last thing you want is to have a man start hitting you."

"If one of them hit me, I would hit him back."

"No, honey; you can't compete with them physically. That's like taking a knife to a gunfight. If there's one thing they know how to do, it's fight. If you hit him, he probably won't even feel it. But, if he hits you, it's going to hurt."

"Has one of them ever hit you Meg?"

"A man might hit you sometime without meaning to, and if he gets on his knees and begs for forgiveness, you might let it go. But, never twice honey; you just walk away. There is nothing worse than a hitter."

"Did your last husband hit you? Is that why you are divorcing him?"

"No. He had a girlfriend. I thought I could get him back, but I couldn't. She was a smart cookie. She had him on his knees, licking her butt. He didn't know what hit him."

"Au…, that makes me sick."

"There is nothing wrong with a man licking a girl's butt, honey. He was just licking the wrong one."

"When you found out he was going with another woman, you didn't leave him right away?"

"No! Hell, you can't let some gal take your man just because of a little squirt of sperm. That's the cheapest stuff in the world, and it might not even be his fault."

"What? I don't believe a woman could rape a man."

"A gal doesn't have to rape a man. If she pulls her panties down, he's going to do it. You just have to be sure he doesn't go back to her again."

"Why not; if sperm is so cheap?"

"Because you are going to lose him. She's going to be working on him, just like you did, and you have to remember, he's really dumb. As long as he sees boobs and bottoms, he's going to be sniffing along after her. First, you lose his heart and soul, and then you lose his paycheck."

"Do you ever do it with another guy too?"

"No. That is the stupidest thing a woman can do."

"Why? Tell me why?"

"Because, it's harder for a man to forgive you, than it is for you to forgive him. And, even if he does forgive you, you probably lose your power over him. And, there's something else. He might kill that guy, and you too."

"Why is it different for a woman, than for a man?"

"It goes back to some primeval instinct. You see, a woman always knows who her kids are. But, a man can't be sure, unless he's the only one she's with."

"That doesn't make sense, Meg. You don't even have any kids."

"Honey, you have to remember, they are stupid. It doesn't do any good to try to make sense with them. Anyway, a woman can control herself a lot easier than a man can."

"Why is that?"

"Look! If some man gets his cock out and shows it to you, you are going to be disgusted, and maybe call the police. If a girl pulls her panties down in front of a man, he isn't going to be disgusted. He is going to be sniffing around down there, right away."

"So, how do you get one?"

"Well," her aunt replied, "you just go around acting like you're not trying to get them—they are too dumb to figure that out—and wait until you get one on the line. Then, you look him over, and if you don't like what you see, you just flip um' off the hook, and keep trolling. You might see one that doesn't notice you, so you find out where he hangs out, and just happen to be there. If you are desperate, you can touch him."

"Touch him? Ugh, I would never do that!"

"Oh, I don't mean like that! You just touch his arm with your finger! You do it very nonchalant, you know, as if it were an accident. It's like giving them an electric shock. If they don't come after you then, you might as well forget it."

"An electric shock; just touching his arm with your finger?"

"You have more power in that little finger than you know. If you touch an old one, it might give him a heart attack," the woman laughs.

"But, I'm not pretty like you, Meg."

"Honey, first of all, you are pretty. And, second; a girl is as pretty as she thinks she is. If she thinks she is beautiful, men will fall all over themselves trying to get her. And, remember; after a few hours they can't see how you look anyway. They just see this thing they have created in their mind. If you smile at them, they will think you are the most beautiful woman in the world."

"I don't believe that Meg. The guys are always after the cute girls, and they don't pay any attention to me."

"That's because you decided you hate them. You don't want to look beautiful for them. If you think of yourself as a girl a man would want to be with—that he would think is beautiful—then he will want to be with you, and he will think you are beautiful."

"Really, Meg; really?"

"Really!"

"**A**fter you get a guy you want on the line, what do you do?"

"It's like bringing in a big fish with a little fishing pole. You give him plenty of line, and play him until he is too tired to fight. I told you what he would be thinking. Well, you don't let him do it. But, you flirt with him a little, so he thinks there may be some tiny chance."

The woman stops to laugh. "And, he will start scheming on you. Of course, you know exactly what he's doing, but he doesn't know you know. You let him touch your arm, or put his arm around your waist, and when he tries to touch your cheek, you brush his hand away, very gently, as if that's just too fast for you."

She laughs again. "You make him work two or three days, just to touch your cheek. And, then you let him give you a tiny kiss on the lips, and send him home thinking you may not let him see you again."

The girl joins her laughter. "And, then you let him play with your boobs, pulling his hand away occasionally, and pant as if you are so sex starved you can't stand it. And, all this time, you are checking him out. You make sure he has a job, and goes to work every day. If he doesn't work, he isn't worth a hoot in hell. And, you see how he treats older women, and little girls. If he doesn't treat older women with respect, or if he ever looks at a little girl, with that look in his eye, you dump him on the spot."

"Once you get him, how do you keep him?"

"Well, honey. I've never been very good at that, so maybe you better ask your mom."

"Really Meg, tell me."

"Well, I can tell you what I'm going to do next time. I'm going to keep him well fed, and keep his house clean, and flirt with him constantly. And, when he comes home from work, I'm going to screw his brains out, and wake him up in the middle of the night and screw his brains out again. I think sex is the main thing, honey. I'm going to get as much of his juice in me as I can, and make sure he doesn't get bored with it."

"What if he looks at another woman?"

"You can't stop that. You just say, hey, she's really pretty, isn't she? I wish I were that pretty. And, then you take him home and screw his brains out."

"What if he is thinking about the other woman, while he is doing it with you?"

"You can't control what they think, and you don't need to. Hell, let him look at pornographic pictures if he wants to. Just be sure he keeps his pants zipped up, while you're not around."

"What if he tries to rape you?"

"That is a terrible thing honey, but what happened to you was much worse. They can never do that to you again. You are not a little girl anymore. They may hurt you, and they may even kill you, but they can't make you cry that way."

Aunt Meg continued, "If it happens, well, you just have to pick yourself up and go on. There isn't much you can do about it. You scream if you can, but just remember, any man that will rape you, will probably kill you if you fight him. But, I can tell you that most men wouldn't do a thing like that. Like I told you, they only enjoy it if they think you do too. And, most of um' would rather cut their hand off than touch a little girl."

When Aunt Margaret left the family, the girl's mother thanked her. "You saved my daughter, and you put a smile back on her face."

WHAT THE HELL IS JOHNNY'S GAME: ECUADOR, THURSDAY, AUGUST 13

I plan another trip inland. Shirley will have to teach again today, so I decide to have a look at cacao and African Palm production. I want to know whether the crop is produced on small farms by families, or on large plantations, and if so, where the workers come from and how much they pay them, and how they get the stuff out of there to the world market. During breakfast we are surprised when Johnny joins us. "I'm going into town with you guys this morning. I have to confirm our tickets home, and I need to hit a bank—I'm almost broke. I thought maybe we could all have dinner together at Casa Garibaldi this afternoon."

"That's a great idea, baby." She says.

"Yeah, Johnny; that's great. Hey, as long as you are going in, maybe I'll get off the truck at the highway, and go back up hill. They grow African palm up there I want to check it out, and I think there is some cacao too. I'll be back in Esmeraldas for dinner at Garibaldi's. Maybe, you could meet Shirley at the school, and I will see you both at Garibaldi's for dinner."

"I don't think she needs anyone to meet her at the school," Johnny says. "She is quite capable of getting a bus to the beach, all by her little helpless self."

She laughs, "It's okay Johnny, he thinks he's protecting me." She gives me the 'mother accepting the grammar school art work' look.

"So;" Johnny says, "what is cacao?"

"We call it cocoa, for some reason—chocolate, you know. I really didn't see any cacao trees, but there were drying racks with sliding lids, they use to dry cacao, up the road."

"Ray is a scientist, Johnny. Yesterday, he was up river studying bamboo, and today it's this chocolate stuff. Simple folk like us wouldn't understand." She giggles at me.

On the truck, I think about Johnny. He seems to be more comfortable with me. Maybe he's glad to know you have something to do around here, besides trying to get Shirley's panties down, I tell myself. Obviously, he doesn't want a sexual relationship with her, and yet he seems to care about her a lot. Why would he care about Shirley? I don't have an answer.

I get off the truck at the highway, and wave good-bye. A bus headed uphill is passing; I run to catch up and jump aboard. There is an empty seat in the front row next to the driver and I take it. The driver is typical: a mestizo with a dirty T-shirt and three days growth on his beard.

"Hey chauffeur, I just want to ride up a few dozen kilometers with you. I'm looking for a plantation where they grow African Palm. Can you drop me when we see a plantation?"

"Of course, gringo; but why would you want to see a plantation of palmas?"

"No, well; you know. I'm just hoping to find a pretty girl up there. What else is there to do?"

"Well, there is nothing more important than pretty girls!"

The driver's helper comes up the isle to my seat and want me to pay for the ride. The driver says no, he's just going up the road; let him ride free. I don't like the situation. Why should I ride free while poor people have to pay? I offer to pay. Again, the driver says no.

"Hey man; I don't need your generosity. But, there are a lot of other people around here who do."

The driver doesn't appreciate my comment. He ignores me, but drops me at a side road when I request that.

I check out the African palm plantation, but have little success. Apparently the crop is produced only on plantations—strictly commercial—and they seem to think I am a spy or something.

By late morning, I am back on the road, still headed inland, and having no luck with a ride. I walk for a while. Finally a jeep comes by and gives me a lift. The driver is a veterinarian, and is checking cattle at several ranches along the highway. He completed his medical degree at the University of Iowa, and is more than willing to have a gringo companion. His English is not as good as my Spanish, but he wants to show it off, and I am his guest. It is a good opportunity to see how the cattle business works, so I stick with him.

We visit three ranches, and I watch him work with the cows. His work is sloppy, compared to that of veterinarians working on the ranch in Texas. He explains that people are not willing to pay for expert care; "Cows are cheaper than good medicine," he says.

He tells me he will return to Esmeraldas by two or three in the afternoon, and will drive me to Casa Garibaldi, to meet my friends. I agree to the plan. Actually, we reach the restaurant at about four PM. I insist he join us for a beer.

"This is Doctor García. He is a veterinarian," I say. "Allow me to introduce my friends. This is Shirley and Johnny." I am suddenly shocked and embarrassed to realize I don't know their last names.

"How do you do," the veterinarian says, in very careful English, shaking hands with Johnny.

"Let me get you a beer, Doctor," I say.

"Just one," he replies. Being so formal with García makes me even more embarrassed that I cannot introduce Shirley and Johnny properly. But, the simple fact is that I can't. It has not occurred to me to wonder what their last names were. The doctor doesn't seem to mind.

The 'just one' ploy was a farce, of course, and García is with us through wine and dinner. I regret having asked him to join us because, he is drunk quickly, and wants Shirley's attention.

"We have to go now," I tell him. "We have to take the 5:30 truck to Atacames."

"No, stay; I'll drive you back later," he says.

No way! I tell myself. He is too drunk to drive himself home. I pay the bill, and ask the owner to be sure we have a taxi outside the door.

"Okay folks, let's go," I say.

"Wait, I'll drive you! Stay! I'll be right back," Garcia says, and staggers off to the bathroom.

"Okay," I say, "let's get the hell out of here."

Shirley is embarrassed by my insistence upon leaving him. "Look, love. These guys will never stop drinking. We would be here till midnight, and there is no way we are getting into that jeep with him."

Johnny agrees. "Ray's right, baby; we have to ditch him."

"How can we do that to him, after he helped you so much?"

"Love, tomorrow he won't even remember what happened—assuming he makes it home alive tonight, and there is nothing we can do about that. Let's *chogi* out of here, before he comes back." I hurry her to the door, and into the cab.

"Tell Roberto to take care of him," She yells to me, from the back seat of the cab. I do, and tell the taxi driver to get going. The 5:30 truck has left, and our cab catches up a few kilometers down the highway. We transfer to the truck.

"I can't believe we did that," Shirley tells us, "just leaving him without saying good-bye, or anything."

"Believe me, we did the right thing. Down here drinking is a contest. No one will quit till they fall down and vomit. It would ruin our whole next day. Believe me, love, this is the way you do it—you *escapar*—you just escape when you can."

"He's right about this." Johnny says. "I've been through it, baby. You can't believe how bad it gets, when they are all sloppy drunk. And, it gets harder to leave. You have to make the break when you can. They all do it, so there is no problem."

She seems satisfied we have done the right thing. "Jeez, it makes me not like this country so much. They peek at you through the cracks in the wall, and they fall down and vomit. You know about them, but you still love them, don't ya?"

"Every culture is different, love. We have our bad side too. Don't think there aren't things about us that make them want to throw up. Like, the way we treat anyone with other than lily-white skin, and our xenophobia for anyone who has a tiny accent in their English. You have to take them the way they are, and there are so many good things about them. You just have to take them the way they are. But, you have to protect yourself, too."

"Ray's right about this Shirley," Johnny says. "There are goods and bads with all people. I wish everyone could understand that." Johnny glares at me, and I think I know the kind of people he is referring to.

Shirley is content again. She puts on her I love you face, and gives me a tiny lip motion kiss. We get off the truck at the Costa trail and walk. She insists that we walk on each side of her. She puts one arm around each of us, and continues to talk, obviously a bit high on the wine and beer.

It's so great having two guys that care for her, and who want to protect her—hell, she can protect herself. We are so sensible and understand the culture so well; she will always listen to our advice. She will study the culture more, and try harder to understand.

Meanwhile, I am wondering what's going through that screwed up mind of Johnny's. Why does she care for him? And, why does he want to protect her from me. What the hell is his game?

"We are headed for the Amazon country tomorrow, Johnny." I say. "Want to join us."

"We are?" Shirley asks, as if awakened from a dream.

"Yeah, love. Remember? We decided to do the Rio Napo thing."

"I'm not going down to the Amazon," Johnny says. "That place is crawling with snakes."

"Snakes?" Shirley perks up. "There are plenty of snakes right here on the coast."

"There are no snakes down here," Johnny says.

"Are you kidding?" I say. "There are just as many snakes here as in the Amazon. You just don't see them."

"Yeah," Shirley adds, "but, they see you. And, you are walking over there on the edge, where the snakes are."

"Oh shit!" He says, and pulls away from us. He moves to the middle of the path in front of us.

"You have to watch out for the middle of the road snakes, Johnny," I say.

"What are they?" he asks. He must know I'm bullshitting him, but his fear of snakes extends to the mythical ones in my imagination.

Shirley fills in for me. "Well, I just wouldn't want to be the first person in the path. They come right down the middle of the trail, baby. The only thing you can do is jump into the bush, with the other snakes."

"Oh shit, you guys!" Johnny says. He decides to drop in behind us.

"I'm sorry Johnny," she tells him, looking back. "We are just putting you on about the snakes."

"Thanks a lot, Shirley! Maybe you guys have some irrational fears too."

"Yeah, we do." She says in a serious tone, and I'm pretty sure I know what she is thinking.

"Especially me, Johnny," I tell him. "I'm afraid of my own face. I live in fear of a dog that crawls out of the back of my brain sometimes. I'm the basket case here. I'm sorry about the snake thing." She holds me closer.

We climb the stairs to the deck, and enjoy the view of the Pacific Ocean. Johnny joins us. "I don't like it baby," he says. "I don't want you going down to the Amazon."

"It's okay," she says.

"Look, irrational fear is one thing, but this dog in the brain shit is something else." He says.

I regret spilling the dog story, but now I have nothing to say.

"Baby, Ray was in the war in Korea. He has some problems with that, but we are working on it, and it's going to be okay. Trust me baby, it's going to be okay."

"No fucking way, Shirley! I know about this war shit, and I don't want you going down there with this guy." Again, he speaks as if I am not present.

"Please Johnny, Norma knows all about it. I'm working with her on this, and I know everything is okay. I love you for being concerned about me, but please, trust me on this, okay?"

Obviously he does not thrust her on this. He waves his arm and leaves the table. She seems disappointed.

We go to our hut. I feel our time that night is spoiled. I don't even try to caress her. She sleeps, and I feel miserable. My stupid veterinarian friend; all that talk about culture; the silly snake stuff; and my confession to Johnny. How could I have been so stupid? And, I will lose her in just ten days. I am miserable. I just want her back tomorrow.

CADILLACS AND LINCOLNS: KOREA, SUMMER, 1953

The mood in bivouac was different. In his hooch, Corporal White filled him in. While he was in Japan, a Chink patrol had broken through both the lower and upper perimeter wires, and had inflicted ten casualties on the company, including three men killed.

That attack had been followed by two days of almost continuous artillery fire that produced eight more casualties, including three more dead. Among the casualties in Weapons Platoon were Private Ringer, probably paralyzed for life by shrapnel in his back, and Sergeant Hart, dead. Hart had been killed while trying to carry Ringer to safety after the first round hit. Hart was to be awarded the Silver Star, posthumously.

He went over to his old hooch, and found the men somber, and somehow resentful that he had missed the action. He left them quickly, and went to Patterson's hooch. "Hey Pat, I heard you guys caught hell while I was gone."

"Yeah, man," Patterson responded in a low voice. "They put fucken hell fire down on us. Lucky you missed it, Rich."

"Shit man, I wasn't trying to miss it. We've been in this shithole almost a year, and only taken nineteen casualties, and then I leave for two weeks and fucken hell fire comes down on us—shit."

"Well, it wasn't your fault, Rich." Patterson said. "How was your wedding?"

"I'm embarrassed to tell you, Pat. I'm over their living it up, and you guys are getting hell kicked out of you."

"Don't sweat it man. Most of us didn't see anything. Shit, we just hunkered down in our bunkers and prayed."

The Commanding Officer called a formation and had the men sit in bleachers. He spoke of the past week's events. Reading the names of the men who were killed, his voice broke, and he had to choke back tears. Some of the troopers cried too, but the officers and NCO's, and many of the young soldiers, were disgusted by the CO's sniffling.

When the company was dismissed, Lieutenant Snider ordered the weapons platoon to remain seated. The Lieutenant intended to set the record straight on how the army felt about the action. "Men!" The Lieutenant yelled. "The fucken Chinks are going to hit Zebra again, and we are going to be ready for them. It's pay-back time, men," the Lieutenant harangued. Many of the men cheered.

"Yeah," someone yelled. "We'll kill those fuckers," yelled another man.

"Weapons Platoon doesn't sleep at night any more, men. We sleep in the daytime—one man sleeps while his buddy is on guard. At night, every man is going to be alert. Let um' come, goddamn it! We are going to blow every one of those sons-a-bitches off the side of that hill."

The men were worked into frenzy. They yelled and cursed, with many standing up and shouting. He found the scene disgusting, but said nothing because he had missed the action. He returned to his hooch, sick with anger at the army, the Lieutenant, and himself. You should have taken the job at division, he told himself. And then put that notion out of his mind.

Baker Company moved up to Zebra on Thursday morning before sunrise. They had anticipated an attack, and hoped to surprise the enemy with two companies on the hill rather than one. Both companies remained for ten days, in terribly cramped quarters. Later, each company would get a few days rest occasionally at a temporary bivouac at the base of the hill.

All transfers were carried out at night, and no regular routine was maintained. The returning company would carry double rations of ammo. They shelled Chink positions almost around the clock, and took return fire frequently.

For Lieutenant Snider, weapons platoon was the pivotal force that stood between the Chinese Army and the California coast, and he was hungry for battle. The Lieutenant asked for, and received, permission to send 15 men down to fetch more 81mm ammo each day, leaving his platoon at about two-thirds strength for several hours while they were away.

Having assumed the role of forward observer, Snider spent most nights and many days in one of five outposts located on prominent points at or near the lower perimeter wire. Outposts were reached by commo trenches that extended downhill two hundred and fifty to three hundred yards from the Main Line of Resistance trench at the crest of the hill. Outposts were nothing more than deep trenches reinforced with sandbags. They were within range of enemy mortar fire, but could usually withstand all but a direct hit, assuming you were hunkered down in a bunker or at the bottom of a trench.

Outposts were also within range of sniper fire if Joe Chink decided to put a man at risk of our mortar fire and our own snipers. The zing of a Chink sniper's round was mother's milk for Snider. He would call in tens of thousands of dollars' worth of mortar fire in response. "Teach the goddamned Chinks a lesson," he would say.

Corporal Raymond Richards was Snider's radioman, and therefore a reluctant participant in the Lieutenant's escapades. He would follow the Lieutenant down a commo trench in the early evening. They would remain at an outpost that night, and usually the next day. Snider would search the hill in front of him, and call in fire on anything that moved. At night, flares would light up the sky at five to fifteen minute intervals, and they would continue to call in mortar fire. "Fire mission!" He would say repeatedly, into the mike of his radio. The following night, they would return up the trench to the hill.

His sleep time had been reduced to two or three hour periods, at random intervals—and almost no sleep at all between sunset and sunrise. He usually had no more than one hot meal, or cup of coffee, in two days. The rest of the time he ate cold C-rations from the can, and drank water from his canteen. The relatively comfortable bivouac was forgotten—as was his weekends with Donna at Division. He had no way to tell her about the change in orders, and could only hope she would know. He dreaded the thought of her waiting for him at the guest housing office. Even more disturbing was the fact that she would be terrified by the possibility of him becoming a casualty.

Three weeks passed with the men at a level of intensity that could not be sustained. Men began to fall asleep on guard. Rumors spread through the unit that sleeping on guard would be punished by firing squad. Actually, offenders were given company punishment; PFC stripes were ripped off, or offenders were assigned to digging trenches. Company morale slumped, and bitching spread through the unit like a virus.

He had begun to hope the attack would come soon. They were consuming themselves. There was a risk that, at some point, there would be no fight left in them. He had terrible visions of Joe Chink overrunning them, and killing everyone. Part of the problem, he decided, was men like Lieutenant Snider, who were overzealous and cocky. But, the real root of the problem was the Commanding Officer, who was indecisive and very obviously scared.

The attack came a week later at four AM. Baker Company was on the hill, with Charley Company in reserve below. He was with the Lieutenant at outpost three. They had abandoned the outpost and scrambled up the commo trench, grateful that the attack had not come up that side of the hill. The barrage of artillery fire was so heavy, that virtually all the men had taken cover in bunkers. Apparently, the CO had panicked and ordered the company to evacuate the hill—meaning retreat and leave the hill to the enemy. Other officers tried to rally the men. "Hold your positions Men; hold your positions," they yelled. But, conflicting orders confused the men, and drained courage. Some men abandoned their positions, and run back off the hill.

When he and Lieutenant Snider reached the Weapons Platoon bunkers, most of the men had abandoned the position, taking the mortars with them. The Lieutenant could not control the situation. Sergeant Jordan stood with his face a few inches from the Lieutenant's and shouted back. "We've been ordered off the hill, Sir. I'm following orders! My men are following orders, and you can't countermand the orders of the CO. NO Sir! NO SIR! I will not countermand the orders of the CO! Sir, my men are evacuating this position, Sir!"

He had moved with the other men, instinctively following Jordan's orders. "Richards, get back here! You're my radio." The Lieutenant shouted to him. He stopped and looked at Jordan, hoping for some indication that he should disobey the Lieutenant's orders. But that indication did not come. Jordan is trying to save the grunts, he told himself. He can't worry about you; you're a NCO—an expendable professional. He had treasured his time at the Guest Quarters that his NCO status had made possible; now he would pay the price. There was no decision to make; he simply followed orders. He moved back to Snider.

"Let's go, Richards!" The Lieutenant said, and they jogged toward the northeast side of the hill. The shelling had stopped, and the attack could be expected almost immediately. But, there was no small arm's fire, and no apparent break in the wire in their sector. Both the fourth and weapon's platoon positions had been abandoned. He followed Snider across the hill to the third platoon position. The third platoon was at the main trench, ready to repel an attack.

A group of officers had gathered behind a bunker; Snider and his radioman joined the group. The company Executive Officer was there, as well as the platoon leaders for the 1st, 2nd, and 3rd platoons. Apparently, the Exec had countermanded the CO's orders to withdraw. As he and Lieutenant Snider ran up, the Exec officer yelled, "Where is Weapons Platoon, Snider?"

"They bugged out, sir; the captain ordered them out. I was just getting back from the forward observation position. By the time I got there, it was over." Snider replied.

"Goddamn you Snider! Why weren't you with your men?" The Exec screamed. "You son-of-a-bitch—playing cowboy out there. If we had any kind of CO in this fucken outfit, he would have kicked your fucken ass up between your shoulders. Christ! Now, we've got no mortars! How about Fourth Platoon?"

"They bugged, along with Headquarters Platoon" Snider replied. "There's no one over there."

"Christ!" The Exec screamed. "What about Lieutenant Young?"

"He must have bugged out with his platoon, Sir; I didn't see him over there." Snider said.

"I'll see that son-of-a-bitch in hell!" The Exec screamed. "Erickson, get two squads from your platoon, and cover those positions, and be sure your radio is working."

"Yes, Sir." Lieutenant Erickson jogged away.

"Two squads?" Snider said. "You can't cover that area with two squads."

"That's all we have, Snider—thanks to you and Young, and your fucken Captain. Anyway, the attack is going to come from over here. They blew out the lower perimeter wire."

"Sir," Snider said. "I can get artillery fire on that position from outpost five, if you patch me through to Division."

His heart sank. Snider is going to try to be the whole Weapons Platoon. He wants to be a hero, and you're going to get your ass shot off, he told himself.

The Exec considered the offer. "You can command that whole sector from five?"

"Yes Sir! I was down there on Monday, and could get mortar fire anywhere in that sector," Snider responded.

"Do it!" The Exec said, and yelled, "Watson, get that radio over here." A soldier ran up with a radio. "You are Baker One, this is Baker Five. I want them patched through to Div Seven. That's your job Watson—your only job. You keep that fucken patch working."

"Yes Sir," the soldier responded.

He and Snider jogged past white-faced soldiers. They reached the commo trench and continuing down the hill, now scrambling along to keep their heads below the top of the trench. At outpost five, they found the position abandoned.

Snider lay over the top of the trench, exposed above the bunker, with binoculars glued to his eyes. He sat in the bottom of the trench, removed his radio and extracted his spare battery from his pack, placing it beside the radio.

"Contact Baker One," the Lieutenant ordered.

"Baker One, this is Baker Five; how do you read me?" He said into his radio.

"Baker Five, this is Baker One; I read you five-by-five. You are patched through to Division Artillery—that's Div Seven. Give um' fucken hell man, blow those cock suckers out of there!" The urgent reply came from a man who knew his own life was on the line.

Snider had heard the reply, "OK Richards, give me a round in sector three; wire plus two-fifty, hit it."

"Div Seven, this is Baker Five, Fire Mission!"

"Baker Five, this is Div Seven; Fire Mission!" The voice on the other end was sing-songy and professional, as if he had ordered a pizza. Clearly, this man did not have his butt on the line. "What is your position, Baker Five?"

"Div Seven, this is Baker Five, at Zebra outpost five. Give me a round in sector three; wire plus two-fifty."

He listened to the reply, "fire mission, sector three, wire plus two-fifty." Thirty seconds later, he heard the whistle of the round pass over, and the dull explosion off in the distance.

"Right one hundred, back fifty, fire!" Snider barked, without looking back.

"Div Seven, this is Baker Five. From Outpost Five, right one hundred, back fifty, fire!" He repeated, and listened to the pizza man repeat his request. Again, a single round whistled overhead and exploded much closer.

"Right fifty, back twenty-five, give me a pattern there," Snider yelled.

"Div Seven, this is Baker Five. Right fifty, back twenty-five, give me a pattern," he said into the mike. Several rounds whistled overhead and explosions occurred in quick succession.

"Hold that!" Snider said. "Prepare to fire for effect on my command. I want everything they've got, and prepare to walk um' up the hill to the wire."

He repeated the commands, into the mike of his radio. "WillCo," the pizza man said. "Prepared to fire for effect at your command; prepared to walk it up the hill to the wire. We're giving you Cadillacs and Lincolns my man, and lots of um'. At your command, my man; and, you can tell Mao Z Toon he better start counting his children."

A senator visiting Korea, on a mission to cut costs of the war had recommended naming each artillery round by the car that had the same cost as the shell. In theory the men would be impressed with the cost of artillery rounds, and would use them more sparingly. In practice, no one ordered a Ford, if three Cadillacs were available. He had found the whole idea to be humorous, when he first heard it. Now it filled him with bitterness.

Snider remained glued to his binoculars, and said nothing. At last he had time to think. He was certain he would die. The thought of Donna crying and grieving filled him with pride and dark pleasure. Then, he took even that good thought away from himself. She won't cry. She will hate you for not taking that job at Division, just because you wanted to be a goddamned hero. You don't deserve to have her cry for you, he told himself. For a moment, he was afraid his emotions would overwhelm him. He had to control himself. No, he told himself, you didn't do it because you wanted to be a hero. You just never thought you would die. Dying was never a consideration.

"Okay Richards!" The Lieutenant said. "I think I see some activity out there. Let's show um' what we've got. Give me a five minute barrage."

He repeated the command and a minute later the pounding began. The noise was thunderous and the ground shook under him. He put his head down and covered his face, as if he needed protection from the noise.

After the noise stopped, he wanted to ask the Lieutenant if they had hit Chink troops, but he didn't. He expected the Lieutenant to move down away from the exposed position at the top of the trench, but the man had remained in place. Thirty or forty minutes later, the Lieutenant called for another barrage, and the ground shook again.

Through the morning and early afternoon, he continued to call in fire at the same location.

"Fire Mission!" He would say, and the pizza man would repeat, Fire Mission. And, the ground would shake. He would think only of Donna. He pushed all other thoughts out of his mind. He had to think of her as much as he could. Soon, he would be cold and empty, and he would never be able to think of her again.

A mortar round exploded a hundred yards to his right. He was disturbed because he knew the mortars had been evacuated. But, there was little time to consider that thought. In a few seconds his life would be changed forever.

For the third time, in the brief period since he had joined the army against his parent's wishes, he would be transformed. The high school football team second-string tight-end was hardly a memory. The young soldier that had left Uncle Bob's house, with a mix of fear and wonder at his new life as a soldier, was no more. The young man, who had held his new wife with tenderness and the certainty of a future filled with love and free of all grief and pain, would have found it hard to recognize the new self about to emerge. He would be transformed again—this time with devastating consequences for himself, and his new bride.

IT'S AS IF YOU ARE VIOLENT: COSTA DEL SOL, FRIDAY, AUGUST 14

At dawn I kiss her lips. "Don't kiss me, honey."

"I don't care about your damned breath. I'm dying, and I can't stand it any longer." I hold her tight, and kiss her mouth. "I'm so sorry about all that stuff yesterday. Please forgive me, and be the way we were."

"There is nothing to forgive. I love you more than anything. Of course, we are the same way."

I relax. My imagination had run wild all night for no reason. I didn't really have to fight the dog.

We pack for our Amazon trip. Shirley is in good spirits, and soon I am too. We catch the first truck from Atacames to the Esmeraldas road. In twenty minutes, a bus for Quito passes, and we climb aboard. At the bus station in Quito, we put on warm clothing, and take a fast *colectivo* taxi, one that carries multiple passengers, to the town of Ambato, arriving at sunset.

We check into a hacienda hotel, on the outskirts of the town. It is a nice place—a refurbished hacienda "Big House" enclosed within high adobe walls. The very old stone building has high ceilings and huge doors. There is a very large fireplace in the common living area.

We go into town and take a quick look around. Not finding a restaurant we like, we return to the hotel, and eat dinner there. We learn breakfast will not be served until 8:30 AM, which probably means nine or nine-thirty, and arrange, at a considerable surcharge, for our breakfast at 5:30, which we know probably means six o'clock.

We have a shower with hot water in our room. She agrees to shower with me, but I am not to look. I would have agreed to anything; the past two days had become an eternity and I am dying for her. I hold her close in bed, and listen to the hum of her breathing. Her shyness about menstruating surprises me. She had seemed so casual about sex—almost flippant with the let's pretend, and when it's over it's over—as if she had been with dozens of lovers before. I thought I knew her, but now I'm not so sure.

I wake up sometime past mid-night and go to the bathroom, and fail to close the bathroom door. I had always closed the door before, and think about going back to do that. Hell man, she knows you piss, I tell myself. I make a loud noise passing gas, and wished I had closed the door. When I return to bed she is awake, sitting up.

"You made that sound." She says.

"What?"

"You made that sound, and you knew I could hear it. You didn't even close the door."

"I farted. Guys do that; don't make a big thing out of it. I'm sorry I didn't close the door."

"I know what it means." She says.

"What it MEANS? It means I had gas and I farted. What the hell else could it mean?"

She is quiet for a moment, and then says, "Guys never do that when they're dating a girl, because they are just thinking about her. And, then later they realize there are other girls, with boobs and bottoms, and then they start doing that right in front of you."

"What the hell are you talking about? I just farted, for Christ's sake."

"It's okay." She sighs. "I just didn't think you would start noticing other girls so soon."

"Shirley! That's the most childish thing I have ever heard in my life!"

She continues her pensive mood, "Do you know what it means when a girl does that in front of a guy?"

"No, Shirley! NO! I don't know what that would mean! Certainly, it wouldn't mean she had gas!" I am disgusted. "Does it mean she hates your guts? She's going to murder you in your sleep? What, Shirley? Tell me what it means!"

"Ray, it means..." She begins to laugh. She rolls over on her back and rocks back and forth laughing, and says, "I couldn't think of anything stupid enough to say."

I have stepped on that damned snake again. "It's so easy to trick you." She says. "You take it so seriously. It's so much fun." She chokes the words out through her laughter. She is right, and I have to laugh with her.

I bang on the manager's door. The 5:30 breakfast we had paid for in advance is not ready at six AM. I insist he return the thirty pesos. Shirley is not happy with my attitude.

We go on to the bus station and have coffee there. "You have to teach these damned people a lesson. You pay for something and they don't deliver."

"You have to take them the way they are," she says. "Remember?"

"Well, yeah, maybe. But, I need breakfast in the morning, damn it!"

"We aren't in Texas, honey. You have to take them the way they are. And, another thing; I don't like you getting mad that way."

"Okay, Shirley. You're right. It's no big thing. So I didn't get my scrambled eggs and jalapeño peppers this morning. Course, I'm probably going to feel terrible all day, and get seasick on the bus. But, it's no big thing."

"I don't like that part of you," she says. "Getting mad and threatening people; it's as if you are violent or something."

"Jeez, Shirley; I didn't threaten that man."

"Well, you sure had him fooled—and me too."

"I just wanted my money back. Give me a break, Shirley."

"Call me Shirley love, if you please."

Suddenly, I feel shame, and disgust with myself. The breakfast problem is so trivial, and my response so extreme. How can I concern myself with that silliness, when I have her love? And, only for a few more days! Why are you trying to be the biggest shit-head in the country? I ask myself.

We get a *colectivo* taxi headed down the eastern side of the Andes to the town of Baños. I hold her close. "I'm sorry, Shirley love. Sometimes, I'm just a shit-head. I'm sorry."

"You are not a shit-head. I wouldn't be in love with a shit-head, so stop saying that."

"Well, I was kind of crude back there. Missing my breakfast is a major deal with me, ya' know."

"Yeah, I know. Breakfast really is important for you, isn't it?" I know she wants to change the subject.

"Yeah, it's my favorite meal. I could just about skip all the others, as long as I have my scrambled eggs and jalapeños in the morning."

"Ya' know I usually don't have breakfast at all. Maybe a cup of coffee sometimes—but I never miss it."

"You're sick, Shirley love. In Texas they would take you out and shoot you."

She giggles. "Would they, honey?"

"For sure, love. They are all armed, and anyone who doesn't get up at six o'clock, and eat breakfast, is shot on sight."

We reach the town of Baños before noon. It is a resort featuring hot springs, perched on the side of the Andes, about half-way down to the Amazon basin. Shirley wants to go into town and look around, but I insist on moving downhill. The bus stop is on the road above town, and the ride down and back will consume too much time. "There's just a bunch of hot baths down there anyway," I tell her.

There are no buses, so I scramble around, and get a truck headed down hill to Puyo. Shirley agrees, but insists she will sit by the window, with me in the middle. Sitting in the middle makes me uncomfortable; everyone knows the woman sits in the middle. "I don't want him to touch me." She says, referring to the driver.

"If the son-of-a-bitch touches you, I'll kill him!"

"I don't want you to kill anyone. I just want to get down there without some man touching me."

I sit in the middle, and again think about the terrible burden, of being a woman in Latin America.

In Puyo, I hire a pickup to take us to Misahuali, the end of the road on a tributary of the Napo River, and the jump-off point for the Amazon. We stand in the back of the truck, so I won't have to sit in the middle.

At Misahuali, we get a room in a small hotel, and go over to the restaurant. It is on a raised deck and has a loud jukebox. We order dinner and beer. A dodge carryall pulls up in front of the hotel, across the road, and a young man begins to off-load plant presses.

"Those guys are botanists. We should talk to them." She looks at me inquisitively. "They might know something." I stand at the edge of the deck of the restaurant and yell at them, "Hey!" I call to them, figuring they were Americans or Europeans.

"Yeah," the young man yells back.

"Come on up and have a beer. We need some information about plants."

The young man continues to work with the plant presses, and a middle-aged man comes over to the deck, and sits at our table. He is a botany professor from LSU. He is a fine fellow, and wears a baseball cap. We talk about plants while he drinks beer, and waits for his dinner.

"And, there is a plant they call *barbasco*," I tell him, "they use it to stun fish in the river."

"Yes," he says, "*barbasco* is a generic term. It just means a plant that stuns fish. There are a number of plants that can be used in that way, but the one I think you saw is the type where they use the leaves and berries. Well, that plant reproduces only vegetative now, as far as we know. It probably lost the ability to produce viable seeds hundreds of years ago."

"You mean everywhere you find it, people have planted it there?" I ask.

"That's right. We know that plant is native to Amazonia, but it was found in almost all the Caribbean Islands. So, people have planted it all over tropical America, for the past thousand years or so."

"So, that means these people we think of as non-agricultural, really know all about plants, and how to reproduce them."

"Of course, they do. These people out in the forest know more about the plants out there than we do—much more. That's the main reason we are down here—to learn from them."

I am excited with the conversation, and have failed to notice that Shirley is falling asleep. "I'm so tired, I can hardly keep my eyes open," she says. "I'm going over to the hotel; you don't have to hurry."

"It's that tropical sun working on you, love. It drains your energy. I'll be there in a few minutes." I finish with the botanist quickly and go to the room.

"**G**et out of here!" she yells at me. I had opened the bathroom door and walked in without thinking, and caught her on the toilet. I close the door and sit on the bed.

I know she is really sensitive about that. We both were at first, and had established an unspoken rule to ensure privacy for that personal business. Hotels usually don't have locks on the bathroom doors, unless they are communal. So, we would always leave the door ajar except when one of us wanted that privacy. Walking through a closed bathroom door was strictly forbidden.

She comes out of the bathroom and stands with her arms crossed, and her forehead wrinkled. I endure the hard stare for a few seconds. "I'm sorry, love. I didn't know you were in there."

"Then, where did you think I was? And, why did you think the door was closed?"

"I'm sorry. I wasn't thinking."

"You don't give me any privacy, Ray!"

"I'm really sorry. I won't do it again." I endure a few more seconds of torture. "Excuse me, I need to use the bathroom." I try to escape into the bathroom.

"Don't go in there! Can't you see the door is closed?" She screams.

"But, you aren't ..."

"Will you get it through your thick head? I don't want you to see that and I don't want you to smell that!"

I sit on the bed again and decide to try to reason with her. "We use the same outhouse in Costa, and it stinks to high heaven."

"That's everyone's smell!" She exclaims.

Forget reason, GI, I tell myself. She isn't finished with me. "And, I told you not to kiss me before I brush my teeth, but you do it anyway!"

"I'm sorry; I just didn't realize you were so sensitive about that stuff."

"It's not a question of sensitivity! It's common courtesy!"

"That was a poor choice of words. I meant, I'm sorry to be so discourteous." I say, trying to look contrite. "I'm going outside to take a piss."

"If it's an emergency, I'll go in there and strike matches!"

"It's not an emergency, love. I just need to piss."

I rush out the door, to her loud exhale. I take more time than I need outside, hoping she will cool off a bit. When I return to the room, she is in her PJ's on her side facing the wall.

"And, anyway Shirley, I only kissed you one time before you brushed your teeth, and that was when I thought you were mad at me, for Christ's sake."

"One time?" She turns to me. "You do it every morning!"

"Well, what do you call morning? It isn't morning till the sun comes up," I say.

"Sun comes up? Since when have I not brushed my teeth by the time the sun comes up? You have me up at the crack of dawn, stuffing scrambled eggs down my throat! I might as well be in your fucking Eighty-Second army."

I have to laugh at that, and she turns toward me with the wrinkled forehead look. "Come on Shirley; don't tell me I can't kiss you when we make love."

She tries to maintain her stern look, but blurts out a sudden giggle. "Okay," She says, changing to a smile. "We'll say it's not morning till the sun comes up." After a few seconds she continues: "So, you might as well forget about the no kissing rule. If I haven't brushed my teeth by the time the sun comes up, we might as well both forget it."

"Well, what about the PJ's?" She pulls her PJ's off quickly, throws them off the bed, and rolls on top of me.

THE HERO: KOREA, SUMMER, 1953

He was transferred to an army hospital in Japan. Donna resigned her volunteer position in Korea, and joined him two days later. He was given VIP treatment, including a private room, expert medical attention, special food, and overnight visiting privileges for his wife.

The VIP treatment had not surprised him, nor was he surprised that he would not be charged with dereliction of duty or cowardice. He knew how much power Mama had. But he was surprised that doctors and nurses did not treat him with contempt—the treatment those with connections usually get, and deserve, when they receive special care.

He complained of severe headaches. The diagnosis was brain concussion. A neurology specialist examined him, and an army psychologist was added to his medical team. There were many examinations, and many questions. The psychologist seemed to be trying to extract information. He remembered the advice of the medic: 'Don't tell um' anything'. He didn't. He would let Donna and Mama take care of everything. He was alive and safe, and he had Donna. Don't tell um' anything; tell um' you want a lawyer; fuck all of um'; he would tell himself.

Papa arrived. "How are you son," shaking his hand. "Son, you've made me real proud. You've made me proud to have a boy like you in the family." Donna beamed at her father. "Son, we are going to get you out of this damned place forthwith." The General yelled to the doctor, "This boy is ready to check out." And, said to him, "We're headed for Tokyo, son. You have a two-week leave coming to you, and you deserve it. Anyplace you want to go son—here in Japan, I mean. There is nothing too good for you son. You name it."

"Sir," the doctor said. "Our tests are inconclusive. I strongly recommend an additional week here in the hospital. This man may have a severe brain concussion. We need to keep him here for observation."

"Nonsense; he's fit as a fiddle! The army doesn't buy into the shell shock myth. You're looking at an airborne soldier here!" Papa said.

The doctor tried to pull Papa aside for a private talk, "Sir, our staff psychologist feels this man needs a considerable period of convalescence and counseling."

Papa would hear none of it. "Counseling; what the hell do psychologists know about war?" The doctor gave up and walked away.

"Son, you are going to receive the Silver Star for bravery under fire—above and beyond the call. Your Lieutenant—what's his name—will also receive the Silver Star. His parents will be here to accept his medal. I can't tell you how proud I am to have you in the family. I always said, my Donna knew how to judge a man, and get herself a real man. I'm proud of you son." Again, the handshake, with Donna beaming at her father and at him.

When Papa left, everything swirled around him. His head pounded as if shells were exploding nearby. You should be happy, he told himself. Instead of a firing squad, you get a medal. You're a hero. Donna believes the story.

"What's the matter, baby?" Donna asked.

Maybe you are a hero, he told himself. How would you know? You don't know shit. What difference does it make? You have Donna, and you have a two-week leave. What more do you want? Don't tell them anything; tell um' you want a lawyer; fuck all of um'.

"What's the matter, baby?"

"It's nothing, honey."

They arrived at the General's quarters at Camp Drake. Mama rushed to him, "Oh, my poor baby," she said, smothering him with kisses.

"Welcome, son." Papa said, shaking his hand, and sloshing the martini in his left hand. "Welcome home. Have a drink."

"No, the doctor said ..." Papa wasn't listening. No one was listening. He felt as if he had entered a mad house. Donna was on the couch with her mother, their arms around each other, yelling and shrieking about something.

"Don't pay any attention to them son." Papa said, handing him a martini. "They'll drive you crazy."

"Jesus!" he said; but, no one heard.

They decided to repeat their honeymoon trip. They took the same trains, and stayed in the same Japanese hotels. The idea was perfect. They would repeat the most wonderful experience of their lives. But, the honeymoon trip could not be repeated. They both understood that quickly, and told each other they didn't expect the same magic to be there. They would be more mature, and just enjoy their time together, and remember the past. But, things went sour frequently.

He woke up sitting upright on the futon, and heard a terrible scream. It was a scream of some terrified person—some lunatic. Donna held her hand over his mouth, and he realized that what he heard was his own scream. The Japanese Inn owners burst through the sliding door, their faces filled with terror.

"It's okay," Donna told them. "It's okay." They stood dumbfounded. "It's okay, he was in Korea. He is all right now; please leave."

He fell back on the futon mat, and began to cry. He cried as he had not cried since childhood. She comforted him, but he felt alone. "Oh God, Oh God, Oh God," he said;

and, he cried; not for Snider and not for Doyle, and not for Donna; he cried for himself. He was alone. He could hear and feel Donna's efforts to comfort him, but he was alone.

The days passed, some pleasantly and some marvelously, but bad times were there, waiting for an opportunity to occur. She wanted him to tell her everything. "No, you wouldn't understand."

"I can understand. I'm your wife. I love you."

"Nothing happened baby, nothing at all. I don't want to think about it. I just don't want to do that medal thing."

"Why not? You deserve it. You risked your life to save your platoon. You deserve that medal."

"I didn't risk anything. I did what I was told, and little of that. I was scared shitless, and I was no hero."

"That's always the way it is. Papa said the same thing, when he got his medal. No one expects you to be superman! Of course you were scared. Who wouldn't be scared?"

"I just don't want to do the medal thing, Donna."

"Look honey, I know how you feel." She said. No! You don't know how I feel, he told himself. I don't know how I feel! "You don't feel as if you were a hero—even though you were. You feel as if it would be cheating to accept the medal. I respect you for that honey. If it were just me, I would say fine, tell them you don't want it. But, you know how important the medal is for Papa. Just do it for him. Have I asked you for anything before?"

"No baby, you haven't."

"Well, just do this for Papa. And, if you can't do it for Papa, do it for me."

"Okay."

Papa plied him with martinis before the ceremony. His head pounded. He was not sure whether it was the same headache he experienced so often, or it was because of the drinks. They took his picture. He knew his face was contorted and unreal. They read the citation.

On July 23, 1953, Second Lieutenant James Arnold Snider and Corporal Raymond Lewis Richards, having been ordered to evacuate Zebra Hill positions, voluntarily remained behind, and moved to an advanced, unprotected position within range of enemy small arms and mortars fire, and remained at that location, calling in artillery fire on enemy positions. Their actions prevented an imminent attack on an undermanned United States unit. In that action, Second Lieutenant James Arnold Snider was killed, and Corporal Raymond Richards was wounded. For bravery above and beyond the call of duty, and for wounds received in battle, the United States awards Lieutenant James Arnold Snider, and Corporal Raymond Lewis Richards, the Silver Star, and the Purple Heart.

The citation almost seemed true. Maybe, you are a hero, he told himself. At least, he would not be arrested and charged with cowardice. Snider's parents wanted to shake his hand, and talk to him. He could not speak to them. He was desperate to leave the reception, following the ceremony.

"I have to go to bed," he told Donna. "I feel drunk and my head hurts."

"Honey; you can't leave! This party is for you. It's so important for Papa. Do it for me."

After an hour and another martini he couldn't stand the party any longer, and went to his bedroom. He drifted into a fitful sleep, and woke with Donna at his side. "Damn you! Why can't you do this for Papa? After all he has done for us." She was angry with me for the first time.

"Donna, please! I have a terrible headache. I can't stand it. I think it was the martinis. I'm sorry baby, I don't want to make you sad."

"But, you are doing it." Yes, you are, he told himself. But he could not return to the party.

In the following days, Donna insisted that he receive counseling. He attended the sessions reluctantly. They wanted him to remember Zebra; he wanted to forget it.

Donna told him he would get a medical discharge from the army. He would receive a monthly disability payment, and free medical and psychological care. He didn't want that. His Korea time was filled. He had only ten months left on his hitch, and wanted to complete that with an honorable discharge.

Donna insisted, "I can't let you be away from me while you have this problem, and I'm not going to follow you around army posts, and live on a corporal's salary."

She was right, he reasoned.

At the ranch in Texas, he tried hard to love Donna, and the great fortune that had fallen to him. Why do you have to try, he asked himself? This place is more than anything you have ever wanted. You love Donna more than your life. Why do you have to try? But, he did have to try. He tried hard.

He woke before dawn each day, and had breakfast with the workers. He worked with the veterinarian, and learned the various treatments for cattle, and how to help the cows calve. He repaired fences, and mended gates. He checked fence lines when they didn't need to be checked. He worked with the Mexican hands and gained their confidence.

Mama got him a job with the newspaper in Austin. He worked hard at that job, and pleased his boss. He would return to the ranch, and work till sundown. He loved Donna, and tried to make her know he loved her.

In his dreams the dog would crawl out of that hollow place in the stem of his brain, and he would push the dog back. Someday he would have to fight the dog, and he planned that battle. He would thrust his hand down the dog's throat, and grab its tongue, and choke the dog to death. The dog would not be able to bite his arm—to chew his hand off. Maybe, he would not be able to grab the dog's tongue. Maybe, the dog would chew off his hand. Maybe, the dog would win. He continued to push the dog back down in there. Sometimes he would wake up groaning and whimpering.

Donna would comfort him, "Was it the dog?" She would ask. You have to tell the psychologist about that, honey. He can explain it. He can help you."

"I don't want to talk to those people, baby."

Most of all he resented the picture. He was in his dress uniform, with the Silver Star on a blue ribbon around his neck. At first, the picture had been placed in the entry hall of the house. He asked the maid to remove the picture, but it reappeared.

"Donna, I don't want that picture on the wall," he said.

"Papa want's it there. This is his house."

"Papa isn't even here most of the time. Why does it have to be there?" he complained.

The picture was removed from the entry, and placed in Papa's office. When he was home alone, he would go into Papa's office, and look at that picture. The contorted face would fill him with disgust and dread of the dog.

Aunt Meg Told Me About You: The Amazon, Sunday, August 16

Shirley is wide-awake, looking at me. "You were looking at me, weren't you?" She nods. "It ain't a cute face, is it?"

"No honey, it isn't. But, it is a tender and loving face." She replies.

"I don't think so."

"It's the face of a guy that cares a lot for Shirley love, isn't it?"

"Yes, it is that." We are lying on our sides, arm's length apart. I kick the sheet down so I can see her naked body. She looks at me, too.

"We are the same height," She says. "But, look how different we are."

"Vive la difference!"

She isn't listening to me. She is mostly talking to herself, out loud—the way she does sometimes.

"How much do you weigh?"

"About a hundred and seventy; maybe one sixty-five now."

"That's thirty pounds more than me. And, it's all right here." She taps my shoulder. "I probably weigh as much as you from the waist down. Men have little butts, don't they?"

"Compared to what?"

"That's because they never have to worry about popping a baby out of there." She says, and continues, "You are a lot stronger than me."

"You're really strong, Shirley. You are the strongest woman I have ever met."

"Not compared to a man. Johnny is stronger than me too, but he doesn't know it. But, look at you. There is no fat on you. That's because of the army, isn't it?"

"Maybe."

"It would be really stupid for me to try to fight you. That would be taking a knife to a gun fight, wouldn't it?"

"Are you thinking about fighting me?"

Again, she ignores me. "I don't have to compete with you physically. I just have to remember which of us is stronger, and remember which one knows the difference between up and down."

"So which one knows the difference between up and down?" I have no idea of what she is talking about. "I don't think we are so different. We think alike."

"Ha! That's how much you know about it. We don't think alike, at all!"

"Yeah? Well, tell me something we think differently about."

"That's a good example, right there. The fact that you don't know, and I do. In fact, you don't notice anything about me. You even think I'm beautiful—that's a laugh! I could have a terrible emotional problem and you would never know."

"Yes I would. Anyway, you don't have any emotional hang ups."

"You don't think so, huh? Maybe my parents were missionaries in Africa when I was a little girl, and the natives murdered them and kept me as a slave for ten years, and I escaped through the swamp and down the river on the African Queen with Humphrey Bogart." I shake my head. "You would have no idea." She says.

Suddenly, I am concerned, "Shirley, if there is something you want to tell me, well hell, I would help you in any way, if I could."

She moves her leg over so that her toe touches my foot. "We better let Norma take care of the surgery, honey. You just stick with your snakebite doctor stuff. That's what you're good at."

"What the hell are you talking about?" I ask.

She opens her mouth slightly and moves her tongue around her lips. She has my complete attention.

"See," she says, "I know what makes that happen. At first, I thought it was because you were looking at my body, but it isn't. It doesn't even matter whether I have my clothes on or not. It's because I'm touching you. See? My toe is touching your foot. And, you're looking at my mouth. You can't even hear what I'm saying."

"Yes I can." I say, but she isn't listening to me.

"At first, I wondered what was going through that flat brain of yours, when you get this way. I thought you were thinking about some other girl. But you aren't. The blood that fills that thing up drains out of your brain. You are too retarded to think of anything but what my mouth reminds you of."

"What the hell are you talking about?"

She rolls on top of me, and continues to talk. "Here, you can look at my mouth." She opens her mouth and moves her tongue around. It had never occurred to me that her mouth excites me, but it does. "See? Your IQ is down to fifty now; pretty soon you'll start making those noises."

"Shut up." My voice sounds as if it is coming from the bottom of a well.

"I don't have to worry about what it means," her voice sounds gravelly too. "If it looks like a duck, and sounds like a duck, and acts like a duck, then it's a duck!"

I can hear what she says, but the words coming out of her pink mouth are meaningless. "Will you shut up?" I say.

"The blood runs out of my brain, too, and goes down there. But, it's not your mouth that gets me. It's your glazed eyes and retarded face and your noises."

I can't stand any more talk and cover her mouth with mine.

"**W**e satisfied each other, didn't we? It will just make it worse later."

"Make what worse?" I ask. "What the hell are you talking about?" She is still lying on top of me, and we are both too exhausted to move.

"Later I will touch your arm or something, and you will look at my mouth. And, then we will both be frustrated because we will be on a bus or a boat and we won't be able to do anything."

"That's the way it's supposed to be."

She pushes herself up, and looks at me, "No, Ray! That's not the way it's supposed to be! We are not supposed to be thinking about sex and playing with each other all day long!"

"So? What are we supposed to be doing?"

"You're supposed to go out and work in the fields from sunrise to sunset. And, I'm supposed to change the baby's diaper and cook for our six kids, and then can peaches all afternoon, so we'll have something to eat besides cornbread and beans in the middle of the winter!"

"And, then I would come back to the house and play with you. And anyway, I would shoot a pheasant or a squirrel or something so we wouldn't have to just have cornbread and beans for dinner every night."

"No Ray! Then you would chop the wood and fix the leak in the roof, and I would make another quilt, so our kids wouldn't freeze to death in the middle of the night. And, when we finally get in bed, at MIDNIGHT, we would be so tired the last thing we would think of is playing with each other, and we would be thankful that we had the cornbread and beans so our kids wouldn't be starving to death."

"So? How would we have six kids if we weren't playing with each other all the time?"

"You don't have to do it two or three times a day to make babies, Ray! It would be more like once a month or once a week, at the most."

"Once a week? No way, Jose! I would go feed the pigs, and then come back in and play with you. And, you would change the baby's diaper and then come back and we could do it again. And, when I'm plowing the fields you could come out there and pull your dress up and we could do it out there, too."

"How could we do it while you are plowing the fields?" she huffs.

"We would figure out a way to do it. You could sit in my lap, and drive the tractor."

"Sit in your lap and drive... Good lord, Ray; that proves it! You are a complete sex maniac! No wonder you can't remember anything; your brain is filled with sperm! And, now you are making me a sex maniac, too."

"You don't have to thank me for that."

"I'm serious, Ray. You're driving me crazy with this. How am I supposed to get over it?"

"I don't want you to get over it." I hear her loud sigh. "And anyway, I don't see why we have to have cornbread and beans for dinner again when we have a whole fucken cellar full of canned peaches."

She pushes herself up and looks at me, as if in shock, and then starts laughing uncontrollably. Still giggling she says: "I forgot about the canned peaches Baby." She kisses my eyes and nose: "You can have all the canned peaches you want—we've got um' coming out of our ears; I'm going to spoon feed um' to you baby." She rolls on top of me.

Later she says: "You shave at night now, don't you?"

"I'm not very smart, but I do know which side of the bread the butter is on."

"I never enjoyed kissing anyone as much as I enjoy kissing you; and, I certainly never enjoyed making love with anyone as much as I enjoy it with you. And, I can tell you for sure, I don't know how I'm going to get over this."

We go to the loading area on the river. None of the larger boats—dugouts thirty or more feet long and six feet wide—will be leaving before noon. We look for something earlier. A man tells me a smaller dugout will be leaving immediately. He introduces me to the boatman, using an Indian language. The boatman speaks very little Spanish. I am a bit worried, but the man assures me the Indian has been 'Christianized'. I ask the guy to make a deal with the Indian for our ride. He does that, and then says I can pay him now, and he will pay the boatman. No way! I tell myself.

"I pay you in Coca," I say to the Indian, in very slow and careful Spanish. The Indian nods. I give the man who made the deal for us a twenty-peso tip. We climb aboard. A few minutes later the Indian starts his outboard motor and we head downstream.

Shirley is also apprehensive about the boatman, and I assure her everything will be okay. Soon, we are enjoying the fabulous sights and sounds of a tributary of the Amazon. She wears my cap; apparently, she enjoys my cap when no one is around to see her. I like her wearing the cap too. She cocks her head up so she can see me under the visor, and flashes the 'we have a secret' look.

Although we travel on a minor tributary to the Napo River, which is just one of many tributaries of the Amazon, it is a substantial river. We are still losing considerable elevation so the flow is very fast. Where the river turns sharply, it almost seems to be banked, as a highway is banked on sharp curves. I know that must be an illusion, but the illusion is very striking; Shirley comments on that as well. The boatman frequently pulls his motor back so the prop will clear the water; apparently he is fearful of breaking his prop on logs and other debris in the river. Indeed, the river is thick with debris, including huge tree trunks floating downstream.

The sound of the outboard is very loud, but we can still hear some of the sounds of the forest. There are many sounds, none of which seem to repeat. Perhaps they do repeat, but the repertoire is long we cannot remember any particular sound. Some of the sounds suggest large animals or human cries. But, almost certainly most or all the sounds we hear are birdcalls. Interestingly, our boatman can make many of those sounds, and apparently can't resist calling back.

There are small clusters of huts every few miles down the river. Most of the women and young people are naked—the adult men usually wear boxer under-shorts. Some are in small dugouts, working hand lines or a spear for fish. At one small cluster of huts, a man with short pants and a tee-shirt waves to us. We stop.

Shirley and I take advantage of the stop to examine the layout of the small camp. Two families seem to live here. Each family has a garden around their hut, with a great variety of plants from low ground cover to larger banana and papaya plants. I sample some of the berries on a bush, and an Indian woman rushes over to tell us to stop; she points to her stomach and shakes her head.

"Why do they keep a plant with toxic berries around the house?" Shirley asks.

I ask the man with the pants and shirt about that, but he doesn't seem to understand the question, or just doesn't want to answer.

"I'll bet it's a medicinal; could be a kill or cure treatment for some serious illness," I tell her.

"What about the kids? Isn't it dangerous to have plants like that around the kids?"

"The kids probably learn fast—you know, a slap on the hand, or a good case of diarrhea. Just like city kids learning to watch for traffic on the streets."

Incredibly, there is a very large field of cassava—at least three acres. I point that out to Shirley, "That's enough cassava to feed ten families."

"Ten families on just three acres?"

"Yeah; you can get a huge amount of that stuff on a small plot, and down here it grows year-round. What the hell do they do with all that cassava? They sure don't export it out of this place."

When we get back in the boat, the man with the tee-shirt joins us. He speaks some Spanish, so I ask him questions and fill in the translation for Shirley, when she misses something. He is a medic, trained by missionaries to provide medical service to settlements along the river. He demonstrates his medical kit. It is a three-pound coffee can, with some medicines and a hypodermic needle.

I want to know how many kids the people down here have and how many survive childhood, and puzzle over how to frame the question. "Ask him how many children women have when they are forty-five years old." Shirley suggests, and I do. The man ponders the question for a moment, and then responds. I am shocked by his response.

"There aren't any women forty-five years old." I translate.

"Why not?" She asks, and then answers her own question, "My God! They die before they reach forty-five. Why do they die?" She looks almost as if she will cry.

"He says mostly infection from childbirth. But, it must be a hard life for women out here. I'll bet it was that way in the pioneer days in the States, but maybe not this bad."

"It would be as if my life were more than half over already," she says. That has taken some of the shine off the sights and sounds of the river for her, and I regret having translated the man's response. We drop the medic at another cluster of shacks, and continue down river.

At one point the boatman turns up a small tributary of the main river. I ask him where we were going, but cannot understand the response. Shirley is very worried. "Where is he taking us?"

"I don't know, love. But don't worry about it. Now, if we were in New York and the cab driver took us down the wrong street that would be the time to start worrying."

We reach an even more isolated settlement where the boatman changes boats, for reasons he cannot explain to us in his limited Spanish. Again we have an opportunity to examine an Indian settlement. This one appears to be a single family, or perhaps extended family, because there is only one house. It is a round hut made with thatch. It is perhaps twelve to fourteen feet in diameter and is a single room with a small section blocked off at the back. I figure that small section is to provide some privacy for Dad and Mom. They have an open fire pit in the middle of the room, and the thatch ceiling is black with the smoke of many fires. Soon, we were back on the main river, headed downstream to Coca. We reach the town, with just a little twilight remaining. The trip has taken almost twelve hours.

We get a nice clean hotel in Coca. The structure is old and made of wood, but incredibly there are no cracks or holes in the walls. There is only one relatively decent restaurant in the town and we go there. During dinner, a Major in the Ecuadorian Army joins us. Where are we going? Do we have passports and visas? If we were missionaries he will not be pleased with us. Not at all, I tell him. We are Catholics. I had learned in Mexico that having the wrong religion could cause serious problems.

The Major is happy with us. Yes, he can recommend an interesting trip. A group of Alama Indians have recently been resettled from the forest to a place just twenty kilometers down river. They will be happy to receive us, and we will see the naked savages for ourselves. He will arrange for a boat for us early tomorrow morning. Later at the hotel Shirley asks, "Will he really do that? Get a boat for us to that Indian village?"

"Count on it, love. Being Catholics, we deserve only the best!"

"What do you mean Catholics?"

"I told him we were Catholics. Down here the only thing worse than a baby killer is an atheist, and the only thing worse than an atheist, is a Protestant. It's the same

261

thing in Colombia; these people resent the rich Protestant missionaries. That's why he questioned us in the first place. He thought we were missionaries."

"Do you think we should really do it? Go to a village of wild Indians?"

"Love, it is the opportunity of a lifetime. You can wait for me here if you want to; but, I have to go."

"We go together."

In bed, I lie on top of her and slide down a little. "This is the one I saw through the sleeve of your blouse, on the bus. She's a sex pot."

"She's not a sex pot, and she's probably mad at you for peeking at her."

"Nah, she's not mad at me. She wanted me to see her. She would be a sex pot all the time, if her boss would let her."

She laughs, "You know, my Aunt Margaret told me all about you."

"She did?"

"Yeah; she told me about how you two were in Paris when the Nazis came in, and how you escaped to Portugal, and then caught a boat to Brazil. And, how you guys had so many adventures and how much you loved each other, and how much fun you had together."

"Oh, I remember, good old Margaret. She was almost as pretty as you."

"Ha! She's a thousand times prettier than I am. But, she told me you wouldn't notice. She said if I smile at you, you would think I'm beautiful. And, you do, don't you?"

"Yeah; what else did she tell you about me?"

"She told me what you would be thinking—when we first met—and what you would try to do. And, she was exactly right. You were thinking exactly what she told me, and you did exactly what she told me you would."

"So? What was I thinking?"

"You were thinking about how you would get my panties down."

"Shirley!" I say in mock shock. "How could you think that? And, on the first day I met you!"

"That's exactly what you were thinking. Admit it!"

"I'm not collaborating with the enemy, love. Name, rank, and serial number, is all you're going to get from me."

"It doesn't matter, I know anyway. She told me how to read your mind."

"How do you do that?"

"I'm not going to collaborate with the enemy either, honey." She continues, "Do you remember when we were on the deck, at the table, those first days? Remember how I would smile, when you said something, or did something? Well, I was reading your mind. And, I always knew exactly what you were going to do next. First, you touched my arm, and then you put your arm around my waist, and I knew you were going to try to touch my cheek next. Aunt Meg told me to push your hand away, and make you work for three days to touch my cheek." She laughs.

"Yeah; and you did, too!"

"Nah, I let you do that on the second day. I really wasn't trying to get you. If I had been trying to get you, I would have worked you like a big fish on a small fishing pole, just like she told me to."

"How do you do that?"

"Well, honey. You give um' plenty of line, and play um' till there is no fight left in um', and then you just pull um' in, and snag um'. But, I'm giving away secrets to the enemy."

"So, you weren't trying to get me, huh?"

"No. In fact, I had no intention of getting involved with you, or anyone else, for that matter."

"Why did you change your mind?"

"It was when I realized it was really you—the same guy Meg told me about. I just couldn't help it. Do you know when I knew it was really you—when I decided I wanted you?"

"It was on the boat with Margarita."

"Nah, that's when I decided I wouldn't bother to be civilized about it; I had already decided I wanted you. It was when you asked me to forgive you for what you said that night. Meg told me, if you ever hurt my feelings, or made me cry, you would feel really bad about it, and you would beg me to forgive you, and you would really mean it. And, you did, didn't you?"

"Yes, I did."

"Aunt Meg never told me how you looked, so I made up my own *beau ideal*. You were supposed to be tall and dark, with black wavy hair, and be really sexy with a French accent."

"Well, at least I turned out to be sexy."

"Sexy?" She says. "Sexy is not thinking about sex all the time! It's being suave and sophisticated. And, what happened to your French accent? You are more like a hick from Texas! And, wearing that silly cap! Some *beau ideal* you turned out to be." She giggles. "And, I'll bet I'm a thousand miles from your dream girl, too."

"You are the spitting image of my dream girl, Shirley."

"Ha! I'll bet your dream girl was cute and dainty, like Shirley Temple. How about Peggy Rice? Wasn't she the cutest girl in the class?"

"Yeah, she was. But, she taught me a lesson about cute girls. I gave up on the cheer leaders a long time ago."

"And, I'm more like a football player than a cheer leader, huh?" She says, giggling.

"You sure are, Shirley love."

"It's so amazing that I met you. I'm going to tell Aunt Meg you are still down here bumming around. You know, she left you because she thought you were going to settle down and have a bunch of kids, and she just wanted to keep having adventures. She's going to be so disappointed when she finds out you stuck around down here."

"Well, love. I tried to get her to stick with me, but you know how wild women are. But, I'm sure glad she sent you down here. It has been a long dry spell since the Nazis were in Paris—and here I thought I was in the third grade when that happened."

"**S**hirley, I want to ask you something personal, okay?"

"Okay."

"You are always asking me personal stuff. Now, I'm going to ask you something. Promise you won't get mad at me."

"How personal is it?" she asks, sitting up in the bed as if preparing to defend herself or run.

"It's the same stuff you ask me all the time." She doesn't respond. "You said you were married once, and it didn't work out." She nods yes. "What happened?" She relaxes and lies back on the pillow. "Well, what the hell did you think I was going to ask you?"

"A man like you, who knows?" She responds.

"Whata' ya mean, a man like me?" I laugh and she nods her head with that 'what next look' on her face; then she responds.

"I just couldn't stand to be around him. We were married for a year and a half. Course, that last year we weren't living together. You know something? I bet we have had more sex together in the last few days than I did with him all the time we were married. He was my first boyfriend, and I was dumb enough to marry him without knowing anything."

"Was he a queer?"

"NO! You always think that! Anytime someone acts differently than you, you think they are homosexual. Anyway, he wanted to have sex with me all the time. I just didn't like it."

"Was he mean to you? Did he hit you?" She shakes her head. "Maybe, you just didn't love him."

"I just didn't like it. You know something? I didn't think I would ever like it. But, Jerry—you know, my guy in San Francisco—he helped me to get over that. He is really gentle and understanding—the opposite of you, Ray!"

"You sure have changed, love. Married your first boyfriend; I can't believe it. Anyway, I thought I was gentle and understanding."

"Not about that! But, that's okay; I like you the way you are. And, I would like you even more, if you would stop trying to be a psychologist. You are a lot better at curing snakebite than therapy."

"Whata' ya' mean curing snakebite? Are you snake bit?" I ask.

"You wouldn't understand."

"Try me! You mean the way I make love with you?"

"No!" She says emphatically. "It's just the way you feel about me."

"Because I love you."

"No. You would feel the same way about any woman." She says.

"You aren't just any woman."

"I told you wouldn't understand." She talks in riddles, I tell myself. Don't pay any attention to her; she'll drive you crazy.

TITS ON A BOAR: COASTAL ECUADOR, SUMMER, 1956

The teachers met in the assembly hall with the principal. The hall was in the largest of three old wooden structures that surrounded the school playground. A series of long wooden tables with small chairs faced the raised platform at the front. The hall would seat two hundred children, with girls on the left and boys on the right. The floors were worn by the scuffling of thousands of little feet over the past quarter century, and they creaked under the weight of an adult. Almost every square inch of each table was marked with names and drawings—carved into the wood with sharp pencils.

There were sixteen teachers present, mostly male and mostly Mestizos from the highlands. Only three teachers, all of them women, shared the black skin of the children in this coastal town of Ecuador. They met the day before classes began so the principal could discuss school policy and objectives.

The principal was a small woman who wore a long black dress and starched white blouse, buttoned at the wrists and neck. She was a foreigner—an American. She had worked at the school for eighteen years, much longer than any of the other teachers, and she understood the culture as well or better than any of them. She spoke Spanish without a trace of accent, and she could speak the Spanish dialect of the Black children as well.

She was a Catholic Nun. She had been a missionary in Latin America most of her adult life. At age sixty-two she had been encouraged to retire and return to the United States. She requested, and received, permission to remain at the school as long as health permitted. Her parents were long dead, and she had no siblings. The Church was her home, and the school was her life. She would spend her declining years in a convent in the Highlands, and her body would be returned to the coastal town. She would be buried in a plain wooden casket, and a small stone would be placed at the head of the grave with the words, *Hermana Norma.*

The principal introduced a volunteer teacher. *"She is a high school teacher from the United States—San Jose, California, our Sister City. She will be teaching English with Maestro Gonzalez and Sister Juana,"* the Principal said. *"Her transportation to Ecuador was provided by the Sister City Organization. She is paying her expenses while in Ecuador, and volunteering her time. We will try to repay her, in a small way, by providing her with Spanish language classes."*

Maestro Gonzalez stood and spoke in English. He would be more than happy to provide Spanish classes for the volunteer teacher. He was concerned about the young woman, because she might be assaulted, in this town filled with Black men. He would try to be sure she would be safe in the community.

The volunteer from San Jose did not like Maestro Gonzalez; he had already made his intentions toward her quite clear. She intended to set him straight. She didn't like the principal, either. She had decided the Catholic Church was responsible for the slaughter and pillage of the Indians during the colonial period. She would not have volunteered to work at the school had she known of the affiliation with the Catholic Church. She especially didn't like Nuns—worthless as tits on a boar—she had said, many times. She would set the nun straight, too.

"Señor Gonzalez!" She said, standing and speaking loud enough for all to hear. "If you find some man one morning, with his throat cut and his testicles stuffed in his mouth, you will know he tried to rape me."

Sister Juana gasped and Maestro Gonzalez's face flushed. There was a murmur of whisper around the room, as those who didn't understand English, were informed of what she had said. She had hoped to shock the Principal too, but the nun was not shocked. It would take a lot more to get to the old woman, the young volunteer thought, but she had plenty of time.

After the meeting, the volunteer teacher met with the Principal in her office. The young woman did not approve of the teaching methods being used by Maestro Gonzalez or Sister Juana. She would teach her classes in her own way.

That would be fine, the Principal told her.

The volunteer would prefer to receive Spanish language instruction from some of the older students. "The best way to learn Spanish is to speak Spanish, not English!" she informed the Principal. "And, the best way to teach English is to speak English, not Spanish!"

That would be fine. Could the Principal assist her in finding a place to live?

"I can manage."

Would she care to have dinner with the Principal?

"I thought I would go to one of these bars, across the street, and get a beer first; would you care to join me?"

"No, but thank you for the invitation." The principal was pleased this young woman was willing to volunteer her time to assist the children.

"Fine; will that be all?"

Yes, that would be all.

The young woman enjoyed working with poor Black children. She threw herself into the work, and felt she was making good progress. She concerned herself with other aspects of the children's welfare, as well. Learning the children were being charged one peso per week, for the school lunch—which was surplus food donated by the US Government—she complained to the Principal.

The one peso charge is nominal, even for the poorest families, the Principal told her. The payment provides parents the dignity of paying for the support of their own children. The money is for art supplies, used by the children to paint murals on the walls, and beautify the school.

The young woman objected to the murals. "They have religious motifs; there is no place for religion in the public schools," she told the Principal.

This is not a public school. "We are supported by the Catholic Mission." The Principal was sorry the young woman had not been informed of that fact, when she had agreed to volunteer. The Principal understood her concern about religion in the school. However, she should be aware that virtually all the children were Catholics, and the fact that the church was an integral part of their cultural. No parent had ever objected to the religious motifs of the murals.

The volunteer teacher became aware that some of the children were punished severely by their parents, and sometimes by their teachers. She complained to the Principal: She would not tolerate teachers hitting the children.

The young woman was absolutely correct, the Principal told her. Hitting a child was prohibited. The principal was not aware that had happened, and would certainly put a stop to it. The young woman wanted an investigation of parents who sent children to school with bruises on their faces and arms.

"We must be very careful when we intervene between children and their parents," the Principal told her. "We must always remember that we cannot be with the child twenty-four hours a day. We will do everything in our power to educate parents in the proper methods of disciplining their children, but criminal charges are usually counter-productive."

That would not be good enough to satisfy the young volunteer. The Principal was sorry, but would not sanction a police investigation of a parent. The volunteer teacher should report cases of suspected abuse to the Principal, who would speak to the parent personally. That would not be good enough to satisfy the young woman. The Principal was sorry.

One day the young woman was asked to meet with the Principal. Maestro Gonzalez would no longer be teaching at the school, the Principal told her. Until another English teacher could be contracted, the Principal would greatly appreciate having the young woman teach some of those classes. The Principal would teach the other classes.

"Of course."

For two weeks both women worked very long hours, teaching classes through the day, and grading papers in the late afternoon. The volunteer was pleased to have been given the added responsibility.

On a late afternoon, the volunteer teacher was leaving the school, having finished grading almost two hundred pages of homework. The Principal had also just finished a similar stack of homework, and was leaving at the same time. They met at the door.

"Thank you for all this extra work," the Principal told her. "I hope we will have another English teacher soon, and we can get back to a more normal schedule."

"Well, you seem to be holding up your end of it. I guess I can hold up my end, too."

"I just want you to know we appreciate your help." The Principal responded.

"Sure," she said, walking away, and over her shoulder, "how about going over to the tienda, and having a beer with me."

"Okay," the older woman said.

She had been certain the nun would decline; now she was stuck with her. Having a beer with a nun would be an embarrassment. The two women sat together and ordered beers. "Ummm, refreshing," the older woman said, as she sipped her beer. The younger woman gave her a disbelieving look. "You didn't think I would take you up on your offer, did you?"

"Frankly no, I didn't. I thought you people had to spend your spare time praying."

The older woman continued to smile. "Sometimes even a nun needs a break from work and prayer. Perhaps I'll come over here and have a beer with you every afternoon."

"You're putting me on, Sister." But, she had to smile back at the older woman. "So, why did Maestro Gonzalez quit?"

"He didn't quit. I fired him."

"You fired him? Why?"

"Because one of the girls told me he had touched her."

"That son-of-a-bitch," the young woman snapped. "He was trying to scheme on me the first day. I should have slit his throat."

"You are a tough girl," the older woman said, smiling.

"That happened to me when I was thirteen. It took me three years to get over it. And, I can tell you, I would still love to get my hands on one of those bastards."

"You were just thirteen. I'm so sorry that happened to you. How did you get over it?"

"My Aunt Margaret; she helped me get over it. She saved me. I don't know what would have happened to me if she hadn't come along when she did."

"How did your Aunt Margaret help you get over it?"

"Well, Meg is a woman of the world. She knows all about men, and how to deal with them. She's about as different from you as a lioness from a pussycat. She just laid the whole thing out in plain English, and told me to get myself together."

"How wonderful for you that she came along at the right time."

"Ha! I doubt if you would think she is wonderful, or approve of any of the stuff she told me."

"If she helped you to get over that terrible thing, then she was wonderful. And, if what she told you put that smile on your face, after what happened to you, then she was a blessing."

"Do you really think that?"

"Yes, I really think that." The Principal told her. "You don't approve of the Catholic Church, do you?"

"No!"

"Do you want to tell me why?"

"Because of what the Church did to the Indians. They slaughtered and raped and plundered the Indians. And, they still exploit them. And, frankly, I think nuns are about as worthless as tits on a boar."

The older woman took a long breath. "Well, you certainly didn't sugar coat it for me."

"It was not my intention to sugar coat it!"

"No, I guess not. But, thank you for speaking your mind plainly." The older woman paused a moment, and then continued: "I know those terrible things happened. And, I know bad things still happen. But, the Church didn't do it then, and the Church isn't doing it now."

"Oh, really; then, perhaps you can tell me who did?"

"The Church isn't a building, or a group of priests and bishops. The Church is the people—the faith community. The Church—the people—suffered the slaughter and rape and plunder. Some of those who committed the crimes were priests and bishops. But, they were certainly not part of the Christian faith community, no matter what they said, or who they said they represented. They certainly did not represent Jesus Christ, did they?"

"No, they didn't!"

"We have to be sure the leaders of the Church—the leaders of the faith community— never do that again. And, we have to do what we can to make up for those terrible crimes." The young woman remained silent, and the older woman continued: "Do you object to the work I am doing here in this community?"

"No! Of course not! And, I'm glad you fired that son-of-a-bitch. I just wish I could have been there when you did it."

"So you could have slit his throat?" The older woman asked, smiling again.

"You bet."

"I reported him to the police, but I knew I couldn't prove it. I had a friend of mine put the story and his picture in the local newspaper, and in the Quito paper—where he's from. I told the reporter to say I thought he molested boys, too. That probably wasn't true, but I wanted to hurt him as much as I could, and these men down here absolutely hate a man who molests boys. I wanted to be sure it would follow him, and he would never be able to teach in a school again. But, I guess it would have given me a lot more pleasure to slit his throat."

"You; a nun would think about slitting the guy's throat?"

"You bet! Even a nun can think about slitting the throat of a man that would do that."

The two women sat for a minute sipping their beer. "You are not angry with me, are you?" The young woman said.

"No."

"I have been hateful to you; why aren't you angry with me?

"You had a reason."

"I think I was wrong. You know, when you refused to tell the police about the parents of the kids that had been mistreated, I knew you were right; I just wanted to be mad at you." The older woman did not respond. "I'm sorry I did that."

"You don't need to be."

"Why do you treat me this way? I'm not a Catholic; I'm not even a Christian. Why do you treat me like...you treat me like you like me. Why do you do that?"

"I can see your work; you love the children and you are doing your best to help them." The principle replied.

"But was wrong about you."

"Well, you are right about nuns in one way." The Principal stopped and looked at the young woman for a bit, and then she continued, "I guess my breasts have been about as worthless as tits on a boar." The young woman laughed aloud and the older woman chuckled to herself.

After a few moments the younger woman broke the silence: "Do you ever regret having become a nun?"

"Yes. But I don't dwell on it; I've had an exciting life and I believe I have served the Lord. But, I never had children, and I never had a man to love me."

"Well, you didn't miss much—not having a man, I mean. And, anyway you've had hundreds of children—thousands!"

"Don't you ever think about having children of your own?" the older woman asked.

"We already have more children in this world than there are people to take care of them; I would think we would take care of the one's we already have before we start thinking about having more."

"It's not healthy for a girl your age to be afraid of sex."

"I'm not afraid of it. I was married once, you know; I divorced him."

"Was he a bad person?"

"No. I just couldn't stand it—always trying to touch me; and as far as I'm concerned they can stick that thing up their own butts."

"That would be hard to do since it's mounted in the front. Looks like God designed it to go into a woman."

The young woman looked shocked: "I'm surprised you could say that! Maybe your profession has kept you so innocent you don't know how many thousands of women and children have been raped and molested by that thing—by men!"

"Sex is the glue that holds men and women together and causes them to have children and become a loving family. Something that has so much power for good will also have great power for evil when it is misused, wouldn't it? Would you have that otherwise?" The older woman paused for a few seconds, and then continued: "Think about your mother's love and how great a gift that has been for so many people. Isn't that why it is so terrible for a child when a mother fails in that duty? Can you really have good without bad? Why is it that those people you love the most—your parents, your siblings, your spouse—why is it that those are the persons who sometimes hurt you the most?"

"So, you're a psychologist too?"

"I studied psychology; and, I've spend a good part of my life working with many women and children who have been raped and molested; I know how terrible that is. But it wouldn't take much of a psychologist to see why you are troubled with sex, after what happened to you."

"Anyway, I thought you people didn't believe in divorce! Aren't you going to condemn me for that too?" The young woman asked.

"Doesn't sound like you were very married in the first place. And, anyway it's not my job to condemn you or anyone else."

The young woman did not respond for a few moments, and then said: "You're not—not what I thought."

"Well I'm certainly glad of that."

"I have to go catch my truck to the village; they always leave late, but the one time I'm not there they will probably leave on time."

"Go ahead. I'll pay for our beer."

"No; I'll pay; I invited you." She got up and walked over to the counter to pay. She returned to the table: "I'm embarrassed to say this, but after paying for the beer I don't have enough money to pay for the truck; can you loan me three pesos?"

"Sure." The older woman gave her a five-peso note.

"This is so stupid. I didn't bring any extra money; I usually just bring enough to pay the truck and maybe have a coke or something. This is so stupid."

"It's not stupid. There is no reason to carry more money than you need; and anyway, you never dreamed I would take you up on your offer to have a beer."

"I'm going to think about what you said. Maybe we could have dinner sometime and talk more—Norma. I'm sorry I was so rude. I knew I was wrong; I can see how you work for the children. I don't know why I did that."

"Don't worry about it; it's nothing. I can see how you work with the children too. You are a very good person Shirley; we are on the same team."

SNAKES EVERYWHERE: THE AMAZON, MONDAY, AUGUST 17

Tell me about Donna." I have just opened my eyes, and she is wide-awake beside me.

"What about her?"

"You two lived together for a whole year?"

"More like two years."

"Did you hang on to each other like this, all that time?"

"I don't want to talk about that, Shirley."

"I don't mean THAT! I don't have a filthy mind like you, Ray! I mean, just being together all the time, and holding on to each other."

"Well, yeah. But, we weren't together all the time. We had to go to work, you know. I would drive her to the hospital every morning, and then go work at the newspaper."

"You drove her to work? And, then you picked her up after work?" I nod. "And, then what?"

"I don't know; sometimes we would have dinner in town and go dancing at one of those country and western bars."

"So you would dance with her. Did you dance with other girls? Did she dance with other men?"

"No! You don't let some other guy dance with your wife in Texas, Shirley. Maybe that's the way it is in California, but not in Texas."

"And, then you go home and hold on to each other all night long. And, how about on weekends? What did you do? Just hold on to each other day and night?"

"Sure we did things together, but not necessarily. Sometimes I would go hunting, or work on the ranch, and she would go shopping or something. What are you getting at? If you're married to someone, you are supposed to be together."

"You are not supposed to be together all the time. People are supposed to have their own lives, Ray."

"We are together all the time."

"Yes, I know! I'm just wondering how long we can keep doing this."

We met the Major at the river at seven am. He introduces a boatman, and we are off. On the way down river, I tell her about how the government of Ecuador, and all the other countries around the Amazon, is rounding up the wild Indians, and forcing them into settlements, so the oil and lumber companies, and the farmers, can take the land.

"My Anthropology Professor in Mexico says these Indians usually live in clans of no more than a dozen or so and move every few months when the game becomes scarce. When they are forced to live in large villages, there won't be enough game for everyone. And, diseases spread through the villages, because wild Indians have never been exposed to most of those diseases and they have no immunity."

We continue talking and exchanging impressions of the river and the forest. The river is much wider than upstream from Coca; I figure another major tributary must have joined. It runs fast and carries huge logs and other floating debris. The boatman is always alert, and pulls his outboard motor up when we bump over a log or something, so it won't damage his prop. About an hour downstream, the boatman pulls into a clearing on the river and beaches the boat. He will wait for us there.

We get out of the boat and walk along a trail to the village, about two hundred yards from the river. The huts are in a very large circle. We pass between two huts, and walk into the central grounds. There are several women and children in the nearby huts. The women are nude from the waist up, and the children and young people are completely nude.

Shirley wants to stop and talk with them. "Not yet. We better get permission from the headman first. Anyway, these women probably won't speak Spanish." We walk into the middle of the common ground and stop.

"What now?" She wants to know.

"I don't know, love. They *speaki'* first."

A few children are running from hut to hut—probably informing the people of our presence. From across the clearing, a man emerges from his hut, carrying a shotgun. He wears only jockey shorts, and has his hair in a long braid down his back. He looks lean and mean—reminding me of Jack Palance in the movie *Shane*, and walks directly toward us with his shotgun at the ready.

"Let's sit on this log. We'll try to look more non-threatening—if that's possible". I tell her. We sit. The man begins to yell at us in a high-pitched Indian language, as he approaches. We can't understand a single word, but we know for sure he is unhappy to see us in his village.

"*No entiendo, Señor,*" I say to him. He yells louder.

"Should we leave?" She whispers.

"Love, we ain't moving off this log until he lowers that shotgun." To the man I say, "*No entiendo, Señor.*" The man turns and yells back at the huts. A young naked boy joins us. The man shouts at the boy.

"*What you doing here?*" The boy asks, in poor Spanish.

I reply in very slow and careful Spanish. "*We were just coming down river from Coca, and wanted to stop and meet some of your people here.*"

The boy chatters to the man and the man barks back. The boy says: "*My uncle says, you get out of here!*"

"*Please tell your uncle, we will leave immediately. Tell him, we are very sorry to have disturbed his village. Perhaps, we could pay your uncle fifty pesos, for this inconvenience.*"

The boy chatters again and the man barks. The boy says: "*My uncle says, you get out of here!*"

"*Tell him, I wish to say to him, Yes Sir. We are leaving now.*" Shirley has understood enough to know we were leaving immediately. She stands and turns back in the direction we came. "Walk in front of me." I say calmly. She does.

The man is joined by several others—some with shotguns and others with spears or machetes. They walk along with us. Some of the younger men, mostly naked, run up and touch or slap Shirley or me on the back.

"Don't pay any attention to them, love. Just keep walking." I say, trying to keep my voice calm.

As we approach the boat, some of the Indians begin to yell. Our boatman pulls out a shotgun from under his seat.

"*Put the shotgun away,*" I yell to him. He continues to hold the shotgun. "Shirley, stop! Just stand right there." To the man in the boat I yell, *"Put the shotgun away. We are not going to get into the boat until you put the shotgun away."*

"You're telling him to put it away aren't you?" She asks with her voice shaking.

"Yes, love. Don't talk."

Finally the boatman puts his shotgun away, and we continue to the boat. Shirley gets in, and I push us off the bank, and scramble aboard. The boatman starts his motor. The men on shore are all jumping up and down, and yelling at us in shrill, high-pitched tones.

"Sit down in the bottom of the boat." I tell her.

"There's water in the boat," she responds.

"I don't give a damn if there are snakes in there! Sit on the bottom!" She does. "Now lie down—put your head below the freeboard." She does. I sit on the bench, and yell to the boatman, *"Go out into the river; move away from them."*

"You get down here!" She yells at me.

"I don't think that would be a good idea, love."

"Then why did you tell me to get down here?"

"It's always okay for a woman to be scared. I'm not sure they would take to a man doing the same thing. We have to play the odds."

"Damn you, Raymond! Sitting up there with that stupid baseball cap on your head like a cowboy: Get down here! If you don't get down here, I'm going to get up."

The boatman begins to laugh. I start laughing, too. "Damn you, Raymond! Don't laugh at me! I'm getting up!" And, she does.

"It's okay now. We're out of range."

She looks back at the Indians, "THEY ARE RIGHT THERE!"

"Out of shotgun range; now, if they had Garands, they could pick us off at two hundred yards. But then, if they had Garands, they would never have been rounded up and put into that pen in the first place."

"Garands?" She asks, with disgust.

"Yeah, a Garand is ..."

She interrupts me. "I don't want to know anything about your army stuff! You scared me half to death! And, it looks as if I've peed on myself." She looks around at her wet bottom. I have to laugh at that, and her fright becomes a nervous giggle.

"Love, if we had half a brain between us, we would all have peed on ourselves."

The boatman is having a big laugh. "Why is he laughing at us?" She asks.

"He's not laughing at us. He's laughing with us. Down here people always laugh, after a close call. I've seen it a dozen times. Once in Guatemala I saw a guy crossing a street without looking and a car slammed on the brakes and barely hit him—enough to knock him down. But the dude stood up and was unhurt, and started laughing, and then everyone started laughing like crazy."

"That doesn't make sense."

"Well, in a way, it does. There is a great release of tension, and since no one got hurt, they just let the tension out with laughter." I put my hands out, palms up, and shrug my shoulders, and then turn to the boatman with the same expression. He roars with laughter. We begin to laugh along with him.

"Put the shotgun away, or we won't get into the boat." The boatman yells, reenacting the scene.

"He's copying what you said, when you wanted him to put the gun away, huh?" She says. I nod.

"Women and children below deck," I yell back at him. *"Prepare to repel boarders."* The boatman roars.

"What about women and children?" She asks, wanting the rest of the translation.

"Below deck; and, prepare to repel boarders." She enjoys the joke too.

"We must look like idiots coming up the river in a dugout, all yelling and laughing."

When we arrive back at Coca, Shirley jumps into the water. "What are you doing? Aren't you wet enough already?"

"I want the whole thing wet, so people won't think I peed on myself."

I translate that to the boatman, and he begins to laugh again. It is contagious, and we laugh with him. Soon all the people around the docks are laughing too. They have no idea of what we were laughing about, but apparently don't want to miss the fun.

We have lunch at the restaurant. Shirley is elated. "No one will ever believe I did that. I would be silly to tell anyone, because they could never believe it."

"I know what you're saying, love. I've had lots of things happen to me down here that no rational person could ever believe."

"Ya' know honey, if I hadn't been with you, you would probably have just gone down there and joined that tribe. You would have been out shooting wild animals in the forest with them, wouldn't ya?"

"No way; I don't know if those people were really inclined to shoot us, but I can tell you for sure, if you hadn't been there the probability would have been a hundred times higher."

"Really; you mean they don't shoot ya, if you have a woman with you?"

"No. I mean, I doubt if they would shoot a woman. They would keep her for sex, just like we probably would. But, they have to know that hell fire would come down on them if they tried that with a White woman."

"So, why did you make me sit in the bottom of the boat?"

"When the shooting starts, anyone can take a round. Besides, this is all theory. For all I know, these people shoot the women and kids first. You have to play the odds."

"You and your damned odds; and, your stupid baseball cap," she says, smiling at me.

The Major comes in the restaurant. The boatman has told him about our close call. The Major says he will teach the naked savages a lesson. I try to tell him there was no problem, but he insists something must be done. He cannot have tourists threatened in his district.

"No," I explain to the Major. *"They didn't threaten us. We were treated kindly. It's just that our boatman misunderstood and pulled out his shotgun. It wasn't his fault; he just misunderstood. Really Major; there is no problem."*

Yes, there is a problem.

Shirley is apprehensive. She has picked up enough to know the consequences for the Indians could be serious. She wants the whole story. I fill her in and she is devastated.

"I can't live with that! It means we have caused it. I won't live with that, Ray!"

"I'll talk him out if it, don't worry." I try to find a way to get to the Major. I notice he has US paratroop wings on his shirt, and ask where he went to jump school.

"Fort Campbell, Kentucky," he replies, obviously proud of that fact.

"With the Hundred and First; the Screaming Eagles?" I ask.

"Yes." He says, obviously proud of the nickname for the 101st Airborne Division, and begins to tell jump stories. When I can, I tell Shirley I'm trying to get him off the Indian's case, and onto jump stories.

"This better work; if he is going to bomb that village, I swear I will go in the kitchen and get a knife and stab him." She says, in a low serious tone.

"Whoa, love, he wouldn't consider bombing the village, and he knows some English—be careful." I share a couple of my jump stories with the Major, and tell him I fought in Korea. He is impressed. Had I been an officer? Of Course, a First Lieutenant. Had I lost soldiers in battle? Of course, a third of my command. Had we killed enemy soldiers? Of course, many hundreds—perhaps more than a thousand—and taken 872 prisoners of war. He is more than impressed. He has a plane going to an army outpost, on the Peruvian border, in the afternoon which will return early evening. He will be delighted if we will join him. I tell him we would love to join him, but have to be back in Quito by noon on Tuesday. That is not a problem. He will send us on a military plane to Quito, early Tuesday morning.

Shirley is worried sick. I tell her I am making progress. *"Major,"* I say. *"We are really concerned that our trip to the Indian camp may have caused problems for those people. My wife is so romantic about the Indians. She would simply die if we have caused the*

Indians to suffer in any way. The Indians treated her with such kindness and politeness. Some of the Indian women kissed her, and even the men covered themselves so she would not be embarrassed."

There is no problem at all, the Major said; the issue is closed. *"I need to explain this to my wife, Major; please excuse me." Of course.*

"Love, the issue is closed. I told him they treated us with such kindness, you simply loved them, and could not stand the thought, they may suffer in any way. He bought it. He isn't going to do anything to the Indians."

"How do you know he won't do it after we leave?"

"I'm going to tell you the truth. Sooner or later he will find a reason to go down there and bust heads. But, it won't be because of us. Anyway, it isn't something he is personally responsible for. It's a process, like a train rolling down the track that no one can stop. The Indians stand in the way of progress, just as they did in the States in the 1800's. There is nothing anyone can do about it. It's the world market, the oil companies, the almighty US Dollar. It isn't fair to try to lay it off on this fellow. The people in California, who put gas in their cars, are just as guilty as he is, maybe more." She seems convinced. "And, there is more," I continue, excited, "You are not going to believe this. He has a plane going out to the Peruvian border."

"Why do I have the feeling, I'm going to regret this?"

"No, really; he invited us to fly with him, and he is going to fly us to Quito tomorrow, so we will be back in Esmeraldas by tomorrow night."

"We just get out of one crisis by the skin of our teeth, and now we jump into another one." She apparently puts the word jump together with my paratrooper stories, "My God, Ray! We are not jumping out of a plane."

I translate her statement that we are not going to jump out of the plane, and the Major laughs. To her I say "Don't be silly. We are just riding down there. We will have a fantastic view of the rainforest. I mean, it's the chance of a lifetime, and we are leaving right now."

The Major stands to leave. "Come on, love. The plane is leaving."

There is a C47 near the end of a grass runway. The Major parks his jeep at a tin building. He tells us to go ahead and get aboard the plane, and he walks into the building. We walk across the field toward the plane.

"Ray, tell me why we are doing this. I know there is a very important reason. Are we doing it to save the *whole free world*? I thought the French were already doing that in Indo-China."

I begin to laugh, "You don't have to go. You can wait here in Coca."

Suddenly she seems to smile: "Oh, yes! I remember why we have to go. Otherwise, the Major would bomb the Indian village."

"What are you talking about?"

"It's either us or the Indians, isn't it? Frankly, I couldn't have lived with myself anyway, if we had let him bomb the Indian Village."

"Shirley! What on earth are you talking about? He wasn't going to bomb the village, and anyway this trip has nothing to do with that. Jeez, love! It's the chance of a lifetime—to see the rainforest from the air; that's all."

She gives me a hug, and an obviously fake smile, "I know you are trying to make me feel as if nothing is going to happen. Thank you for that."

"Shirley! I'm not going to let you get on the plane thinking this way."

She runs to the stairs and climbs to the door of the plane. "Don't try to keep me from getting on this plane. I swear I won't be able to live with myself if I don't do it." She turns and looks at the interior of the plane, "Oh, lord! There are no seats on the plane, and the whole thing is filled with bombs."

"For Christ's sake, Shirley; you sit on these web seats against the side. Those aren't bombs. That's the food and supplies he is carrying down there. So, he's carrying some ammo; hell, this is a military flight!"

"It doesn't matter. I would rather stand, anyway."

"You can't stand up. You have to have your seat belt on for takeoff. Just like any other plane."

"Ray, what difference could it possibly make?"

"You're getting off this plane!" I take her arm, and try to pull her toward the door.

She sits on the net seat. "Okay, strap me down."

"Strap you down? It's just a seat belt!"

"I really didn't want to die sitting on a net like this," she says.

"We are not going to die! Jeez, these C47's are the safest airplanes in the world. You could hold them together with baling wire."

She turns and holds my face in her hands, "Darling, if it is possible to hold it together with baling wire, then we know for sure what the Ecuadorians are using to hold it together with, don't we?"

"That's just a figure of speech. This plane is in good shape."

"Look," she says, pointing to the static line cable above us, stretching from the front to the back of the plane, "they are using baling wire to hold the back of the plane on."

"That's the static line cable! You hook your chute up to that cable so your static line will pull the parachute open. That's not baling wire! Oh lord, I'm getting you off this plane." She holds me back, and refuses to get up.

Several soldiers come on board with boxes and bags. The door is closed, and the engines start. The plane shakes and rattles—as C47's do.

She speaks as if she is resigned to her fate. "We aren't even going to make it to the runway. The plane is blowing up right now."

"There's no problem! I've jumped these planes lots of times. They always make this noise."

"Then, where are our parachutes?" I think I catch a tiny smile in her face. Good lord! She's going to her death smiling!

Suddenly, I remember how military pilots always rev the engines up to one hundred percent at the end of the runway and then release the brakes with a head-snapping jerk. I figure that will scare hell out of her.

"Look, love. When we are at the end of the runway, they are going to give the engines full power and hold the brakes, and then let go for a fast start. That's totally normal—don't worry about it."

"I want you to know, I don't regret falling in love with you."

"I swear to you, everything is okay!" I say.

We are at the end of the runway. The pilot gives the engines full power and then releases the brakes. The plane rattles and shakes. The noise is boisterous. I figure she must be terrified.

She turns to me calmly, and yells over the noise, "There is only one thing I regret."

"Oh shit!" I say, disgusted. "Okay, tell me what you are going to regret, as we take our last breath of life."

"If I go to heaven, I will never see you again." She says.

I am in a state of shock. It is so unlike her, to say such a thing. Indeed, it is so unlike her to think the plane is going to crash. Then, I notice the tiny smile is spreading across her face. The plane clears the runway and we hear the wheels lock up. She smiles broadly, and then gives me my idiot look, with her head cocked sideways, tongue out, and hands extended, with palms out.

"I can't believe this. You had me worried sick, and you were just putting me on. You aren't afraid of this plane, are you?"

"You mean a C47? Oh hell, honey," she says, in a deep authoritative voice, "these are the safest planes in the world. You could hold them together with baling wire. Everyone knows that," she laughs.

"Why the hell did you have me snort'en back there? How can you say things like that with..."

"With a straight face?" She fills in for me. "It's called putting coals of fire on their heads—check your bible." She is laughing so hard, she can hardly speak.

"How can I ever take you seriously again? No matter what you say, I'll think you are just putting me on."

"Welcome home, love." She says, continuing to howl.

The snake has tagged me good. You knew that snake was out there GI, and you were going to step on it sooner or later. So, what's your fucken problem, I ask myself, and join her laughter.

"You know the problem with the damn snakes?" I say. "I mean, I don't really care about them, ya' know, but, they always pop up just when you don't expect them, and they scare the shit out of you."

"I jerked on your chain real good, didn't I?" She laughs.

"You surely did, Shirley love. You surely did."

The view from the window is fabulous. The forest canopy stretches out forever, like the ocean. The Napo River and tributaries snake across the almost flat land. We see the Indian village we visited in the morning. That village constitutes the largest clearing we will see between Coca and Rocafuerte. Other occasional clearings are no more than a quarter acre, with one or two round huts. Sometimes we see a small dot, standing or moving across a clearing.

"They are wild Indians." She says. "For them to see our plane...it would be like us seeing a UFO from Mars, wouldn't it?"

"I guess they have seen many planes. They are right on the flight path to Rocafuerte. But, I guess they would have no more idea about what we are, than we do about UFO's."

She insists we look out the same window so we can see the same things, even though there is hardly room for two faces. After fifteen minutes into the flight she becomes quiet, just turning to me occasionally, to make sure I see a clearing or a canoe on the river. After about a half-hour, she turns to me, and I think she may have tears in her eyes.

"Those are real people out there." I nod. "They live out there in the forest, with the animals." I nod. "They have always lived out there, haven't they?" I nod. "And, now the Major and his people are going to go out there and kill them, or round them up, and make them live in those villages, where they will die." I don't nod, but I know it is true. "It isn't really the Major, is it? It's us. We are causing it."

"Yeah, I guess we are causing it." She turns back to the window and looks down.

At Rocafuerte the Major drives us around in a jeep while supplies are off-loaded from the plane. It is a military outpost, with a grass airstrip and a few buildings and bunkers. There are a few Indians around the camp—mostly women. Probably prostitutes and workers for the men, I assume. It is a sad place to visit.

By the standards of the U.S. Army I know, the place is a joke. Almost all the gun emplacements are focused on the river on the downstream side. Obviously, they expect an attack by Peruvians to come up the river. But, just as obviously, any enemy with half a brain would come ashore a mile down and flank the base, or attack from the rear. I figure a couple of platoons of soldiers from the Eighty-Second could parachute in just before daylight and kill or capture all of them in half an hour and sustain no more than a handful of casualties. Perhaps there is something here I don't see, but I doubt it.

We are back on the plane headed for Coca in less than an hour. Again, we stand and look out the window and mostly say nothing. I know it had been a strong emotional experience for her, and I don't want to disturb her thoughts. She wants to see our Indian villages again, and we change to a window on the other side of the plane, as we approach Coca.

Neither of us is in the mood for drinks and dinner with the Major, and he is sure to invite us. I suggest telling the Major she is a bit airsick. She agrees. After the plane is on the ground, I thank the Major, and politely decline his invitation for food and drinks, using the air-sickness excuse. Perhaps, if she feels better, we will come down to the restaurant later. We shake hands, and the Major apologizes to Shirley for the bumpy ride. He will have a plane leaving for Quito tomorrow at about ten AM. We should meet him at the restaurant at nine, and ride with him to the airstrip.

We have dinner at a *tienda* across from the hotel. They serve us fried fish and cassava. I have three beers with dinner, and decide to order another.

"I've figured out why that man planted so much cassava." She says. I give her a questioning look. "Back on the river, where those people had that big field of cassava."

"So, you figured it out, huh? How did you figure it out?"

"Just sitting here watching you."

"Watching me?"

"Yeah, just watching you." I wait for her to continue. "Just thinking about how many acres of barley it would take, to keep you in beer."

"Yes! You're right! They can't eat that much cassava, but they can drink it! They could probably even ship the booze up river by canoe, just like hillbillies in Kentucky making corn whiskey. They could afford to ship it to New York if they needed to, or just drink it themselves. Of course, sure—it's obvious! It's so simple; why didn't I think of that? Perhaps, I could take you on as research assistant."

"How much does the job pay?"

"Two hundred and fifteen a month; but, you have to provide my breakfast and beer out of that, and buy me a new baseball cap, if something happens to this one."

"Sounds as if my expenses would exceed my salary."

"Yeah, but I will throw in all the loving you can stand, as a bonus."

"Well, that sweetens the deal. Do I get two weeks paid vacation every year?"

"No, love; you never get to be out of my sight, except for five minutes a day in the bathroom."

"Hum, I'll have to talk to my agent about it. I may get better offers, you know."

I put my hand on hers. "I mean it, Shirley."

She jerks her hand away. "Stop it! It's one thing to joke and have fun."

"I'm just kidding," I lie.

That night in bed she wants to do therapy. "You live sort of dangerously, don't ya?"

"Nah; well hell, you have to take a calculated risk once in a while, otherwise, you might as well stay home with your mother."

"No, I mean, you do things that put you at risk. Like fishing with those men, and going down to the Indian village—as if you want to see if something will happen."

"No! That's not true. I go fishing with those guys because I want to learn about that, and hell, I can swim. I admit that trip to the village was a mistake, but it was a calculated risk. I'm not trying to kill myself, if that's what you mean. I don't get this line of questioning. What are you getting at?"

"It's nothing honey." And, then, "Well, to tell the truth, Norma wanted me to check on this, and I'm glad the answer is negative. You know, it's hard for her to understand when I tell her about some of the things you do. For her it sounds completely bonkers, ya' know. She just can't understand how a person could do the things you do. But, I understand it. I do some of those things too, and I'm not..."

"Not suicidal?" I fill in for her.

"No. Well, yeah; that's what Norma was concerned about. But, I told her she was wrong on that. Anyway, I'm glad I can tell her I was right."

I wake up at moonrise—probably about 3:30. We are lying on our sides, facing each other. While sleeping she usually makes a light hum sound with her breathing, but now she makes no noise at all.

"Are you awake?" I whisper. She nods her head. I put my hand on her cheek. "You know something?" She lifts her head slightly to indicate—what? "I can't believe how happy I am to have you, and to be in love with you. And, you know what makes it really great?" She lifts her head slightly again. "I have all of you to love, and be with." She nods, yes. "And, you know what makes it even better? I think you enjoy loving me, and being with me, as much as I do you."

"That's right."

"Do you know where your very best part is?"

"It's the bottom part of the curves," she whispers.

I have to laugh at that, and then say: "You have a part that is even better."

She thinks for a moment. "If you try to make a joke, or say something crude, I'm going to be *really* disappointed."

"No, love," I chuckle, "your very best part is right here." I touch her forehead, just above her nose. "Right behind there, where the real you sits in a captain's chair and a big control panel with dials and levers, and runs this whole apparatus." I rub my hand down her body. "Having that little Shirley in your head is what makes the rest so important to me."

"That's a really neat thing to say!" She props her head up with her hand, resting her elbow on the bed. "You know; I've thought about that. Not just about the real you in the captain's chair thing, but about having someone's inner person—someone you love—for yourself."

Suddenly, she is awake and interested, and wants to talk. I prop my head up on my hand, and listen. "You know; without that, it's just sex. It wouldn't mean anything. I mean, if that's all we wanted, we could just masturbate ourselves to orgasm, and wouldn't even need each other at all." I nod. "Do you know why I liked you—you know, from the beginning? I knew you didn't just want to hit on me. Oh, I knew you wanted that too, but you wanted more than that. You wanted closeness, didn't you? What we have now." I nod. "And, that's why I wanted to be in love with you. That's what makes it so great."

We lie together in silence for a while. "Do you know how rare this is?" She says. I wait. "It's really rare. I know lots of women who have never had anything like this." I feel she is talking about herself, and it makes me sad. She continues, "Why do we get to have this, when there are so many people, walking around their whole lives, without ever having someone to really love."

"I don't know. Maybe, they just don't know it can be this way."

"You know, I've thought about the little me in my head that runs this whole apparatus, as you put it; I never had her in a captain's chair, with a control panel. She was always just in there, kind of running things. She didn't have to pull any levers, or tell me anything. Do you know what I mean?"

"Maybe, everyone has the same feeling."

"Yeah, maybe they do. Maybe they do, because it's really true."

We are quiet for a long time.

"I want to tell you something important." She says. "I want to ask you to do something for me—to stop doing something. Will you listen, and try to understand?"

"Yes."

"I want you to stop trying to take that little Shirley in my head." I don't respond. "I didn't know you would try to take that. I didn't know anyone could ever take that."

I don't want to respond, but she waits. "I will never do anything to hurt you." I say.

"How do you know? Maybe, you would take that, and then you wouldn't give it back. Maybe, I wouldn't be able to get it back, even if you did give it to me." We are quiet again while she waits for me to respond, but I don't. "I'm not trying to do that to you. You have to promise not to try to do that to me, either." I can't respond. I feel I already have the little Shirley, and she is asking me to give her back. "Promise me, Ray. Promise me, now."

"I promise I will let you go; I will let you go completely, when you guys leave next Tuesday." Saying that makes a tear come into my eye. Somehow she knows, and uses her finger to wipe it away.

"You have already taken my little Shirley haven't you?" She says, and then adds, "I knew you had."

We lie close together on our sides. The pale moonlight through the window reflects off a long tear-streak on the left side of her face. I feel closer to her than before. I like it, but it scares me. In my pursuit of her I have been reckless; I have assumed she would always maintain some degree of balance. Now, I'm not so sure.

"Don't stand up in the canoe, Shirley. You'll tip it over and dump both our butts overboard. And, frankly, I doubt if I could save you."

"You've been standing up in the canoe from the beginning, so don't tell me what to do. Anyway it's not saving me that I'm worried about."

"You knew what I meant, didn't you?"

"I always know what you mean, and what you're thinking. So, don't ever tell yourself you can think something and I won't know about it."

We continue to lie there without talking for a long time. Finally, I feel the crisis has passed. "You know the problem with the little guy up there in your head, that's running you?"

"That little gal up there," she corrects. "I don't have any guy running me."

"Yeah, that's what I mean. The little gal up there would have to have another tiny gal up in her head, running her."

The serious tone is broken, and she begins to giggle. "And, I suppose there would have to be a wee little gal inside the head of the tiny gal too, huh?"

"Exactly."

"Hey," she says, mischievously; "it's like 'bugs have little bugs on their backs to bite um'."

"A perfect analogy."

"Honey you are so damned crazy, I'll be lucky to survive it."

THEN ONE DAY HE STOPPED THINKING ABOUT HER: TEXAS, AUTUMN, 1955

Donna didn't have enough to do on the ranch. She insisted on taking a job at the hospital. Having her spend her days with other people made him jealous. She had grown into an even sexier woman than the girl he had met in Korea, and she still had the innocence he remembered, when he had seduced her with a few quick words and kisses. He tried harder to love her. He met her at the hospital when she finished her shift, and took her to dinner. He bought cowboy boots and clothes, and took her out to the local country music dance halls. He suggested she should get pregnant.

"Not till you have your problem under control."

But the real problem was the ranch, and the tremendous wealth she controlled. He often wished the ranch and wealth were somehow lost; then he could be the husband—then she could depend upon him. He had to ask himself day after day; did I marry her for her money? Did I want her to help me get out of the fighting in Korea? Am I the lowest shit-head guy in the world? Why don't you get off your stupid ass and take control? But he could not take control. He lived on HER ranch. He was supported by HER. He was just a worthless piece of shit.

He stopped telling her about the dog, and became more isolated than ever. His problem was not under control. He was dependent upon her and on Mama and Papa.

His salary at the newspaper was just enough to pay for their dinners and dance hall time, and other personal expenses. He could not have dreamed of paying rent on their portion of the ranch house. He could not pay for plane tickets to places she wanted him to take her. His job at the paper was a dead end. There was little chance he would ever do more than write about local crime and political scandal.

He convinced himself that if he could be his own man, he could handle his problem. Dependency became central to his lack of self-worth and depression. He would have to make the break. He would go to Mexico City and study journalism. His GI bill and the disability check would be more than sufficient to cover tuition and living expenses. He would perfect his Spanish, and specialize in US-Mexico border issues. She would go with him. They would live modestly, without support from Mama. They would be as they had been in Korea, without thought of fine clothes and cars, and no concern with maintaining their position in Austin society.

"No!" Living poor had no appeal for her. She had paid her dues in Korea, and she had a right to enjoy her status in Texas society. She would not be a part of his running away from his problem. Why had he not taken advantage of the excellent medical care available to him? Why couldn't he show a little gratitude for the things Mama and Papa were doing for him? After all, they had asked nothing of him, and have given him anything he wanted. She didn't believe in divorce. It was time for him to conform—to give up his silly ideas, and become a real member of the family.

"No!"

In Mexico, he was excited by the exotic flavor of the city. He loved the people and the language. Many of his fellow students were also vets of the Korean War, and he felt camaraderie with them. The ex-GI's, all living on the GI Bill, became an informal clan. Membership was limited to guys who could speak Army without an accent. Other fellows would try to fake Army-talk, but it would come out stilted and awkward. He had been surprised that ex-Marines and airmen spoke almost the same dialect of Army he did. Members of the clan didn't care about his problem, and many had problems of their own.

They all received their GI checks on the same day of the month. One guy would always buy one of those big three liter, wicker-covered bottles of Bacardi rum, three dozen limes and a case of cokes. They would drink and talk about the funny things that happened in the service, and generally raise hell.

Late in the evening when most of the guys were drunk, someone might start talking about the killing and dying, and the mood would turn somber. Arguments, and sometimes fights, would break out. He, and some of the other guys, would leave the party 'when that shit started'. "This is the kind of conversation I walk away from," he would say, when the blood and guts stories began.

He called Donna regularly. Come down for a visit, you will love it. "No! Come back home." "No!" Sometimes he would forget to call her for a couple of weeks. That panicked him at first. He thought about the men in Austin, following her around with their tongues hanging out. He would lose her. How could he not remember to call her?

Then, one day, he stopped thinking about her.

Many of the girls in the college were wild and free. Many were Americans. They were great fun, and mostly wanted no commitments. "I've died and gone to heaven," he told his friends. But, he didn't like it. Sometimes, when he was with a girl, he would hear Donna's voice telling him 'it's just cheap and dirty, when you do it with someone you don't love'. He especially didn't like hearing friends compare notes about a girl he had been with.

Mexican girls were more fun, and more challenging. But, the ones he could get seemed to be looking for a ticket to the U.S., or looking for extra money. He was not in the market for a wife, and the money thing seemed too much like whoring.

He thought about his buddy Patterson, and decided to phone him. There was half a page of Patterson's in the St. Louis phone book, and he could not remember Pat's first name. Being unable to remember his best buddy's first name produced panic; you must be going crazy, he told himself. Nevertheless, he could not remember. It had always been Patterson, or Pat.

He tried several calls, and finally got Pat's sister, and the number. Pat was married, 'with two kids and one in the hopper.' He had just bought a house in a new subdivision, and could not afford furniture. He had found it necessary to take a part-time job in the evenings, to make ends meet. Forget a visit to Mexico City.

"Now there are five of us in this fucken shithole," he told his former buddy. Pat didn't understand him. Perhaps, Pat didn't want to understand him.

He began to travel. First, he took weekend trips in Central Mexico. Soon he was missing classes for visits to Southern Mexico and Central America. He found himself in the Guatemala town of Livingston, on the Caribbean Coast, drinking beer with a young Black Carib man named Francis. Francis spoke Creole English, as well as Spanish, and the Carib language. Francis had a dory—a large dugout canoe with an outboard—that he used for fishing and diving, and transporting local people across the bay to British Honduras. There were Black Carib villages along the coast of British Honduras—Barranco, Punta Gorda, Punta Negra, Monkey River Town, and Stann Creek, where people lived off the sea and bush. There were other people there too: East Indians; Maya Indians; Creoles; Hispanics from Honduras and Guatemala; and even a community of Americans—offspring of southern expatriates from the Civil War.

To keep his GI Bill money flowing, he returned to Mexico City College, and arranged an independent research project with an anthropology professor. Soon he was back in Livingston, and then on the dory across the bay to Barranco, British Honduras.

He found the Black Carib people to be even more exotic than Mexicans. They were very Negroid in race, but spoke the Carib Indian language, as well as Spanish and Creole English. They were offspring of runaway slaves in the Caribbean, who had taken Carib Indian women, and formed a new society of Black people with an Indian culture and language. After losing a war with the English on one of the islands the survivors were taken by ship to Roatan Island off the coast of Honduras. From there they slowly spread up the coast into British Honduras. The men were fishermen, and the women maintained gardens of fruits and vegetables, and fields of bitter manioc, from which they made their manioc bread.

He found an old hotel in the coastal village of Punta Gorda. It was a wooden structure with a verandah, overlooking the Caribbean. He made the hotel his central location. He learned to fish and net turtle, and to dive for conch and lobster, with young Carib guys. He visited Kekchi Maya Indian villages in the forest and talk with East Indians in town and on their farms. He learned to cut the high forest and plant corn. He ate corn-flour tortillas and beans in thatched huts with Indians to the light of candles. He traveled up rivers—poling dugout canoes through the rainforest—to places where old Maya temples were overgrown with forest, and where rivers boiled out of caves, or up from underground aquifers.

At first it seemed the Black Carib girls were free and easy. Few Caribs were married, and almost all the men had multiple sex partners. No one seemed to be concerned about which girl he might be with. If a girl had three kids, there would likely be three different fathers. This time, you really did die and go to heaven, he told himself.

But, then he learned the rules. A man was expected to give a portion of his earnings to each girl that had one of his children. On payday, the men would stand in the company line to get their wages, and the girls would be there, waiting. Some guys would have two or three girls with their hands out, and some girls would have their hands out to two or three guys. A girl would pick out a man she figured would have a paycheck coming, and be careful enough to be sure she knew he was the father of the child.

Sometimes, the fellow would try to deny fatherhood, and the girl would take the baby to his mother or father. The parent would examine the child carefully. Yeah, that's one of ours, the unfortunate fellow's father would say, and he would be stuck.

All the girls knew the White man would have a paycheck coming—a huge paycheck! And, there would be little doubt about the father of a mulatto kid. For the first time in his life—the first time in any man's life, he thought— he was pursued by girls who wanted to have sex with him. But, there was no way. He knew he would not be able to pack and run and he didn't want the responsibility. You're lucky you figured it out before the hammer fell, GI! Oh lord; water, water everywhere, and not a drop to drink.

The Maya people were very different. Almost all were married, and apparently faithful to their spouses. The girls were so shy they couldn't look at him. Most of the men spoke Creole English, as well as their Maya language, and some spoke Spanish as well. But, the girls usually spoke only the Maya language. Most married by age fifteen or so, and were worn-out by age thirty-five. He decided he would not even think about Maya girls.

One of his Maya friends had a young unmarried daughter named Concha. Concha would fix his tortillas and beans in the morning and evening, and do his laundry. He would always pay the girl a small sum for her work. That small sum turned out to be a very large sum for her. Without knowing, he had sent a strong message. He became aware of the problem, but decided to ignore it. Even the girl's father told him he should stop giving her money. "I'm not giving her money," he responded. "I'm paying her for her work."

Arriving at the village one day, he was accosted by a village boy, about eighteen years old. The boy was a foot shorter than him, and little more than half his weight. But, the boy carried a machete, as villagers always did, and seemed prepared to use it. He was not sure he could match the boy with a machete—even if he had one—and was not about to swing a machete at the young Indian boy, in any case.

What was the boy's problem? There had never been a single bad word from anyone in the village, and now this boy was going to kill him. He backed away from the boy. The boy had said the word *concepción* several times, but he could not connect it with anything that might have caused a problem. He felt lucky to have escaped with his head on his shoulders.

At his friend's hut, the source of the problem became clear. His friend told him *Concepción* would go with him. It hit him: Concha is short for *Concepción*.

"Go with me where?"

"You can take her," his friend said. "I am giving you permission to take her."

"I'm not taking her! She is just a child, and I am a married man! I have never touched her, and never said anything to her. I gave her that money because she earned it. She has to go with that boy—down the lane there. And, my friend, you have to explain to that boy, I am not taking Concha anywhere."

He wanted to explain to the girl how impossible her dream was, but there would be no way to do that. He found another family to eat with, and thought about the danger of living in a world where he did not understand the culture.

Each month he would travel to Belize City by boat. There he would meet an American or English fellow, and talk about the news and world events. He would visit the bars and listen to American Country music. He would go the bank and cash a check, each time checking on the growing balance. He received $150 for the GI Bill, and $215 for disability payment. His expenses were running under one hundred per month.

Most important, he would look for a White girl. Once he had met an English girl named Kathleen. He met her in a store, and she had favored him with her presence for dinner. She wore a tight, low-cut blouse, and the tops of her breasts were luscious.

He could hardly force his eyes away, and had to hold his right hand with his left, to keep from trying to touch her. He knew he was making a complete ass of himself, but couldn't contain his excitement. Your fucken tongue is dragging the ground GI, and she isn't going for it. He told himself.

And, she didn't go for it! After dinner she said, "I'll pay my own check, thank you." But, Kathleen. "No, I can walk home by myself, thank you." But, Kathleen. "You Americans are disgusting!" Yeah, I know, he told himself. But how the hell did you know? She knew!

When he was informed the GI Bill payment had stopped he was little concerned. He had almost four thousand dollars in the bank, and without the GI Bill, he had no reason to even pretend he was doing research. He could go anywhere. He did.

I WON'T FORGET: THE AMAZON, TUESDAY, AUGUST 18

We stay in bed till long past sunrise. We have decided to leave just enough time to pack, and have something to eat, before leaving with the Major for the airstrip. "You don't like me calling you Shirley, unless I say Shirley love, huh?" I use her technique of soliciting agreement, at the end of my statement.

"Yeah, because when you do, it sounds as if you're mad at me."

"That's why you called me Raymond on the boat, wasn't it? You were mad at me, huh?"

"Yes! I was trying to get your damned attention; showing off up there, like a cowboy."

"I wasn't showing off, I was playing the odds."

"I don't want to hear any more about your odds."

"Look, what good would it have done for me to get down there with you? That probably would have increased the chance they would blow the boatman away, and if they did that we were both dead. There is no way I could have reached the motor in time to get out of range." She thinks about that. "So you have some troopers at risk, okay? That doesn't mean you don't try to save the ones you can save. It's better to lose a few troopers, than lose them all."

"I guess you're right," she replies.

"So, I wasn't being a cowboy, was I?"

"Maybe not, but, I'm still going to throw that baseball cap away."

"It's therapy time, honey." She lays her head on my chest, and is absolutely quiet for about two minutes. I have the feeling something heavy is about to drop. It does.

"Did you kill anyone in the war?"

I think about the question for a bit. "No; not the way you mean."

She lifts her head and looks at me. "What do you mean, not the way I mean?"

"I didn't blow anybody's brains out, or slit their throats, or bash their heads in with a rifle butt."

"What did you do? Electrocute them?"

"Jesus, Shirley, we weren't the fucken Nazis."

"Well, what did you do?"

"I called in fire on them. I guess they were just as dead as if I had blown their brains out."

"You put fire on them? Isn't that against the Geneva Convention?"

"Oh Christ!"

"Wouldn't they just do the same thing back to you?"

"Yeah," I say, sarcastically. "But, we had more matches than they did."

She puts her head back on my chest. In a low, soft voice she asks, "Did they try to burn you?"

I let her question sink in for a minute. "Lieutenant Snider blew up right in front of me. He was about that far away." I point to the chair beside the bed. "And, he blew up; his head was gone, and his arm; his brains were all over my face and my fatigue jacket." I turn on my side and look at her. She has a shocked look on her face. "He just fucken blew up." I hear my voice flat and emotionless.

"What did you do?" she whispers.

"I ran. I ran and crawled and hid. I didn't want to die; can you understand that?" She nods in frantic acknowledgment. "I didn't want to die. I didn't even take my carbine. I ran like a madman--like a goddamned coward." I roll over on my back, overcome with emotion.

She lays her head on my chest again, and remains quiet for a long time.

"That's enough therapy for today, honey. You weren't a coward or a madman. Anyone would have done that."

Suddenly, I am filled with bitterness and anger. I turn back and roll over on top of her. I put my hands on each side of her head, digging my fingers into her hair, and hold her head.

"I'm not going to let you leave me; do you understand that?" I tighten my grip on her hair, and shake her head. I can see fear in her eyes, but I don't care. "I won't let you leave me. Not next Tuesday, not next month, not ever. If you leave me, you'll have to kill me first, do you understand that?" My voice sounds shrill and ugly, even hateful, but I don't care.

She says nothing, and waits for my anger to subside. I release my grip on her hair, and roll off her, and onto my back. For a long time, I lie on my back staring at the ceiling.

"You were violent. You hurt me, and you scared me."

"I didn't hurt you!" I say.

"You hurt me, and you don't even know you did it."

"How did I hurt you?"

She pulls herself up and looks at me. Her expression is one I have not seen before—a mix of fear and anger. "You pulled my hair. I thought you were going to pull it out! And, you threatened me. I thought you were going to start hitting me."

"Oh, no; I would never do that, never!" She lies back on the pillow. "Forgive me,"

"I forgive you." She responds immediately, but her voice is harsh.

I lean up and pet her head softly. "Does it hurt?"

She pushes my hand away. "No, it's okay."

"So, I'm forgiven?" She nods. "Will you forget I did that, love?"

"No."

"Please," I say softly.

"I forgive you, but I won't forget."

"Oh shit!" I hear myself say, and lie on my back staring at the ceiling.

In the morning she wants to talk: "You know something? I've figured something out about you. You always do everything at one hundred percent. You laugh and love and cry, and make crazy jokes all the time. You're running all the burners, all the time. You're always so intense and emotional. I know why those things that happened in Korea are hurting you so much now. Do you know why?" I shake my head. "Because, you didn't deal with it at the time. You had Donna and her Mama smothering you, and you didn't deal with it. You're not that way. You have to do everything spontaneously." She continues: "That's why that dog is coming out now? You have to face the whole thing, and deal with it. You have to talk about it, and deal with it."

"I'm talking about it with you."

"Yeah, and, it's helping you too."

The sun is shining in the window, and there is no breeze. We kick off the sheet and lie naked on the bed. The heat and humidity, and lack of air circulation, are too much. We get up and shower and dress. We walk down all the streets of the small village, and down to the riverfront, to see if either of our two boatmen is there. Neither is. We walk back to the restaurant, and have coffee and a big breakfast.

"You're starting to eat your breakfast, like a good girl. Maybe, the Texans won't shoot you on sight."

"I'd better. Hanging around with you, I may not get anything else to eat for the rest of the day."

"Well, you look pretty healthy to me. You know; you are probably the healthiest woman I have ever known. Hell, you are the only woman I have known, who could do this shit we're doing."

"You mean put up with this shit we're doing." She continues: "You know, yesterday was really something. I still can't believe it. First, we go down to the Indian village, and you say just sit on this log and look non-threatening." She laughs. "And, then they chase us out with guns and spears, and we're lucky they don't shrink our heads and put them on poles. And, then you make me sit in the bottom of the boat, so it would look as if I had peed on myself." She stops to laugh again. "And then, we have to talk the Major out of bombing the village. And then, we take the plane across the whole Amazon, and … And then, I jerk on your chain so bad you almost have a heart attack." She continues in a high pitched voice, "Oh sweetheart, I'm so afraid of these planes. Maybe they hold them together with baling wire." She cocks her head sideways and sticks her tongue out, giving me my idiot look. She has a good laugh at my expense, and I have to join her.

"You know something? If I told Norma about all this, she would have both of us committed to the loony bin forever."

The Major arrives, and is in a hurry. The plane will leave for Quito early, and we need to get aboard immediately. He drives us to the plane, which already has both engines running, and says good-bye. "Give him a little kiss on the cheek, love. He really helped us." She shakes his hand.

After we are on the plane the ramp is removed immediately, and the plane taxies toward the end of the runway; we sit and buckle in. She puts her arm around my head and pulls my ear to her mouth, yelling over the noise of the plane.

"I know he helped us, and I don't blame him personally for what they're doing to the Indians. But, I'm not about to kiss the son-of-a-bitch. And anyway, I thought you were too jealous to have me kiss some man." I am too jealous to have her kiss any man, and am glad she didn't.

We reach the airport in Quito at 10:30 AM, and take a cab to the Esmeraldas road.

We will flag a bus there, rather than take the extra time to go into the city to the bus station. I tell her the bus will probably be full, and we will have to stand up most of the way down to the coast. But, she is more concerned with Johnny worrying about her back at Costa if we are late.

We wait on the side of the road for a bus. We aren't lucky. There is a tienda about a hundred yards from the road, where we can get a coke or beer, but I am afraid our bus will pass. I ask her to get us something to drink while I wait by the road, and then think better of it, "You stay here, love. They are more likely to stop for you. I'll go get us something to drink."

We have a long hot wait by the road. I make three trips to the tienda, beer for myself only after the first trip because she worries about someplace to urinate if she had too much beer. Of course, I urinate behind the tienda, and kept drinking beer. I think about the burden of being a woman in Latin America, with no place to urinate.

A bus finally arrives. There are no seats, so we stand. A man offers Shirley a seat, but she declines. Standing isn't so bad, but we can't see out the windows without bending over, and there isn't room, because of other people, who are also standing. We stand leaning on each other, and holding onto the railing on the roof of the bus and talk.

I have always thought foreigners were rude to speak their foreign language in a crowded place, but I am so wrapped up in her that I don't care. We don't get a seat until we reach Santo Domingo.

"I need to tell you something," she says, after we sit. "I don't want you to feel bad about this, but I have to tell you. When you pulled my hair, I forgave you, but I told you I wouldn't forget. That's the one thing I won't forget."

"I'm sorry I did that."

"Yes, I know you're sorry. I wouldn't be here with you now if I didn't know for sure that you were sorry. I really did forgive you, and I won't ever mention this again. But, I want you to know, I will not forgive that twice."

"I will never do that again, Shirley. I promise I'll never do that again."

"You don't have to promise me anything. But, I want you to know I won't try to compete with you physically. I won't be hit."

"Shirley..."

She puts her hand over my mouth. "You don't need to say anything. I already know you didn't mean to do that, and I already know you don't intend to let it happen again."

She sleeps with her head nestled against my chest. I can look down at her, and see her face. I have looked at her face almost constantly for the past few days, but have not been able to see it. Now I can. She has her relaxed confident look, and her breathing hums quietly. Her face is beautiful, I think. Not pretty, not cute, not lovely— just beautiful. I wonder if her face looks beautiful to other people as well, and decide that it does.

I have just six days left with her. Seven nights and six days, and then she will leave me. Just as sure as the sun comes up next Tuesday she will leave me. I hate the thought, and try to blame her for the way I feel.

She wants to leave you, I tell myself; the sooner the better, because you're a shit-head. She is just stringing you along for another week, and then she will go home, happy to get you out of her life. That guy in Frisco doesn't deserve her. He just wants her to take care of his kids. He doesn't really love her, and she doesn't really love him. She really wants to stay with you. My rationalizations don't work. None of them are true. I can't fool myself. I have to stop thinking about her leaving or face that damned dog again.

We reach the Atacames road after the truck has passed, and have to walk. There is no moon, but the stars are bright. We enjoy the walk, but she reminds me that Johnny is going to be worried sick. We reach Costa at about 8:30 and see Johnny on the deck, finishing his umpteenth beer. He is mad, and walks away from us without speaking.

"Come on Johnny, we're sorry. We just couldn't make the last truck. Jeez, Johnny!" she yells after him. "It's not as if I'm a little girl, and you have to start worrying about me when the sun goes down." But, he isn't responding.

After dinner, we walk down the beach and make love.

"We are going to do therapy."

"Do we have to?" I ask.

"Yes, that's part of the deal." I turn, and face her.

"Tell me about Zebra hill."

"It was just a hill."

"Why were you up there?"

"It was fifty-three. The war had stalled, and the politicians were chit-chatting about which hills we would keep, and which ones they would get. There were too many hills. We couldn't man all of um' adequately, and they couldn't either. Zebra was our hill. Charley Company would hold the hill for a week, and then we would go up and relieve them, and they would go back in reserve at bivouac. And, then the next week Charley would come back and relieve us, and we would go back to biv. The Chinks knew what we had, and we knew what they had. So, when they attacked, they would come with overwhelming force. They would send three or four companies up at us. We would fire everything we had, and bug out. Then, we would pound the hell out of them, for a couple of days, and retake the hill—the same way they did. And, they would bug out, because they knew we would be coming in with overwhelming force."

"And, then they would pound the hell out of you," she fills in.

"Nah, they didn't have that much stuff. They would hit us some, and then move on to another hill."

"When the Lieutenant blew up—I'm sorry, I don't know how to say that—were just the two of you there? Where was everyone else?"

"My platoon had bugged out—fourth platoon too."

"Bugged out?"

"Yeah, they ran like rabbits. The Old Man was so chicken-shit he tried to pull the whole company off the hill. They busted the son-of-a-bitch out of the army, I think."

"Why did they have that old man up there, and why did they run away and leave you?"

"They didn't run away and leave me! The Old Man is the commanding officer of the company; we always called the CO the Old Man—jeez Shirley!"

"So, why were you and the Lieutenant alone? Why didn't you bug along with them?"

I burst into laughter. "I can't talk to you about this stuff. You don't understand."

"I'm trying to understand, and I will if my patient will cooperate."

"The Lieutenant wanted to be a hero. When the Old Man—the company commander—ordered the retreat, our platoon bugged, but Lieutenant Snider stayed behind, and because I was carrying his radio I had to stay too. We joined the Exec Officer who had the rest of the company—the other platoons. Then, Snider wanted to play cowboy, and we went down to a forward observation post and called in fire on the Chinks. He wanted to burn the sons-a-bitches as they came up the hill. You know, he wanted to throw matches down on um'."

"Don't treat me like a fool. I don't know about war, but I'm not a fool."

"Anyway, I was carrying his radio, so I had to stay with him. The son-of-a-bitch took us right over to the northeast side of the hill, right where they would be coming up. And, then he started calling in fire—that's artillery fire—you know, big shells that blow up."

"Is that when it happened? Is that when the Lieutenant blew up?"

"Yeah, that's when it happened."

"You felt terrible, didn't you? Seeing the Lieutenant with his head blown off."

"No."

"I don't understand."

"I don't either. But, I didn't feel bad about the Lieutenant, and I didn't feel bad about Doyle either."

"Who is Doyle? Did he blow up too?"

"That next morning I found Doyle in a bunker, dead. I took his food and water, and I took his rifle. And, I didn't feel bad about him. I was just glad to get his food. Can you understand that? No, Shirley, you can't understand that! You know something? I don't understand that either. What would you do if you saw someone you knew, dead? Would you just take their food and run away? Would you do THAT? That's what I did!"

"I don't know what I would do. I have never seen anyone get their head blown off."

"Well, I don't think you would take their food, and run away."

"Maybe, I would, if I were hungry, and people were after me. Maybe, I would take his food and run, and not feel bad about him. Were you hungry?"

"I was starving, and I was scared to death."

"I think you were right to run. Everyone else had left and you were by yourself. Why shouldn't you run? I would have run so fast; I think anyone would have."

"Yeah, but the trouble is, there was no attack. There really weren't any Chinks up there. They just feigned the attack. They hit us with a patrol, and the Old Man panicked and ran. I was in about as much danger as sucking on my mother's tit. But, I ran like a rabbit."

"But, you didn't know that, did you?"

"No, I surely didn't know that."

"Then, you didn't do anything wrong. You did what anyone would have done."

"Yeah?"

"Are you really a hero?"

"Yeah, I'm a fucken hero." I say in an ugly tone.

"Did they really give you a medal?" she asks.

"Yeah, they fucken gave me a medal. A fucken Silver Star."

"You say that word too much. I say that too, sometimes; but you say it too much."

"It comes with the territory."

"I don't like war, but I think we should have real respect for soldiers who fought for our country, and were brave in the war."

"I wasn't brave in the war. I just ran like a rabbit."

"Then why did they give you the medal?"

"Mama did it!"

"I don't understand. How could she give you a medal?"

"Mama runs everything! She had the general put me in for the medal. She wanted her Donna to have a hero."

She is quiet for a whole minute. "Is that it? Is that why you are so bitter? You just don't feel you deserve the medal? Is that it?"

"I don't give one shit about the medal. They can stick it up their asses, if they want to."

She is quiet for another minute. "You know something?" she asks softly. I don't respond. "I think we've made some progress on your problem."

"My problem is you are going to leave me next Tuesday!"

"This is therapy. Don't mix things up."

She wants us to sleep in the hammock, but worries about being cold in the early morning. I arrange the blanket to lap over the back of the hammock and have her get in first. I'll pull the blanket over us when it gets cold, I tell her. We take a long time to arrange our arms, so they won't go to sleep, because of the other person lying on them. She puts her right arm under my neck, and I put my left around her, taking advantage of the space between her arm and chest. Our foreheads touch, and I can see her eyes sparkle in the starlight.

"You know something?" I tell her. "I know a lot more about you than I did a couple of days ago. And, I think that makes me love you more."

"I'm glad you love me more. But, you don't know anything about me."

"Sure I do. I know as much about you, as you know about me."

"Ha! I know what you're thinking before you do. And, you have no idea about what I think."

"Oh yeah?"

"Oh yeah! When I put you on, in the plane, you had no idea. And, you know something sweetheart, you have never, never fooled me about anything. Even your stupid scheming on me, when we first met. I knew exactly what you were trying to do."

"So, why did you fall for it?"

"Because, I wanted to fall for it, and, that's more than I can say for you. Any girl with a nickel's worth of brains could lead you down the garden path."

"Well, hell. Maybe, I don't mind being led down the garden path."

"Ahh, you're hopeless." After a few seconds she says, "You have to go in to see Norma tomorrow."

"Tomorrow?"

"Yes, tomorrow! And, don't give me any excuses."

"What for; what is she going to do?"

"Oh, she will probably just tie you to a post, and beat your brains out with a club." She responds.

"Really, what the hell does she want to see me about?"

"Since when do the grunt soldiers know what the generals are thinking."

"I don't know."

"YES, YOU DO KNOW! You promised you would do this, and you are going to do it!" she lifts herself up, as if to get out of the hammock.

"Okay, okay, I'll talk to the woman." We relax again.

The problem with two people in a hammock is, when one needs to change position in the night, it is a major operation. She decides she will have to lay on her other side. She turns, and cradles her head in her arms, her back to me. I feel her back. I push her hair away, so I can kiss the back of her neck. Her butt pressing against me feels wonderful. Later in the early morning, I feel her shiver, and pull the blanket over her. I get the blanket over our legs, and over most of her, but can't cover my chest without covering her head. Rather than wake her for the rearrangement, I decide to tolerate the cold air, but snuggle against her, and enjoy her warmth.

What Else Could He Do? Esmeraldas, Summer 1956

Two women stood in a school courtyard talking above the din of dozens of playing children. Both were dressed in white blouses and long black skirts; one was small and frail, forty years senior to the younger women, but they would both have immediately been recognized as nuns in any Catholic country. A young woman rushed toward them in a quick walk and called to them some twenty feet distant: "Norma, I have to talk to you."

"Okay," the older woman said.

"At 10; I have to go to my class now; can I see you in your office at 10?"

"That will be fine."

She took the older woman's hand and bowed to kiss it, and then turned to the younger nun: "I didn't mean to interrupt." She hesitated and then added: "Actually, I did mean to interrupt; I'm sorry, but I need to talk to Norma, and I have to run to my class." And she turned and rushed away.

"What a miracle worker you are, Norma; I can't believe the change in that girl. How did you manage that? When she first came here she had nothing but contempt for the Church, and us too." The older woman smiled and shook her head. "What do you suppose she wants to talk to you about?"

"I think I already know."

"Yes, I think I know too. I never trusted that man; I told you that."

"Let's not gossip, Juana." With that the younger woman turned away. She did not like being corrected.

Shortly after 10 O'clock the young woman knocked on Norma's office door. "Come in." The young woman walked over to the desk and sat. "You want to talk to me," the older woman stated rather than asked.

"Yes, but I'm afraid to tell you."

"Why?"

"I'm afraid you won't want to be my friend anymore."

"I will always be your friend."

"It's pretty bad."

The older woman took off her glasses, rubbed her eyes and sighed: "You are having sex with Ray."

"Yes, how did you know?"

"You're radiant Shirley!"

"Oh my God, is it that obvious?"

"It's obvious to me, because I know you very well. It is not obvious to other people."

"I didn't mean to do it; I couldn't help it." She was silent for a few seconds and then added: "Well, actually I did mean to do it; I did it on purpose." The older woman nodded. "He loves me Norma; he thinks I'm beautiful."

"You are beautiful."

"Norma! I know what I am!"

"Do you think he's beautiful?"

The young woman turned away and huffed into the air above her. Then she turned back and said: "He is beautiful." When the older woman nodded again, she added defensively: "When he comes in to see you, you can judge for yourself!"

"Are you going to tell him you told me about this?"

"Yes, I've already told him I would."

"And, he didn't like that." The young woman shook her head. "He said it is none of my business." The young woman nodded affirmatively. "And, you said?"

"I told him if we didn't tell the truth about this, we would just be wasting our time on his problem; and, I'm more worried than ever about his problem."

"I don't think he will want to come in to see me."

"He promised he would; and I intend to hold him to his promise!"

"Yes, I believe you can." The older woman said.

"You won't hold this against him, will you? I can understand if you don't want to be my friend anymore, but please don't hold it against him. It's my fault as much as his— actually it's all my fault. I let him flirt with me from the beginning. I let him kiss me and I let him feel me; and, when I decided to have sex with him I just took my clothes off right in front of him. What else could he do?"

"You don't need to make excuses for him. You don't need me to tell you adultery is wrong; and he doesn't need me to tell him that. I don't judge either of you, and I am not your confessor. And, DON'T YOU EVER QUESTION my friendship again."

"I'm sorry; I won't do that again. And, thank you. I know you can help him; he needs your help so much."

"I will do all that I can to help him."

"Thank you." The young woman waited a few seconds and then continued: "There is something else—I am completely over my problem."

"I'm thankful for that."

"I never wanted to have a man touch me, let alone... I didn't know people could do it that much.

"Are you going to get pregnant?"

"No; I'm using birth control. You don't approve of that either, do you?"

"I told you I don't judge you; I'm concerned about your physical and emotional health! Are you going to try to keep him?"

"No. I'm going to leave him and go home just as I planned; and that's going to be another problem."

"Why?"

"I'm afraid of what he will do when I leave him. You were right; I should never have done this. But, anyway I can't keep him."

"Why?"

"Because in the first place he already belongs to someone else; I may be a cheater, but I'm not a thief.

"You MAY be a cheater?"

"Okay, I am a cheater! I'm cheating on his wife and I'm cheating on Jerry; but that does not make me a thief." She wiped tears from her eyes with her hand.

"No, it doesn't."

"Anyway, I could never keep him."

"Why?"

"Because some morning he is going to wake up and realize he is stuck with an ugly girl." The older woman shook her head. "Girls are after him all the time—flashing their boobs at him." Again the older woman shook her head. "I've seen them do it! You think he doesn't notice that? In the States they would probably be showing their butts; I can't compete with that! I have to have a man who can be satisfied with just me."

"Like Jerry?"

"Yes; if he will forgive me for this."

"You're going to tell him about this?"

"Yes, I have to. He'll know anyway; I'm not the same person as before."

"I think he may like this new Shirley more than he liked to old one."

"Yes; I intend to make sure he does."

"I will do anything I can for your young man; you know that, don't you?"

"Yes, but I'm so worried. He's out there somewhere right now hurting all over because I'm not with him; at 3 O'clock he'll be waiting for me at that front door. He's so dependent on me. I should never have done this; I've just made everything worse for him. When I leave him I'm afraid he will just start crying; if anything happens to him it will be my fault." She lays her face in the hands of the older woman. "Please take care of him; please don't let anything happen."

"I will do all I can for him."

WHAT'S MY LAST NAME? Costa Del Sol Wednesday, August 19

"**S**o, it's loony bin time for me." She doesn't respond, but gives me her arched eyebrow, eyes up, and loud exhale treatment. We are sitting at our favorite table, and having breakfast. "So, when is zero hour?"

"She wants to see you at three, after the kids are out of school. And, you be there, damn it!"

"I'll be there! Why don't we go in together, and stay at the hotel on the beach for a couple of days. I can kick around the dock, and visit the poor community down by the river."

"What about Johnny?"

"Hell, he can get a room there too."

"I don't think so. We are both running out of money, and that place is expensive."

"I'm paying, love. I have plenty of money. Don't sweat it."

"I'll check with Johnny—be right back for my breakfast." She runs off to Johnny's hut. The woman serves breakfast, eggs over rice with *arepas* for me, and just *arepas* for Shirley. I think about waiting for her, but she doesn't emerge from Johnny's hut. She doesn't mind if her breakfast is cold, GI, I tell myself. I do mind if my breakfast is cold, so I eat.

Finally, she and Johnny emerge from the hut, with her pushing him along.

"So? Why the hell are you bugging me?" he is saying, as he reaches the table.

"We want you with us." She tells him. "We will have dinner at Casa Garibaldi tonight."

"I don't have the money, and I don't want to take money from this son-of-a-bitch," he says. I am not present as far as he is concerned. That suits me fine; since I am not present, there is no insult intended, and none taken.

"Don't talk that way Johnny. I love him."

"Hey, Johnny;" I say, "no sweat, man; just consider it DIA money." He glares at me.

"He's just kidding." She says to him, and to me, "Stop that!"

"Really, Johnny," I say: "We want you to join us in town. That fellow at Garibaldi's—what's his name—will really give us a fine dinner."

"His name is Roberto—not that you would give a damn."

He probably doesn't want to, but decides to go with us. We take the path to the road, and catch the truck into town. We get off the truck together, at the stop near the school. Johnny turns to leave.

"Hey Johnny, I'll get rooms at the hotel, and we'll meet there at five o'clock, and go to dinner together, okay?"

"Look," Johnny says. "I don't want you to pay for my room. I can stay in your room—on the floor. It doesn't matter. I don't give a damn what you kids are doing."

"Yeah;" Shirley says, "but, we care about who's watching."

"I'm not going to watch; jeez, Shirley!"

"I don't know how you would be able to help it, Johnny. We are going to be in there, naked and playing with each other, all the time." Obviously, she enjoys bugging him.

He heads off for places unknown, and I walk her to the school. She reminds me about not holding hands and kissing—the kids ya'know.

I turn to leave, and then yell back. "What the hell is his last name anyway?" She gives me a questioning look.

"I have to get him a room, and I don't know his last name."

"Tucker."

"Okay, love. See you at three."

"Ray!" she calls after me. "What's my last name?"

I turn and yell back, "Love." She smiles at me, and we go our separate ways.

I insist on a room with a balcony, overlooking the sea. Then I decide Johnny should have the same treatment, and get two of the most expensive rooms they have. I walk down to the dock, and check on boats going north and south, and upriver. There is nothing moving that would get me back in time for my meeting with the shrink. I decide not to go to the community by the river, because I would have a tough time turning down a beer, and I don't want that on my breath, when I talk to that woman. She'll paddle your fucken butt, GI! I tell myself.

I go to the room and put on a bathing suit, and then go out for a swim in the ocean. Later I return to the room and shower, and then sit on the balcony and watch the ocean. At two PM, I walk back through town to the school, and sit on a bench in the main building.

At three, the kids come running out, and I am still there waiting. I get bored and walk through the building, and into the schoolyard. Some kids are playing basketball, and the ball bounces to me. I try a jump shot from the sidelines; it's a lucky shot.

A little Black girl comes over to me, "*Juega con nosotros,*" she says.

"*Sure.*" He responded in Spanish.

BUT I HAD A GIRL ON MY SIDE: ESMERALDAS, WEDNESDAY, AUGUST 19

Two women walked down stairs holding hands. One was a small frail woman, in her mid-sixties. She wore a black dress, reaching to her ankles, with large pockets on the sides, stained with white chalk dust, and a starched white blouse, buttoned from the neck down. Her hair was short and gray. A silver cross was pinned to her dress, just above her left breast, although there was only a hint of those female features in the front of her blouse. The younger woman was a full head taller, and with long arms and legs. She wore a full cotton skirt, and a short-sleeved blouse. She had long, light brown hair and her face and body radiated youth and vigor.

Seeing the two women together, hand in hand, one might have thought they were mother and daughter, if not for the fact that the older woman was a Nun. And, of course, the tall, strong girl could not have shared the genes of the small older woman.

The two women walked into the courtyard playground of the school. Some twenty yards away, a young White man dribbled a basketball, and talked with four Black children in school uniforms. One was a girl about ten years old with a black pleated skirt and a white blouse. The three others were boys about twelve or thirteen years old, wearing khaki trousers and short-sleeved brown shirts, old and torn, but clean. The two women stopped to watch.

"What is he saying to them?"

The older woman smiled. "He chose the little girl to be on his side, and the boys are saying that's not fair."

"I could have told you he would choose the girl."

The little girl suddenly put her hands on her hips, and began to protest. The older woman laughed quietly.

"What's he telling them now?"

"He's being really silly. He says he and the three boys will be against the girl. Look at her; she's devastated." The older woman said, shaking her head.

"He's an idiot. He's always doing stuff like that. Let's let him play with them for a few minutes; it will be good for him." The two women watched the young man play with the children.

The young man took the rebound, and dribbled out on the court. He passed the ball to the little girl. She bounced the ball with both hands, and tried to shoot the basket, but the shot was pitifully inadequate. One of the boys took the ball, dribbled to the hoop, and made a basket.

The young man took the ball out of bounds, and passed to the girl. He danced around her, keeping the boys away, while she bounced the ball with both hands, and walked down the court to the hoop. Under the hoop the girl tried to heave the ball up from between her legs, but the ball did not reach the hoop. One of the boys recovered the ball, and made another basket.

The young man took the ball out of bounds again, and motioned for the little girl to come over for a conference. He whispered in her ear. The little girl took the ball, and from out of bounds, passed to the young man, and then ran down the court and stood under the basket. The young man dribbled around the boys, and ran for the basket. He put the ball into her hands, and picked her up and held her to the rim; she dropped the ball in. The little girl cheered.

The older woman laughed softly. The younger woman smiled at her and said, "He's charming that little girl. And, oh boy is he good at that! He can't stand to have a female around somewhere, who doesn't love him."

"I can see why you fell in love with him. Maybe, I would have too."

"You; you could have?"

"Yes. I wasn't born an old woman you know, and even nuns have feelings. I can understand how you can feel that way."

The young man walked over to the two women. The children followed. "*Sigue jugando con nosotros,*" one of the boys said. He divided the kids into two teams, and sent them back to play. Then, he turned to the women.

"Who won?" The young woman asked him.

"They did," he replied, smiling broadly to the younger woman. "But, I had a girl on my side."

"You mean," she said, with a sly smile. "You lost because your teammate was a girl? Or do you mean, you don't care if you lose, as long as you have a girl on your side?"

"Both."

Like A Sister To You: Esmeraldas, Wednesday, August 19

"Ray, this is Sister Norma." I take the woman's limp hand and squeeze softly, almost afraid I might crush it. The woman smiles at me, and says hello in American English.

"You're a Nun." My words are a statement rather than a question, but she responds.

"Yes."

"You're a Catholic Nun." I say, realizing my statement is redundant.

"Yes I am, young man. But, I minister to all of God's children." She waits for me to respond, but I don't.

Shirley breaks the nervous tension. "Don't let him tell you he can't remember that he can't remember!" she says, smiling at me.

The woman turns to Shirley, "Think about your statement."

Shirley thinks, and then blushes. I have never seen her blush before. Then, I also recognize the silliness of not remembering what you can't remember.

"Perhaps," the woman continues, speaking to Shirley, "you could have him stop by my office, before you leave." The woman returns to the building and walks up the stairs.

"Jeez, that's Norma?"

"Yes. What did you expect?"

"Well, I didn't expect her to be a Nun. You didn't tell me she was a Nun."

"Being a Nun has nothing to do with it. She's a smart woman and she wants to help you. That's the important thing."

"She really put you down."

"She didn't put me down. She doesn't do that. She was just telling me not to say stupid things. And she was right; that was really stupid! How could I have said that?"

"She's going to do brain surgery on me now?" I ask.

"She just wants to talk to you for a couple of minutes, and she just needs to ask your permission to check on something."

"Check on what?"

"I told you I'm just a soldier in the trenches. Don't expect me to know what the generals are doing in headquarters. Go on up there and talk with her."

"Jeez!" I respond, turning away.

She grabs my arm, and gives me a hard jerk. "Damn it, Raymond! You promised you would do this. It's not going to hurt you to walk up those stairs and talk to her for a few minutes. She is just going to ask you permission to check on some things in Texas. If you don't want her to, then you can tell her not to." We stand looking at each other for a couple of seconds, "Don't be such a damned coward, Raymond!"

"Raymond love—if you please!"

She ignores my joke and pushes me toward the building, "Give me that stupid cap!" She jerks my cap off. "It's the third door on the left, from the top of the stairs. And, watch your language!"

"**C**ome in." She opens the door and shakes my hand again. She leads me to a wooden bench, against the wall. "Sit down Ray. I want to ask you some things, but first I want you to know who I am, and why I'm doing this."

I sit. "Yes ma'am."

"You may call me Norma, or Sister."

"Yes ma'am."

She removes her glasses, and rubs her eyes, continuing to talk. "You have an older sister, don't you?" I nod. "How much older is she?"

"Four years."

"So, she took care of you sometimes, when you were growing up?" I nod. "Does she still love you, the way she did when you were growing up?"

"I guess so; yeah, sure."

"I want to ask you something. Did you ever go to your sister and tell her something you didn't want other people to know—to ask her advice, or get her help?"

"Well, yeah, lots of times."

"And, your sister always tried to help you, didn't she?" I nod. "Even if she really should have told your parents what you did, or made you face up to your failings; she just wanted to protect you, and help you, didn't she?"

"Well, yeah. She's always that way. I guess she would do anything for me, even if I am a shi…"

"That's the way sisters are—and brothers and parents, too. They will protect you, even when you don't deserve to be protected. That's why you can tell them things you would never dare to tell anyone else." I nod. "Ray, I have taken a vow to be a sister to you; to be to you, just like your sister."

She pauses as if to let that sink in. "Even if you were to tell me you did something really terrible, I would never reveal that to anyone. Even a court of law cannot make me reveal what you say to me. I want to make this very clear to you. Even if you me you were a rapist, or a murderer, I would never reveal that to anyone."

"Jesus; I'm not a damned rapist, or a murderer."

She puts her hand over my mouth. "Please don't use the Lord's name in vain. I know you are not a rapist or a murderer, but we have all sinned—you and me and everyone else; we all have things we are ashamed of, and would not want other people to know. I want you to know you can tell me things, the way you can tell your sister. I want you to trust me."

"I trust you."

"Good. Do you have your passport with you?" I nod. "Can I see it?" I remove the document from the pouch around my neck, and hand it to her. She opens to the first page. "Is this your picture?"

"Yeah;" I say, shrugging and shaking my head.

"Is this really the way your face looks?"

"Sure, of course."

"Remember the dream you had on the bus—the first day you met Shirley—the dream where you see yourself?" I nod. "In the dream, do you see yourself as you really are, or the way you look in this picture?"

"Well, I look kind of strange. Yeah, the way I look in that picture."

"Yes, because, you comb your hair this way." She brushes her fingers across my head from left to right. "And, you always have this little dimple here in this side." She touches the left side of my face. "But, here in the picture, you have your hair combed backwards, and the dimple is on this side."

"Yeah, that's right."

"Come over here; I want to show you something." She leads me to a mirror hanging on the wall, and stands behind. She points to the mirror. "This is your real face, isn't it?" I nod. "And, you look normal, don't you?"

"Sure!" shaking my head.

"But, you don't look normal to me there." She points to the mirror. "See, you look as if your hair is parted on the right side." She turns me around to face her. "But, it isn't. It's parted on the left." She turns me around to face the mirror again. "And see, that little dimple is on the right side of your face in the mirror, but actually it is here on the left side." She puts her finger on the left side of my cheek.

"You are the only person who sees yourself this way." She points to the mirror. She turns me around, and puts her hand on my face. "Everyone else sees you this way. And, like this." She demonstrates the passport picture. "The camera doesn't lie, but the mirror does."

"Jeez!" Again she puts her hand over my mouth.

"Where was the picture hanging? The one you see in the dream?" I don't respond. "Was it at the ranch in Texas? Is the picture on the wall in the living room?" She waits. "When you open the front door and walk in, can you see that picture on the wall?"

"No. They had it there in the entry, but I asked Donna to take it down. She put it in her Papa's office, so I wouldn't have to look at it."

"Did you ever go into the office and look at that picture?" I nod. "Why?"

"Because I hated it."

"In the picture, you have your army uniform on, don't you?" I nod. "And, there is a medal—a Silver Star—pinned right there on your shirt." She puts her hand on my chest.

"No. It's hanging around my neck, on a ribbon."

"You didn't deserve the medal, did you?" I shake my head. "Why did you accept it?"

"I had to; Donna made me to do it."

"Why don't you give the medal back to the army, and tell them you don't deserve it?"

"That would kill Papa. And, then Donna would hate my guts forever. Her Papa wants me to be a fuc...to be a hero."

"Ray, listen to me. You are going to have to live with that medal, or give it back to the army." She says, and then continues, "I want you to think about that, and the next time you come in here to see me, I want you to tell me what you are going to do about that."

"Jeez!" Again, she puts her hand over my mouth.

"When Lieutenant Snider, and the other boy died, you didn't feel bad about them, did you?"

"Shirley told you that."

"Shirley tells me everything. And, she told you she would, didn't she?" I nod. "But, she didn't have to tell me that; I already knew."

"How could you know that?" My voice sounds angry.

"I know, because that happened to me."

"To you? You don't know about this stuff!"

"Sit down." She says. I do as I'm told, and she sits beside me. "I do know about this stuff. War is not the only time you see people die. That's not the only time you escape, when someone else is unlucky."

"It was a long time ago," she begins: "I was in Mexico, and I shared a room with Sister Dianne. I didn't know her very long, but she was a good person, and I loved her. We were teaching school in a little village down there, and we lived in an old adobe house. One night there was an earthquake, and that old house fell down. Somehow, I managed to get out, but a beam that held the roof fell on Dianne's bed and crushed her.

She was killed, right in front of me. And, you know something? I didn't feel bad about Sister Diane. I just felt glad I was still alive. When it happened, I just thought about myself. Can you understand that?"

"Maybe, everyone feels that way."

"Yes, they do! I already knew that, because I had studied about those things. But, knowing wasn't enough. I felt real bad. Maybe, the way you feel." I can't stand to look at her, and look away. "You know what I did?" She waits, but I don't respond. "I went to all my sisters, and told them exactly what had happened, and told them exactly how I had felt, when Dianne was killed. I told them I was sorry I had just thought about myself, at that moment." She waits again. "And, you know something? Almost all of them understood, and told me it was okay. I was able to leave that burden behind me, and continue to do the Lord's work."

We sit quietly for a bit. "What are you going to do to rid yourself of that burden?"

"I don't know."

"Maybe, you could try to contact the families of those boys who were killed, and explain how you felt at the time."

"I tried that Sister. It was terrible—it just made it worse."

"The war has been over for several years. Maybe they will feel different now. And, if they don't understand, that will be their burden, not yours."

"I don't know."

"I want you to think about that, and the next time we talk, I want you to tell me what you are going to do about that."

She waits a bit, and then says, "Shirley is going home on Tuesday." I nod. "What are you going to do when she leaves?"

"I don't know."

"You should go home, too. You should go home to your wife."

"She doesn't want me back, Sister."

"She sure wouldn't want you back if you couldn't deal with your life there, would she?" She pauses. "But, if you could deal with your life back there, maybe she would want you back." She waits, but I don't respond. "It isn't your wife's job to hold you up, Ray! That isn't Shirley's job either! You have to stand on your own feet!" I remain silent. "I want you to think about whether you can deal with your life back there in Texas, and whether you want to ask Donna to give you a chance to do that. I want you to think about that, and tell me what you are going to do about it the next time you come to see me, okay?"

After a few seconds, she continues: "Donna and her parents are Catholics, aren't they?" I nod. "I have a friend in Austin. He's a priest. I can call him, and find out about some things that I need to know. He will never tell anyone I called; not Donna, and not her parents. Can you understand how I can do that?"

"Yeah, I guess so."

"But, I'm not going to do that unless you tell me it's okay. Can you understand why I cannot do that, unless you tell me it is okay?"

"Yeah, I guess so.

"If there is something I can use to help you, I will tell you. But, I will never tell anyone else. I want you to give me permission to do that."

I stand up. "Sister Norma, thank you. And, it's okay with me for you to do that." I walk outside and down the stairs.

"**A**re you going to be okay?" Shirley asks.

I don't respond to her, and walk on ahead. I am embarrassed because I know my eyes are red. We come to a small park with trees and benches, and I sit. She sits beside me.

"You have to give her a chance Ray, she is really smart."

"I know she's smart!"

"She jerked on your chain, didn't she?"

"Jesus, she jerked on my chain. How does she know this stuff?"

"I told you she knows everything."

She seems to sense I don't want her to see my face. She leans her head on my shoulder, and rubs my back. We sit for several minutes. After I regain my composure, I put my arm around her. "At least, she didn't paddle my butt. Do you want to take a cab to the hotel?"

She puts my cap on my head. "Why don't we walk? We aren't meeting Johnny till five—the walk will do us good."

We reach the hotel at a quarter to five and Johnny isn't there. We go up to see our room. She is thrilled. The room is beautiful, and the view is magnificent; it must cost a fortune to stay here; and Johnny has a nice room too; and we have hot water! The bed is enormous—she doesn't think she will be able to find me in there.

We return to the lobby to wait for Johnny. He is twenty minutes late. A wheel—not a TIRE, he emphasizes, A WHEEL—had rolled off the bus, down the street, and almost killed a pedestrian. He had to walk the rest of the way, watching out behind, he said, to be sure no wheels were coming his way. "These goddamned people don't know how to put the wheels on their buses. Shit, you could be killed by a wheel just walking down the street." We think his story is funnier than he does.

Our dinner is lavish. We are seated at the best table, facing the window to the sea. Apparently, Johnny has already arranged everything. Dinner is on me, he says. Fine Chilean wine is served in long-stemmed glasses. Cloth napkins are placed in our laps. There is enough silverware on the table for a party of twelve. We are served steak and lobster, and incredibly Brussels sprouts. I love Brussels sprouts, and have not seen any since leaving the States. The change from white to red wine brings fresh wineglasses. Johnny is asked to test the red wine; he approves. We talk together, and I find Johnny's conversation interesting. Shirley is pleased.

After dinner we walk back to the hotel. She is a bit high on the wine, and insists on walking between, with one arm around each of us. It is so great to have two guys who love her, and want to protect her—hell, she can protect herself. The dinner was so great. And, wait till you see the rooms, Johnny! She will never forget this night. She insists on Johnny coming up to our room, to see the view from the balcony. "And, you have a room just like this one."

"Thanks, Ray. You didn't need to do that."

"We wanted to do that, Johnny. Actually, Ray did it. I didn't even know," she explains.

He is dying to get out of our room, and I am more than willing to see him go. Finally, she says, "Well, Johnny. We're down for the count. See you tomorrow." He leaves us.

Our room affords a level of luxury that we have not experienced together. "Maybe we should ask them to put a hammock on the balcony for us; I may not be able to find you in this bed." She says. There is no moonlight so we leave the balcony light on, to simulate the moon. We lie together in the bed, and I love her as much as I can, and feel she loves me as much as she can, too.

Later she says, "I want to talk to you. I want you to be serious."

"No therapy tonight, love."

"This is therapy for me." She says. She turns on her side and pulls me onto my side, facing her. I know she isn't joking.

"You want therapy from me? If you need therapy, I need a padded cell. You're the most self-secure person I have ever met, and I'm whacked out. Anyway, if you want to talk to a psychologist you better see Norma."

"I don't need a psychologist. I need a bush doctor!"

"Snake bit, huh?"

"Don't joke about this, Ray. I want you to tell me something; about how you feel about something." She waits for a couple of seconds, to get my full attention. "You couldn't rape a girl, could you?"

"I'm not a damned criminal, Shirley!" I don't like her question, and try to pull away, but she holds me.

"Wait. What if it wasn't against the law to do that? This is just hypothetical."

"What do you mean, not against the law? How could that not be against the law?"

"But, what if...let's say some woman deserves to be punished—maybe to be executed. Would you think about raping her then?"

"Jeez, Shirley; what is this? Anyway, No! If she should be executed, then execute her. That has nothing to do with rape. Besides, I probably wouldn't even be able to get an erection."

"Why? That's what I want you to tell me! Why couldn't you get an erection?"

"Hell, I wouldn't want to have sex with a woman that didn't want me to."

Apparently, I have said something significant, and she is intent and excited. "One more question; just one more. I have to ask you this." I nod. "I know you would never touch a little girl, okay? But, what if you thought about doing that? What would you do?" I frown at her. "You have to tell me. This is hypothetical. What would you do, if you did think about doing that?"

"I wouldn't think about it."

"Maybe, you are dead drunk, and suddenly you realize you are thinking about doing that." She insists.

"Shirley, I would cut..." She says the words with me, "my... hand...off."

She rolls back on her pillow. "I knew you would say that!" Her voice shakes with emotion. "Meg told me. Everything Meg told me is true!" I am mystified, but know this is something important for her.

"I was molested by a man when I was thirteen."

"Oh, Shirley; I'm so sorry."

"Yes! Everyone is sorry! But, it still happened."

She has tears in her eyes, and her voice shakes. This is a part of Shirley I did not know—would never have guessed. Shirley is vulnerable; she can be hurt; she can cry for herself. Shirley is like you, I tell myself.

She continues, "I didn't tell anyone for three years, and then my Aunt Meg helped me to get over that." She pauses to control her voice. "She told me most men are the way you are. She helped me. But, I wasn't really over that until now. You know why? Because, everything Meg told me is true! She told me exactly what you would say! I guess I didn't really believe it. I don't have to hate men anymore. Can you understand that?"

"Yes, maybe I can understand."

The sun is shining when we wake up. "I have to teach today, what time is it?" She rushes to the shower. I join her, but she doesn't have time for my petting. "I better skip breakfast."

"You have plenty of time. Go have your breakfast, and I'll scare up a cab. I promise you will be there by nine." When I return, she is finishing her coffee and toast. My ham and eggs are on the table.

"Eat your breakfast honey, I'd better go." I insist on going with her. "If you don't eat your breakfast, the Texans will shoot you on sight," she says.

"I'll take that chance," I tell her, and ride with her to the school.

I return in the same cab and order a new breakfast. Later, I go to the poor community by the river, and walk around for a while. The men are mostly gone, and the women are doing laundry and watching kids. They all look at me as if I am there to buy something. It makes me uncomfortable and return to the hotel.

I sit on the beach and think. I have just four days left with Shirley. I love her and want her and need her so much. But, she is leaving in just four days. She belongs to me. What right does she have to take herself away from me? She thinks it's a game. She will laugh with her Aunt Margaret, about how she had fun and then left me.

You're trying to fool yourself, GI. She told you she has a man in the States. She told you it would be over in three weeks. She told you she would love, and then let go. You wanted to play the game, now it's time to pay up. Stop being a cripple, and stand on your own feet.

What about the medal? What are you going to do about the medal? I'll give it back to them, and tell them to stick it up their asses.

That will kill Papa, and then Donna will hate your guts forever.

Maybe, I could explain to Papa. He was a soldier in the trenches once. He knows what it is to be scared shitless. Donna doesn't care about the medal. She just cares about Papa.

It won't work! Don't tell um' anything; tell um' you want a lawyer, fuck all of um'.

What about Snider and Doyle? What are you going to do about Snider and Doyle?

Snider's parents will understand. I will tell them he was the hero; he was the one who tried to save the company. I was just doing what I was told, and then ran when he was killed. I'll tell them I'm returning the medal, because I don't deserve to share it with Snider. They will understand.

What about that screaming Doyle woman? Are you going to face her again? Don't tell um' anything, tell um' you want a lawyer, fuck all of um'.

What am I going to do about Donna? Maybe, I could go home and Donna will take me back.

What about the girls? Are you going to tell her you were screwing around with girls in Mexico a month after you left her?

I'll tell her I was just dicking around with them; she will understand that and forgive me.

What about Shirley? Are you going to tell her you were just dicking around with Shirley?

I can't tell her about Shirley. I won't lie to her, I just won't tell her.

She will find out someday, and then she will know you were lying to her.

Maybe, I will tell her about Shirley, and I just won't tell her I was in love with her. Maybe, she won't want to know the details, and she will forgive me.

Fat chance, GI; you're a shit-head, and she will hate you. She probably has another man by now. She probably has divorce papers waiting for you when you get there. Don't tell um' anything, tell um' you want a lawyer, fuck all of um'.

Nothing works. You are walking down a path that will dead-end in four days. You can't go on, and you can't turn back. What can you do? I will hold her. I won't let her go.

Don't even think about that, man. She won't tolerate that. Forget it!

Then, what can I do? I would have been better off if I had stayed on that bus. At least, I wouldn't be a cripple. At least, I could take care of myself. But now, what can I do?

I leave the hotel at one PM, walking slowly down back streets to kill time. I am at the school early, and wait in the playground shooting baskets with the kids. When Shirley finally arrives I am hurting to touch and kiss her. No touching or kissing—the kids, ya' know. We leave the school, and I insist on taking a cab to the hotel.

Later we meet Johnny. Shirley tells him we want to have dinner at Garibaldi's again, and want him to join us. He declines. "You kids go on; I have some things I want to do in town." I think he is allowing us to be alone, and appreciate his thoughtfulness.

I tell Roberto we want a quiet table. He understands, and provides a small, secluded table for two. We have a fine dinner, with good Chilean wine. We return to the hotel, take a long shower together, and then lie together in bed and talk for a long time.

"**L**et's stay here till noon." Her plan sounds perfect. We enjoy the luxury of the huge bed and the warm water in the shower. But, by 8:30 we are ready to get up. We dress and go down for breakfast. We sit in the hotel dining room, facing each other across a small table. The table has large place mats, and lots of extra glasses, plates and silverware. It's the fanciest restaurant in town.

Everything is funny, and we laugh and giggle. "The bugs have little bugs on their backs to bite um, love." Somehow that sounds funny to us.

She leans across the small table to kiss me. "I can't stand to have you so far away from me. Move your chair around to this side."

"I'm not so far away; I can feel you under the table." I demonstrate.

"You're too far away, I can't stand it."

"There isn't enough room for two plates on that side of the table." I say.

"Then we'll both have to eat from the same plate. Get around here—I can't stand it any longer. If you don't move around to this side, I'm going to pull off all my clothes, and start screaming."

We laugh, and I take the challenge. She is trying to be as crazy as bat shit, but nobody can do bat shit better than I can.

I call the waiter over. *"Perdon, if you will do me the favor,"* I say, in Spanish, *"move my plate and chair over there beside her."* She understands what I said, and giggles. The waiter is dumbfounded.

"There isn't room, Sir. Two plates will not fit here."

I know she has a pretty good idea of what he said, but I translate anyway, "He says, there ain't enough fucken room on this side of the table." And to the waiter: *"Well, we will eat from the same plate. Of course, you may charge us for two."*

The waiter is shocked. *"Perdóneme un momento, señor."* The waiter says, and walks away, to discuss the problem with the maître d'.

"What did you tell him?" she giggles.

"I told him he could just pile the food on the table, and we would eat with our hands," I whisper. Her laughter causes her to spit coffee across the table. She turns away, unable to remain serious.

The maître d' comes to our table. "Que *es el problema, señor?"* he asks, in a strict and formal voice.

She knows what he said, but I give her my personal translation anyway: "He said, what's your fucken problem shit-head." And to him, in my most formal Spanish, I say, *"There is no problem señor; we just want to sit together, on this side of the table."*

"Perdóneme señor; there isn't room for two places on this side of the table. But, of course, we have larger tables that you are very welcome to use; if you please, sir." He gestures for us to move to another table.

I know she has picked up most of that, but gave her my version. "He says this is a family restaurant, and if we want to play grab-ass, we can get the fuck out." She turns her head completely away, unable to contain her giggling.

"Perdon señor," I say, speaking as formally as I can. *"But, my woman insists on this table, and she obligates me to be at her side at all times."* And, to her, "I told him, you are crazier than bat shit, and if he doesn't move me to that side, you are going to pull off all your clothes, and start screaming."

She buries her face in her hands, with laughter so violent that it could be taken for crying. All the customers and waiters have stopped their activities, to observe the spectacle.

"You see!" I say to the maître d', *"She is beginning to cry, and then who knows what*

will happen. I hope you will resolve this situation for me very quickly." And, to her, "I told him you are starting to have a fit, and we may need a pair of pliers to hold your tongue, so you wouldn't swallow it." She chokes and begins to make gasping sounds.

The maître d' turns sharply and barks orders to the waiters. *"Two small plates on this side. Take those things away."* He has two waiters rearranging our table.

I sit beside her, and she continues to bury her face in her hands. "Here, sit up, love." I say, in a serious voice. She sits up, and then bursting into laughter, goes back to her crouched position, holding her face in her hands. She makes high-pitched crying sounds that came out as short gasps.

"Calma, calma," I say, for the benefit of the people at the other tables, rubbing her back. I pull her arm around my waist, and place mine over her shoulder. Lifting her head, I put a fork to her mouth, loaded with scrambled eggs. The eggs fly across the table, in a spate of laughter.

"Ray, I have to get out of here. I need to go to the bathroom. Right now!"

"Perdon," I call the waiter. *"The Señora prefers to have her coffee in the room, if you will do me the favor."* And, to her, "I told him you were peeing in your pants, and he could expect to see our attorney."

"Oh lord! You damned idiot! These people think I'm crazy."

"Like bat shit," I say.

She is almost unable to walk. She covers her face, maybe because of the laughter, or maybe because she doesn't want to be seen. I am trying hard to be serious. After a few steps, she makes an effort to straighten up and look serious, too.

As we pass a table, an elderly woman smirks at us. Knowing Shirley is watching me, I screw up my face and stick my tongue out at the woman. Shirley presses her face against my neck, and insists we run from the room. She runs up the stairs and me after her.

Inside the room she rushes inside the bathroom. The waiter comes in, and sets our table with coffee and toast. I give the man twenty-five pesos for a tip and another twenty for the maître d'. After the waiter leaves the room, she comes out of the bathroom.

"You idiot; you damned idiot!" she screams, and grabs me around the neck. At last, I allow my laughter to explode and we fall on the floor rolling and laughing. "You idiot; I can't believe you did that! They think I'm crazy," she says.

"Like bat shit," I tell her.

We roll about on the floor, laughing. "And, you stuck your tongue out at that woman. I'm never going back in there. I'm going to climb out the window. I can't face them," she laughs. She tries to control herself: "Why is bat shit so crazy?"

"There's nothing crazier than bat shit, love."

"How do you know?"

"We did an extensive study on the subject. Complete library research, laboratory and field-testing, the works. And, there is no question about it. There is nothing crazier than bat shit."

"Who is we?" she asks, trying to control her giggling.

"The second squad of weapons platoon, Baker Company, the fucken Eighty-Second Airborne; and, there is no higher authority than that on bat shit." We roll on the floor, laughing.

In the afternoon we walk down the beach. Rock outcrops reach the ocean, and we scramble and climb over, to find another stretch of sandy beach. We had hoped to find a beach sufficiently isolated to swim nude, but there is always someone nearby. Around one rock outcrop, we find an alluvial skirt of gravel and sand, reaching the sea. A large round Black woman is standing in the surf, moving a large wooden plate in the waves.

"What's she doing?"

"If I didn't know better, I'd say she's panning for gold."

We walk over, and speak to the woman. Incredibly, she IS panning gold. The woman comes ashore and sits with us. She works the sand and gravel from the alluvial skirt that has washed out of the hills over the millennia.

She loads her wooden dish and wades out into the surf. Floating the dish on the water, she allows the waves wash out the lighter sands. She sells her gold to a local dentist, who pays one and one-half times the government price. Apparently, dentists are required to pay two or three times the government price when they buy gold from the government. She can make as much money panning gold as she can doing laundry—about thirty cents US per day—and sometimes she finds a small nugget worth a couple of dollars. Once, she found a nugget worth twenty-five dollars. She finds panning gold more pleasant than doing other people's laundry, and always has the hope of finding another big nugget.

Shirley wants to try her luck, and the woman is delighted. They fill the wooden dish with sand, and wade out into the surf. The woman stands behind Shirley and holds her arms—and it seems to me, other parts as well—as she guides the waves over the dish. The woman giggles and makes whooping sounds, obviously enjoying herself.

I watch Shirley turn and look at the woman in a strange way, and wonder if something is going on below the water line. They come ashore, and Shirley demonstrates the absence of gold flakes in the dish. The woman says she has done marvelously. She puts her arms around Shirley and hugs her ferociously, making the whooping noises again. We thank the woman and walk back down the beach.

"You know? That woman was feeling me."

"Really?"

"Yeah; I think she just wanted to know if white girls are built the same way. You know, sometimes they feel your nose or hair, because it's different."

"Yeah, I can understand that. I've been conducting the same study myself. Just checking to see if they are all built the same way, ya' know; purely academic, love."

She looks at me. "Do you think she was... If you thought that, why didn't you jump in there and stop her?"

"Well, hell. She didn't seem to be doing any harm."

"No harm?" she says, indignantly.

"How could a woman do you any harm, love?"

Back at the hotel, we take advantage of our hot shower again, and then go down to Casa Garibaldi for an early dinner. We sit at the same table as the night before, and have the sea food platter, which includes lobster, shrimp, clams, mussels, octopus—every sort of seafood we have ever heard of, and several we haven't. The meal is delicious. We are back in our beautiful bed, with the balcony doors open to the sea, and our fan running, by 8:00 PM.

"No therapy tonight, love; I want to examine you."

"What do you mean examine me?" she asks, as if I were the county property tax assessor.

"I want to check out all your girl parts."

"Don't look at me there, it's ugly."

"It's not ugly. Which part do you pee through?"

"Get away from there!" she pulls my head to her stomach.

"I want you," I say, in a harsh voice.

"You have me."

"I want more."

"There isn't any more."

"I want you more."

"We're already together twenty-four hours a day."

"That's not enough," I say. "I want more." I hear her loud sigh. "I'm going to crawl up there, and just curl up, and stay in there."

"Oh, lord! It's back to the womb for Raymond. Freud would have a field day with this."

"What the hell would that old queer know about normal people?" I ask.

"Normal people?" she screams, lifting her head to look at me. "You mean like us?"

"Yeah, we're normal."

"Normal people don't have wild Indians chasing them around with spears."

"There are no Indians chasing us."

"They don't go into a restaurant full of people and make a huge spectacle about bat shit. And, they don't forget where they are going or wear baseball caps around in Ecuador!"

"There's nothing wrong with wearing a baseball cap."

She becomes more serious. "And, I'll tell you something else. Normal people don't hang on to each other twenty-four hours a day. Jeez! Even when we're sleeping we are hanging all over each other, and blowing our bad breath in each other's faces, as if we think the other one is going to run away in the middle of the night. And, we're holding on each other all day long, and looking at each other like idiots. Like idiots, Ray! Haven't you noticed all the people looking at us, as if we were completely bonkers?"

"They're just jealous."

"Jealous? One of these days, I'm going to jump into the bush with the snakes, just to get away from you!" She begins to giggle: "but, you would probably jump in there after me." And, then she adds in a sing-song voice, "You probably like snakes."

"There is nothing wrong with snakes, love."

"Nothing wrong with snakes?" she huffs. "The snakes down here are deadly, Ray! Deadly!"

"Bush doctors can cure snakebite."

"Bush doctors? You would be dead in ten seconds—how would you find a bush doctor?"

"You exaggerate, love."

"Yes, Shirley exaggerates," she says, as if resigned to my idiocy. She lies back on the pillow, and rolls her head back and forth, laughing. "You could probably stagger around, and foam at the mouth for a whole minute, while you look for a bush doctor, huh?"

"At least."

"And, we haven't been chased by wild Indians for a couple of days now. And, today you gave me five minutes of privacy in the bathroom—course now that you want to know which part I pee through, I probably won't get that privacy any more."

She presses her lips together and wrinkles her brow, as if to indicate just how demented she considers me to be. "And, they're all just jealous, aren't they?" she nods her head up and down. "We are the ones who are normal, huh? Everyone else should be locked away in the loony bin. And, we should just dance around their cages like clowns, and act normal, huh?"

AMERICAN CUSS: ESMERALDAS, FRIDAY, AUGUST 21

The common people of Ecuador bare great burdens, and yet they endure. To an uninformed visitor from a wealthy society, the poor people of Ecuador might appear helpless and floundering. But, that perception could not be more wrong. The proof of their strength and resiliency is in their very existence. A lesser people would not have survived at all.

The norm of poverty is interrupted only by periodic extreme deprivation. They suffer contempt and exploitation from the wealthy elite. They endure official decrees, and legal papers and documents, with costly stamps and seals, from lawyers and judges requiring bribes and other payments. They live with police and army forces that have powers of confiscation, and sometimes power to rape women and force men into involuntary servitude.

As if those burdens were not enough, the Lord saw fit to send them foreigners. Some of the foreigners are missionaries with gods that are powerful and mysterious. A radio can pick up the 'Christ of the Andes' transmission in mountain valleys where no other radio station could be heard. Indians hear the staccato cadence of an English-speaking preacher, without understanding a single word, but knowing the powers of God Almighty are being called down into their villages.

The missionaries are hated by the elite, but common people accommodate themselves to these new conquerors, as their ancestors had to Spaniards. The more religion the better, they tell themselves, as they allow their children to be baptized or prayed over. One could cook, or sew, or clean, or do laundry, for one of these foreigners, and receive a huge payment in return. And, they had the power to cure a sick child or heal a terrible wound.

There were powerful men in long cars wearing uniforms or business suits. These men caused huge pits to be carved into the earth, and trains loaded with ore, to move toward the coast. They caused the very sky to be lined with ribbon clouds, behind silver planes. Even the wealthy Ecuadorians respected these men. And, common men would pray for a chance to work in one of those pits. A man would face terrible danger and a life shortened by congested lungs. But, he would earn wages twenty to fifty times more than he could make in the potato and cornfields.

There were young foreigners who moved through their communities with impunity. They were on vacation from a world of leisure, and privilege. Yet, they seemed unaware of contamination by the poverty around them.

Many of the foreigners were middle-aged men who had come from the United States to seek their fortunes. In that southern tier of the States that face the Gulf of Mexico recovery from the Civil War would require several generations. In the meantime people with ambition looked elsewhere for opportunities. Black men and women moved to northern cities. Some White women also moved north, or moved west with their men. But the cities of the north and west had little to offer men whose education was acquired on farms, and in gas stations and machine shops. Many of these men looked south, attracted by the same *El Dorado* and *Fountain of Youth* that motivated Spaniards four hundred years earlier. The *Dorado* was that business opportunity always tantalizingly just out of reach. The *Fountain of Youth* flowed in the form of women and cheap booze.

Almost every Ecuadorian had seen one of the *Norteamericanos*, and many had seen and interacted with them on many occasions. Notwithstanding the vast difference between the *Norteamericanos*, they were somehow the same. They seemed to have wealth and power, and usually a complete ignorance of the language and culture. But they were friendly and laughing, and they were mostly unaware or unconcerned with paying two or three times the going rate for anything they purchased. Mr. Alabama was a rustic prototype of the *Norteamericano*; he lived and worked in a small coastal town in Ecuador.

A large man dressed in Levis and cowboy boots, sat at a table in a small beachfront cafe. He had not removed his hat—an old cowboy hat discolored by years of sweat and wear. The man had a permanent smile on his face, and seemed to think everyone, and everything, was fun or funny.

His vocabulary in Spanish was limited to a few nouns and verbs, and those few words were so poorly pronounced, and so awash in English slang, he might have done as well without them. But, he had no language problem. He was friendly and outgoing. He had plenty of money for the girls, and was always happy to buy drinks for anyone in his company. He was too big and self-confident to be challenged, so everyone made an effort to understand what he wanted. And, of course, he had no interest in, and therefore no reason to understand, anything said by a local person.

He joked and flirted with the waitress, and she was more than happy to flirt back. The tip he would leave on the table would increase her day's income by twenty percent!

A young American couple walked into the cafe. To meet another American in this small town was a novelty. They greeted and sat together for breakfast. The man liked to talk and was soon telling his life story. The man's language was—put generously—colorful. Certainly, much of what he said was in jest, meant to get a laugh from the listener. But, part of his tale was true and taken seriously, at least by himself. The two young Americans identified with his country slang, and enjoyed listening.

He was from Alabama, he said. He worked on a dredge in the harbor. He had been there for a year and a half, and planned to stay. He had been a Marine during World War Twice, and served in the Pacific—four years, two months, six days, three hours, and eighteen minutes, he said.

"Hell, when I went down to join the service, I said shit; don't like to walk, and kan't fly, so I joined the Navy. Well, ya' know, them sum'bitches lined us up, and any feller' that had an IQ equal to his height in inches, was throwed' into the Marine Corps; never was nothing but a police force for the Navy, ya' know. But, we was a fighten bunch'a sum'bitches! When we wasn't fighten' the goddamn Japs, we was fighten' each other. Well, when the fighten' stopped I said, I don't need no more a' that shit, and went home. And, when I got home, all them sum'bitches back there had got rich off the war, and they didn't want no part'a me. The only thing I knowed' how to do was fight, and the first thing ya' know, they got my ass locked up in their fucken jail. Well, I said, I don't need no more a' that shit, and went out to Texas and did some rough-necking on them oilrigs.

Got married to a woman down there in Texas. She already had two boys at the time, and then we had a little girl. Them boys was big—I mean big! Shit, the oldest one was six-four and weighed two hundred and ten pounds, and there weren't a' ounce'a fat on that fucken kid; an hell, the other'un growed up bigger'n him. I'd just knock um' down—shit there weren't no sense in talking to um'. Now that little girl was the sweetest thing you ever saw. If she had been any sweeter, the Lord woulda' kept her for his'self. But, them boys was mean as snakes. Well, that woman up'an left me, for some other sum'bitch, and took that sweet girl with her. Left me them damn boys. Hell, I started a pipeline business over in West Texas, just to work some a' that shit outa' them boys. You workum' hard all day, and they don't get into so much trouble at night. Them boys get home so tired they kain't hardly eat their supper. Hang them Levis on a nail and sleep. Shit, them big o' fucken Levis'ed try to walk away by their'selves. Well, them boys finally got old enough to leave. Hell, I don't know where they are now. They's getten' too big to knock down anyway. And, then I got another woman—married her ya'know—and that was the warshenest' woman I ever saw. You just get your socks ta' where you know which one goes on which foot, and the first thing ya' know, she was a' warshen' um'. Well, I'll be damned if she didn't up'an leave me too, like that other woman. And, I said, I don't need no more a' that shit. I don't know what them women did with all that money. I just come home and laid my paycheck on the table, and never saw another dime. Once I got them women out of my house, I had more money'n I knowed' what to do with—kan't even drank it all up. Shit, one time I let this women in my house, and the first thing you know, she's over there a' worshen' out my coffee pot. Hell, I ain't worshed' that coffee pot in three years, and it was just starten' to taste good. And, here's this woman worshen' it out. And, I says woman, what the fuck are you doing? And, she says, worshen' out this stinken' coffee pot. And, I says, well you can get your sweet ass right out'ta my house. I ain't never having another woman liven' in my house. I don't need no more a' that shit."

The man became aware of the young woman listening to his tale, and apologized. "Excuse me ma'am. But, I ain't gonna' put up with no woman worshen' out my coffee pot. Ain't nothin' to making coffee. You just throw a hand full of coffee in for each cup, and ball' the shit out of it. But, you don't never warsh' the pot, cause it gets better with use. So, I ain't haven' no woman around worshen' out my coffee pot. I don't need no more a' that shit."

The young couple were all smiles, and obviously enjoying his tale. They were interested in the dredging operation, and asked for a tour. Sure'nuff! They walked together to the harbor and took a company-owned motorized skiff out to the dredge.

It was an old dredge, pulled down from San Diego by a tugboat, he said. There were dozens, maybe hundreds, of engines, electrical motors and mechanical devices. And, there was the huge diesel, powering the long arm reaching off the bow to pick up silt and transferred it to barges, pulled by tugs. The silt is used to fill in the swamp region along the river, where the bamboo shacks are built on poles. He said new shacks always spring up on the river-side of the new fill.

His job was to keep all the engines, motors, and mechanical devices operational. He had four Ecuadorian men helping him, with at least one on duty at all times, and other men operating the barges and tugs. His salary was twice the sum of all their wages.

He yelled orders at his workers in a language best described as American Cuss. "*Abre* the goddamn housing and pull them fucken brushes; clean up that shit and get it the hell *fuera*; get off ya' fucken ass boy, and lend a hand with this *cadena*." Incredibly, they understood him. "If a man kan't understand nothin', I fire the sum'bitch. What the hell good is he, if he kan't understand what somebody says?" he explained. More incredibly, the men seemed to like him. He worked with them, unlike an Ecuadorian boss. His hands were dirty—greasy. There was no job he couldn't or wouldn't do.

"Five years ago I went down to Venezuela, and worked them rigs in that shithole they call a lake down there. That's where I learned to talk this Spanish. But, I'd rather work here on this rig. These Black folks is okay. Had a bunch of American kids working down there in Venezuela; shit, you gotta knock them American kids down or they don't pay no attention. Hell, these folks don't give ya' no talk back." His language is the same, whether he is talking to a man or woman, but the young woman just smiled.

He talked about growing up in the South. "Mom wouldn't give us no grits; says that's poor people's food. Hell, there weren't nobody poorer'n us. If it cost a nickel to shit, we woulda' had to throw up."

The man learned the young woman worked at the school, and decided to fill them in on that 'goddamn American Catholic woman'. "That woman's mean as a snake. She comes down here and tells me I gotta' hire some sum'bitch back, cause he has a bunch of kids, and he's a good Catholic. So, I said lady you c'n kiss my sweet ass; that sum'bitch kan't understand a fucken word you say to um'."

The young woman was disturbed by this story, but the young man winked at her, and shook his head. She decided to ignore the comment, and the man continued his story. "So, that Catholic woman goes down to the office and complains to the boss, and that sum'bitch brings this fucken guy back out here, and tells me I gotta' hire him back. And, I said shit, I'll throw his ass in the ocean if you leave um' out here. So, they had to give him a job in town. That woman's got all them sum'bitches buffaloed. Well, I told her to kiss my sweet ass. Hell, I don't need no more a' that shit."

"You folks ain't Catholics are ya?" The man asks suddenly. No, the young man told him. "Well, you kan't be too careful. Hell, there's Catholics all over the fucken place down here. I don't need no more a' that shit."

FOR THE GOOD TIMES: ESMERALDAS, FRIDAY, AUGUST 21

"Why do they pay him so much?" She asks.

"Well, hell, he isn't going to come down here for nothing."

"But they could hire twenty local men for what they are paying him."

"Yeah; and they couldn't keep the dredge operating with a thousand local people. Did you see how many different kinds of electrical and mechanical machines he has to keep going, and all of them junk."

"Yeah, he's a pretty smart man, isn't he? I mean, in his own way. How do you find a man who knows all that stuff?"

"Check any gas station in Alabama, or Texas, or anywhere else in the States, for that matter." I say. "Those fellows have grown up working on every kind of junk machinery known to mankind."

"Yeah, I guess so. But, how can they understand him?"

"You know, I was in Maya Villages in Central America for a while, and almost everyone carries a machete around all the time. And, you know something; you never have a dog come up and nip at your heels. There is one hell of a process of elimination at work. We're talking evolution, big time!"

"So, not understanding Mr. Alabama, is an unhealthy habit," she says.

"Yeah; we were seeing the residual work force out there. I'll bet there are a lot of men around here with no money in their pockets, who didn't understand him."

We sit on the beach and play in the waves, and enjoy our room most of the day. In the evening we walk up the main street of town. We walk hand in hand. The town is dirty, as are most lowland towns. As always, most streets and sidewalks are under construction, or in disrepair. It had rained in the afternoon, and we have to jump over puddles of water and skirt around muddy spots. We walk past paths leading to shacks perched above the swamp on bamboo stilts. There is a tangle of walkways, suspended above the swampy riverbank, connecting bamboo shacks.

"The poorest people live out there. I guess they will use the silt from the harbor to fill here, and even poorer people will move further out on the river." We stop to look.

"You ever been down there?" she asks.

"Yeah; they have bars down in there, some with jukeboxes that—would you believe it—play American country music."

Closer to the center of town, there is a rather nice park with a fountain, and broad acacia trees covering the whole area, almost as if they were umbrellas. The walkways are lined with concrete benches, each with the name of some prominent citizen who had probably paid for it. The grass and flower gardens are roped off, and well cared for. There are sloths in the trees. Obviously, someone has captured them and put them there. They hang upside down and move slowly along tree limbs. Some of the females have juveniles hanging on to backs or stomachs.

We sit and enjoy the curious animals for a while. Continuing our walk, we are again faced with mud obstacles, and broken sidewalks.

"Let's put a shine on this town." She says.

We walk into the next bar we come to and order a beer. I play the jukebox, and select all the country music available. We listen to Jim Reeves songs.

"It's really strange that they would have American country music down here," she says.

"Yeah, only down here on the coast where you find Black people."

"They don't understand English," she says.

"I know, but they usually figure out the words to these songs. Some of these people sing those songs. Black people always know good music when they hear it."

"They've got rhythm; is that it, honey?"

"You can laugh, but it's true."

One of my favorite songs is playing: 'Hold your warm and tender body close to mine...and make believe you love me one more time, for the good times.'

Suddenly, I connect the words of the song with our love, and I know she has too. I drop more coins into the jukebox, and play that song again.

As the song begins the second time, I tell her, "It's my favorite song."

"I don't believe you."

To prove my point I sing along: 'there'll be time enough for severance when you leave me'. I continue looking directly into her eyes, and she puts her hand over my mouth. I continue again: 'And make believe you love me, one more time, for the good times'. She puts her hand over my mouth again. I feel my eyes become watery and think hers might be too.

"Come on honey, let's hit another joint."

We walk on down the street to the next bar. "I never knew country music could be so sad," she says. "I don't want to be sad. Don't play it anymore, okay?"

I play Mexican tunes I know, and sing along with the music, '*Mariquita se llamaba, la que vive junto al rio.*'

"What does it mean?" she asks.

"It's a Mexican song. They don't really say anything, but if you read between the lines, there's all kinds of sexual stuff, you know," I explain. "The man is singing to this girl, he calls Mariquita, and he says, cover me with your *rebozo—your* shawl—because I'm dying of the cold."

"I get the picture," she says smiling.

"And, he says," I continue the translation, "Mariquita give me a kiss, your mother told you to. And, then she says, my mother is in charge of me, but I'm in charge of my mouth."

Shirley enjoys that one and laughs out loud. The other people in the bar laugh with her.

"They know you're translating the words to me don't they?"

"Yeah, I guess so." I respond.

"This place is fun. Let's get another beer."

"It was the last toast by a Bohemian for a Queen," I translate. "The mariachis stopped playing. From my hand, that had lost its strength, my glass fell. She wanted to stay when she saw my sadness, but it was written, that on that day I was to lose her love."

"That's sad. Do they really say it is written, like the Arabs?"

"Yeah; there is a lot of Arab influence in Spanish, and in the architecture too. That comes from the Moors."

"You always know this stuff," she says.

I translate another Mexican song: "We stood there, face to face in the moonlight without speaking, when suddenly he said that I should forget his love because he didn't want to take advantage of me. I wanted to reach out my arms, with desire to hold him. But, my pride impeded me. Then, alone in front of the church, and before the stone crucifix, and crying, and crying, I implore Christ to contemplate my sadness. And, then the crucifix of stone also..." I see tears welling up in her eyes, and stop the translation.

"Also, began to cry." She completes the words for me. I nod. "That's just too sad," she wipes her eyes. "They're all looking at me. They know you're telling me what it means, don't they?"

I look up at the somber men around the bar, who mostly look down to avert my gaze. "Yeah, they do know."

347

"I feel so damn stupid;" she says, turning away to face the door, and wiping her eyes. "I never cry." Her voice is choked.

"You don't have to feel stupid. Down here everyone cries. I guess there is an awful lot of sadness and tragedy down here, so most people can identify."

"Damn you!"

"What love?"

"Damn you!" She repeats in a harsh voice.

"What's the matter, love?" I try to caress her face, but she pushes my hand away.

"You're trying to hurt me." She says, in a choked voice. "You promised you wouldn't, but you're doing it."

Slowly, I come to grips with her words. "You're hurting me, too."

"Why don't we just STOP IT!"

I let that sink in. "I can't." I whisper to her. I feel philosophical. "Only the people you love can hurt you. People who never love anyone are never hurt. Isn't that strange?"

"Let's get out of here. If I have one more beer I'm going to make a complete fool of myself."

I pay the bill, and we walk outside. The shine on the town is gone, and we both know it.

"I'll get a cab."

"No, let's walk. I need the time."

She has her hands in the pockets of her skirt, and keeps them there as we walk. I put my arm around her waist and arms. She walks leaning the other way, with her face turned away from me. I feel her chest heave, and realize she is crying. That makes me cry, too. As we pass people on the street there are stares—some with sympathy and others with disgust or anger. They probably think you've been beating her. Fuck um—I don't care what they think, I tell myself.

That we are breaking up comes over me slowly. She's going to tell you it's over when you get to the hotel. You can't let her do that.

I stop and hold her. She keeps her face away from me. I try to turn her face, gently at first, and then more firmly. She refuses. Feeling her chest heave with grief is too much for me.

"Shirley, look at me." She begins to pull away from me. "Damn you! Turn around and look at me."

I know my harsh words are a mistake. She does turn, but in the glare of the streetlight, I can see her tear-streaked face has an angry look.

"Shirley, don't. I didn't mean that. You can't leave me now. Please, don't do that."

"You're not playing the game fair." She says, wiping her face with her hand.

"I'll play fair. I'll do anything. Just don't leave me tonight." We continue to stand facing each other, and a light rain begins to fall. "Not tonight; I couldn't take it."

I resign myself to her decision. There is nothing more I can say. I look up, so the rain will hide my face, and wash off the tears. She does the same thing. The rain comes harder, with wind. I shiver, and feel her shiver, too.

"Ray." I continue to look up at the falling rain.

"Ray," she says again. "Look at me."

"I can't look at you when you say it." I choke out the words.

We continue standing there for a minute, with me looking up at the rain. "I won't leave you tonight," she says. The release of emotion staggers me. I hear a loud, ugly noise. I realize the noise has come from me, and turn away from her in embarrassment. I walk over to the lamppost and hit it with my hand, and then lean on it for support. I feel relief and anger at the same time. I want to yell at her for doing that to me, but I say nothing.

"You're mad at me now, aren't you?" She puts her arm around my waist, and leans her face against my back. "I paid you back for what you did to me, didn't I?"

"Yes."

"I didn't plan to do it; it just came out that way."

"I know."

"Do you forgive me?"

"I forgive you."

She pulls me away from the post gently, and stands facing me. "Will you forget I did this to you?"

"No, love; I will never forget it."

We walk on slowly in the rain. We are both trembling with cold. She pulls my face around to her, and tries to say something, but it is mostly lost by her chattering teeth. My teeth chatter, too.

"We're fucken freezing to death out here," I say, in a low gravely tone.

Somehow that is funny, and we both began to laugh. We run toward the hotel laughing together. The crisis seems to be over, but I know things will never be the same again.

Sleep comes in short interludes between caressing. Crying is contagious. I try to contain myself, and know she is doing the same for me. My dream is filled with the horror of crawling in trenches and hiding. When I wake, it is with a start, and think I may have made a noise. She is looking at me, caressing my face. It is a bad night.

"Let's see how miserable we can make each other today." She says. It is just daylight, and we are lying on our sides looking at each other.

"My love," I respond, "I'll bet I can make you more miserable, than you can make me."

"Honey, you just don't know how vindictive and bitchy I can be, when I put my mind to it."

"Let me tell you something, my love. I put fire on people and burn them, and pull their hair out."

"My dearest sweetheart; how would you like a handful of brains splashed in your face?"

"Uhh," I say. I can't top that one.

"We're not funny are we?"

"No."

"That last thing I said was really cruel, wasn't it?"

"Yes. I said a terrible thing to you, too."

We dress, and walk into town for breakfast. Shirley won't consider the restaurant at the hotel, after the bat shit incident. We have our breakfast at a beachfront café.

"Any tribes of wild Indians around here?" She asks.

"I don't think so. Why?"

"Oh, I thought we might provoke some wild Indians into a fight."

"Shirley, I'm not in the mood for this."

"Say bat shit." She orders. "Say it!"

"Bat shit."

"Say it loud. Say, Shirley is crazier than bat shit."

"Come on, Shirley."

"Say it!"

"Shirley is crazier than bat shit."

"Say it loud. I want those people across the street to hear it. Yell it." I do, and have to smile. "Do you feel better now?"

"Yeah." I say.

"Well, let's get on with the problem of screwing up the lives of the wild Indians."

"Maybe we could go down to the dock, and see if there is a boat going somewhere. You never know, sometimes if you just poke around, something interesting will happen."

"Great idea, let's do it," She says.

I know she is looking for something to keep us too busy to think about having only two days left. I am too. We take a bus to the dock and check for passenger boats up the coast. Nothing will leave till noon, which probably means two PM, and we will have no way to get back. We poke around the dock, and spot a powerboat with a very large outboard motor. There is a young mestizo fellow, obviously from the highlands, loading gas containers into the boat. We stop to talk. Seeing Shirley, he is more than willing to have us as passengers.

He is well-educated and middle class, and is here to supervise a logging operation. He will be headed up the coast to check on the operation, and of course, we are welcome to come along. His name is Roberto; we can call him Beto. No, he doesn't need any help loading the boat. No, we will not have to bring any food or beer. He has a man who takes care of everything, and we will eat at the logging camp. We stand aside and let him prepare the boat.

Shirley is impressed. "You said if we poked around, something would happen, and it did. You just go around having all these adventures."

"It wasn't me, love. It was you."

"What do you mean?"

"If I had been alone, he would never have invited me. It's you. He just wants to be around you."

"I don't think so. I always know when a guy is looking at me that way."

"He's not looking at you that way, because he knows I would kill him if he did. He just wants to show off his boat to you. Maybe he will get a chance to see up your skirt or something, you know."

"That's really pathetic. You guys would actually hang around with a girl, just for a chance to see up her skirt?"

"Well, sure."

"Why? What good is it going to do him? He knows I'm with you. He isn't going to get anything from me."

"Love, you just don't understand."

"Explain it to me."

"Well, that's all he can get. Hell, he's high and dry here, and there isn't going to be anything like you, up the coast. He would rather just have you along in the boat, and think about it, than have nothing at all."

"Having me along is something?"

"Yes, love. Having you along is really something."

"I thought girls were sick. But, you guys are really sick."

Beto's man arrives with a cooler full of beer. He is a young Black fellow, probably in his early twenties, with a body and poise that suggests he has spent the past ten years lifting weights, and studying modern dance. But, of course, he hasn't. He just has a beautiful body, and lots of self-confidence. He wears only shorts, and sweat glistens from the ripples of muscle in his chest, back, and arms. His name is *Mártir.* 'Martyr,' I translate to Shirley. He and Beto sit in the front of the boat, with Beto at the controls. We sit in the back.

"Jeez," Shirley says. "Look at that guy."

"I'm looking at him, love—and trying to figure out how I'm going to kill him. And, I can tell you, it's not going to be a fair fight."

"Stop it! I'm just looking at his body. He's spectacular."

"I know what you are looking at!"

"You're jealous. Come on, Ray. Girls aren't that stupid. If it were a girl with a body like that, you would probably throw me overboard, and be up there trying to look up her skirt."

"If it were a girl with a body like that, I would run for the fucken hills."

Beto is obviously insecure driving the boat through the waves. He powers up a swell, and then cuts the power back at the top, as if afraid we will shoot up into the air. When he reduces power at the top of the swell, we settle into the trough, and the crest passes us, spilling water into the boat. Then, he powers up again. After a while he is apparently satisfied he has demonstrated his skill, or perhaps ashamed of it, and he turns the boat over to Martyr. He comes back to join us. Martyr immediately gives the boat full power, and we skim along bouncing from the top of one swell to the next. Obviously, Martyr knows how to drive the boat.

I explain to Beto that he will have to speak slowly, so Shirley can understand. He is happy to comply. We talk, and I translate as little as possible, happy to have her focus on Beto, rather than Martyr.

Beto is a fine fellow, from a good family. His father sent him down to learn the logging business, when he flunked out of engineering school. He will learn the business, and then go back to school. Someday, he will run the logging industry up the coast and build it into an empire. I figure he has a real good chance to build his empire. If he were insecure, he certainly would not have Martyr as his man, and he is smart enough to know Martyr knows more than he does, at least about the boat. That's a good start on building an empire.

When I have a chance, I tell Shirley, "This is the man you want, love. He's handsome, and he's a White boy, and he's going to be a millionaire someday. Why are you hanging around with an ugly shit-head like me, and looking at that Black dude that doesn't have a pot to piss in."

She doesn't appreciate my humor, and doesn't seem to be sure that it is humor. We have started the day with an ugly tone, and it's not improving much. I wish there were some way that I could find a Margarita or Ines for her. I wish I could thrill her again, and make her love me for being a good guy, rather than hate me for being a shit-head. But, there seemed to be no way.

The logging operation is rustic, but substantial. There are two other highland Mestizos working there—an engineer and a forestry expert—along with numerous Black workers. Everyone defers to Beto as boss, but clearly Beto knows the score. He asks for, and accepts, advice on everything from business to lunchtime. Again, I marvel that he has enough cool, and self-esteem, to recognize the fact that he doesn't know anything, and that he is smart enough to be willing to take advice from people who do know. I decide I like Beto.

After lunch we head back. Beto turns the boat over to Martyr. The waves are higher, but Martyr powers through at a furious speed. I find it scary and think Martyr may be showing off for the foreigners. It is a situation that I would normally object to, in no uncertain terms. I don't like people putting me at risk for frivolous reasons, and I sure don't like having someone put Shirley at risk. I feel confident that if the boat does flip or sink, I can swim to the coast; we are no more than five hundred yards out. But, I'm not sure Shirley could, and wonder if I would be able to save her. I would either save her, or go down with her. It is that thought that causes me to remain silent. If Beto is worried, he doesn't show it. Shirley doesn't seem to be concerned, either. Perhaps she thinks it is normal, and doesn't understand the danger.

We make it back to Esmeraldas without mishap. Perhaps I had overestimated the danger. I suggest to Beto that he and Martyr should join us for dinner at Casa Garibaldi. Beto looks away and thinks about it. Immediately, I know Martyr will not be welcome at the restaurant. Not because of his black skin, but because of his dress, and the obvious fact that he is lower-class. Perhaps we can all have a beer together at the bar near the dock, Beto suggests. I don't translate the unspoken words to Shirley, knowing she would have trouble with it.

At the bar, Martyr is jovial, but very polite. He avoids looking at Shirley. Martyr is smart enough to know he has hitched his wagon to a star, I tell myself. Beto will be the boss someday, and Martyr is going to be there with him. My respect for both of them increases greatly. Martyr has to leave. Beto pays him his wages, and says good-bye. We go to Casa Garibaldi with Beto.

During dinner, I translate as little as possible, so Shirley can be a part of the group, instead of just being with me. We have a nice dinner and conversation, but we don't seem to enjoy it. Beto insists on exchanging addresses, and promises to meet again. I know we will forget one another in twenty-four hours.

Shirley and I walk out to the beach. "I didn't appreciate what you said." I don't know what she is referring to, and decide it will be best not to know.

I'M GOING TO MARRY JERRY: ESMERALDAS, SUNDAY AFTERNOON, AUGUST 23

The slope of the shoreline fell away steeply toward the pounding surf. At the top of the sand berm, that marked the high water level, a young woman sat facing the ocean. The tide was low, but coming in. The strong surf, some ten feet below and thirty feet out, kicked a misty spray up into the sea breeze, which carried it up to where the woman sat. The woman wore a full skirt, which she kept tucked between her widely spread legs.

A young man sat facing her left side. He put his right leg around her back and his left between her legs. He wrapped his arms around her arms and body. He locked his ankles and hands together around her and held her tight. She would not be able to escape. He was surprised she had allowed herself to be held captive.

The young woman sat passively and submitted to the man's display of domination. A few days previous she would not have allowed that. But, it posed no threat to her now. She knew he would be capable of holding her against her will, if he chose to do so. But, he would not.

A few days ago she had come to grips with the fact that she could not physically dominate this man. That had been one of the few times of her adult life she had experienced the emotion of fear. She knew immediately that her pretense of physical equality with men was self-deception. She abandoned that pretense. She had decided years earlier that she would not deceive herself, and she would not wish for the unattainable. At that time, she examined her face in the mirror and made a very deliberate decision. At the dinner table that night she announced to herself, but aloud in front of her parents, "When I was younger I wanted to be pretty, and to be petite and feminine. I don't want that anymore. I like the way I look, and I am happy being the way I am." The decision to abandon the illusion of physical equality to men was made in the same deliberate manner, and announced aloud, to herself more than to the person with her.

Having rid herself of that pretense, being held physically captive was no longer a threat to her. She would use the tools God gave her. She would control herself, and those people with whom she established relationships, with superior intelligence, strength of personality, and will power.

"You shouldn't have let me hold you like this;" he told her, "now I won't let you go."

"Yes you will."

"Tell me you don't love me. Then I'll let you go."

"I won't tell you that."

"Tell me to let you go. Tell me you don't want me anymore."

"No."

"Then I won't let you go."

"You don't want to kiss me as much as before." She said.

"Yes I do."

She ignored his response. She knew he would not have noticed that subtle change in his behavior, nor would he understand why he had changed. She was not informing him of the change. It was not important for him to understand. It was of no concern to her either, except to confirm to herself that she understood his behavior in every detail. "It's because you would rather look at me."

She was informing herself. She informed herself aloud, as she frequently did. Thoughts could be changed or discarded. Statements made aloud were confirmed and fixed. She needed to inform herself of an important decision she was about to take. Allowing him to hear would also serve to dispel any lingering doubts he might have about her intentions.

"You love me. You aren't just pretending. How can you just walk away from me? I would never do that to you."

She ignored his question and continued speaking to herself aloud, calmly and without emotion; "I'm going to marry Jerry. If he will forgive me for this, I'm going to marry him. And, he will forgive me."

"You are going to tell him about us? What are you going to say? I want to marry you Jerry, and by the way, please forgive me for being in love with someone else. Is that what you will tell him?"

"I'm going to marry him." One minute before she had not known she would marry Jerry. Now the decision had been made.

"Marry me."

"I couldn't marry you. It hasn't even been three weeks and already I can hardly stand it. You and I could never tolerate each other. Anyway, you're already married. Perhaps you have forgotten that."

"Maybe I won't be married much longer."

"Are you going to divorce your wife?"

"She probably has divorce papers waiting for me right now."

"No she doesn't. She doesn't believe in divorce."

"How do you know that? Did Norma tell you something?"

"The only way for you to get a divorce is for you to ask her. Are you going to do that?" He did not answer. She continued; "Is that what you are thinking? Because if it is, I'm going to walk away from you right now. That would be as if I had caused it. I can't live with that."

"And, you won't live with it." He completed her statement before she could.

"I told myself it was because I wanted to help you. And, I do. But I probably made things worse for you, and anyway that's not really why I did it. It was because I wanted you to love me. I have never been pretty; I even stopped wanting to be pretty a long time ago. But I wanted you to see me—in your mind—as a beautiful woman. I didn't know it would be so much for you. And, I didn't know you could make me love you back. I didn't know I could love someone. But I can. And, that's why I can go back and marry Jerry now. I'm ashamed of what I did, but not because we loved each other. That was fair for both of us. I'm sorry I made things worse for you. But, I didn't mean to do that."

"You didn't make anything worse. Why are you ashamed of what we did?"

"I'm ashamed because I knew Jerry would forgive me, and that's why I cheated him. If it had been you, I wouldn't have done that. You would have been insanely jealous. You can't even share a couple of hours of my time with someone else. But, Jerry has asked so little of me, and has given me so much. And, that's why I'm ashamed."

"I love you."

"Jerry loves me as much as you do; more than you do. He will love me even after I tell him what I did. Could you do that?"

"Yes."

"Could you really? Could you forgive that, and forget about it? I hope you really can."

"Did Norma tell you something? Are you trying to tell me something?" She ignored his question. "Why would you tell someone something that would just hurt them?"

"You can't start your life with someone with a big lie. Don't you know that?" she asked, and then continued, "Jerry will forgive me, and I'm going to make it up to him. I wasn't good to him before. I knew he loved me and I could do anything I wanted. I didn't think about him. But, I'm going to change that now. I know how to be in love with a man now, and I'm going to be in love with Jerry. I'm going to love him more than I love you; much more."

"How can you just stop loving me? How can you do that? How can you just walk away?"

She tried to free herself from his arms. She pushed against his arms gently, at first, and then harder. She looked into his eyes and read his thoughts. He would demonstrate his power to hold her. He would release her only if she asked him to—only if she ordered him to. He would force her to tell him to release her. But, he was mistaken. It was not a test of strength; it was a test of wills.

She continued to struggle to free herself. She could easily reach his groin and hurt him, and she could scratch his sides and back if she wanted. But, that would be unfair because he could not hurt her back. And, that would be self-deception—taking a knife to a gunfight. She would simply continue to struggle until he released her. General Grant's famous statement came into her mind: 'If it takes all summer.'

The four minutes they sat locked in the struggle seemed without end. Her face became contorted as she pushed against him with all her strength. Tears, born of frustration ran down her cheeks. She began to moan, softly at first and then more loudly, until it became a gasping cry.

Suddenly, he released his grip, and held his arms straight out. She sat for a half-minute panting from exhaustion. Then she unlocked his ankles and pushed his now relaxed legs open. She stood and observed him for a full minute, wiping her wet face with the back of her hand. He sat with his arms as they had been, now stretched out to her.

She turned and walked away, up the beach.

THERE WILL NEVER BE ANOTHER SHIRLEY: ESMERALDAS, SUNDAY, AUGUST 23

I sit on the sand and watch her walk away. She must be going back to the hotel. She would not leave me this way. She would have to say good-bye. Even if she does go back to the hotel, I have just two nights and one day left with her. On Tuesday morning she will leave me. That is now as certain as sunrise on Tuesday morning. I need her. Why is she going to leave me? She is just like me. Yeah, she was molested, just like you. The men did it to her, the same way the war did it to you, I tell myself. But, she doesn't need me, the way I need her. She isn't a cripple like me.

That happened to her when she was just a child, but she can still stand on her own feet. So, what's wrong with you? Why don't you stop crying about your little problems? Shirley can, why can't you? I will! I will stand up. I will stop feeling sorry for myself and stand up and be a man. Shirley knows Donna has another man. Norma told her. Are you going to forgive Donna, the way Jerry is going to forgive Shirley? I will. I can forgive her.

Maybe it's too late. Maybe she won't want you back. Maybe she won't forgive you. Those thoughts make me shudder. I will lose Shirley, and then I will lose Donna.

I walk back to the hotel, and go to the room. I am relieved to see Shirley on the balcony. She is seated in a lounge chair. She did not leave me. I kneel beside her, put my head in her lap, and wrap my arms around her waist.

"I'm not going to ask Donna for a divorce. And, I can forgive her if she has been with another man. You have helped me a lot. I'm going to start dealing with those problems. I have already started to deal with them, and it is because of you. I'm a shit-head Shirley, and I don't blame you for walking away from me."

She goes into the bathroom and turns on the shower. I sit in the chair and think about the medal, and about Snider and Doyle, and about Shirley leaving me, and about Donna with another man. She comes out of the bathroom with a towel around her, reaching from her breasts to the tops of her legs. She is so sexy I could die for her at that moment.

"You didn't join me," she says.

"I was just coming in to join you. I was just thinking about some stupid things."

"That's okay."

I shower alone. Later we lie together looking up at the ceiling. "You know, over the past three weeks, I have been the happiest person in the whole world." She says. "Did you know that?"

"No, I was."

"We were. I never really loved anyone before you. I thought I had, but now I know I didn't."

"So, now you will go back to the States and be in love with Jerry. What about me?"

"You will fall in love with another girl. It's easy for you."

"There will never be another Shirley."

"No! And there will never be another Donna, will there? But, there will be another Judy, and another Elizabeth, and another Megan, and another Janet." We are quiet for a minute.

"That's not fair. Yeah, I've been with other girls, but it wasn't this way."

"I'm sorry. I knew that wasn't true. I'm just trying to be hateful." She continues, "It doesn't matter if you don't forgive me, does it? We are breaking up, aren't we?"

"Shirley, why . .

She interrupts: "Don't say that. I know what you were going to say. And, if you say that, I'm going to walk out the door, right now."

"I'm not saying it."

"Don't!"

"Okay, love. You're ..."

"Don't say that. I'm warning you. You are going to say I'm in charge. You always do that. You always push everything on me. And, later you're going to say Shirley left me; Shirley didn't love me. Ray! Will you just stop?"

"You read my mind so well, I don't need to say anything." I reply. "Are we pretending we're pretending?"

"I'm warning you."

"Is this our last night together?"

"It will be if you make me cry, or if you sing any of those damn Mexican songs."

"And, if I don't sing those songs?"

"Then, we will be together tomorrow."

IT NEVER WENT AWAY: MEMPHIS AIR PORT, AUTUMN, 1955

Doyle was from Memphis, he thought. There would be a four-hour layover before his flight from Memphis to Austin. He finished his first beer and asked the bartender for a second. "I had a buddy from Memphis." He told the bartender.

"You in Ka'Ria?" The bartender asked. The bartender was a Black man about his age.

"Yeah."

"In the fucken Corps?"

"The fucken Corps? Hell no! I was a soldier, man!"

"Shee'it!" The bartender responded. "The fucken soldiers didn't do shit in Ka'Ria."

"Hey man! Eat the apple and fuck the fucken core—I've heard that said!"

The other men at the bar flinched and sat back on their stools. Race relations in the town were tense, and Blacks and Whites rarely spoke to one another. They expected a fight. But, there would be no fight. The two men had established a bond with those few innocuous insults that transcended race and social class. They both spoke the same language.

"When were you there?" he asked the Black man.

"Fifty-one; shit, we were headed for the Yalu when the fucken Chinks came in. When that shit was over there weren't very many guys in my outfit still standing up. I got the million-dollar wound, man; right in the ass. Can't be a brick mason like my old man. Now all I can do is work this fucken bar. Course, I was lucky to get out of that shit with any of my ass left. When were you there?"

"Fifty-two and three; I don't think the front moved more than a couple of miles all the time I was there. Just a bunch of fucken politicians shooten' the shit while we're getting our asses shot off. Well, actually it wasn't that bad; you know, not as bad as before. We were mostly just trading artillery fire, and sending out patrols. We lost some guys, but it wasn't that bad. Hey man, you got a phone book?"

"Sure." The man put the book on the bar in front of him. "Give your buddy a call, huh? Better let sleeping dogs lie, man."

"No shit. But, anyway this dude is doing his sleeping in heaven—or more likely hell. I just thought I would call the family, you know."

There were five Doyle's in the phone book. "Can I use your phone?" The bartender put the phone on the bar, shook his head, and busied himself with another customer.

"Hi, I was in Korea, in the Eighty-Second airborne, and I just wondered if you knew aha ...a guy who was killed there?"

"Who is this? We don't want to buy nothing, and we ain't giving you no money." He heard a click on the other end of the line.

He hung up the phone. "That was stupid." He said to the bartender. "Fucken guy thought I was trying to sell him something."

"Leave it alone, man." The bartender advised.

He called the second number, and a woman answered. "Hi, I was in Korea, and

I just wondered if, maybe you had a son over there." There was a long pause on the other end of the line.

"Who is this?" he heard a man's voice now.

"I was in the Eighty-Second in Korea, and I was just wondering ..."

"Charles was killed in Korea," the man said. "Why are you calling?"

"Well, I was there. I was kind of a buddy of his, and I just thought I would call."

There was another long pause, and he could hear loud voices on the other end.

"Where are you?" It was the woman's voice.

"I'm here in the airport, at (he cupped the phone, what's the name of this place?) at the Highlife Lounge. Yeah, I'll be here for a couple of hours. My plane doesn't leave until eight PM." He hung up the phone.

"That was really stupid." He told the bartender. "Now those fucken people are coming down here."

He knew who they were immediately. He stood and greeted the middle-aged man and woman. "Hi, I called earlier. I'm sorry; I really don't know why I called. I just thought ..."

The woman interrupted. "Did you know Charles?"

"Yeah; he was in the second platoon, but I knew him." The three of them sat at a table.

"Were you in the truck when it blew up?"

"Nah, we were on the hill. There weren't any trucks up there."

The woman started crying.

"What are you trying to pull here, son?" The man said.

"I'm not trying to pull anything, sir. I just called because I thought I should say something to you folks."

"Charles was in a truck that hit a landmine in Korea. He was killed."

"Nah; he was in a bunker up on Zebra. We didn't have any trucks up there."

"What are you saying?" The woman's voice was shrill, and her eyes were flooded with tear.

"I'm not saying anything, ma'am. Maybe, he was in a truck. Hell, I don't know."

The woman grabbed his arm. "Did you see him; did you see him?" she pleaded.

"Yeah, I saw him."

"Where was he?" The man demanded.

"I told you, he was in the bunker."

"Why was he in a bunker?"

"Hell, I don't know. He was dead when I got there."

The woman's anguish burst forth, and the man became angry. "We don't have to put up with this son, we have rights. I'm in the American Legion, and I have connections."

He wanted to leave. "Hey, I didn't mean to trouble you folks. I'm sorry I called." The man and woman held both arms, and pulled him back to his seat.

"Why did they tell us he was killed in a truck, if he was in a bunker?" The woman asked.

"Hell, I don't know; what difference does it make?" The woman shrieked. "Hey, I didn't want to cause this. Maybe it was some other Doyle; I didn't know his first name." He said to the man.

"Just tell us what you saw."

"Well shit. I was lost. I was trying to get back, and just wanted to hide in that bunker. I thought we would be pounding the shit out of the hill, at any minute. I was scared shitless, man."

"Don't use foul language in front of my wife."

"Hey, I'm sorry. I didn't mean to do that."

"Just tell us what happened."

"I just crawled in there to hide. I thought the Chinks were coming up."

"And, Charles was there?"

"Yeah, Doyle was sitting there. He was already dead."

"He was sitting up when he was dead?" The woman shrieked.

"Well, yeah."

"How did you know he was dead?" The man asked.

"Well, hell. I could tell."

"Did you check him?"

"No, it was dark. I waited for the sun to come up, and I could see him. I'm sorry, but he was dead."

"You didn't even check him?" The man demanded.

"Well, I did when the sun came up, and I could see. I took his canteen, and C rations, and his bandage, and I took his M1. That's why I wanted to call you folks—to tell you I took those C rations. But, he didn't need them."

"You took his food!" The woman screamed at him. "What right did you have to take his food?"

He felt as if she had slapped his face. He stood. Most of the people in the lounge had turned their attention to the commotion. "I WAS HUNGRY!" He heard his voice, loud and hateful. "I didn't have any water! The Lieutenant's fucken brains were all over my face. I was scared to death, woman! I didn't cause the fucken war, and I didn't cause your son to be killed." He felt tears run down his face, as he tried to pull away from them.

A man from a nearby table came up behind him, and held his shoulders. "That's about enough," the stranger said, to the seated woman.

He stumbled toward the door of the lounge, with the stranger helping him. The woman came behind screaming and crying, but the stranger held her away. "That's enough, lady! Leave him alone." The husband scrambled to help his wife to a seat, and ran after them. "Leave him alone, mister," the stranger said. "He isn't responsible for what happened."

"I just wanted to say, we're sorry."

"Yeah, everyone is sorry!" He yelled at the man.

The stranger continued to hold him. "It'll be okay, son. It will be okay."

He looked at this stranger who held him; somehow the man seemed to be his uncle—Uncle Bob. "You were a fucken soldier." He said.

"Yes son, I was a soldier. Yes, I was a fucking soldier. And, I'm telling you, it's going to be okay."

"It will never be okay again." He pulled away from Uncle Bob, and ran down the corridor.

The stranger stood for a long moment and watched the young man run through the crowd; he held out his hand: "WAIT; WAIT..." Then he turned and walked back into the bar, where the husband stood waiting for him.

"We didn't mean that, sir; we are sorry. It was because our son was killed in Korea. We didn't mean to treat him that way. We are sorry."

"Yes, everyone is sorry." The stranger answered, and then turned to the people in the bar staring at him, and repeated in a loud, harsh voice, "EVERYONE IS FUCKING SORRY."

The stranger's woman rushed to him. "Darrell! You've never said that word. What's the matter with you?"

He ignored her, and turned to the bartender, "That boy pay his bar bill?"

"There is no charge, Sir." The bartender replied. The stranger pulled a bill from his pocket, crumpled it in his fist and threw it on the bar. The bartender picked up the bill and straightened it, and held it out to the man. "I said no charge, Sir."

"Consider it a tip." The stranger said, angrily

"No Sir!"

The bartender held the bill in his hand with his arm stretched out toward the man. The man accepted the money. Suddenly, his anger turned to grief. He staggered and caught himself on the bar rail. He lowered his head and removed a handkerchief from his pocket, and wiped his eyes.

"What is the matter with you?" The woman demanded, and then, "Oh Darrell, don't let it come back; please, don't let it come back."

"It never went away."

GET OFF ME: ESMERALDAS, MONDAY MORNING, AUGUST 24

She is caressing my face. "You're okay honey." I wake and feel my face wet with tears. She holds me. "It's okay." I regain control of myself, and lie quietly. "You were having a bad dream."

"Yeah." I am embarrassed that she has watched me cry.

"Was it because of me?"

"Nah, it's the goddamned war. I guess I'll never get over it."

"I'm so sorry."

"Yeah, everyone is sorry." The tone of my voice is distant and harsh. I feel the dog come up, snarling at me.

"Please, don't look at me that way. Don't blame me."

I turn to her. "I don't blame you. It's just me—I blame myself." I continue, "Whatever happens—and I know what's going to happen—I don't blame you for anything. You're the best thing that has ever happened to me, and I will always love you."

"Oh, I'm so sorry." We lie quietly for a long time, and I continue to struggle with the dog.

We stay in bed after sunrise and make love. I hear myself make ugly guttural sounds, and hear her make ugly noises too. I know we always make those sounds when we make love, but I have not heard them before. I prop myself up, with my elbows, and look at her face. She has an expression I don't like. Her eyes are flat, and her mouth slightly open. Her face appears haggard, as if she has been through some terrible ordeal—like that woman on the Life Magazine cover from the Oklahoma Dust Bowl. She is whimpering and groaning. I know she always has that look when we make love, but I have not seen it before.

When the sounds stop, I continue to look at her face, and Donna's words run through my thoughts: 'It's just cheap and dirty when you do it with someone you don't love.' Those words had come into my mind in Mexico, when I was with a girl, and I had felt disgust and shame. Now, I have heard those words here, with Shirley.

"Get off me!" Her voice is cold and hard.

Does she know what I was thinking? If she does, it would be terrible. How could I have thought such a thing? I want to apologize to her, but she could not possibly have known. I don't know what to say, so I say nothing.

She gets up immediately, and goes into the bathroom. I hear the shower, but I don't consider joining her. I stay in bed, hating myself for those thoughts that came into my mind, and dreading the notion she knows. When she comes out of the bathroom, she is dressed, and combing her hair.

"I'm going back to Costa. Are you going with me?"

"Of course I'm going with you."

I shower quickly. When I return to the room, she has all our things packed and is waiting by the door.

What is happening? Why is she doing this to you? Depression comes over me like a cold mist. I shudder. She is doing this to you. She wants to hurt you as much as she can. *No! I won't think that way. She wouldn't do that to me. I love her, and I won't think that way.*

She's thinking about herself. She wants to leave you. *No, stop it, I won't think that way.* Maybe she can't help it. She's doing that to you and she doesn't even know. My hateful thoughts continue.

"You guys are late." Johnny is waiting for us in the lobby. "I was about to come up there, and dump a bucket of cold water on you two."

Then, he seems to realize things are ugly. He pulls Shirley aside. "What's the matter, baby? Did he do something to you?"

"Yes. He stopped loving me."

"That's okay baby, you don't need him."

"Yes I do."

He turns to me, "What did you do to her, you bastard?"

"I hurt her."

"No." She says. "He didn't hurt me. He just doesn't love me anymore." She puts her head on Johnny's shoulder: "It hurts so bad."

"I knew this was going to happen." Johnny says. "I'm going to take you home. You don't need this son-of-a-bitch."

"I need him."

I go over to the desk, and pay the bill, and then meet them outside. There is a cab in front of the hotel. "Let's take the cab out to the truck stop." I say.

"Get away from her, you damned bastard." He says. Suddenly he starts swinging his fists at me wildly. The first punch surprises me, and he connects to the left side of my face; but he hits with the inside of his fist rather than his knuckles. His eyes are red and he makes whimpering sounds, as if in desperation. He continues charging forward and swinging his fists at me, but the punches are mostly ineffective. I take a couple of awkward punches in the face and chest, and then hold my arms up to protect my face, and step backward.

"Stop it, Johnny," she says, putting herself between us. She puts her arm around his neck, and pulls his face to her shoulder. "Besides, it's not fair; he can't hit you back."

She is talking to Johnny, but looks directly at me. "You know why? Now he knows you love me. He doesn't love me anymore, but he can't hit you, because he knows you care about me." There was no love or tenderness in her voice; she almost sounds hateful. She continues to stand between us, holding Johnny's face to her, and looking at me, "He could just never believe someone like you could love me. For him, love has to be some big physical and emotional thing."

We continue standing there. I don't know what to do, and they don't seem to know either. She speaks to me again, in a voice no longer harsh. "You're just too much weight to carry around, Ray."

"Let's go back to Costa," Johnny says, pulling away from her.

"Johnny, I'm going to Quito today. Are you going with me?" she asks.

"Yeah, I'm going with you."

It is over. There is nothing I can say. I wanted to keep her longer, and now I have lost the last day with her. I turn and start walking down the street. I don't know where I will go, but first I will walk down the beach to the place where that big woman was panning gold. I will sit out there alone, and cry for myself, for being a goddamned shit-head.

"Ray!" she yells at me. "Come back here!"

I stop, but don't turn toward her. She walks over and grabs my arm, and jerks me around, the way she did on the first day.

"Come back over here! You didn't even take your bag with you!" I shrug, and go back and pick up my bag.

"You're still in that trench! You have the Lieutenant's brains all over your damned face; you can't just walk away from this. Come back here!" she jerks my arm again.

"What is it Shirley? You don't want me."

"You are going to see Norma."

"Why, Shirley? Why?"

"You're going to do this."

"It's over! There's nothing left. I'm sorry, but I just can't do it." I turn to leave. She pulls my arm again.

"No! I can't live with that. I won't live with it! You are going to do this. You can do it for yourself, or because you promised. Or, you can do it for me, and that's not too much to ask; but, you are going to do it. Johnny, will you go back to Costa and get our stuff, and pay the bill?"

"I'm not leaving you alone with this bastard," he replies.

She walks between us and exhales in a loud huff. "Okay, listen up guys. *This is what we are going to do!* Johnny, you are taking the cab to the truck stop, and going on out to Costa to pay the bill, and get our stuff. And, then you're bringing our things back to town, and meeting me at the school in the afternoon. Ray and I don't need the cab. We aren't in a hurry; Norma won't be free till ten O'clock." She turns to me, "Ray, we are going to walk into town. We will have breakfast someplace, so you won't be seasick the rest of the day! Then we will go see Norma at the school. *That is what we will do!*"

"Get going Johnny, I mean it." Johnny gets in the cab and leaves.

Shirley takes my arm. "I mean it, Ray! Come on."

We walk down the street toward town, and stop at a small café. "I'm not hungry; I'll wait for you out here," I say.

"Just get in there and sit down and shut up!" She snaps, and pinches me hard on the back of my arm. I push her hand away and walk into the café. We sit at the counter and a woman comes over to take our order. "*He will have fried eggs over rice with jalapeño peppers,*" she says to the woman, in Spanish, "*and, I will have the same. We will have coffee too; please bring the coffee now.*" I give her a wary look. "I'm getting used to it," she says defensively, and adds, "and I don't want the damned Texans shooting at me because I didn't get up at dawn and have my breakfast."

It's meant to be funny, but I can't get into that mood. "You're a bully! You know that Shirley? You're a damned bully."

"Have you just figured that out? I've been a bully all my life. In grammar school I bullied all the other kids; you know why? Because I was bigger than they were; that's why! And, now I bully my students and I bully Johnny, and I've been bullying you from the first day we met. The only time I wasn't a bully was when I was in Junior High and I realized I was the ugliest girl in the school, and I couldn't stand to even look at anyone, let alone bully them. And then, I decided I didn't care if I was the ugliest girl in the school and I started bullying everyone again. And, what I want to know is, why were you stupid enough to fall in love with someone who has done nothing but bully you?"

"Maybe I just thought that if I loved you enough you would stop bullying me, and start caring about me."

"Well, you sure were wrong about that, weren't you?"

"No," I say. She folds her arms and looks up, as if to summon patients. I continue: "And, I never did get that kiss you owe me."

"You've kissed me ten thousand times!"

"Those were all mutual."

"Oh Lord, here we go again. When everything else fails, turn on the charm. You'll have them groveling at your feet, Ray. They'll sit in your lap and drive the tractor!"

I can't decide whether I should laugh or cry. I shake my head.

"That's not funny, Ray. But, it's good to see you smile again, anyway." She touches my face for the first bit of tenderness of the day.

"Shirley, why can't we..."

She pinches my arm hard. "Yowl! That hurts, damn it!" I pull my arm away, but she reaches over and pinches again. Again I pull away from her; "Stop it! You've got no right to do that to me, damn it; just stop it!" I move to the next stool.

"If you don't stop trying to charm me, I'll pinch that arm till it's bleeding."

"Okay, go ahead," I tell her and move back to my stool. "I don't really give a shit. Go ahead Shirley, pinch away; make it bleed."

"No!"

"No?"

"NO! You will enjoy it too much."

"Well, what the fuck DO you want?"

She looks away for a half minute, and then turns back to me: "Ray, I'm going to explain this to you in little bitsy words so it will sink into your thick head, okay? There isn't going to be another day, and there isn't going to be another kiss, and you are not going to get my panties down one more time. It's over—OVER!" She puts her hands on my face to force my complete attention. "Ray, this past three weeks has been the most fun I have ever had in my whole life. I have never loved anyone the way I have loved you, and I have never been loved by anyone the way you loved me. But, it's over. Our affair is over, Ray. That doesn't mean I'm going to forget about you, and it doesn't mean I'm going to stop loving you. And, I'm still going to make sure you see Norma and take care of your problem. I have an obligation to make sure you do that, and I AM going to make sure you do that. You are not going to just walk down the beach and find some place to sit and cry, because I won't live with that, okay? So get that through your thick skull; and while you're at it, get it through your thick skull that our affair is over."

There doesn't seem to be anything left to say. We have our breakfast and then walk to the school. Shirley leaves me in the playground, and orders me to play basketball with the kids. She will leave my bag in Norma's office. I have to promise to stay there, and wait until Norma can see me. If I leave without talking to Norma, she will never forgive me; even when we are both dead, she still won't forgive me. That would be terrible she explains; it would be as if I did something to my sister, and she refused to forgive me for the rest of my life. She might be a long time with Norma. She needs to clarify her situation for the next year, and she needs to talk to her. Norma is her friend; I will understand that and wait for her, even if she takes a couple of hours. That isn't too much to ask.

She does take a couple of hours. I shoot baskets with the kids. Apparently, some kids are always at recess. Some of the boys are pretty good. I stand under the basket, and pass the ball back to them, as long as they keep making the basket. When a boy misses, I pass the ball to another boy, and he tries his luck. The little girl I had met previously comes out, and wants me to hold her up so she can make a basket. I do, to the dismay of the boys who are convinced she has no business on the basketball court.

A young boy runs up to me and says the *Hermana Norma* wants to see me. I climb the stairs and knock on Sister Norma's door. "Come in." As before, leads me to the wooden bench against the wall, and sits beside me. "Shirley is going home."

I look at her, knowing my face is contorted. "Isn't she even going to say…"

"She will say good-bye to you, before she goes. But, she is going. You know that, don't you?" I nod. "She couldn't stay with you even if she weren't going home. You know that too, don't you?" I nod. "It could never have worked, never! I'm surprised she was able to stay with you as long as she did, and that's a testimony to her character."

"Yeah, I'm surprised too."

"I don't mean to imply, you are a bad person, or that you are a person a girl would not want to love, and live with. No, on the contrary, I think you are a fine man for a girl to spend her life with."

"But not Shirley."

"No, not Shirley; you must know that by now, Ray. Can't you see how different the two of you are?" I don't respond to her. She puts her hand up and touches my face while she talks: "She is a very soft-hearted and kind person, just like you. But, you are so sentimental and emotional. You want things to be fun and beautiful. You want to dream about things. You want people to love you." I say nothing. "Don't you know Shirley is not that way?"

"Shirley is just like that!" I respond harshly. "She is sentimental and kind. She wants to have fun, and she needs me to love her just as much as I need her to love me."

"No. Shirley is more...more like an engineer, than an artist. She wants to build things. She wants to make a real difference in this world, and she thinks she can. Sure she likes to have fun, and everyone needs to be loved. But, she needs something else a whole lot more. She needs to accomplish the goals she has set for herself. It's too bad she will not be able to accomplish all those goals. But, striving to accomplish those things is what makes her happy."

I know what she says is true. "She's not an observer, Sister."

"No she isn't! I am really surprised she stayed with you this long. And, I can tell you she would not have, if she had not felt you really needed her help. She committed herself to your problems. Her love was bound up in the emotion that comes from dealing closely with a person you want to help. But, that kind of love cannot be sustained. There are other projects. There are other people in need. Shirley has to go with her true heart. In her true heart she can't cry over your love together. You can Ray, but she can't. There are too many other things in this world that call for her time and commitment."

"How can you be so sure about this stuff?"

"I have known her for a long time. She worked with me last year. We talk often, and I can see her work. And, you: well, I guess you are easy to know. I doubt if anyone could know you a couple of weeks, and not know what I just told you about yourself."

She laughs softly. "Shirley told me she could read your mind right away. I guess most people know what you are thinking most of the time. And, that's good, because, they know you want to have fun and love everyone. That's why they love you so much. Can't you see that?" I can't. She continues. "This morning, when you decided you didn't want her any more, she knew."

"I didn't think that! I didn't think that! Some stupid thoughts came into my head, but I didn't—I never decided I didn't want her any more. I could never have thought that." I feel tears in my eyes. "I wish I had told her I was sorry, for those stupid things that came into my head."

"In a way she was relieved it was over. She dreaded leaving you tomorrow so much. Don't you know how much that would have hurt her, to leave you with you wanting her to stay?"

I have to turn away from her, and face the other way. "You two played a very dangerous game together, didn't you?"

"Yeah, I guess so."

"It was wrong, Ray; wrong for both of you. You are a married man, and she knew that from the beginning. Much as I would like to think of you as two innocent babes in the wilderness, it just isn't true. You have to take responsibility for your actions; you can't just live recklessly and sinfully and think everything is going to turn out fine." I don't respond. I wait and say nothing. "Shirley has put this whole thing behind her now. Do you know that?"

"Yeah, I guess so."

"Can you? Can you put that behind you?"

"What choice do I have?"

"This is not a question of choice!" she turns me around to face her. "Choice is when two paths divide. There is only one path for you. You have to face up to the truth." She waits for me to respond, but I don't. "You have to let her go, Ray."

Those words make me choke. "Ray, it is possible to give away and have more; it is also possible to try to hold on too tightly and lose everything."

"I'm losing everything, Sister."

"No! You're not losing everything! What you had with Shirley can always be yours; but, only if you let her go." She is quite for a half minute, and then continues: "You can draw strength from adversity. You know that, don't you?" I look at her but don't respond. "When you became a soldier, the training was hard and cruel, wasn't it?" I nod. "But, that made you strong and confident, didn't it? Did the harsh training make all the boys strong and confident?"

"No, some guys couldn't take it. It made them the opposite—weak and pitiful. I felt sorry for them. Hell, I detested them. I would rather face the war, than face that."

"I know it is hard for you to understand right now, but letting Shirley go can make you a stronger and better person. But, if you try to hold on to her, it will make you weak and pitiful, just like those boys in the army who couldn't take it. You don't want that, do you?"

I shake my head. "You know something Sister, the army wasn't all bad. I learned a lot. I wouldn't want to be the guy I was before I went into the Army."

"And, you wouldn't want to be the guy you were on the bus, before you met Shirley."

"No, I don't ever want to be that guy again."

"Those terrible things that happened to you in the war, made you weak and pitiful, didn't they?" I nod. "That was because you didn't stand up and deal with it! You have to stand up to this! RIGHT NOW!"

I think about guys who couldn't take it, who could not command their bodies to stand at attention or carry a pack, and who cried when sergeants yelled at them. I felt contempt for them at the time and still feel contempt for them now. I think about Shirley being molested as a young girl and how proud and strong she is. I see myself, from high above through the ceiling of the room. I look pitiful and helpless. I am ashamed.

"I will; and I'm going to stand up to those other things, too." I say. "I've been thinking, Sister. It's as if I was molested, just like she was. But, I wasn't a child when that happened to me. If she could stand up to that as a child, well, I guess I'm just a sorry shit-head for not dealing with my problem." Then I realize I have broken a confidence by telling her about Shirley. "I shouldn't have told you about Shirley, Sister."

"I know about Shirley. And, I know how important you have been for her, in helping her to get over that. You, and her Aunt Meg, and her man in San Francisco: Each of you came into her life, at just the right moment. I'm thankful to all three of you for that."

"I didn't do anything to help her. I didn't even know she had that problem, until a couple of days ago. When I think about it, I guess I was really mean to her in some ways. But, I didn't know. She was trying to help me, and I was just trying to have a good time with her. I didn't know she wanted me to help her. And, I couldn't have done anything to help her anyway."

"You were just being yourself, Ray. You didn't have to try. If you had tried, it wouldn't have worked. What you two did was wrong—very wrong. But Shirley is a strong girl and she can handle her emotions. Most girls aren't like that. Most are like you—maybe even more emotionally fragile than you are—and they are hurt very much when someone uses them for sex. You will be over Shirley soon, and then you will be looking around for another girl to fall in love with and use. You have to stop that. It's not good for you and it can be much worse for the girl. YOU DON'T LOOK AT ANOTHER GIRL UNLESS YOU WANT TO SPEND YOUR LIFE WITH HER!" She puts her hands on my shoulders and shakes me. "AND, YOU ALREADY HAVE A GIRL YOU ARE SUPPOSED TO SPEND YOUR LIFE WITH!"

The words sting, but having the frail old woman shake me seems almost comical. "Yes Sergeant!" I respond.

She releases my shoulders, smiles and shakes her head. "I don't judge you, or Shirley either. That's not my job. But, it is my job to tell you when I see you walking down the wrong path."

"I guess you don't think much of me; guess I can't blame you for that."

"You're wrong! I think you are a very good person. You have a gift—a very wonderful gift—that I don't have, and Shirley doesn't have, and most people don't have; you make people happy." I am mystified, and know my face expresses that. She continues: "Haven't you ever turned to look at the sea of smiling faces in the wake you leave behind?" I don't know what she is talking about; I just look at her.

"Shirley calls it charming people, to make them love you. That is a very wonderful thing. But, you can't use that gift to get sex from girls—that's wrong, and it can be very hurtful." We stand looking at each other for a few seconds. "Ray, I'm going to ask you to do something for me; okay? I want you to help us out here at this school. I want you to stay for a few weeks, and work with us here." I give her a puzzled look. "This school really needs an organized physical education program. I want the boys to learn how to play organized sports, and I want them to learn to march, and learn discipline. If you can do that for a while, and really make a difference in these kids, I think I can persuade the Mission to make the physical education position permanent."

"You don't want me to help you. You want me to stay so you can help me."

"Yes, I want you to stay for that reason, too. We need to talk, Ray, about those other things, about what you are going to do about the medal, and about those boys that were killed, and about your life back there in Texas; but, this is not the time for that, and I do need a physical education teacher. I think you could do a good job for this school. I watched you playing basketball with the children, and I know you would be good for them. I'm embarrassed to tell you how much the job pays."

"You are going to pay me?"

"Not much, I'm afraid; only about forty dollars a month."

"You don't need to pay me anything, Sister. I'll work as a volunteer, the way Shirley did."

"No, I want the Mission to become used to the idea that this is a paid position. Otherwise, they will think it is frivolous."

"There is no way I'm going to take any money from you. I should be paying you. You can donate the money to the wild Indians, or something; Shirley would like that."

"You know, the first year Shirley was here, she was really mad at me because we don't have basketball and volleyball facilities for the girls. The boys won't let the girls play on that court, and the hoop is too high anyway. I just haven't had the funds to do anything about it."

"Maybe, I can help you out there, Sister. I sure didn't like it when she got mad at me!"

"No! I'll bet you didn't," she chuckles. "It's settled then. You can start tomorrow at nine o'clock. And, I want to talk to you again today. Perhaps you could go out and have some lunch, and come back at about two o'clock. Will you do that?"

"Sure."

I leave her office and walk over to the main street, and take a bus to the beach. I know Norma is talking with Shirley, and I am glad she will tell her I will be working at the school for a while. I want Shirley to know she has helped me, and I will be okay after she leaves.

THANKS, IT HAS BEEN LACKING FOR ME: COASTAL ECUADOR, SUMMER, 1957

"*Where is the tall gringa?*" The owner of the *tienda* had placed a bowl of soup on the table in front of a young foreigner. He had served this foreigner a couple of weeks earlier, and the man had bought him a beer.

"*She left me.*" The young man responded.

"*I'm not surprised.*" the owner said, "*The only ones who don't leave you are the ones that enjoy making you miserable. Are you going to have beer?*"

The young man thought about the statement. It was true she didn't enjoy making him miserable. Nevertheless, he decided the older man's homespun philosophy was in reference to his own life. "*No. I would prefer coffee. But, you have a beer, señor; it's on me.*"

The owner yelled to the back room for coffee, and opened a beer for himself. "*Thanks.*"

The owner's woman brought the coffee to the table. She turned and faced the counter with her back to the young man. She was a tall, muscular Black woman. Very likely, she would defy Shirley's rule about men being stronger than the women. The woman put her closed fists on her hips, and observed her man.

Although the woman had her back to the young man, he was sure he could imagine the expression she would have on her face. There would be the arched brow, and the hard stare. The man stood behind the counter, drinking the beer. He looked back at his woman with apparent disinterest. The woman exhaled loudly, and walked back to the interior room.

The owner looked at the young man, and shrugged and smiled. The young man smiled too, and thought about the fact that he had not smiled very much lately. It felt good.

The young man finished his soup and coffee, and walked up to the counter to pay. *"I may be in town for a couple of weeks or so, working at the school down on the main street; perhaps I will come by for a bowl of soup for lunch sometimes."*

"That would be marvelous. With the profits from soup and beer every day I can expand my business—perhaps add another table, or hire a pretty girl to serve my customers on weekends."

"I probably won't have beer—I will have to go back to work in the afternoon, you know. But, you can have a beer, so the profits will be the same."

"In such a case, the profits will be double. First I will profit by drinking the beer, and then I will profit again with the payment. But, I see no profit for you in such an arrangement. Clearly, money is of no consequence for you; but it is something. And, what is it that you would get in exchange for so much money?"

"I would benefit from your wisdom, señor."

"Of course, the wisdom of age; I'm surprised that you, being a young man, recognize the wisdom of age. Ah yes, I once thought how marvelous to have both youth and wisdom; but, of course the two are incompatible, and in such a case there would be no purpose for old age. It is best that wisdom be reserved for the elderly."

"Señor, you seem to suggest that I would be better served by ignoring your wisdom."

"Of course not; don't preoccupy yourself with the possibility that you may gain wisdom in the simple act of listening to a wise man. You will continue to pursue the unattainable and stumble over the unnoticed. But, such misadventures can make fine memories for an old man one day. I guarantee you that your adventure with the tall Gringa will be a fine memory for you one day."

"You are the second person who has told me that. I'm beginning to believe it may be true. Have another beer, señor. Have two, if you like."

The man immediately put two more bottles on the counter and opened them. *"I guarantee you that the other person was also an old man."*

"A woman actually; but old—older than you I would say."

"You see! The wisdom of age extends even to women. But, take care with their advice— it is a rare woman who will help a man who is not her own son."

"This is indeed a rare woman. Enjoy your beer, señor."

"Thanks, it has been lacking for me."

IS IT GOING TO BE OKAY FOR YOU: ESMERALDAS, MONDAY AFTERNOON

Shirley is standing below. I had returned to Norma's office at two PM and she directed me to the window, open to the street below. Shirley is wearing the same skirt and blouse she had on the first day on the bus, and her small backpack is on her back. Johnny is about fifty feet away, with the duffel bag, and facing away from us.

"I wanted to say good-bye from here." She says. "Is that going to be okay for you?" I nod yes. "Ray, you aren't going to try to find me down here next year, are you?"

"No. And, I'm not going to try to call you, or send you a card on your birthday."

"You're letting me go, aren't ya?" I nod. "You're giving back my little Shirley, aren't ya?" I nod. "I never told you, but I took your little Ray, too. It was that second night at the hotel in Coca; did you know?" I nod. "But, I gave him back to you." I nod. "Are you sorry we fell in love?"

"I guess, if you had asked me this morning, I would have said yes. But, I'm already looking back now. From here it looks so...when I look back now, it's so beautiful." She nods. "Are you sorry?"

"No, I'm not sorry," she says. "It all came in one big package. Life is like that, isn't it? You have to take a chance once in a while; otherwise you might as well stay home with your mother, huh? Otherwise, it's just a big box, with pretty wrapping paper, and ribbons around it, and nothing inside, huh?" I nod. "I just couldn't stand to see you walk away this morning. That would have been as if—as if it were my fault." I shake my head. "You're going to stay here for a while with Norma, aren't you? You are going to let her help you, aren't you?"

"Yes."

"I helped you some too, didn't I?" I nod. "Did you know you helped me to get over that thing that happened to me?" I shake my head. "It was your bush doctor stuff. My Aunt Meg did bush medicine on me, too. But, I never really believed it—you know, completely believed it—until you. I'm going to tell her about you. I'm going to tell her everything. I hope you don't mind, but I own that, and I can do anything I want with it."

"I know."

"Ray, I'm going to remember all the good times we had: The Posada; the ride down the river with that Indian; and how we almost had our heads shrunk and put on poles in the village; and how you made me sit on the bottom of the boat, so it would look as if I had peed on myself; and, Mr. Alabama and Margarita and Ines; and the big woman panning gold at the beach. And, the bat shit, and a whole cellar-full of canned peaches, and millions of Chinese babies with baseball caps on their little bald heads. And, how I tricked you on the plane ride: I really got on your case, didn't I? Taught you a lesson, didn't I?" I nod yes. "I'm going to remember all the good times. But, I'm going to forget about the bad things. It will be as if they never happened." I nod yes. "You say that, too."

I have to clear my throat and swallow to get my voice. "I will remember all the good times we had, Shirley love, but I will forget the bad things. It will be as if they never happened."

"I hope you go back to Donna. You need her." I nod yes. "Wish me luck with Jerry, too."

Again, I have trouble finding my voice. "I hope you are happy with Jerry. It's going to get harder to take care of those boys as they grow up. It won't just be Little League."

"Yeah, I know!" she says, nodding her head as if to tell me she understands how difficult taking care of the boys will be.

She stands there smiling at me for a couple of seconds. "Good-bye, Ray."

I move my lips, "Good-bye, Shirley," but, no sound comes out.

She walks toward the street, and then stops and turns back. She cocks her head sideways, and sticks her tongue out, raises her hands with palms out, and wags her head. I nod to her, and she turns and walks away. Johnny picks up the duffel bag and follows her.

I watch her walk away. I am completely numb, with nothing left to do or think. When she disappears around the corner I close my eyes and exhale slowly. I turn back into the room, and walk over to Sister Norma's desk, feeling the need to say something.

"She's really something, isn't she?" I say, realizing immediately how stupid it must sound.

"She is very real," Norma replies, "and yes, she is really something—something very much."

I choke and turn to face away from the desk. "It hurts so much."

"The hurt will go away after a while; you know that, don't you? But, the memory will be there for the rest of your life. Will it be a good memory?"

"Yes."

"Well Ray, if you are going to have a memory like that to live with, you don't need to be looking for sympathy from me."

"I'm not asking for sympathy; I just can't believe I will never see her again."

"And how much worse for you if you had never seen her in the first place! What if you hadn't been on that particular bus? What if she had gotten off before you woke up? What if—Ray, listen to me: What if her aunt had not told her about that boy she loved in Brazil? You must know that's why she did it. Just think of how many things that had to fall into place for that to happen. Do you think all those things were just lined up like dominoes waiting for you come down here and push the first one over?"

"What are you saying? It was all just meant to happen?"

"NO! That's the coward's way out. That's just a way to avoid responsibility for your actions—a way to avoid facing up to reality. You've been doing that too long, Ray; it's time to stop that. I'm telling you to count your blessings! Shirley has done that. She isn't going away thinking this has been some kind of tragedy. She is going to be a better, stronger person because of this. Ray, look at me!" I turn to her. "Even though what you two did was very wrong, there has been some good that has come out of it for Shirley and you too. She didn't hurt you Ray, did she?"

"No, she didn't."

"And, this has been good for you, hasn't it? I'm not talking about having a good time, Ray! I'm talking about something that has helped you to be a better and stronger person!"

"Yes, she helped me a lot; more than I can say."

"Then stop crying and start counting your blessings!"

The breeze picks up suddenly. The air feels fresh and cool. I wipe my eyes with the sleeve of my shirt. My head feels light, but clean and clear. "You know: She said she always thought her *beau ideal* would be tall and handsome with black wavy hair and be suave and sophisticated with a French accent—and, that I was more like a hick from Texas."

"She said that, did she?" Norma chuckles silently. "Well, I can tell you, as if you didn't already know, that you were her *beau ideal*. Now she can go home and marry the man she was supposed to marry, and she won't have to waste her time wondering about that *beau ideal* she always hoped to meet. You can go home soon too, Ray—and be with the woman you are supposed to be with."

"Yeah; I hope I can." I stand looking at her for a moment. How does she know all this shit, I ask myself? I wait for her to speak, but she doesn't. "Sister, I'm going to find a place to live here in town, and then go out to Costa del Sol to get my stuff. I will be ready to start work here tomorrow morning. Perhaps, we should meet first, so you can tell me exactly what you have in mind for the physical education position."

"That will be fine. I can recommend a place for you, if you want; that might save you some money and time." I nod. "What sort of place do you want?"

"Just a room with a private bath if possible; it would be nice to have a restaurant nearby, for breakfast."

"Why don't you try the Hotel España; just off the main street toward the river, about eight blocks down. They have nice rooms with private baths, and a good restaurant in front. The owner is Reinaldo Juarez. He has a fine family, and he's a good cook. You tell him I sent you, okay?"

"Yes, I will. Thank you."

"And, perhaps we could discuss the physical education program over dinner tonight." She adds.

"Sure! How about Casa Garibaldi's at, say seven o'clock? And, dinner is on me."

"Thank you, Ray. That's an excellent choice. I believe they serve very fine Chilean wine. I will see you there at seven."

"Thank you, Sister."

IT'S GOING TO BE TOUCH AND GO: ESMERALDAS, TUESDAY, AUGUST 25

The boys ran out to the interior courtyard playground, noisily. This would be the first time they would meet their new foreign teacher, and they were prepared to test his limits. The boys stood in a loose bunch, jostling and yelling at each other. From the second story window, Sisters Norma and Juana watched. The older woman smiled in anticipation of the scene about to unfold.

"I wanted you to see this," the older woman said, "I told him to take the younger boys first, just to get the routine set up. He said no, give me the oldest boys first; I'll kick a few asses and the rest of them will fall into line."

Sister Juana cringed. She had come to Ecuador as a missionary, hoping to follow Norma's path. She had changed her name from Jane to Juana, and dedicated herself to her work with the poor children. But, nothing in her past life or training had prepared her for the hard reality of her work in this coastal village. Hearing the person she hoped to emulate use a bad word was especially offensive.

"I wish you wouldn't use bad words Norma."

"I wanted you to know what he said; anyway, no one heard it but us."

"The Lord heard it!

"The Lord has bigger fish to fry." Norma replied, smiling.

The new teacher faced the group of boys and yelled suddenly, "***Atención***!" The boys looked up at him, but continued to mill about and giggle. "*Men,*" the teacher began softly, in Spanish. "*I'm going to demonstrate—ONLY ONE TIME—how you will stand at attention and keep your mouths SHUT. JUST ONE TIME! And, then all of you will stand at attention properly, and keep your mouths SHUT!*"

The biggest boy in the group continued to giggle, and look about for support from the other boys. The teacher walked over and stood with his face a few inches from the boy's. "*Do you know why you will do that?*" The teacher huffed the whisper out, loud enough for all the boys to hear, "b*ecause, I am the meanest and most vicious son-of-a-bitch in Ecuador!*"

The boy's giggling stopped. "*When I speak to you, you will respond: Yes, Coach Richards. DO YOU UNDERSTAND ME?*" The boy stood transfixed. "*WHAT DO YOU SAY WHEN I SPEAK TO YOU?*" the teacher screamed.

"*Yes, coach Richhardes.*"

"*NOT REACH HARD DES! RICHARDS! DO YOU UNDERSTAND ME? WHAT DO YOU SAY, WHEN I SPEAK TO YOU?*" the teacher screamed in the boy's face.

"*Yes, Coach Richards,*" the boy responded.

The teacher continued his instruction.

"**He** is being too hard on the boys." Sister Juana said.

"He is doing exactly what I told him." Norma said. "What those boys need is a swift kick in the butt, and that's just the man to do it."

"That's a very high price to pay for discipline. We could accomplish the same thing in a loving way."

"You think so?" The Principal asked.

"Yes! I think so! And, I don't trust him; you know what he did to Shirley."

"He didn't do anything to Shirley that she didn't want him to." Sister Juana turned away. "You didn't trust Shirley at first either; but she proved you wrong, didn't she?"

The older woman waited for a bit, and then continued: "Juana, you are the kindest and most loving and giving persons I have ever known. Few other persons could do the job you have set out to do as well as you; few people would dare to try. The Church has never had a bride as loving and true as you. But, that's not enough. The Lord has work for us that we cannot accomplish alone. We have to work through other people. Those boys out there are marching to a drummer that we can't even hear. They don't want love and kindness; they want something that only a very tough man can give them." The older woman paused, but the younger woman did not respond. "He calls them men."

"That's just it; they are not men, they are boys!"

"Yes, but they want to be men." Once again the younger woman did not respond. "I want you to watch how those boys respond to this young man. And, after a few weeks, I want you to think about which teacher those boys love the most."

"They aren't going to love him because he is mean to them."

"You think not."

"That's right; I think not."

"Juana, there really aren't very many ways to skin a cat. I couldn't skin one at all; could you?"

"No! I couldn't skin a cat!"

"The Lord wants that cat skinned," Norma said, motioning to the scene in the playground. "What are we going to do about it?"

"Well, I suppose we will just have to let that mean man skin the cat!" Juana replied, as she turned and walked away.

The boys learned discipline from their new coach. They learned to stand at attention and march, and they learned to play basketball as a team, and win. A new concrete slab was built in the recreation area, and lower basketball hoops were installed. New basketballs and volleyballs were purchased, and the eighth-grade boys' basketball team received bright new uniforms and tennis shoes.

Their gringo coach became the instrument of cultural transfer from Mexico: To be real men, he told them, they must have the three F's; they must be *feo, fuerte, y formal*. A man must be <u>ugly</u>; he must accept the face God gave him and never concern himself with what someone else may think about it. A man must be <u>strong</u>; he must be prepared to be a soldier and defend his country, but most of all he must support and defend his own family. A man must be <u>courteous</u>; he must always treat women and older people, and his teachers, with respect, but most of all he must treat his parents and his brothers and sisters, and someday his wife, with respect. "How are we?" he would yell, and the boys would yell back: "FEO, FUERTE, Y FORMAL!"

Grudging respect for the new coach soon became admiration. This coach called them men and demanded a level of performance they did not know they could achieve. Those boys who cowered when the coach yelled at them, or who complained to their mothers or teachers of the coach's abuses, were ridiculed as crybabies. The *real men* can take it, the boys told each other. Soon they could do much more—they wanted to do much more. This coach was a man they could admire, and more than anything else, they wanted to admire a man. They wanted approval from this man they admired. He made them feel strong and confident.

In the evenings the new coach would frequently meet with Sister Norma to talk. At each session, she talked less and he talked more. She listened intently as he told her of experiences Shirley had related to her previously.

He told her about how he would return the medal and explain to Papa. "Papa was a soldier in battle once; he will understand this. He will explain it to Donna. She doesn't care about the medal, she just cares about Papa."

He told her about how he would explain that to Snider's parents, and tell them he didn't deserve to share the medal with their son. "And, I'm going to write to Doyle's parents too. If they can't accept it that will be their problem, not mine."

He would ask her questions, and she would mostly wait for him to answer them. Just keep the train on the track, she would remind herself. Occasionally, he would become emotional, causing him embarrassment.

"You don't have to turn away," she told him, "I'm just like your sister, remember?"

"Yeah, but you're not my sister! I'm not even a Catholic. Why do you do this for me?"

"Why do you work with the boys at the school?"

"Oh hell, that's nothing. I enjoy keeping those kids in line, and kicking their butts once in a while."

"Well, maybe I enjoy keeping you in line, and kicking your butt once in a while."

He smiled at that, "You know, Sister? You have always been a step ahead of me. You're a smart woman."

"You think so?"

"Yeah, I think so. You were probably always a step ahead of Shirley, too. But, you know, I'll bet it took her a while to figure that out." The woman smiled. "You don't know how much she loves you." And, then he added, "Yeah, you do know."

One afternoon, Sister Norma came into the recreation courtyard and watched the basketball team practice. The coach joined her.

"You've done a marvelous job with these boys," she said. "They were so proud when they won the game last Friday. We haven't beaten that school for eight years."

"Well, they just needed a little discipline and training. And, those new shoes and uniforms really did the trick. I told them they would be able to jump a quarter-meter higher with those shoes, and they did."

"They are more courteous to their teachers, especially Sister Juana. Even the younger boys are more respectful. I've never seen Juana so happy. I thought I was going to lose her; she couldn't control those boys, and they tormented her. She prayed so hard, that they would just accept her gifts of time and talent and love," she said, and then added: "I don't suppose you know what made the boys change their attitude."

"Why no, I have no idea, Sister. Perhaps, the Lord answered her prayers."

"Yes, the Lord works in mysterious ways."

"I got a letter from Donna yesterday. I don't know—it's going to be touch and go."

"Sounds as if she isn't totally against the idea."

"No. I don't think she is. But... well, she had a boyfriend. That's over now. She thought she loved him, but later she realized she didn't. She's afraid I won't forgive her for that, but I will, Sister; I have already forgiven her."

"It is not just forgiving; you have to be able to forget. It would be terrible for her if you were to throw that in her face ten years from now."

"I wouldn't do that. I can forgive her, and forget that forever."

"Did you tell her about Shirley?"

"I told her I was dicking around with girls in Mexico."

"Did you tell her about Shirley?"

"I just couldn't tell her about Shirley."

"You couldn't tell her about Shirley because you loved Shirley. Isn't that it? You think it would be easier for her to forgive you, if you were just dicking around." He nodded. "Is that the way you would feel? Would it be easier for you to forgive your wife if she had been just dicking around with men?"

"Well, no. That's completely different."

"You think so? Why don't we have dinner together this evening, and talk about it?"

"Sure. How about Casa Garibaldi's at seven, and it's on me."

"Why, thank you. Yes, that will be fine. I'll see you there at seven." The woman turned back into the building.

"Sister Norma;" the elderly woman turned back, "are you a good witch, or a bad witch?"

An initial look of shock slowly turned to a smile, and then a silent chuckle. "I'll see you at dinner, Ray."

Printed in the United States
By Bookmasters